ALSO BY SUSAN HOWATCH

THE DARK SHORE *1965*
THE WAITING SANDS *1966*
CALL IN THE NIGHT *1967*
THE SHROUDED WALLS *1968*
APRIL'S GRAVE *1969*
THE DEVIL ON LAMMAS NIGHT *1970*
PENMARRIC *1971*
CASHELMARA *1974*
THE RICH ARE DIFFERENT *1977*
SINS OF THE FATHERS *1980*
THE WHEEL OF FORTUNE *1984*

GLITTERING IMAGES

GLITTERING IMAGES

Susan Howatch

ALFRED A. KNOPF

NEW YORK 1987

THIS IS A BORZOI BOOK
PUBLISHED BY ALFRED A. KNOPF, INC.

 *Published in the
United States by Alfred A. Knopf, Inc., New York,
and simultaneously in Canada by Random House of
Canada Limited, Toronto. Distributed by Random
House, Inc., New York. Published in Great Britain by
William Collins PLC, London.*

*Library of Congress Cataloging-in-Publication Data
Howatch, Susan.
Glittering images.
I. Title.
PS3558.O884G5 1987 813'.54 87-45130
ISBN 0-394-56206-2*

*Manufactured in the United States of America
First Edition*

For Barbara,
in memory of our conversations
about the two Herberts

Contents

PART ONE

THE MYSTERY

"The deeper we get into reality, the more numerous will be the questions we cannot answer."

Spiritual Counsels and Letters of
BARON FRIEDRICH VON HÜGEL,
ed. Douglas V. Steere

I

"A bishop, I remind myself, is not quite as other men."

HERBERT HENSLEY HENSON,
Bishop of Durham, 1920–39,
THE BISHOPRICK PAPERS

I

MY ordeal began one summer afternoon when I received a telephone call from the Archbishop of Canterbury. It was a hot day, and beyond the window the quadrangle of Laud's shimmered in the hazy light. Term had ended; the resulting peace provided an atmosphere conducive to work, and when the telephone rang it was with reluctance that I reached for the receiver.

A voice announced itself as Lambeth Palace and proclaimed that His Grace wished to speak to Dr. Ashworth on a matter of extreme urgency. Apparently the Archbishop was still infecting his chaplains with his love of melodrama.

"My dear Charles!" Dr. Lang's voice, always sonorous, now achieved a pitch of theatrical splendour. He was a member of that generation which regards the telephone as at worst a demonic intruder and at best a thespian challenge, and when I inquired diplomatically about his health, I was treated to a dramatic discourse on the more tedious aspects of senectitude. The Archbishop, on that first day of July in 1937, was in his seventy-third year and as fit as an ecclesiastical grandee has a right to expect, but in common with all men he hated the manifestations of old age.

". . . however, enough of my tiresome little ailments," he concluded as I added the finishing touches to the mitre I had sketched on my memo-pad. "Charles, I'm preaching at Ely next Sunday, and because I'm most anxious that we should meet, I've arranged to spend the night in Cambridge at the house of my old friend the Master of Laud's. I shall come to your rooms after Evensong, but let me stress that I wish my visit to be entirely private. I have a commission which I wish to entrust to you, and the commission," said the Archbishop, milking the situation of every ounce of drama by allowing his voice to sink to a whisper, "is very delicate indeed."

I wondered if he imagined he could arrive at my rooms without being recognised. Archbishops hardly find it easy to travel incognito, and an archbishop who had recently played a leading part in the abdication of one king and the coronation of another was hardly the most anonymous of clerics.

I said politely: "Of course I'd be glad to help you in any way I can, Your Grace."

"Then I'll see you on Sunday evening. Thank you, Charles," said Dr. Lang, and after giving me a brisk blessing, he terminated the call. I was left staring at the mitre I had sketched, but gradually I became aware that my gaze had shifted to the last words I had written before the interruption.

"Modalism appealed to the Church's desire for monotheism, but in the second half of the fourth century it was propounded that the modalist God metamorphosed himself to meet—"

The impact of Modalism on the doctrine of the Trinity seemed a long way from the machinations of Dr. Lang.

I found I had lost interest in my new book.

My ordeal had begun.

2

"MY commission," said the Archbishop with a reverence calculated to underline the importance of the subject, "concerns the Bishop of Starbridge. Have you met him?"

"Only briefly. He preached in Cambridge Cathedral during Advent last year."

We had achieved the private meeting in my rooms, and I had offered the Archbishop a cup of his favourite tea; one of my London friends, visiting Cambridge the previous day, had brought the tea directly from Fortnum's. Dr. Lang, formally attired in his archiepiscopal clothes, was now sipping from one of my best china cups as he sat in my most comfortable armchair, while I, wearing my cassock beneath my doctoral gown, was busy repressing the urge for a whisky. My cigarettes had been hidden. I had even left the windows wide open all day to banish any hint of smoke.

Lang took another sip of tea. He was a man whose features cast themselves without effort into an autocratic expression, and as I glanced at him I was reminded of the story which had circulated the Church of England after he had displayed his portrait by Orpen to a group of bishops. Lang had mused: "I feel I must object when the critics say the painting makes me look pompous, proud and prelatical!" whereupon Dr. Henson, the caustic Bishop of Durham, had inquired: "And may I ask to which of these epithets Your Grace takes exception?" The Archbishop was not without his enemies in the Church, and as I remembered Henson of Durham my thoughts turned to Jardine of Starbridge who, so Lang now informed me, was the subject of the mysterious commission.

"Before I explain further, Charles, answer me this: what did you Cambridge theologians think of Jardine's speech in the House of Lords ten days ago?"

That was an easy question to answer. During the debate on Mr. A. P. Herbert's Marriage Bill, which advocated extending the grounds for divorce, Dr. Jardine had attacked the Archbishop in a speech which had tossed a fireball into the tinder-box of the Church of England.

"We were all horrified, Your Grace."

"Of course he's a brilliant speaker," said Lang, careful to go through the motions of exercising Christian charity by giving credit where credit was due. "Technically the speech was a masterpiece."

"But a deplorable masterpiece."

Lang was satisfied. He must have been confident of my support, but it was over ten years since I had been his chaplain, and like all prudent statesmen he no doubt felt it unwise to take loyalty too readily for granted.

"Jardine's attack was quite inexcusable," he said, sufficiently reassured to indulge in the luxury of indignation. "After all, I was in the most unenviable position. I couldn't condone any relaxation of the divorce law; that would have been morally repugnant to me. On the other hand if I had openly opposed all change there would have been much damaging criticism of the Church. Caught between the Scylla of my moral inclinations and the Charybdis of my political duty," declared the Archbishop, unable to resist a grandiloquent flourish, "I had no choice but to adopt a position of neutrality."

"I do see the difficulty, Your Grace."

"Of course you do! So do all reasonable churchmen! Yet the Bishop of Starbridge has the insufferable insolence not only to accuse me of 'sitting on the fence'—what a vulgar phrase!—but to advocate that multiple grounds for divorce are compatible with Christian teaching! No doubt one shouldn't expect too much of someone who's clearly very far from being a gentleman, but Jardine has behaved with gross disloyalty to me personally and with gross indifference to the welfare of the Church."

The snobbery was unattractive. Lang might long since have acquired the manner of an English aristocrat, but he came from the Scottish middle classes and no doubt he himself had once been regarded as an "arriviste." Perhaps he thought this gave him a license to be virulent on the subject of class, but I thought the virulence underlined not Jardine's social origins but his own.

Meanwhile he had discarded all grandiloquence in order to deliver himself of the bluntest of perorations. "In my opinion," he said, "Jardine's no longer merely an embarrassment. He's become a dangerous liability, and I've decided that the time has come when I must take action to guard against a disaster."

I wondered if malice had combined with old age to produce irrationality. "I agree he's controversial, Your Grace, but—"

"Controversial! My dear Charles, what you and the general public have seen so far is just the tip of the iceberg—you should hear what goes on at our bishops' meetings! Jardine's views on marriage, divorce and—heaven help us—contraception have been notorious for some time in episcopal circles, and my greatest fear now is that if he continues to parade his questionable views on family life, some unscrupulous newshound from Fleet Street will eventually put Jardine's own domestic situation under the microscope."

"You're surely not implying—"

"No, no." Lang's voice was suddenly very smooth. "No, of course I'm not implying any fatal error, but Jardine's domestic situation is unusual and could well be exploited by a press baron with an axe to grind." He paused before adding: "I have enemies in Fleet Street, Charles. Since the Abdication there are powerful people who would like nothing better than to see me humiliated and the Church put to shame."

The speech was florid but for the first time I felt he was not motivated solely by malice. His words reflected an undeniable political reality.

I heard myself say: "And where do I come in, Your Grace?"

"I want you to go down to Starbridge," said the Archbishop without hesitation, "and make sure that Jardine hasn't committed some potentially disastrous indiscretion—because if he has, I want all evidence of it destroyed."

3

LANG was talking in calculated euphemisms. He was anxious not to blacken the Bishop's reputation too deeply in the presence of a junior member of the Church's hierarchy, but at the same time he wished to signal to me that where Jardine was concerned almost any nightmare was feasible. Jardine was not suspected of a "fatal error"; that meant adultery, a moral failure which would render a bishop, or indeed any clergyman, unfit for office. On the other hand Lang was raising the possibility that Jardine had committed a "potentially disastrous indiscretion," a phrase which could mean anything from an unwise comment on the Virgin Birth to holding hands with a twenty-year-old blonde.

"How much do you know about him?" Lang added before I could speculate further.

"Just the outlines of his career. I know nothing about his private life."

"He's married to an exceedingly feather-brained little lady who must now, I suppose, be in her early fifties. Jardine himself is fifty-eight. Both of them look younger than their years." Lang made this good fortune sound like a breach of taste, and I sensed that his envy of Jardine's youthfulness was mingling with his dislike.

"Any children?" I said, pouring him some more tea.

"None living." He took a sip from his replenished cup before adding: "Ten years ago, soon after Jardine became Dean of Radbury, a young woman called Miss Lyle Christie was engaged by him to be Mrs. Jardine's companion. Poor feather-brained little Mrs. Jardine couldn't cope with her new responsibilities as the Dean's wife, and all was the most inappropriate confusion."

"And did Miss Lyle Christie bring order out of chaos?"

"Miss Christie. We're not dealing here with a double-barrelled name—the misguided parents gave her the name Lyle instead of a decent Christian name such as Jane or Mary. Yes," said Lang, setting aside his teacup, "Miss Christie's been keeping her employers' household in admirable order ever since her arrival. However, although this innocent little ménage à trois would normally be unremarkable, there are three aspects of the situation which—after ten years—can and do cause unfortunate comment. The first is that Miss Christie is a good-looking woman; the second is that she shows no inclination to marry; and the third is that Jardine himself has what might be charitably described as a healthy interest in the opposite sex." Lang, whose own good looks had ensured a steady stream of feminine admirers throughout his long bachelor's life, gazed out of the window at this point in order to appear non-committal. As a Christian he was obliged to approve of a healthy sexual interest which led to marriage, but I knew he found a more pervasive carnal preoccupation with women distasteful.

"In other words," I said, easing him around the awkward subject of Jardine's attitude to the ladies, "you're afraid that if the press start delving into Jardine's private life they may make some embarrassing deductions about Miss Christie. But with all due respect, Your Grace, why should this worry you? Even the gutter-press aren't above the laws of libel, and they'd never print salacious allegations without written evidence to back them up."

"That's exactly why I'm so worried." Lang shed all affectation at last to reveal the canny Scot who still lurked behind his English facade. "Jardine keeps a journal. Supposing some newshound bribes the servants and gets his hands on it?"

"But surely this is a journal of spiritual progress, not an outpouring of girlish chatter?"

"Spiritual progress can encompass confession."

"Yes, but—"

"Let me make my position quite clear. I doubt that any blatantly indiscreet written evidence exists. What I'm much more concerned about is the possibility of an innocent document being quoted out of context and distorted. You know how unscrupulous the gutter-press can be."

In the pause which followed I found I was again sharing his view of an unpalatable but undeniable reality, for I could see that Jardine's private life, no matter how innocent, might well prove to be the Church's Achilles' heel in its current uneasy relationship with Fleet Street. A new king might have been crowned but the memory of the previous king still aroused much sympathy, and Lang's speech criticising Edward VIII for abandoning his duty in order to marry a divorced woman had been widely resented for its priggishness. In these circumstances the last thing Lang needed, as he strove to regain the ground he had lost, was a scandal about a sexually alert bishop who lived in a questionable ménage à trois.

"Well, Charles? Are you going to help me?"

The ringmaster was cracking his whip, but in fact no whip was needed. I was loyal to my Church and despite a considerable ambivalence I was loyal to my Archbishop. "Of course I'll help you, Your Grace," I said without hesitation, and the die was cast.

4

"HOW do I start?" I said, surveying my new role of archiepiscopal spy and at once confronting the depths of my inexperience.

Lang was immediately soothing. "Once you're safely established at the bishop's palace, I'm sure it won't take you long to decide whether I do in fact have cause for anxiety."

"But how on earth do I establish myself at the palace?"

"That's simple. I'll telephone Jardine and ask him to put you up for a couple of nights. He's not going to refuse me, particularly when I tell him you wish to visit the Cathedral Library in order to do some research for your new book. Have you ever been to the Cathedral Library at Starbridge? The chief glory, as you probably know, is that early manuscript of St. Anselm's *Prayers and Meditations*."

"But my new book's about the influence of Modalism on fourth-century Christology—it's got nothing to do with St. Anselm at all!"

Lang was unperturbed. "Then you'd better be writing an article for a learned journal, a reappraisal of St. Anselm's ontological argument, perhaps—"

"And I suppose that during a discussion of the ontological argument I casually ask Jardine if I can sift his journal for pearls of wisdom, heavily disguised as impure thoughts on the subject of his wife's companion!"

Lang gave me one of his thinnest smiles. Knowing that my levity had encountered disapproval, I said at once: "I'm sorry, Your Grace, but I honestly don't see how I'm to proceed. If you could issue me with some elementary marching orders—"

This appeal to his authority smoothed the ruffled feathers. "Ask Jardine about his journal. It's no secret that he keeps one, and as it's unusual to find a clergyman continuing that sort of spiritual exercise into middle age I think you'd be justified in exhibiting curiosity on the subject. I want to know if he uses it as a confessional. Then I also suggest you talk to Miss Christie in an attempt to find out if Jardine writes to her when he's away from home. To be frank, Charles, I'm even more worried about the possibility of indiscreet letters than I am about a journal which is probably kept under lock and key. Men of Jardine's age are capable of almost limitless folly where young women are concerned, and even though I do doubt the existence of any blatant indiscretion, there's always the chance that I could be wrong."

"Surely Miss Christie would burn an indiscreet letter?"

"Not necessarily. Not if she were in love with him—and that's why I want you to take a hard look at this ménage to gauge its potential inflammability." Lang, who had written romantic novels in his youth, began to exercise a baroque imagination. "For example," he said, "it's not impossible that Jardine's wholly innocent but the woman's in the grip of a grand passion. Jardine may long to dismiss her yet be terrified of doing so in case she causes trouble."

The plot was dramatic but not, unfortunately, implausible. The attentions of passionate spinsters were an occupational hazard for all members of the clergy, and after allowing a pause to signify that I was giving his theory serious consideration, I said abruptly: "Supposing I succeed in finding something compromising. What do I do?"

"Report to me. Then I'll see Jardine and order him to take action himself. He'd make a much more thorough job of censoring his papers than you ever could."

I was relieved to hear that my activities were not to include sabotage, but nevertheless I still felt a certain amount of shady behaviour was being sanctioned and I decided that the shadiness should be more precisely defined. I said lightly: "If the journal's under lock and key, Your Grace, I trust you don't require me to pick the lock? Or am I expected to behave like a Jesuit: all things to be permitted for the good of the Church?"

"This is the Church of England, Charles, not the Church of Rome. Good heavens, of course I'm not suggesting you behave in any manner unbecoming to a gentleman!" exclaimed Lang with an indignation which only narrowly failed to ring true, and I knew then he had been hoping I would not press him to define the boundaries of the commission too closely. Naturally he was obliged to repudiate any suggestion that he might be sanctioning shady behaviour. "All I'm suggesting," he said with a very passable attempt at innocence, "is that you 'test the water,' as it were, before I dive in. My problem at the moment is that my suspicions are so entirely unsubstantiated that I'm quite unable to confront Jardine with them; but if you too find yourself suspicious after sampling the atmosphere at the palace, I shall feel I can approach Jardine without the fear that I'm making some colossal mistake."

This statement was credible enough, but I decided the time had come to probe how far he was confiding in me. The more he insisted that he believed Jardine to be innocent of any blatant indiscretion, the more tempted I was to suspect the Bishop was giving him the worst kind of clerical nightmares. "Your Grace, is there any possibility at all that Jardine could be in very deep water?"

Lang achieved a patient expression as if I were a wayward child who had asked a foolish question. "My dear Charles, we're all sinners and the possibility of error must always exist, even for a bishop, but in this case the likelihood of deep water's exceedingly remote. Despite all our differences I'm convinced Jardine's devout; if he'd committed a fundamental error, he'd resign."

This statement too was credible. There might have been loose-living bishops in the past but nowadays no bishop was ever accused of anything worse than senility. However, Jardine had not always been a bishop. "Has there been any scandal in his past, a scandal which was successfully hushed up?"

"No. He would hardly have received regular preferment if that had been the case, Charles."

"Yet you mentioned this 'healthy interest' in the opposite sex—"

"Occasionally at a dinner-party he makes it a little too obvious that he finds a woman attractive, but in truth I find that reassuring. If anything were seriously amiss I'm sure he'd be at pains to conceal it."

This struck me as a shrewd judgement, and in the knowledge that I was once more dealing with the canny Scot who inhabited the bottom layer of his personality I decided to risk prolonging my cross-examination. "What about the feather-brained wife?" I said. "Do we know for a fact that he's discontented with her?"

"No. There's a persistent rumour that the marriage has its difficulties but he always speaks of her loyally enough, and the gossip may merely have arisen because they seem an ill-assorted couple. Don't jump to conclusions about that marriage, Charles. Very clever men often marry very stupid women, and just because the Jardines are ill-matched intellectually you shouldn't automatically assume they're unhappy."

After this wise warning that I should avoid approaching my commission with preconceived ideas, I felt there was only one question left to ask. "When do I leave for Starbridge?"

"As soon as Jardine's prepared to receive you as his guest," said Lang, well satisfied with my commitment to his cause, and finally allowed the warmth to permeate his thin dry politician's smile.

5

I THOUGHT he would leave then but he stayed. For a time we talked of College matters; he wanted to know whether the undergraduates were still susceptible to the evangelical Christianity of Frank Buchman's "groupists," but I said I thought that influence was on the wane.

"The tragedy of such movements," said the Archbishop, who had sanctioned the Buchmanites in 1933 and had probably lived to regret it, "is that their good intentions are so vulnerable to abuse. Troubled young men should seek to purge their souls in private confession before a priest, not in the so-called 'sharing' of painful experiences with a group who may be spiritually no wiser than they are." So subtle was his manipulation of the conversation that it was not until he asked his next question that I perceived the drift of his thoughts. "Do you hear many confessions, Charles?"

"I never seek them. I always stress that the Church of England says only that one may make confession, never that one must. But of course if an undergraduate comes to me, I hear him."

"And you yourself? I was wondering," said Lang, finally revealing the core of his curiosity, "if you might wish to take advantage of this rare private meeting by raising any problem which you feel would be eased by a confidential discussion."

I allowed only the briefest silence to elapse before I replied, but I knew my silence had been not only noted but reserved as a subject for future speculation. "How very thoughtful of you, Your Grace," I said, "but I'm happy to say that the only serious problem I have at present is to decide what to put in my new book."

"A problem which I'm sure your intellect will be more than capable of resolving in due course! But may I ask who your spiritual director is nowadays?"

"I still go to the Abbot of the Fordite monks at Grantchester."

"Ah yes, Father Reid. I wish I had the time to call on him while I'm in Cambridge, but alas! One is always so monstrously busy." Lang made a theatrical gesture of despair, glanced at his watch and rose to his feet. My audience was drawing to an end.

I asked for his blessing, and when he gave it to me I was aware of his gifts as a churchman. I remembered how his care and concern had sustained me during the difficult years both before and after my ordination; I recalled how his generosity of spirit, glamorously displayed, had sparked my understanding that Christianity could be not a pallid priggish way of life but a glittering realisation of one's finest possibilities. People can be led to Christianity by infinitely diverse routes, and there was no denying that I had been led by Lang's worldly success to the creed which rated worldly success unimportant. Beyond the glittering image lay the stark absolute truth. It was a juxtaposition which had fascinated me ever since I had decided to be a clergyman, but as I now looked without effort past Lang's worldly glamour to all the flaws of his powerful personality I was conscious of amazement that he should have had such an influence on my life. How had this vain, pompous, arid old bachelor ever inspired me to a discipleship which emphasised the humility and simplicity of Christ? The inspiration struck me as little short of miraculous, but then guilt assailed me because although I owed Lang so much I could no longer view him through those rose-tinted spectacles which I had worn with such unquestioning ease in the past.

He departed. The ensuing solitude came as a relief, and retiring at once to my bedroom I stripped off both gown and cassock before pausing to light a cigarette. At once I felt more relaxed, and as soon as I was dressed with the minimum of formality I returned to my sitting-room, mixed myself a substantial whisky-and-soda and began to contemplate my mission to Starbridge.

6

THE more I considered the situation, the less enamoured of it I became. It would involve me in deception; although it could be argued by any student of moral philosophy that the welfare of the Church justified a little espionage by the Archbishop's henchman, I was averse to involving myself in one of those situations where the end was held to justify the means. When I had cited Jesuitical casuistry earlier, Lang had all but quoted Shakespeare's line: 'This is the English, not the Turkish court,' but nevertheless I did wonder, as I recalled our conversation, what game Lang was really playing.

Jardine had humiliated him during that debate in the House of Lords ten days ago. "What are the ordinary people of England to think," the Bishop had demanded in fury, "when on one of the great moral issues of the day the Archbishop of Canterbury says with a conspicuous lack of courage that he can vote neither for this bill nor against it? Is this leadership? Is this the great ecclesiastical pearl of wisdom which so many people have been eagerly awaiting? Is this the ultimate fate of the Church of England—to be led into the wilderness of moral confusion by a septuagenarian Scot who has apparently lost touch with those whom he purports to serve?"

I thought Lang would want to get rid of Jardine after that performance, and the only way Lang could rid himself of a turbulent bishop without a scandal was to find evidence of a disabling impropriety so that a resignation could be extorted in private. In other words, I suspected that I was being used not merely to safeguard the Church but to promote a secret war between two of the country's leading churchmen.

This was a most unedifying thought. As I followed my Sunday evening custom of making myself a cheese sandwich in the little pantry attached to my rooms, I wondered if I could extricate myself from Lang's scheme, but I could see no way out. I had committed myself. I could hardly admit now that I was suffering debilitating doubts. Lang would be most displeased, and incurring my Archbishop's displeasure was a prospect on which I had no wish to dwell. I decided my best hope of resolving the dilemma lay in proving Jardine's private life was as pure as driven snow with the result that the Archbishop's Machiavellian plans would collapse in an unconsummated heap, but the next moment I was asking myself how likely it was that Jardine was an episcopal saint. Even if one ruled out the possibility of a fatal error, there was still room for a variety of smuts on the driven snow;

the thought of flirtatious behaviour at dinner-parties was not encouraging.

I finished my second whisky, ate my sandwich and brewed myself some coffee. Then I decided to embark on some preliminary research by talking to two people who almost certainly knew more about Jardine than I did.

My first telephone call was to a London friend who worked for *The Church Gazette.* We had been up at Cambridge together as undergraduates, and later when I had been Lang's chaplain and Jack had begun his career as an ecclesiastical journalist, it had suited us both to maintain our friendship.

"I confess I'm ringing you out of sheer vulgar curiosity," I said, after the conventional inquiries had been exchanged. "I'm about to stay at the episcopal palace at Starbridge—what can you tell me about its current tenant?"

"Ah, the vampire who feeds on the blood of pompous archbishops! Brush up your theories on the Virgin Birth, Charles, take a gun and shoot straight from the hip—after dinner at Starbridge when the Lovely Ladies have withdrawn the conversation will be guaranteed to put you through your theological paces."

"Are you deliberately trying to frighten me?"

"Oh, don't despair of survival! He likes theologians—they give him a good run for his money. But why are you offering yourself to Jardine for shooting practice?"

"I'm beginning to wonder. Tell me more about these lovely ladies I shall meet at the dinner-table."

"The gossips say no man receives an invitation to dine unless he has an attractive wife, but I dare say that's an exaggeration."

"What's Jardine's own wife like?"

"She's a wonderful fluffy little thing with a heart of gold and a stunning selection of tea-gowns. Everyone adores her. Her favourite topic of conversation's the weather."

"That must make a welcome change from the Virgin Birth. And isn't there a good-looking companion in the household? What do I talk about with her?"

"Don't get excited, Charles—curb your natural inclination to indulge in impure thoughts! Miss Christie's the original ice-maiden. Starbridge is littered with the bones of those who have died of unrequited love for that particular lady."

"Well, I wasn't seriously expecting to find a nymphomaniac lodged at the episcopal palace—"

"No, Jardine knows when to play safe. Lovely ladies, preferably titled and always chaperoned by their boring old husbands, are more in his line than nymphomaniacs and ice-maidens. No scandal, of course. He just likes to look and chat."

"No doubt he enjoys the chance to talk of subjects other than the weather."

"Ah, so you've heard the rumour that the Jardines' marriage has died of boredom, but don't you believe it, old chap! Mrs. Jardine's still pretty as a picture and I shouldn't think Jardine gives a damn about her intellect once the lights are out in the episcopal bedchamber."

"Jack, are you still working for *The Church Gazette*? You're sounding exactly like a hack from *The News of the World*!"

"Nonsense! There's nothing scandalous about a bishop who sleeps with his wife. *The News of the World* would only bat an eyelid if he started sleeping with someone else, but as far as I know—"

"Yes, how much of this prurient rigmarole of yours is hearsay and how much is firsthand information?"

"Well, naturally I'm in league with the chaplain, but since he always presents his hero as a cross between St. Paul and Sir Galahad he's hardly a source of spicy gossip. However I do have firsthand experience of the Jardines. Last March I was invited down to Starbridge to report on a Church committee meeting which was discussing special Coronation services in the Southern Province—Jardine, as chairman, was playing host. Of course he's rumoured to eat journalists on toast for breakfast, but in fact he was very civil to me and Mrs. Jardine was a poppet. She gave me some ginger biscuits and said I reminded her of her nephew."

"And the luscious Miss Christie?"

"She gave me a cool look and told me where to find the lavatory. But I think you'll like both the Jardines, Charles, and I see no reason why you shouldn't survive your visit with ease. Just gird your loins when the sinful vintage port starts circulating, and take a deep breath if the Bishop begins to hold forth on the Virgin Birth . . ."

7

I NEXT telephoned a man whom I had met at Theological College and who was now the incumbent of a rural parish in the Starbridge diocese. Although our paths had diverged since our ordination, we had maintained our friendship by letter and I felt I could express without insincerity the hope that we might meet during my visit. However, a meeting was to be impossible; he and his family were about to take their first holiday in five years. Keeping quiet about my spring visit to France I said I was sure Bournemouth would be delightful, but I was still repressing a shudder at the thought of the cheap boardinghouse which awaited him when he asked why I was visiting Starbridge.

To reveal that the Bishop had invited me to stay at the instigation of Dr. Lang would have seemed, in the circumstances, an unforgivable piece of bragging, so I merely mentioned my desire to visit the Cathedral Library and said I would be calling at the palace as a courtesy. "What's your opinion of Jardine, Philip?" I added. "Do you find him a good bishop?"

"I find him an embarrassment, quite frankly. That speech in the Lords! I felt sorry for Lang. A bishop's got no business to attack his archbishop in public."

"But what's he like when he's doing his job instead of chasing every headline in Fleet Street?"

"Why ask me? I usually only see him once a year for confirmations."

"But don't confirmations give a good indication of a bishop's conscientiousness? There's a world of difference between a bishop who can barely disguise the fact that he's treading a very well-worn path and a bishop who makes the candidates feel the occasion's as special for him as it is for them."

"True," said Philip reluctantly. "Well, I have to admit Jardine can't be faulted there—although when he first became Bishop five years ago he did seem 'distrait.' However, I put that down to lack of experience. The next year he was quite different, very much in command before the candidates, very relaxed behind the scenes, but all the same . . . I've heard he can be an absolute terror."

"In what way?"

"Well, he's supposed to be at his worst when a clergyman wants to get married. He's got a bee in his bonnet about clergymen being ruined by unsuitable wives, and if he doesn't think a clerical fiancée's going to make the grade as a vicar's wife he has no hesitation in saying so. It makes one wonder about his own marriage—rumour has it that Mrs. Jardine's delightful but incompetent and that the real power at the palace is her companion."

"Yes, I've heard about Miss Christie. Jack Ryder paints her as a femme fatale."

"What rubbish! She wouldn't have lasted ten years in a bishop's household unless she was propriety personified!"

"But she's attractive, isn't she? Wouldn't it have been safer to engage a companion who looked like the back end of a tram?"

"Jardine's the kind of man who would baulk at confronting the back end of a tram every morning at the breakfast-table."

"Philip," I said, amused, "I'm receiving the clear impression that you don't like him, but is this solely because he attacks his Archbishop in public and demolishes clerical fiancées? Neither of these unfortunate habits can have affected you personally."

"No, thank God Mary and I tied the knot while Jardine was still Dean of Radbury! I don't dislike him, Charles—he's always been charming both to Mary and to me—but I do disapprove of him. I think he's far too worldly, and he's got a very flashy nouveau-riche streak which should have been ironed out before he was let loose on an income of several thousand a year. I'll never forget the garden-party he gave for the diocesan clergy two years ago—talk about extravagance! I was shocked. I kept thinking what all the catering must have cost and calculating how many poor people in my parish could have benefited from the money."

"My dear Philip! Aren't you being a little churlish about your generous Bishop?"

"Perhaps. And perhaps you live in an ivory tower, Charles, and don't know what's really going on in the world. How long has it been since you visited a house where the husband's been unemployed since the Slump, the wife's half-dead with TB and the children have rickets as well as lice?"

There was a silence.

At last Philip said rapidly: "I'm sorry—" but I interrupted him. "I'm very conscious, believe me," I said, "that I lack experience at the parish level."

"Nevertheless I shouldn't have implied—"

"It doesn't matter." There was another pause before I added: "Well, I'm sorry I shan't be seeing you, Philip. Perhaps next time—"

"Oh yes," he said. "Next time."

But we both knew "next time" was a long way away.

8

ON the following morning the Archbishop telephoned to inform me that I should present myself at the palace early on Wednesday evening. Jardine had professed delight at the prospect of offering me hospitality, a profession which Lang cynically suspected derived from a guilty wish to make amends for the bellicose speech in the House of Lords. ". . . and I'm sure he'll give you a warm welcome, Charles," was the Archbishop's dry conclusion.

"Did he remember meeting me last year?"

"Of course! When I mentioned your name, he said: 'Ah yes, the young

Canon from Cambridge who thinks the world began not with Adam and Eve but with the Council of Nicaea!' "

So Jardine had at least glanced at the book which had made my name in theological circles. He himself had published no work of historical scholarship, but that never deterred him from writing trenchant reviews of other people's efforts, and I had been surprised as well as relieved when my own book had escaped his characteristic literary butchery. How the escape had been achieved I was uncertain, but possibly he found any discussion of Arianism boring and had decided to rest his pen.

These thoughts about scholarship reminded me that I had not yet decided why I should need to consult the library of Starbridge Cathedral, and aware how important it was that my need should be convincing, I spent some time pondering on the problem before I devised a stratagem which would enable me to tell the truth. I had long been contemplating the revision of my lecture notes on medieval thought. I now decided that my undergraduates were going to learn more about St. Anselm, and as a conscientious lecturer I naturally felt obliged to cast a glance over Starbridge's early manuscript of *The Prayers and Meditations.*

I suffered a further moment of uneasiness as I contemplated the duplicity inherent in this decision, but then I pulled myself together with the thought that no harm could come to me even if Jardine were steeped in apostasy. On the contrary, Lang was bound to be grateful for my help with the result that I would inevitably emerge from the affair with my future prospects in the Church enhanced.

Casting my last doubt aside I began to prepare for my journey.

9

SO I came at last to Starbridge, radiant ravishing Starbridge, immortalised by famous artists, photographed by innumerable visitors and lauded by guide-books as the most beautiful city west of the Avon. I could remember clearly from my previous visit as an undergraduate the medieval streets, the flower-filled parks and the languid river which curved in an arc around the mound on which the Cathedral stood. The Cathedral itself dominated not only the city but the valley. Wider than Winchester, longer than Canterbury, set in a walled precinct which was even larger than the Close at Salisbury, Starbridge Cathedral was renowned for embodying in pale stone and vivid glass the most glittering of medieval visions.

The city itself was small, and being encircled on three sides by the river it still gave an impression of compactness despite the recent housing development to the east. It lay snugly in the middle of its green valley like a jewel displayed on velvet, and the smooth slopes of the surrounding hills added to the impression that the landscape had been designed in order to show the city to its best advantage.

The diocese was primarily rural but it included the port of Starmouth with its sprawling slums, so there was a dark underside to the tranquillity which formed the stranger's immediate impression of the area. Nonetheless I thought Jardine was probably well pleased with his latest preferment. The diocese was rich; his income was well to the fore among episcopal salaries. London was easily accessible by train, a fact which meant he could keep in close touch with the centres of power, both secular and ecclesiastical, and the bishopric conferred an immediate right to a seat in the House of Lords, a privilege not accompanying the majority of bishoprics where the incumbents had to wait their turn for an ecclesiastical seat to fall vacant. Starbridge was not Canterbury and it was not York, but it was plush, privileged and pleasing to the eye, and no doubt there were many among Jardine's episcopal brethren who envied him.

I had decided to travel to Starbridge in my car, not the sports car which I inevitably found myself driving whenever I dreamt of motors, but the respectable little Baby Austin which was cheap to run and easy to manipulate out of tight corners in the busy streets of Cambridge. Whenever I hankered for an MG, I reminded myself how fortunate I was to have even an Austin. Most clergymen could not afford a car, and in fact motors were still regarded by the older bishops as an evil which lured parsons on jaunts away from their parishes.

The road began to curve among hills as I approached Starbridge, and soon I glimpsed the Cathedral in the distance. The road curved again, the spire vanished, but at the next twist it was once more visible, slim and ethereal, a symbol of man's inchoate yearning to reach upwards to the infinite. As the road continued to wind I felt as if it were mirroring life itself, granting glimpses of transcendence only to rush on before the transcendence could be fully experienced, but finally the last fold in the road lay behind me and I could see the entire city shimmering in the valley below.

This view over a settlement was very old. The Romans had built their city Starovinium on the ruined encampment of the British tribe the Starobrigantes, and the ancient name still survived in city landmarks and on official documents. The Bishop, who was theoretically married to his diocese, was entitled to use the surname Staro in his correspondence, and I had proof of this tradition in my pocket. Jardine himself had sent a letter to welcome me to Starbridge.

"My dear Dr. Ashworth," he had written in a bold, striking hand,

The Archbishop of Canterbury has informed me that you wish to pursue your studies in the Cathedral Library, and may I now confirm that you would be most welcome to stay at the palace from the evening of July the seventh until the morning of the tenth. His Grace thought you would probably arrive by motor, but should you prefer to travel by train, please send a wire to my chaplain, Gerald Harvey, who will arrange for my chauffeur to meet you at the station. His Grace also thought that you would not wish to stay more than three nights, but if you should decide to prolong your visit I hope you will assist me at the early service of Holy Communion in the Cathedral on Sunday. In looking forward to the renewal of our acquaintance, Dr. Ashworth, I send my best wishes for a safe journey and assure you that I remain yours very sincerely,

ADAM ALEXANDER STARO

The auguries for my visit could hardly have been more favourable. Descending from the hills I drove across the floor of the valley and finally entered the city.

10

THE crooked medieval streets were confusing but the way to the Cathedral was signposted and I soon found myself at the gateway of the Close. Slowing the car to a crawl I asked the constable on duty to direct me to the palace; my memory of the Close was hazy.

I drove on, and the next moment the Cathedral was towering above me in an overpowering display of architectural virtuosity. There had been no later additions, no ill-judged alterations. Built during the short span of forty years, the Cathedral was uniform, untouched, unspoilt, a monument to faith, genius and the glory of English Perpendicular.

I drove down the North Walk with the vast sward of the churchyard on my right. On my left the ancient houses, dissimilar in style yet harmonious in their individual beauty, provided the perfect foil to the Cathedral's splendour, and as I turned south into the East Walk I experienced that sense of time continuing, an awareness which is never more insistent than in a place where a long span of the past is visually present.

At the end of the East Walk the palace gates stood open, and within seconds I was confronting the palace itself, a Victorian "improvement" on the original Tudor building which had been destroyed by fire in the last century. Dr. Jardine's home was a mock-Gothic travesty built in the same pale stone as the Cathedral, but it was not unpleasing. Smooth lawns and ancient beech trees framed the house, and above the porch the arms of Starbridge were carved in the stone in a brave attempt to unite medieval custom with a wayward Victorian illusion.

Parking my car in a secluded corner of the forecourt, I extracted my bag and paused to listen. The birds were singing; the leaves of the beech trees were a brilliant green against the cloudless sky; the town beyond the walls of the Close might have been a hundred miles away. Again I sensed time continuing. I was standing in twentieth-century England yet at the same time I felt a mere pace away from a past which contained the seeds of an alluring future, and suddenly I forgot the harsh realities of the present, the horror of Hitler, the agony of the Spanish Civil War, the despair of those whose lives had been ruined by the Slump. I was conscious only of my privileged good fortune as I allowed myself to be seduced by the subtle glamour of Starbridge, and running up the steps to the front door I rang the bell with all the eagerness of an actor who could barely wait for his cue to walk onstage.

The door was opened by a butler who looked like a character from a Trollope novel—a worldly version of Mr. Harding, perhaps—and I stepped into a vast dark hall. Beyond some mock-Gothic furniture of varying degrees of ugliness a handsome staircase rose to a gallery. The walls were adorned with dim portraits of nineteenth-century gentlemen in clerical dress.

"If you'd care to come this way, sir . . ." The butler had already taken the bag from my hand when a woman emerged from the far end of the hall. As the butler paused at once I paused beside him, and the woman moved swiftly, smoothly, silently towards us through the shadows.

"Dr. Ashworth?" She held out a slim hand. "Welcome to Starbridge. I'm Miss Christie, Mrs. Jardine's companion."

I took her hand in mine and knew without a second's hesitation that I wanted her.

II

"I pleasantly assured him that in my belief, based on the experience of a long ministry, it would be roughly true to say of the married clergy of the Church of England that probably fifty per cent were ruined by their wives and fifty per cent were saved."

Letters of
HERBERT HENSLEY HENSON,
ed. E. F. Braley

I

NO one had described Miss Christie to me, and Jack's reference to an ice-maiden had evoked an image of a tall blonde. However, Miss Christie was small, no more than five foot two, with slender ankles, a slim waist, reddish hair and black-lashed dark eyes. She also possessed high cheekbones, a delicately moulded but very firm chin, and a subtle mouth which somehow reinforced this hint of a determined character while conveying an impression of sensuality. Her make-up was discreet; her grey skirt and white blouse were restrained in taste, as befitted a lady's companion in a clerical household. I thought her alluring beyond description, and my first coherent thought was: how could he resist her? Yet I knew that this was a wild question which failed to reflect the reality of the situation. Unless he was an apostate Jardine had no choice but to resist, but such was Miss Christie's allure that for the first time I seriously considered the possibility of apostasy.

She showed me to my room. I managed to maintain a polite conversation as we ascended the stairs, but all the time I was thinking about Jardine in the light of what I now knew of Miss Christie. As I calmed down I dismissed the melodramatic notion of apostasy, but I now began to wonder if Jardine's inclination to form harmless friendships with good-looking women was his way of deflecting an inclination which was not harmless at all.

I roused myself from these speculations as Miss Christie led the way into a large bright room, sombrely adorned with more massive Victorian furniture. Beyond the window the garden stretched downhill to the river, and on the far side of the sparkling water cows were grazing among the buttercups in the meadows. Starbridge lay east of this outmost curve of the river, and to the west the farmlands stretched across the valley to the hills.

"What a beautiful view!" I said, as the butler deposited my bag and departed. Miss Christie had moved to the vase on top of the chest of drawers and was restoring the symmetry of the flower arrangement by adjusting an errant rose.

"The bathroom is at the end of the corridor," she said, evidently finding my comment on the view too mundane to merit even a murmur of agreement. "Dinner is at eight but we assemble for cocktails in the drawing-room at any time after quarter-past seven. The water's hot every evening from six o'clock onwards. I trust you have everything you require, Dr. Ashworth, but if by any chance something's been forgotten do please ring the bell by your bedside."

I thanked her. She gave a brief formal smile and the next moment I was alone.

There was a Bible placed on the bedside table to remind visitors that despite the grandeur of their surroundings they were in a clerical household, and in an effort to distract my mind from the temptation to meander down carnal byways I opened the pages in search of an edifying quotation. However, this random dip produced only Ezekiel's diatribe against the harlot. Still thinking of Miss Christie I ploughed forward into the New Testament and eventually found myself lingering on the text: "For there is nothing covered, that shall not be revealed; and hid, that shall not be known."

That seemed like a good omen for an espionage agent. I closed the Bible. Then after visiting the regal lavatory, which remained as a sumptuous memorial to Victorian plumbing, I unpacked my bag and sat down with my prayer book to read the evening office.

2

WHEN I closed my prayer book the time was half-past six. I stripped, washed at the basin to erase all trace of my journey, and decided to shave. I did not usually shave twice a day but I wanted to appear thoroughly well-groomed, not only to impress Miss Christie but to impress the Bishop. I sensed Jardine might have strong views on the obligation of a clergyman to present a neat appearance to the world; he himself had been very smart, very dapper, when I had encountered him in Cambridge eight months ago.

The evening was warm and the prospect of encasing myself in my formal clerical clothes was not appealing, but naturally I had no choice but to martyr myself in the name of convention. I spent some time in front of the glass as I coaxed my hair to lie flat. I have curly hair which I keep short, but it has wayward tendencies which water can rarely subdue for long. However, I never use hair-oil. It makes me look like a bounder, and I was always unaccountably nervous in case my appearance reflected the wrong image in the mirror.

Yet that evening I found my reflection reassuring. Here was no bounder, no shady character from a modern "shocker," but a clergyman who was thirty-seven and looked younger. Playing squash and tennis had curbed an inclination to put on weight as I left my twenties behind, and although I was a little too fond of good food and more than a little too fond of good wine, my appearance proved I had these weaknesses well in control. I saw no heaviness around the jaw, no pouches beneath the eyes, no giveaway lines around the mouth. I looked like the man I wanted to be and the image in the long glass seemed impregnable as I surveyed it in the golden evening light.

Glancing at my watch I saw that the time had come for me to make my appearance downstairs. The curtain was about to rise on the stage at Starbridge, and leaving my room I headed for the wings to await my cue.

3

I HAD no trouble finding the drawing-room. As I descended the stairs I could hear the murmur of voices drifting towards me through the open door on the far side of the hall. A woman gave an attractive laugh, a man protested: "No, I'm serious! I've always thought *Peter Pan* was a most sinister story!" and I deduced that the conversation had arisen in connection with the recent death of Sir James Barrie.

"But, Henry, you can't possibly describe an innocent fantasy as sinister!"

"Why not? Captain Hook reminds me of Mussolini."

"Everyone reminds you of Mussolini. Oh darling, I do wish you'd forget Abyssinia and look on the bright side for a change—after all, think how well we're doing! We've survived the War, the Slump and the Abdication—and now that dear Mr. Chamberlain's poised to turn the country into a vast version of Birmingham with that divinely businesslike efficiency of his, I'm sure we're all set for a rosy future!"

"This sounds like another of Barrie's fantasies. No wonder you enjoy *Peter Pan,* my dear."

I walked into the room. The first person I saw was Miss Christie. She was standing by the French windows and looking formidably aloof. In contrast, the other three occupants of the room were exuding that easy camaraderie which arises when people have enjoyed an unaffected friendship for a long time. By the fireplace stood an elderly man with a frank mild face and that air of self-confidence which can only be acquired from a lifetime spent in privileged surroundings. He was drinking a cocktail which appeared to be a dry martini. Perched on the arm of a sofa a handsome woman was also toying with a martini glass, and beyond her a plump, pretty, grey-haired little woman in a lavish lavender evening gown was selecting a water-biscuit from a silver dish nearby.

Everyone turned to look at me. Miss Christie at once moved forward to make the introductions, but she was a long way away and the plump, pretty little woman forestalled her.

"Dr. Ashworth!" she exclaimed, beaming at me. "How nice to see you! I hope your motor journey wasn't too difficult but it must have helped that the weather was fine. Isn't the weather beautiful? All the sunshine's so good for the garden."

I did not need to be told that I was being addressed by my hostess. "How do you do, Mrs. Jardine," I said, smiling as I took her hand in mine. "It's very kind of you to have me to stay."

"Not at all, it's splendid for Alex to have someone clever to talk to! Now let me introduce you to everyone. Miss Christie you've met, of course, and here"—she turned to the couple who had been debating *Peter Pan*—"are Lord and Lady Starmouth who have always been so kind to us ever since Alex was Vicar of St. Mary's Mayfair. They have such a delightful house in Curzon Street and Alex stays there when he has to be up in town for the debates in the House of Lords—oh heavens, perhaps I shouldn't mention the Lords debates, especially as you're a friend of the Archbishop's—Lyle, am I dropping some frightful brick?"

"Dr. Ashworth," said Miss Christie, "is probably only thinking how pleasant it must be for the Bishop to stay with friends whenever he's up in town."

But in fact I was thinking that the good-looking Countess of Starmouth might well be one of Jardine's "lovely ladies," faithfully chaperoned by one of the gentlemen whom Jack had described as "boring old husbands." However, this unflattering description hardly did justice to the Earl of Starmouth, who looked alert enough to be entertaining even though he might have been on the wrong side of seventy. Perhaps Lady Starmouth kept him young; I estimated that she was at least twenty years his junior.

"My wife collects clerics," said Lord Starmouth to me as we shook hands. "She'll collect you too if you're not careful."

"I adore clergymen," agreed his wife with that aristocratic frankness which never fails to make the more reticent members of the middle classes cringe with embarrassment. "It's the collar, of course. It makes a man seem so deliciously forbidden."

"What can I offer you to drink, Dr. Ashworth?" said Miss Christie, middle-class propriety well to the fore.

"A dry sherry, please." No ambitious clergyman drank cocktails at episcopal dinner-parties.

A young man in clerical garb bustled into the room, muttered: "Bother! No Bishop," and bustled out again.

"Poor Gerald!" said Mrs. Jardine. "I really wonder sometimes whether we made the right decision when we installed a telephone. It's so terribly hard for the chaplain when people ring up at awkward moments . . . Oh, here's Willy! Come and meet my brother, Dr. Ashworth."

I was introduced to a Colonel Cobden-Smith, a hale gentleman in his sixties with a pink face, white hair and a cherubic expression. He was accompanied by his wife, a thin energetic woman who reminded me of a greyhound, and by a very large St. Bernard dog who padded majestically through the room to the terrace on his way to water the flower-beds.

"I know nothing about theology," said Mrs. Cobden-Smith to me as soon as we had been introduced. "I always say to Alex that I know nothing about theology and I don't want to know anything either. As far as I'm concerned, God's God, the Church is the Church, the Bible's the Bible and I can't understand what all the arguments are about."

"Funny business, religion," mused her husband, uttering this dubious remark with such an ingenuous admiration that no clergyman could have found him offensive, and began to talk about a Buddhist monk he had met in India.

The young chaplain bustled back into the room. "So sorry, Mrs. Jardine, but you know what the Archdeacon's like when he rings up in a panic . . ."

I was introduced to Gerald Harvey. He was a short bespectacled man in his early twenties who seemed to be perpetually out of breath, and I wondered whether the Bishop of Starbridge regularly reduced his chaplain to this state of wild-eyed anxiety.

". . . and I've heard about your book, of course," he was saying, "but I confess I haven't read it because all those ancient arguments about the Trinity simply make me want to tear off my dog-collar and enlist in the Foreign Legion—oh my goodness, there's the doorbell and the Bishop's still not down! I'd better go and see if anything's wrong."

He dashed away again. I was surprised that Jardine had selected such a plain, unsophisticated and clearly unintellectual chaplain, but before I could speculate on the existence of sterling virtues which would have qualified Harvey for his post, the butler announced the arrival of a Mr. and Mrs. Frank Jennings. Jennings, I soon discovered, had just been appointed to teach dogmatics at the Theological College in the Close. He himself was unremarkable in his appearance but his wife was a pretty young blonde, and remembering Jack's gossip I wondered how far her looks had qualified the couple for an invitation to the episcopal dinner-table.

"I found your book most stimulating," Jennings said to me agreeably, but before he could continue, his wife exclaimed: "Good gracious, Frank, look at that gigantic dog!"

"Alex had a dog once," said little Mrs. Jardine as the St. Bernard made a stately return to the room. "He called it Rhetoric. But we were living in London at the time and poor little Rhet was run over by such a vulgar Rolls-Royce—really, I've never felt the same about motor cars since . . . Do you have a dog, Dr. Ashworth?"

"No, Mrs. Jardine."

"Do you have a wife, Dr. Ashworth?" called Lady Starmouth, giving me a friendly look with her fine dark eyes.

I was acutely aware of Miss Christie's hand pausing in the act of pouring out glasses of sherry for the newcomers.

"I'm a widower, Lady Starmouth," I said.

"All clergymen ought to be married," said the authoritative Mrs. Cobden-Smith, offering a handful of water-biscuits to the St. Bernard. "They say the Roman Catholics have frightful trouble with their celibate priests."

"They say the Church of England has frightful trouble with its married clergy," said a strong, harsh, well-remembered voice from the doorway, and as we all turned to face him the Bishop of Starbridge made a grand entrance into his drawing-room.

4

DR. *JARDINE* was a man of medium height, slim and well-proportioned, with dark greying hair and brown eyes so light that they were almost amber. The eyes were set deep and wide apart; by far his most arresting feature, they were capable of assuming a hypnotic lambent glaze in the pulpit, a physiological trick which Jardine used sparingly but effectively to underline his considerable gifts as a preacher. His quick abrupt walk revealed his energy and hinted at his powerful restless intellect. Unlike most bishops he wore his gaiters with élan, as if conscious that he had the figure to triumph over the absurdity of the archaic episcopal costume, and when he entered the room he was radiating the electric self-confidence which his enemies decried as bumptious and his admirers defended as debonair.

"Don't be alarmed, everyone!" he said smiling, after the opening remark which had won our attention. "I'm not about to secede to Rome, but I can never resist the urge to counter my sister-in-law's scandalously dogmatic assertions . . . Good evening, Dr. Ashworth, I'm delighted to see you. Good evening, Jennings—Mrs. Jennings—now, Mrs. Jennings, there's no need to be shy. I may be a fire-breathing bishop but I'm extremely tame in the company of pretty ladies—isn't that so, Lady Starmouth?"

"Tame as a tiger!" said the Countess, amused.

"We used to have some good tiger-shoots in India," reflected Colonel Cobden-Smith. "I remember—"

"I saw such an adorable tiger at the zoo once," said Mrs. Jardine, "but I'm sure it would have been so much happier back in the wild."

"Nonsense!" said the Bishop robustly, accepting a glass of sherry from Miss Christie. "If the unfortunate animal had been in its natural habitat, your brother would have come along and murdered it. Did you arrive in time for Evensong, Dr. Ashworth?"

"I'm afraid I was late getting here. The traffic around London—"

"Don't worry, I don't award black marks for missing services. Now, Mrs. Jennings, sit down and tell me all about yourself—have you managed to find a house yet?"

As his wife was purloined by the Bishop, Jennings began to tell me about his arduous quest for a property in the suburbs. Occasionally I offered a word of sympathy, but for the most part I sipped my sherry in silence, eavesdropped on the other conversations and kept a surreptitious watch on Miss Christie.

Lady Starmouth suddenly glided into my field of vision. "I think you must be the youngest canon I've ever met, Dr. Ashworth! Does this mean the Church is at last beginning to believe it's not a crime to be under forty?"

"The canonry came with the job, Lady Starmouth. When Archbishop Laud founded Laud's College and Cambridge Cathedral in the seventeenth century, he stipulated that the College should appoint a doctor of divinity to teach theology and act as one of the Cathedral's residentiary canons." I suddenly realised that Miss Christie was looking straight at me, but when our glances met she turned away. I continued to watch as she picked up the sherry decanter again but Colonel Cobden-Smith cornered her before she could embark on the task of refilling glasses.

"... and I hear you were Dr. Lang's chaplain once," Lady Starmouth was saying. "How did you meet him?"

Reluctantly I averted my gaze from Miss Christie. "He gave away the prizes during my last year at school."

"You were head-boy of your school, of course," said Jardine from the depths of the sofa nearby.

"Well, as a matter of fact," I said, surprised, "yes, I was."

"How clever of you, Alex!" exclaimed Mrs. Jardine. "How did you guess Dr. Ashworth had been head-boy?"

"No boy attracts His Grace's attention unless he shows signs of becoming a walking advertisement for Muscular Christianity."

"I adore Muscular Christianity," said Lady Starmouth.

"If Christianity were a little more muscular the world wouldn't be in such a mess," said the forthright Mrs. Cobden-Smith.

"If Christianity were a little more muscular it wouldn't be Christianity," said the Bishop, again displaying his compulsion to argue with his sister-in-law. "The Sermon on the Mount wasn't a lecture on weight-lifting."

"What exactly *is* Muscular Christianity?" inquired Mrs. Jardine. "I've never been quite sure. Is it just groups of nice-looking young clergymen like Dr. Ashworth?"

" 'Angels and ministers of grace defend us!' " said the Bishop, raising his eyes to Heaven as he quoted *Hamlet.*

"More sherry, anyone?" said Miss Christie, finally escaping from Colonel Cobden-Smith.

"Dinner is served, my Lord," said the butler in a sepulchral voice from the doorway.

5

THE dining-room was as vast as the drawing-room and it too faced down the garden to the river. I had wondered if the gentlemen were required to "take a lady in" to dinner, but Mrs. Jardine gave no instructions and as we all wandered informally into the dining-room I was hoping I might claim the chair next to Miss Christie. However, there were place-cards, and a quick glance told me I was to be disappointed. The Bishop had taken care to encase himself between his two Lovely Ladies for the evening, Lady Starmouth and Mrs. Jennings; I was also placed next to Lady Starmouth, and on my right sat the formidable Mrs. Cobden-Smith, with Frank Jennings on her other side and Gerald Harvey taking the place between Jennings and Mrs. Jardine who sat at the far end of the table.

Opposite me, next to Mrs. Jennings, sat Lord Starmouth, and on his left Miss Christie once more found herself trapped with Colonel Cobden-Smith who had been assigned the chair between her and his sister Mrs. Jardine. The St. Bernard, behaving immaculately, adopted a commanding position on the rug in front of the fireplace and fell asleep.

After the Bishop had said grace we all embarked on a watery celery soup, a disaster which was subsequently redeemed first by poached trout and then by roast lamb. The main course was accompanied by a superb claret. I almost asked the Bishop to identify it, but decided he might subscribe to the view that in Church circles a keen interest in wine was permissible only for bishops or for archdeacons and canons over sixty. With a superhuman exercise of will-power I restricted myself to two glasses and was aware of Jardine noticing as I declined a third.

"Leaving room for the post-prandial port, Canon?"

"Oh, is there port, Bishop? What a treat!" I assumed an expression of innocent surprise.

The dinner surged on, everyone talking with increasing animation as the claret exerted its influence. Mrs. Cobden-Smith asked me about my background, and having established the exact shade of my class she was sufficiently reassured to give me the benefit of her opinions, which ranged from the futility of giving the working classes houses with bathrooms to the folly of listening to the Indian natives who wanted independence. When I could escape from Mrs. Cobden-Smith's attentions, Lady Starmouth pounced and I found myself being subjected to a far more subtle inquisition. Lady Starmouth wanted to know about my wife, but when I volunteered little information in response to her oblique inquiries she decided to probe my views on a topical subject affecting matrimony. I was asked what I thought of A. P. Herbert's celebrated Marriage Bill which had triggered Jardine's attack on Lang in the Lords.

The knowledge of how much I owed the Archbishop was never far from the surface of my mind. I said politely: "I'm afraid I disapprove of divorce being made easier, Lady Starmouth."

"My dear Dr. Ashworth, you surprise me! I thought you'd have very liberal modern views!"

"Not if he's the Archbishop's man," said our host, breaking off his conversation with Mrs. Jennings.

"I'm no one's man but my own, Dr. Jardine!" I said at once. I felt unnerved as well as annoyed that he had seen straight through my dutifully conservative stance.

"Well spoken!" said Lady Starmouth.

"Do you approve of divorce at all, Canon?" said Lord Starmouth with interest.

This placed me in a fresh dilemma. If I wanted to be entirely loyal to Lang, who followed the teaching on divorce in St. Mark's Gospel, I would have to say that I believed marriage to be indissoluble, but I was now anxious to show Jardine that I was no mere sycophantic echo of the Archbishop. On the other hand some loyalty to Lang was essential; I could hardly espouse Jardine's extreme and controversial views. I decided to seek the diplomatic middle course by jettisoning St. Mark in favour of St. Matthew.

"I believe," I said, "that adultery should be a ground for divorce—for both sexes, just as Our Lord said."

"So you disapprove of the rest of A. P. Herbert's Bill?" said Jennings, coming late to the conversation and manifesting the teacher's desire to clarify a clouded issue. "You don't believe that the grounds for divorce should be extended to include cruelty, insanity and desertion?"

"Precisely."

"So!" said Jardine, unable to remain silent a moment longer, his amber eyes lambent at the prospect of debate. "You would approve a divorce, would you, Dr. Ashworth, if a man spends ten minutes in a hotel bedroom with a woman he's never met before—yet you would deny a divorce to a woman whose husband has subjected her for years to the most disgusting cruelties?"

"I'm not denying the remedy of a legal separation in such a case."

"In other words you'd condemn her to a miserable limbo, unable to remarry! And all because you and the other clerics who tow the High Church line insist on clinging to an utterly fallacious interpretation of Our Lord's teaching in the Synoptic Gospels!"

"I—"

"You don't seriously think Our Lord was talking about divorce as a lawyer, do you?"

"I think Our Lord was talking about what he believed to be right!" I was aware that all other conversation in the room had ceased; even the servants were transfixed by the sideboard.

Jardine said truculently: "But he wasn't talking legalistically—he wasn't, in advance of Christian history, claiming to be another Moses, the supreme law-giver. He was a life-giving spirit, not a legal code personified!"

"He was indeed a life-giving spirit," I said, "and he illustrated the true life of Man—he made clear the principles of right human action, and I think we ignore his teaching at our peril, Bishop!"

"But what exactly was his teaching on divorce?" demanded Jardine, ripping open the hole in my argument. "The Gospels don't agree! I think the clause permitting divorce for adultery was inserted into St. Matthew's

Gospel in an attempt to correct the legalistic way in which the Early Church had thoroughly misunderstood the teaching of Jesus—"

"That's Brunner's theory, of course, but Brunner's notorious for remodelling Christianity to suit the twentieth century—"

"Brunner's *reinterpreting* Christianity *in the light of* the twentieth century, and what's wrong with that? Every generation has to interpret Christianity afresh—"

"Bishop, are you saying that A. P. Herbert has a license to rewrite St. Matthew?"

"—and one of the outstanding aspects of Christianity is that Christ preached compassion and forgiveness, not an inflexible hardness of heart. How long were you married, Dr. Ashworth?"

"Three years. But—"

"And during those three years," pursued Jardine, "did you have no glimpse of what the state of matrimony could be like for others less fortunate than yourself?"

"That's absolutely irrelevant to the theological point under discussion!"

"You *were* happily married, I assume?"

"Yes, I was—and that's exactly why I'm opposed to debasing the institution of marriage by a set of fashionable divorce laws which go far beyond the teaching of Christ!"

"It's people who debase marriage, not laws—people who would keep a couple yoked together in circumstances which would have made Christ weep! Tell me, how long have you been a widower? It must be hard for you to remain single when you regard marriage as such a blissfully ideal state!"

I hesitated. I was by this time very profoundly disturbed. I sensed I was losing control not only of the debate but of my inner equilibrium, the equilibrium which I had to maintain in order to be the man I wanted to be, and although I knew I had to terminate the conversation I could not see how to do it without a disastrous loss of face.

"Well?" demanded Jardine. "Why the long silence? Let me ask you again: how long have you been a widower?"

I saw the trap he was setting to expose my hypocrisy but I saw too that there was no escaping it. Pride and prudence combined to make an outright lie impossible. In defiance I said finally: "Seven years."

"Seven years!" The amber eyes widened as I gave him the answer he wanted. I felt as if my soul had been X-rayed. Nausea churned in the pit of my stomach. "You surprise me, Dr. Ashworth! You talk so sanctimoniously about the institution of marriage yet apparently you have little desire to marry again! Is this because of a belated call to celibacy?

Or are you perhaps not quite such a stranger to marital unhappiness as you would have us all believe?"

He had tied me up in such a knot that I had no choice but to grab the sharpest knife to slash myself free. "I'm certainly no stranger to marital tragedy," I said. "My wife was killed in a car crash when she was expecting our first child, and I often think I'll never recover from the loss."

There was a silence. The light went out of Jardine's lambent eyes, and for a second I saw the grief mark his face as a memory seared his mind. Around the table no one moved. The room seemed suffocating.

At last Jardine said: "I'm most extremely sorry, Dr. Ashworth. I've no personal experience of losing a wife but I do know what it's like to lose a child. Forgive me for trespassing so intolerably on what must be a very deep and private grief."

I was so conscious of shame that I was unable to speak. Jardine might not have exposed me as a fraud to his guests but he had exposed me as a fraud to myself, and I knew that to preserve my fraudulent mask I had taken the cheapest way out when I had had my back to the wall.

I was still groping for composure seconds later when the ladies withdrew and Colonel Cobden-Smith immediately announced his intention of retiring to the smoking-room. Lord Starmouth offered to accompany him, and after helping themselves to a glass of port apiece they departed in search of tranquillity after the debacle at the dinner-table.

"I've such a strong aversion to smoking," Jardine explained to Jennings as the door closed behind the last servant, "that I insist on confining it to one room of the house." He turned to me with careful courtesy. "But perhaps you'd care to join the Colonel and Lord Starmouth, Canon. Are you a smoker?"

"Yes, but not when I'm wearing my clerical collar." My voice sounded astonishingly casual.

"How admirable. And you, Jennings?"

"I'm a non-smoker, my Lord."

"Even more admirable. Jennings, you may address me as 'Bishop' or as 'Dr. Jardine' but leave 'my Lord' to the servants, if you please. I think bishops suffer quite enough from delusions of grandeur without being addressed as if they'd been born to the purple . . . Well, gentlemen, you've just seen me at my worst and now I must make every attempt to display myself at my best. Dr. Ashworth"—he passed me the decanter—"I beg you to help yourself to the largest possible glass of port and to tell me about your new book. His Grace muttered something about fourth-century Christology and St. Anselm, but as there appears to be no connection between the two subjects I confess I'm mystified—or are you perhaps hoping to prove that the seeds of the ontological argument were sown at the Council of Nicaea?" And he gave me his most charming smile.

I smiled back to signal that I had every intention of supporting his attempt to restore a convivial atmosphere, and began to explain my plan to revise my lectures, but it was Jennings, not Jardine, who talked to me about St. Anselm. The chaplain interposed a remark about the Cathedral Library but sank into silence as the discussion of St. Anselm's theology degenerated into the dreariest type of academic debate.

Suddenly I said to Jardine: "I'm sorry, we must be boring you."

"Not in the least." He sipped his port. "I was merely wondering why you turn your back on the present to bury yourself in the remote past. But perhaps modern Church history would involve you in modern Church politics, which is a subject best avoided if your views are unlikely to please the people in power."

I recognised that this subtly dangerous statement was not an attack but an inquiry; he was giving me the opportunity to state that my career had not been distorted by the most unwholesome form of ambition, and I said at once: "I happen to find Arianism and Modalism more stimulating than the Oxford Movement."

Jardine picked up the reference to Anglo-Catholicism. "Does that indicate a certain ambivalence about the High Church party?"

He was inviting me to disassociate myself from Lang, and suddenly I knew he would once again see straight through any profession of loyalty which was not entirely sincere. "I was sympathetic to Anglo-Catholicism when I was ordained," I said in a clumsy attempt at evasion.

"So was I—that'll surprise you, won't it! But I can see now that I was merely trying to reject my Non-Conformist background." He turned suddenly to his chaplain. "Gerald, I've promised to lend Mr. Jennings that book by Brunner, *The Mediator.* Take him to the library, would you, and look it out for him."

That disposed of Jennings and Harvey. I was alone at last with the Bishop and almost before the door had closed I found myself saying: "I'm beginning to think you see straight through everything."

"I have a first-class try. I sometimes think I know what life must be like for a musician who possesses perfect pitch. I have a well-nigh infallible ear for detecting false notes in a conversation."

"During our debate—"

"During our debate you tried to conceal that your private views on divorce are rather different from your public views. Yes. I know. And that's why I couldn't resist the temptation to tear you to shreds, but I am indeed most sincerely sorry that the debate went so wrong."

"It's all right. My hypocrisy got what it deserved. Sorry I took such a cheap way out." The conversation was now so far removed from any dialogue I could have foreseen that I was unable to sustain it. Moving to the hearth, the glass of port in my hand, I pretended to examine the carvings on the chimneypiece.

"Now that," said Jardine, "is a very remarkable apology. You're beginning to interest me exceedingly, Dr. Ashworth." Although I had my back to him I heard the splash as he refilled his glass. "First of all I was tempted to write you off as just another of Lang's bright young men," he was saying, "but the truth's more complicated than that, isn't it? You no longer find the required mask of sycophancy easy to wear."

I finished my port before saying: "I'm very much in Dr. Lang's debt."

"Of course you are. Men of power have a knack of building up extensive credit, but if one is in a position of power," said Jardine, moving over to me with the decanter in his hand, "one must always be scrupulously careful not to bankrupt one's debtors by demanding inappropriate methods of repayment. More port?"

"Thank you." I held out my glass with a steady hand.

"May I give you a word of advice? Your first duty, debts or no debts, is not to the Archbishop of Canterbury. Your first duty is to God who created you as a unique individual in His own image, not as a miraculous facsimile of Dr. Lang. Be yourself, Dr. Ashworth. Be the man God intended you to be, not the sycophant His Grace's vanity would prefer. And now," said Jardine, having refilled my glass, "I shall stop preaching and we shall divert ourselves very briefly, before we join the ladies, by ruminating on an issue which to me is of far greater interest than dear old St. Anselm's meditations. I refer to the search for the historical Jesus—do you think we can ever see beyond the shining image of the Gospels to the man he really was?"

"I think it can be unproductive to probe behind glittering images," I said, "and with all due respect I believe your generation has been too preoccupied with Christ's humanity at the expense of his divinity."

Jardine smiled. "You think that in pursuing the concept of the immanence of God in mankind we've wound up losing sight of God and following mankind, as represented by Christ, down a historical blind alley?"

"Exactly. Speaking for myself, I'm much more interested in the modern doctrines asserting God's transcendence and the importance of revelation—I think we should focus on the message Christ presented, not on the shadowy figure behind the glittering image," I said firmly, and escaping with profound relief into the world of scholarship I began to talk of the writings of Karl Barth and the challenge of Crisis theology.

6

ON our return to the drawing-room, Jardine announced: "I'm glad to say that Dr. Ashworth and I have quite resolved our differences so there's no need for anyone to remain embarrassed by our debate . . . Lady Starmouth, come outside and take a turn with me on the terrace."

"Coffee, Dr. Ashworth?" called Miss Christie.

"Yes—thank you." I was just moving towards her with alacrity when I was intercepted by a distraught Mrs. Jardine.

"Dr. Ashworth, I'm so very sorry—my husband was terribly upset afterwards, I know he was—it was when you mentioned the baby—" As she broke off I saw to my horror that her eyes were full of tears.

"My dear Mrs. Jardine, please, don't distress yourself—"

But Miss Christie had come to the rescue. "It's all right, darling," she said to Mrs. Jardine, and I was struck by her use of an endearment. "Dr. Ashworth understands. Come and sit down—Mrs. Jennings and I were just discussing the choirboys' concert." And passing me my cup of coffee she steered Mrs. Jardine to the cluster of chairs where Mrs. Jennings was waiting. I found myself abandoned to the company of the Cobden-Smiths, but Lord Starmouth was no more than six paces away by the fireplace and as our glances met he said without emphasis: "The Bishop's passions get the better of him sometimes, but he's a good man."

"One doesn't look for passion in a bishop," said the Colonel with unexpected tartness. "Bad form."

"Very bad form," agreed his wife, "but then of course if one's not brought up to know the difference between good form and bad form, one's bound to cause chaos in later life."

"Steady on, Amy!"

"But my dear, Alex is the first to admit his upbringing left a lot to be desired! That peculiar old father and that dreadful little villa in Putney—"

"The great thing about the Bishop," said Lord Starmouth, "is that he'll own to the little villa in Putney. A lesser man would simply draw a veil over it."

"He had the veil firmly in place when he met Carrie," said Mrs. Cobden-Smith.

"Steady *on,* Amy!" The Colonel was now clearly nervous. He shot a wary glance in my direction, but I was more interested in Miss Christie; she had left Mrs. Jardine, now happily talking about choirboys to Mrs. Jennings, and was approaching us with the coffee-pot.

"Is Carrie all right?" murmured the Colonel as his cup was refilled.

"Yes, all's well, Colonel, don't worry."

"Dr. Ashworth still looks a little white around the gills," said Mrs. Cobden-Smith.

"That hardly says much for the power of the Bishop's port," said Miss Christie dryly, sweeping away again with the coffee-pot.

"That's a very strange girl," mused Mrs. Cobden-Smith, "but so good with Carrie."

I said casually: "She must be a great asset in the household."

"That hardly does her justice. When I think of that time at Radbury before her arrival—"

"My dear," said the Colonel with surprising firmness, "I don't think we'll talk about that at present, if you please."

I was disappointed, and with reluctance I realised that it might pay me later to cultivate Mrs. Cobden-Smith.

I had apparently resumed my role of spy. Did this mean I was regaining my equilibrium after the bizarre scene with Jardine? I supposed it did, yet I had no wish to think of spying and no desire whatsoever to dwell on bizarre scenes. Easing myself away from the Cobden-Smiths, I succeeded in cornering Miss Christie at the side-table where she was stacking the coffee-cups onto a tray.

"What time is Communion tomorrow?" I said, offering the most inoffensive question I could devise.

"Eight o'clock. Breakfast is at nine." She looked past me at the drawing-room door. "Here come Mr. Jennings and Gerald—will you excuse me? I must order fresh coffee for them."

I lost her, and it occurred to me then that a quiet mild approach was going to make no impression whatsoever on Miss Christie. However, if she thought she could brush me aside merely by juggling coffee-cups, she had made a big mistake.

I resolved to adopt a much tougher line in future.

7

IT was after eleven when I regained the sanctuary of my room, and having stripped off my clothes I smoked a cigarette as I tried to work out what had happened. Some strange bond seemed to have been forged between me and my host but it seemed to be my duty to ignore it. It was not my business either to like or to loathe Jardine; my task was merely to estimate how vulnerable he was to scandal.

However, I found I now had a stronger desire than ever not to connive with Lang in any secret plan to oust Jardine from the Bench of Bishops. Jardine was clearly innocent. A man of such integrity would be incapable of living a secret life as an apostate steeped in adultery, and I was also sure he was far too shrewd to engage in any middle-aged folly which fell short of an adulterous liaison. It seemed obvious that he exercised his flirtatious streak harmlessly with his Lovely Ladies and had long treated Miss Christie as part of the palace furniture.

This conclusion was reassuring enough, but I still had to answer the question of what went on in Miss Christie's mind while Jardine behaved like the good man he undoubtedly was. I reminded myself that Jardine could still be vulnerable to scandal if Miss Christie decided to play the neurotic spinster by transforming herself into a furnace of frustrated passion, and although she hardly gave the impression of being a neurotic spinster I felt there was something odd about her extreme self-containment.

I decided I had a moral duty to investigate Miss Christie further and an absolute moral duty to discover how likely she was to transform herself into a furnace of passion.

No Jesuit could have achieved a more satisfying casuistry. With a smile I stubbed out my cigarette, retired to bed and began to plot my espionage for the morrow.

III

"I have seen so many clerical careers arrested, and (to all outward seeming) definitely marred, by the clergyman's marriage, that I never hear of a clergyman's becoming 'engaged' without a shiver of anxiety."

Letters of
HERBERT HENSLEY HENSON,
ed. E. F. Braley

I

I AWOKE violently at seven. Naturally I had been dreaming of Miss Christie. I wanted to smoke a cigarette, but I decided that I had no excuse for breaking any of the minor rules by which I achieved self-discipline, and one of those rules was that I never smoked before breakfast. With an effort I read the morning office. Then making another random dip into the Bible I eventually encountered the appropriate words: "Seek and ye shall find."

As I dressed, it occurred to me that I still had to seek and find a great many facts about Jardine before I could report convincingly to Lang that the Bishop's private life was as pure as driven snow; my impression of innocence would carry little weight unless it were supported by a thorough understanding of Jardine's psychology, and I could hardly establish a psychological portrait without much more information about his past. Apart from gauging Miss Christie's ability to become a furnace of passion, my main task was clearly to talk to as many people as possible about the Bishop without making them suspect they were being interrogated, but I doubted that this would prove difficult. People always enjoy a gossip about a famous man, and when a famous man is personally known to them the temptation to reveal how much they know is all the greater.

Leaving my room I padded downstairs. I met no one, although I could hear the distant rattling and banging of servants pursuing their early morning rituals. Opening the front door I stepped out into the porch, and the brilliant sunlight flooded into my eyes so that for a second I saw only a shimmering green pattern of beech leaves and grass. Beyond the drive the pale stone of the Cathedral soared into a cloudless sky, and opening the white gate which was set in the wall of the churchyard I headed along the north side of the building to the porch.

A passing verger directed me to St. Anselm's Chapel where the weekday Communion services were held. There was no time to gape at the glory of the nave; I wanted to clear my mind in preparation for worship, and as soon as I had chosen my seat in the chapel I knelt to sharpen my concentration. However I had instantly noted Miss Christie's absence.

This failed to surprise me. Weekday Communion is seldom attended by hordes of laymen, and in fact I saw no one I knew from the palace in the small congregation. Then Gerald Harvey hurried into the row behind me, and seconds later at eight o'clock the Dean and the Bishop appeared, preceded by the verger.

As the service progressed I thought how preposterous it was to imagine a bishop administering the sacrament when he was not in a state of grace, and again I remembered the integrity which had emanated from Jardine during our private conversation over the port.

My moment came to receive the sacrament. Erasing all thought of my commission, I focused my mind on the spiritual reality confronting me, and it was not until I had returned to my seat that I allowed myself to think again of Jardine. I vowed to remember that my first duty was not to the Archbishop of Canterbury. I asked for the strength to overcome my weaknesses. And at the conclusion of the service I let the familiar prayer of Christ echo in my mind: let thy will, not mine, be done.

Lang's will immediately became as unimportant as my own. I felt comforted, and rising to my feet at last I left the chapel to find Gerald Harvey hovering in the side aisle.

"Waiting for the Bishop?" I inquired with a smile.

"No, for you."

I was impressed by this courtesy and at once I felt guilty that I had written him off as ineffectual. "How nice of you," I said. "Sorry I've kept you hanging about."

"Oh, you mustn't apologise for taking extra time for prayer!" said Harvey shocked. He was so young and ingenuous that he made me feel old and world-weary. "How did you like the service?"

I paid the Bishop a suitable compliment and was glad I did not have to be insincere for the sake of politeness. We walked through the porch onto the sward. Beyond the wall of the churchyard the houses of the Close basked in the sun and a horse was drawing a milk-cart slowly along the North Walk. I could hear the birds singing in the cedar tree nearby.

"I must confess the Bishop intrigues me," I said idly at last. "What would you say was the fundamental nature of his belief? God-centred? Christ-centred? Rooted in the Trinity?"

"Well, it's all those things," said Harvey, "but I suppose he's fundamentally Christocentric. He has an overriding belief not just in Christ's compassion and forgiveness but in Christ's honesty and truth, and that's why he can't bear hypocrisy—he sees it as a re-enactment of the Pharisees' behaviour in the Gospels and he feels called to attack it just as Our Lord did." He shot me a shy glance. "Please forgive him for last night," he said rapidly. "He didn't mean to hurt you. He just misjudged your sincerity—I think he suspected you'd only adopted your point of view out of loyalty to Dr. Lang and of course he was wrong, but anyone can make a mistake, can't they, and he really is the most wonderful man, absolutely the best, believe me."

I realised belatedly that he had sought my company in order to defend his hero, and I knew I should signal that I was willing to be convinced of Jardine's heroic qualities. I said with interest: "He's been good to you?"

"That's an understatement!" In his enthusiasm Harvey became confidential. "When I was at the Cathedral School at Radbury my parents died and Dr. Jardine—he was Dean of Radbury then—simply took me over, paid my school fees, had me to stay in the holidays, and it wasn't as if I was one of those appealing children who look like angels and win all the prizes. Then later when I wanted to be ordained I wasn't sure whether I'd be able to pass the exams but Dr. Jardine just said: 'Nonsense, of course you can!' and when he offered to coach me in his spare time I knew he really believed I could do it. I'd never have passed if it hadn't been for him, and afterwards when he asked me to be his chaplain . . . Well, you can imagine how I felt! Of course I was terrified I'd be no good and in fact I'm sure he could get someone better, but I try very hard and I seem to muddle through somehow."

"I'm sure you do very well." It was impossible not to be touched by his honesty, and suddenly I knew why he had appealed to Jardine.

Meanwhile our conversation had taken us through the palace gateway and I was rapidly framing some questions which would take advantage of his confidential mood. "Tell me about life at the palace," I said. "Miss Christie evidently has an important role in the household—she seems very close to Mrs. Jardine."

"Oh, Mrs. Jardine thinks of her as a daughter, I know she does."

"How does she get on with the Bishop?"

"People always want to know that," said Harvey, pausing to extricate his latch-key as we approached the front door, "and they're always surprised by my reply which is: 'Better than they used to,' and not the expected 'Magnificently well.' "

"There's been friction?"

"Well, not exactly *friction* . . . but they've had their cool spells. The first was after she came to Radbury—that was around the time I started staying with them in the holidays—and then there was a second cool period after they arrived in Starbridge five years ago. I remember saying to Lady Starmouth once that I was afraid Lyle might leave if the Bishop became much cooler, but Lady Starmouth told me not to worry. She said it's not always easy for a married couple to live in close proximity to a third party, and of course Lyle's much more involved with both the Jardines than I am. I'm fairly peripheral in their private life, even though I see so much of the Bishop in his professional role." He finally found his latch-key, but when the front door swung open it became wedged against a pile of envelopes. "Heavens above, look at all this post!"

"Is this abnormally substantial?"

"Yes, we're still dealing with the correspondence on the A. P. Herbert Bill. We even had to engage additional secretarial help last week," said Harvey, becoming flustered at the memory, and bustled away into the library as if he feared the envelopes might multiply in his hands.

I made a mental note to ask Lady Starmouth about the difficulties of a married couple obliged to live in close proximity to a young and attractive third party. Then I retired to the dining-room in pursuit of breakfast.

2

I WAS early. I found no one in the dining-room, but the morning papers were laid out on a side-table and I began to browse among the cricket reports in *The Daily Telegraph.* I was still digesting the unfortunate news that Oxford had defeated Cambridge by seven wickets when Jardine walked in.

"I was glad to see you at the service," he said after we had exchanged greetings. "I was glad to be there myself. Sometimes one so strongly needs to wipe the slate clean in order to come fresh to a new day."

There was a pause while we both thought of the dinner-party, its unhappy memory now purged from our consciences, and before either of us could speak again the Starmouths entered the room. They were followed by Miss Christie, immaculate in a navy-blue skirt and white blouse, and at once I noticed the discreet, perfectly proportioned curves of her figure above the waist; I even found myself toying with the erotic image of a pair of empty champagne glasses.

"Good morning, Dr. Ashworth," she said formally while I was grappling with these most unclerical thoughts, but the next moment she was turning to Jardine. "Carrie's decided to stay in bed for a while, Bishop, and she's asked me to have breakfast with her."

The Bishop showed no surprise but Lady Starmouth inquired in alarm if Mrs. Jardine were unwell. Miss Christie, however, had already retreated to the hall and it was left to Jardine to answer idly as he turned a page of *The Times:* "It's merely the aftermath of insomnia. At two o'clock this morning, acting out of a strong sense of self-preservation, I was obliged to retire to my dressing-room in order to resume the bliss of unconsciousness. The chief disadvantage of Carrie's insomnia is that she's always overcome with the urge to share it with me."

My immediate reaction was to reflect that Jack had been right in assuming that the Jardines still shared a bedroom. My second reaction was to accuse myself of becoming more prurient than any reporter from *The News of the World,* and in an effort to beat back all thoughts which were unbecoming to a clergyman I began to consider how I should spend my morning. I would have to go to the Library; it would look too odd if I postponed my encounter with the St. Anselm manuscript, but I thought I could use the fine weather as an excuse not to linger indoors. During breakfast the Earl announced his intention of fishing in the river at the bottom of the garden while the Countess confessed an urge to paint a water-colour of the long herbaceous border, and I thought both of them might be in the mood for a little casual conversation about our host.

"Do you have any special plans for this morning, Mrs. Cobden-Smith?" I asked as I finished my eggs and bacon.

"Oh, I shall write some letters, go to the shops, 'fill the unforgiving minute,' as Kipling would say . . ." Mrs. Cobden-Smith spoke with such energy that I immediately felt exhausted. "Willy will take George for a walk"—the St. Bernard looked hopeful as his name was mentioned—"and then . . . What are you going to do after that, Willy?"

"Nothing, I hope," said Colonel Cobden-Smith.

"Good man!" said Lord Starmouth.

"Well, at least the clergy are preparing for a morning of unremitting toil," said Lady Starmouth, and gave me yet another of her radiant sophisticated smiles.

3

THE most notorious fact about the work which passes under the name of *The Prayers and Meditations of St. Anselm* is that it is uncertain how much of the material can be attributed to St. Anselm himself. In 1932 Dom

Wilmart had ascribed nineteen of the prayers and three of the meditations to the saint, who had been Archbishop of Canterbury at the time of William Rufus, but the matter was still of interest to scholars and much of the interest had always centred on the Starbridge manuscript which showed the work before the insertion of many of the additions.

After the required exchange of courtesies with the librarian, I embarked on my reading. The manuscript was written in a clear hand which I mastered without trouble, but there were slips in the Latin which indicated that the scribe might have been a young monk who suffered from wandering attention. To support this thesis I found some entertaining embellishments in the margin, in particular a sketch of a prancing cat with a mouse in his mouth, and I thought how odd it was that this manuscript, perhaps regarded as no more than a tedious copying chore by its scribe, had survived to become a document of profound importance. The young monk had been dead for centuries but his work for God lived on; idly I speculated how I might introduce the subject into a future sermon, and at once I thought of the famous text from Isaiah: "The grass withereth, the flower fadeth but the Word of Our God shall stand for ever."

I took notes for over an hour as I compared the text with my copy of Wilmart's book, and then leaving the Library I returned to the palace, parked my briefcase in the hall and strolled outside again into the garden.

I saw Lady Starmouth at once. She was sitting on an artist's folding stool, her sketchpad in her lap, and gazing meditatively at the long border which stretched downhill in a blaze of colour towards the river. When she saw me she smiled, beckoning me to join her, and as I crossed the lawn I could see the Earl fishing in the distance by the willows.

"I thought it was going to be a water-colour?" I said as I saw the pencil in her hand.

"I always do a rough sketch first and I've only just begun—I've been chatting to poor Carrie."

"Is she better?"

"Yes, but still distressed about that ghastly scene last night. I'm afraid that sometimes she's much too sensitive for her own good and never more so than when the conversation turns to lost babies . . . Did you know about the Jardines' child?"

"Dr. Lang only mentioned that they had no children living. What happened?"

"Am I being given the chance to gossip about the Bishop? Yes, I am—how delightful! Do sit down, Dr. Ashworth, and help me postpone the dreaded moment when I have to open my paint-box and pretend to be an artist!"

To encourage her I said: "If you're in the mood to gossip, I'm certainly in the mood to listen—after my clash with the Bishop last night I find I'm gripped by a curiosity to know more about him."

"In the circumstances," said Lady Starmouth dryly, "I'd say curiosity was an admirably charitable reaction. Now let me see, shall I launch straight away into the saga of the baby or shall I begin with Jardine's arrival in Mayfair? I warn you, I'm rather a menace when I start talking about the Bishop because I find him so intriguing that I tend to prattle away happily for hours."

"I'm sure you never prattle, Lady Starmouth—I can only imagine you discoursing alluringly!"

She laughed. "How wonderful to have such a flattering audience! Very well, let me try to discourse with all the allure at my command!"

Lounging on the lawn beneath the hot sun I prepared to give her my fullest attention.

4

"*JARDINE'S* had the most unusual life," said Lady Starmouth. "I'm not sure how much you already know about his career, but twenty-one years ago in 1916 he was promoted from an obscure chaplaincy in North London to St. Mary's Mayfair—and of course that's one of the smartest parishes in the West End. Henry and I did our best to welcome the new vicar, and because he was unmarried I made a special effort to introduce him to suitable girls. Did you know Jardine married late? He was thirty-seven when he met Carrie, but before the move to St. Mary's he couldn't afford a wife. Unfortunately he had a most peculiar father who had wound up heavily in debt, and Jardine had to support the family on his small stipend."

"Someone mentioned a peculiar father—"

"The whole family," said Lady Starmouth confidentially, "was most odd. In addition to the peculiar father there was a very strange Swedish stepmother and two sisters, one of whom went mad—"

"This sounds like a Jacobean tragedy."

"No, they didn't all kill each other—unfortunately—but you're right to relate it to literature. It was like a novel by Gissing about the ghastliness of genteel poverty."

"Were the Jardines so genteel? What did the peculiar father do for a living?"

"Nobody knows. In fact I've never plumbed the depths of Jardine's lurid family background because he prefers not to talk about it, but the sister—the one who didn't go mad—was painfully genteel, poor thing, a very refined accent and a ghastly way with a teacup—and my guess is that they were all upper-working-class but trying to be lower-middle. God, how crucified so many people are," said the aristocratic Lady Starmouth carelessly but with genuine feeling, "by the English class system."

"Did the whole family accompany Jardine to Mayfair?"

"No, the peculiar father and the mad sister were dead by that time, but Jardine moved into the vicarage with his surviving sister and his sinister Swedish stepmother and immediately began to cast around for a wife—"

"—Whom you obligingly provided for him!"

"Not quite! But I did go to the dinner-party where he and Carrie met for the first time. The meeting was wildly romantic, love at first sight, and four days later he proposed."

"Four days?"

"Four days," said Lady Starmouth, enjoying my astonishment. "Carrie's family were in a tremendous tizzy, of course, because of Jardine's odd background, but on the other hand he had this stunning position as Vicar of St. Mary's and that made it hard to object to him as a suitor."

"Did the family make trouble?"

"They somehow managed to restrain themselves. I suspect it was because Carrie wasn't so young any more and the family had begun to worry that she might wind up on the shelf."

"It's hard to imagine someone as pretty as Mrs. Jardine winding up on the shelf."

"True, but one of the cruellest facts of life, Dr. Ashworth, is that men prefer pretty women to be under thirty. After that women need to rely more on other resources."

I sensed the implication that Mrs. Jardine had no other resources on which to rely, but all I said was: "So nothing impeded Dr. Jardine's stampede to the altar?"

"On the contrary, the Swedish stepmother then made a scene and said she wouldn't live in any house where Carrie was mistress. So she retired with the poor plain sister to a flat in Putney—which Jardine had to pay for, of course."

"But surely wasn't this a good thing? Isn't it better for a woman to start married life without a stepmother-in-law breathing down her neck?"

"Of course. Carrie was thrilled. But Jardine was dreadfully upset. He adored this stepmother, although God knows why—she was twenty years older than he was and she weighed sixteen stone and she had very pale eyes and a very thin mouth and she spoke with a very heavy foreign accent—oh, she was *sinister,* she really was! After the row I thought she'd refuse to come to the wedding but she turned up looking wrathful—what a death's-head at the feast! The poor sister was hardly cheerful either—she wept throughout the service, but at least she was only crying out of sentimentality. I liked the sister. Poor thing, what a wretched life she had! She died of cancer eventually, of course. I say 'of course' because she was the sort of person who inevitably dies of something beastly . . . But I must stop digressing. You're being wonderfully patient, Dr. Ashworth, but I really am getting to the baby now, I promise—"

"Don't apologise, Lady Starmouth. I'm enrapt by the sinister stepmother."

"Well, after the wedding she sank into darkest Putney, thank God, and the Jardines floated off on their honeymoon. When they came back Carrie immediately started planning the nursery, so of course we all thought . . . But nothing happened. However, finally the baby started. We were all so relieved, and no one was more relieved than Jardine—apart from Carrie herself, of course. He started talking to Henry about which schools the child should go to and Carrie started adding the finishing touches to the heavenly nursery—oh, what a mistake it is to count one's chickens before they're hatched! Eventually the worst happened and the baby, a boy, was born dead."

Lady Starmouth paused as if to choose her next words with care. "I wonder how I can convey to you how dreadful this was for the Jardines. Of course a dead baby is always a tragedy, but in this case . . . You see, Carrie was so absolutely sure that her one talent was for motherhood. It's not easy for any woman to be married to a brilliant man and Carrie thought that motherhood would give her the chance to excel in a way which would command Jardine's very special respect. And Jardine himself was longing for a family. He wanted to recreate the family life which he could remember existing before his mother died—a life which he'd almost certainly idealised but which represented to him some intensely desirable goal of domestic bliss. So both he and Carrie were united by these very urgent and powerful dreams—and that was why it was so terrible when the stillborn child tore those dreams apart."

She paused again and I allowed the silence to lengthen to signal my sympathy before I asked: "There were no other children?"

"No, and in a way that was the ghastliest part of all because no doctor could tell her why nothing happened. So she went on hoping and so did he—in fact Alex once told me he went on hoping until . . . well, until no hope was possible any more. There! I'm calling him Alex—very improper, isn't it, to call a man by his Christian name when he's not a member of one's family, but I've known him so long now and we're such good friends and Henry doesn't mind if I call Jardine Alex occasionally . . . I expect you've wondered about my friendship with the Bishop, haven't you?" she added, giving me an indulgent smile. "Perhaps you're even a little shocked!"

"Not at all, I'm deeply envious! I've heard about Dr. Jardine's so-called 'Lovely Ladies,' and obviously you're the Lovely Ladies' leader!"

She laughed. "I simply must add you to my clerical collection," she said. "You're such an exceptionally charming listener!"

"I could listen to you indefinitely, Lady Starmouth. Tell me more."

She sighed. "It really is too dreadful how little encouragement I need . . . But what shall I tell you next? I've told you about the ghastly background and the romantic marriage and the stillborn child—"

"Strike a lighter note," I said, "and tell me about Dr. Jardine's Lovely Ladies."

5

"OF course Alex has numerous acquaintances among the opposite sex," said Lady Starmouth, adding another line to the obscure pattern on her sketchpad, "but there are only three of us who could truly be described as friends. We all met him in 1916 during his first year as Vicar of St. Mary's."

I was immediately intrigued. "Why was he so prone to friendship in 1916?"

"Moving to Mayfair was a huge change for him, and at first he was very lonely and unsure of himself."

"Who are the other two ladies?"

"Sybil Welbeck and Enid Markhampton. Alex liked us because we were all absolutely safe—happily married, churchgoing women, firmly anchored to the conventions . . . Heavens, how dull that sounds! But we're all tolerably amusing, I promise you—"

"You hardly need to assure me of that, Lady Starmouth, but what amazes me is Dr. Jardine's luck in finding three safe Lovely Ladies all at once! Did he never add to his collection?"

"No," said Lady Starmouth, examining the point of her pencil. "He didn't."

"Was that because he felt you were all so incomparable that no other woman was fit to join your ranks?"

We laughed before Lady Starmouth said easily: "He married soon after he met us, and perhaps he was afraid Carrie wouldn't take too kindly to any new close friends of the opposite sex."

"Speaking as a clergyman," I said, "I find the whole idea of close friendships with married women fraught with the most hair-raising possibilities."

"Ah, but you're of a different generation, aren't you?" said Lady Starmouth. "Such friendships may seem strange now but when I was young they weren't so unusual. The War changed so many things, and one of the first casualties of the new freedom afterwards was the concept of the 'amitié amoureuse.' "

"Nevertheless I can't help thinking that if I'd been Dr. Jardine I might have had a hard time preventing myself from falling in love with one of you."

Lady Starmouth gave another indulgent smile but answered seriously: "I can assure you that Alex has never been in love with either Enid or Sybil or me. At the risk of sounding horribly snobbish, I'll say that we're not in the league which he would consider accessible as far as the ultimate intimacies are concerned."

I was again much intrigued. "I'm not sure I understand you," I said, wondering how I could lure her on over such delicate ground, but Lady Starmouth had no need to be lured. I had forgotten that the aristocracy, unlike the middle classes, fail to find the subject of sex embarrassing.

"When Alex was growing up," she said, "the women in his life were—at most—lower-middle-class. Then his years up at Oxford gave him enough confidence to marry an upper-middle-class girl like Carrie Cobden-Smith. But I think if he'd been offered the chance of deep intimacy with someone from the aristocracy, he'd have backed away. He'd have found the prospect too intimidating."

I knew at once that this was a vital detail in the portrait I was constructing of Jardine. The Bishop was safe with his Lovely Ladies, not necessarily because of any indestructible virtue on his part, but because there was a psychological barrier keeping him in check. Jardine would be aware of this; a clergyman is taught to know himself well so that he may learn the best way to control his weaknesses, and Jardine, liking the company of the opposite sex, would only have trusted himself with women who he felt were ultimately beyond his reach.

"Talking of lovely ladies," said Lady Starmouth, adding another line to her sketch, "have you fallen in love with Miss Christie?"

"Miss Christie!" I was so startled that I sat bolt upright.

"I saw the smouldering looks you were giving her in the drawing-room last night. My dear Dr. Ashworth, will you allow me to take advantage of my numerous years of seniority by giving you some friendly advice? Don't bother with Miss Christie. She's spent the last decade proving she's quite uninterested in men."

I said lightly: "She doesn't nurse a secret passion for the Bishop?"

"I suspect it's much more likely she nurses a secret passion for Carrie."

I exclaimed appalled: "But that's impossible!"

"My poor Dr. Ashworth, you *are* smitten, aren't you! Of course I'm not implying the passion's reciprocated—Carrie adores Alex. But you tell me this: why is an attractive, intelligent girl like Miss Christie content to remain as a companion when she's had numerous proposals, some of them from very eligible men?"

I said suddenly: "How do the Jardines explain Miss Christie's continuing spinsterhood?"

"Well, the official story is that she suffered a broken engagement before she met them, and that this left her perpetually disenchanted with the opposite sex. But I find that hard to believe—Miss Christie strikes me as the sort of woman who would consider it a matter of pride to recover completely from a broken engagement."

"Does Dr. Jardine ever talk to you about her?"

"Her name comes up occasionally, but not as much as it used to. Of course there have been moments in the past when he's found the situation a bore."

I sensed we were approaching the difficulties of a married couple who had to live in close proximity to a third party. "A bore?" I repeated, anxious to lure her on again. "Why was that?"

"Oh, I'm afraid it's class again! Alex didn't grow up in a house where certain employees lived 'en famille' and the presence of a third party tended to grate on his nerves, but fortunately the move to Starbridge seems to have solved that particular problem. There's more space here for third parties than there was in the Deanery at Radbury—and besides, when all's said and done the Jardines' marriage is quite successful enough to withstand the presence of a stranger . . . Dr. Ashworth, my husband's waving at you. I expect he's getting bored with the fish and wants to be diverted—but come back and see me again after you've entertained him!"

We exchanged smiles. I said: "Am I securely in your collection now?" and when she laughed I scrambled to my feet, dusted some flecks of grass from my trousers and strolled off down the garden to interview my next witness.

6

"I WAS hoping a little conversation would disturb the fish," said the Earl as I approached. "They all seem to be either asleep or dead."

Beyond the river the herd of cows was grazing again in the meadows.

It was a very English scene which the Earl in his country clothes enhanced, and as I leant against the trunk of the nearest willow I was once more aware of the subtle allure of Starbridge as the morning melted into a shimmering afternoon. It was a day conducive to mirages. I was conscious not only that I was a clergyman pretending to be a spy—or was I a spy pretending to be a clergyman?—but that the Earl was a great landowner pretending to be a humble fisherman. The Earl himself, with his open countenance, looked as if he were a stranger to play-acting, but the atmosphere of that Starbridge noon was reminding me how hard it was to know the truth about even the simplest individuals.

"I dare say my wife's been chatting to you about the Bishop in an effort to ensure you weren't put off by last night's glimpse of the rough diamond," the Earl was saying. "He was undoubtedly a rough diamond when we first knew him, but he's got plenty of gentlemanly polish nowadays when he puts his mind to it."

"He certainly put his mind to it over the port . . . Were you disconcerted, Lord Starmouth, when a rough diamond turned up at St. Mary's in 1916?"

The Earl smiled. "I was more intrigued than disconcerted."

"You hadn't met him before?"

"No, but I'd heard of him. He was always writing letters to *The Times*. However, I had little idea what sort of man he was until I came home from my club one night and my wife told me the new vicar had called. She said: 'He's got beautiful yellow eyes and a harsh ugly voice and he's not sure how to behave and I'm mad about him!' Well, my wife's always had a soft spot for clergymen so I didn't take her too seriously, but then next Sunday when he preached his first sermon I suddenly saw what all the fuss was about. I was used to dozing during the sermons, but this time I stayed awake all the way through—and in fact at the end I was sitting on the edge of my pew. Damn it, I can even remember the text! It was: 'I am not come to call the righteous, but sinners to repentance,' and when he was hammering home his message his voice seemed to make the church vibrate and his eyes glowed like a cat's. Extraordinary. Of course I saw at once he was going to go a long way."

"What did you think when you had the chance for a private conversation with him?"

"I was surprised how shy he was—shy and awkward. He spoke all right; Oxford had ironed out any suburban accent, but he had the trick of either talking too much and too aggressively or else not talking at all. However, that was just nervousness. Once my wife took him up and petted him and tried to marry him off, he very quickly blossomed. All he needed was a bit of social self-confidence."

"Perhaps Oxford had given him a chip on his shoulder."

"More than likely, yes. The Varsity can be hard going for someone who doesn't have the right background—well, I must admit to a bit of prejudice against him myself during the early days of our acquaintance, but then one day he spoke up to me; it was a criticism, a justifiable criticism too, I might add, and suddenly I thought: it took courage to say that. And I respected him for it. He was no sycophant. He was willing to accept a bit of patronage in the form of my wife's kindness but he wasn't going to let that stop him speaking the truth as he saw it. Very exceptional. A man of high moral principle. He's deserved his great success."

"How very gratifying it must have been for your wife to see her protégé go all the way to the top of the Church of England!"

"Yes, I always say she made a small but significant contribution to his career. He needed someone who would invite him to the right dinner-parties and ensure he developed the essential poise his position required. Mrs. Welbeck and Lady Markhampton also helped him in that way, but Evelyn was the one who did the most."

"Your wife's just been telling me about Dr. Jardine's devoted band of Lovely Ladies—I must say, I'm deeply envious!"

The Earl laughed. "I have moments of envy myself! Do you know either Mrs. Welbeck or Lady Markhampton?"

"I'm sorry to say I don't."

"They're both charming. But to tell you the truth, the Lovely Lady I really fancied in the old days was Loretta Staviski. No doubt my wife mentioned her. She's arriving from America next weekend to stay with us, and I'm greatly looking forward to seeing her again."

There was a silence. The river went on flowing and in the meadows the cows continued to graze. I looked at the Earl, who was still peering into the water for a glimpse of a fish; I looked back at the Countess who was still sketching by the herbaceous border, and at last I heard myself inquire in the most casual voice I could muster: "No, your wife didn't mention her. Who is she?"

IV

"Who does not know that no clergyman, however hard-working and devoted, can maintain his spiritual influence if his domestic life be ill-ordered and unhappy?"

HERBERT HENSLEY HENSON,
THE BISHOPRICK PAPERS

I

WHEN I returned to Lady Starmouth, I found her looking critically at her sketch. "I'm afraid this is no good," she murmured. "I seem to have lost my touch . . . How were the fish?"

"According to your husband, they're all either asleep or dead." For a moment I remained motionless, watching her. Then I said casually: "Lady Starmouth, I hope you won't think me impertinent, but may I ask why, when you were telling me about Dr. Jardine's Lovely Ladies, you failed to mention Professor Staviski?"

Lady Starmouth's reaction was swift. "Loretta?"

"Your husband's just mentioned her. There were four of you, weren't there? Not just three."

"Only for a short time, during the War." Lady Starmouth tore the sketch from the pad, crumpled the paper into a ball and put her pencil away in a wooden box. She said nothing else, and her silence was in such stark contrast to her earlier fluency that I felt obliged to say: "I'm sorry—obviously I've given you offence."

"My dear Dr. Ashworth"—Lady Starmouth spoke in the voice of one who finds herself in the most tiresome of dilemmas—"of course you haven't given me offence! I'm merely annoyed with myself for not mentioning Loretta because of course it's only natural that you should wonder why I left her out when I was prattling so freely about the Bishop's past. However, the truth's very simple. I didn't mention her because Alex hasn't seen her since she returned to America in 1918 so she hardly qualifies now as one of his Lovely Ladies."

"She hasn't visited England since then?"

There was another silence.

"Forgive me, I'm being intolerably inquisitive—"

"Pardonably inquisitive, you mean. Of course you're wondering why I'm tying myself up in such knots." Suddenly and most unexpectedly she laughed. "Good heavens, anyone would think I had a guilty secret to hide whereas all I want to cover up is a little private embarrassment!"

"Lady Starmouth, please don't feel obligated to say another word! I'm only sorry that I—"

"My dear young man, now *you're* the one who's behaving as if there's a guilty secret to hide! I can see that the most sensible thing I can do is to enlighten you before you're tempted to exercise a colourful imagination, but you must promise me you'll be discreet. The story's not scandalous, just sad, and I don't want it repeated."

"I give you my word I shall hold everything you say in the strictest confidence."

"Very well, then let me say that Loretta has indeed returned to England for visits since the War, but she and Alex no longer have any communication with each other. I'm sorry to say that although Alex always treated her with absolute propriety, Loretta fell in love with him and their platonic friendship went very disastrously wrong."

2

"*FORGIVE* me, Lady Starmouth," I said, "but in fact I'd been unable to resist wondering if Dr. Jardine's platonic friendships were just a little too good to be true. I still say that any clergyman who dabbles in close friendships with the opposite sex is playing with fire."

"Well, in this case I have to admit he got singed . . . Dr. Ashworth, do sit down again—I find you disconcerting when you tower over me like this. It makes me feel I'm being interrogated."

I sat down at once on the grass but she cut short my apology. "No, I know you're not really interrogating me—it's all my fault for encouraging your questions earlier, but before I close up like a clam let me just say a little more about Loretta so that you can see why for her sake I prefer to treat the incident as closed. She and I first met in 1917 but I'd heard about her for years because my mother, who was American, had been friends with her mother in childhood and they'd always kept in touch. When Loretta finally came to England, she was in a terrible mess. She'd been married young to this man Staviski who was a diplomatist; when America entered the War he was transferred from Washington to

London, and almost as soon as he and Loretta arrived in England the marriage went to pieces."

"He left her?"

"She left him. But she was the innocent party—he'd made life quite impossible for her, so I had no hesitation in coming to her rescue. She stayed with us while she recovered, and of course she soon met Alex. Well, to cut a long story short, I'll just say that she was so successful at concealing her true feelings that for a long time neither Alex nor I had any idea she was in love with him, but eventually the truth surfaced and Alex was obliged to end the friendship. Loretta was dreadfully upset. I felt so sorry for her. It was all horribly awkward and pathetic, just as any unreciprocated attachment always is, and later we agreed never to speak of it again."

"What happened to her afterwards?"

"When she returned to America she embarked on an academic career and now she teaches history at some college on the Eastern Seaboard. She's never remarried but I still wonder if she might one day. She's much younger than me, perhaps only a few years older than you, and although by fashionable standards she's plain she's by no means unattractive . . . However, a lot of men don't like a woman to be too clever."

But I thought of Jardine, enjoying with Loretta Staviski all the intelligent conversation he was unlikely to encounter at home, and I was unable to resist saying: "Dr. Jardine must have been sorry to lose her friendship—was he never tempted to see her again during her later visits to England?"

"How could he? How could he possibly have renewed a friendship which had been so painful to her and so potentially dangerous for him?"

"But was she herself never tempted to—"

"This *is* an interrogation, isn't it! My dear Dr. Ashworth, aren't you taking rather too much advantage of your very considerable charm?"

I privately cursed my recklessness and attempted to beat a smooth retreat. "I'm so sorry, Lady Starmouth, but many a clergyman has to deal occasionally with the sort of difficulty Dr. Jardine faced here, and I'm afraid my personal interest in the subject got the better of me. I do apologise."

She gave me a searching look but decided to be indulgent. "I've no objection to a sympathetic interest," she said, "but perhaps it's lucky for you that I have a soft spot for clergymen . . . Heavens, here's Mrs. Cobden-Smith!" Rising to her feet she folded the stool and picked up her artist's satchel. "For your penance, Dr. Ashworth, you can listen with an expression of rapturous attention to the stories of how she and the Colonel civilised India."

"You two seem to be having a very cosy little tête-à-tête!" called Mrs.

Cobden-Smith as she approached us. "I've just been urging Carrie to get dressed. It's no good lying in bed after a touch of insomnia—I told her to get up and have a busy day so that she'd be thoroughly tired by bed-time. I remember when I was in India—"

"I was only saying to Dr. Ashworth how interesting you were about India—but do excuse me, I must go and see Carrie myself," said Lady Starmouth, and escaped adroitly across the lawn.

My next witness had delivered herself to me with an admirable sense of timing. Fighting my reluctance, I smiled at Mrs. Cobden-Smith and suggested that we might sit on the garden bench to enjoy the sunshine.

3

"IT'S nice to sit down for a minute," said Mrs. Cobden-Smith. "I've been rushing around the town trying to buy horse-meat for the dog and the right cough-syrup for Willy. If Willy doesn't have a dose of cough-syrup every night he coughs like a chimney-sweep and if George doesn't have horse-meat three times a week he gets lazy—and talking of laziness, it seems you've been shirking your work, young man! I thought you were supposed to be closeted in the Cathedral Library, not dancing attendance on Lady Starmouth! You're as bad as Alex—he likes to dance attendance too, but of course in his case he's just savouring the fact that Adam Jardine from Putney is now the clerical pet of a peeress. Did you know Alex spent the first thirty-seven years of his life being called Adam? It's his first name. But when Carrie fell in love with him, we said to her: 'My dear,' we said, 'you simply can't marry a man called Adam Jardine—it sounds like a jobbing gardener!' So she found out his second name was Alexander and we rechristened him Alex. His stepmother was livid, I can't think why."

I finally had the chance to speak and I thought I had been offered a promising opening. "What a coincidence!" I said. "Lady Starmouth was just telling me about Dr. Jardine's stepmother."

"Everyone was always rather appalled by the old girl," said Mrs. Cobden-Smith comfortably, quite uninhibited by any desire to be discreet about a dead relative of her husband's brother-in-law. "She was a very strange woman—Swedish, and of course we all know the Scandinavians are peculiar. Look at their plays."

I ignored this dismissal of the giants of the modern theatre. "But I'm told the Bishop was very fond of his stepmother."

"Devoted. Very odd. Carrie hated her, but when Alex's sister died something had to be done about the old girl, who was by then confined to a wheelchair with arthritis, and so of course Alex announced: 'She's coming to live with us!' Ghastly. Poor Carrie. I can't tell you the havoc that decision caused."

"How did Mrs. Jardine cope?"

"You may well ask," said Mrs. Cobden-Smith, using a phrase which I was soon to realise was a favourite of hers. "It was five years ago, just after the move to Starbridge from Radbury, and Carrie was going through the—well, it was an awkward time for her—and everything was at sixes and sevens. I said to Willy: 'Carrie will have a nervous breakdown, I know she will,' but of course I'd reckoned without Miss Christie. The old girl took to Miss Christie in the biggest possible way, gave Carrie no trouble and died good as gold six months later. I said to Willy: 'That girl Christie's a miracle-worker.' "

"Is there any problem Miss Christie can't solve?"

"You may well ask," said Mrs. Cobden-Smith a second time. "It was strange how she tamed the old girl, I must say. I remember it occurred to me once that there was a curious resemblance between them—not a resemblance in looks, of course; the old girl weighed a ton while Miss Christie's so small and slim, but there was some odd resemblance of the personality. I suspect that the old girl, when she was young, had that same cool competence which Miss Christie now displays so noticeably. Alex's real mother died when he was six, the father was left with eight children under twelve, or something frightful, and the stepmother restored order to the home—rather as Miss Christie pulled the Deanery together when she first came to Radbury."

I was now offered a choice of two openings. I was tempted to ask about Radbury, but I was also curious to discover more about Jardine's obscure background. Finally I said: "What happened to all the other little Jardines?"

"One sister went mad and died in an asylum, three brothers went to the Colonies and died of drink or worse, one brother went bankrupt in London and hanged himself and the last brother simply disappeared. That left the younger sister, who eventually looked after the old girl, and Alex."

"Dr. Jardine obviously had a miraculous survival!"

"It was the hand of God," said Mrs. Cobden-Smith with that matchless confidence of the layman who always knows exactly what God has in mind. "Of course none of us knows for certain what went on in that family, but I've pieced a few lurid details together over the years and there's no doubt the background was a nightmare. I used to talk to Alex's sister Edith—a nice woman she was, terribly common but a nice woman—and she occasionally let slip the odd piece of information which made my hair stand on end."

"Lady Starmouth liked her too, said she'd had an awful life—"

"Unspeakable. The father was a lunatic—never certified, unfortunately, but quite obviously potty. He suffered from religious mania and saw sin everywhere so he wouldn't let his children go to school for fear they'd be corrupted."

"But how on earth did Dr. Jardine get to Oxford?"

"You may well ask," said Mrs. Cobden-Smith once more, enjoying her attentive audience. "It was the stepmother. She finally got him to school when he was fourteen and kept his nose to the grindstone until he'd won the scholarship."

"In that case," I said, "since Dr. Jardine owed her so much, wasn't it a rare and splendid piece of justice that she should spend her final days with him in his episcopal palace?"

"I dare say it was," conceded Mrs. Cobden-Smith with reluctance, "although Carrie didn't see it that way at the time. Thank God Miss Christie tamed the old girl before poor Carrie could have another nervous breakdown!"

"Another nervous breakdown? You mean—"

"Dash, I shouldn't have said that, should I, Willy would be cross. But on the other hand it's an open secret that Carrie's a prey to her nerves. I've often said to her in the past: 'Carrie, you must make more effort—you simply can't go to bed and give up!' But I'm afraid she's not the fighting kind. I'm quite different, I'm glad to say—I'm always fighting away and making efforts! When I was in India . . ."

I let her talk about India while I waited for the opening which would lead us back to the subject of Mrs. Jardine's nervous breakdown. The characters in Jardine's past were revolving in my mind: the eccentric father, the doomed siblings, the surviving sister who had "a ghastly way with a teacup," the mysterious Swedish stepmother who had exerted such a vital influence—and then after the years of darkness, the years of light and a new world with new people: Carrie and the Cobden-Smiths, the subtle charming Lady Starmouth, the clever American girl struggling from the ruins of a disastrous marriage—

"—disastrous marriage," said Mrs. Cobden-Smith, remarking how fortunate it was that Carrie had avoided marrying an officer in the Indian Army. "She would never have survived the climate."

"No, probably not. Mrs. Cobden-Smith, talking of survival—"

"Of course Carrie's had a hard time surviving marriage to a clergyman," said Mrs. Cobden-Smith, playing into my hands before I could risk a direct question about Mrs. Jardine's difficulties at Radbury, "although the ironic part is that in many ways she's cut out to be a clergyman's wife—everyone likes her and she's a very good, devout, friendly little person, but she should have been the wife of an ordinary parson, not the wife of a fire-breathing adventurer who periodically runs amok through the Church of England. It's a terrible tragedy there are no children. Of course children can drive one up the wall, I'm not sentimental about children, but they do give a marriage a focal point, and although Alex and Carrie are devoted to each other any stranger can see they don't have much in common. How ghastly it was when that baby was born dead in 1918! No wonder Carrie went to pieces, poor thing."

"Was that when she had her nervous—"

"Well, it wasn't really a nervous breakdown," said Mrs. Cobden-Smith fluently. "I was exaggerating. A nervous breakdown means someone climbing the walls, doesn't it, and having to be whisked away to a private nursing home, but Carrie's collapse was quite different. She just lay weeping on a chaise-longue all day and when she finally had the strength to leave it she started consulting spiritualists to see if she could get in touch with the dead child—terribly embarrassing for Alex, of course, to be a clergyman whose wife consulted spiritualists, so it was arranged that Carrie should have a little holiday with her parents in the country. That did her the world of good, thank God, and afterwards she was fine until they moved to Radbury."

"Someone did mention that she found the move a little difficult—"

"Poor Carrie! If only Alex had been made vicar of some quiet little parish in the back of beyond! But no, off he went to Radbury to run that hulking great Cathedral, and Carrie found herself put on public display as Mrs. Dean—hundreds of new people to meet, all the residents of the Cathedral Close watching critically to see if she made a mistake, new committees to master, endless dinner-parties to organise, Mrs. Bishop looking down her nose from the palace, all the canons' wives trying to interfere—"

"When did Mrs. Jardine make the decision to engage a companion?"

"Alex made the decision, not Carrie. Carrie was soon in such a state that she couldn't make any decision at all—although of course," said Mrs. Cobden-Smith, "she wasn't having a nervous breakdown. Not really. She just went shopping every day to buy things she didn't need—I think it took her mind off her troubles—and when she wasn't shopping she was always so tired that she had to stay in bed. Finally she bought some really frightful wallpaper—the last word in extravagance—and Alex decided she needed someone to keep an eye on her during her little shopping sprees. Miss Christie turned up and was an immediate success. Alex used to refer to her simply as 'The Godsend.' "

"The Bishop must have been concerned about his wife," I murmured, selecting an understatement in the hope of luring her into further indiscretions, but Mrs. Cobden-Smith merely said: "Yes, he was," and shifted restlessly as if aware for the first time that a stranger might read into her frank comments rather more than she had intended to reveal. I suspected that like most people of little imagination she found it difficult to picture what was going on in any mind other than her own.

"Where does Miss Christie come from?" I said, changing the subject to soothe her uneasiness.

"Rural Norfolk—one of those places where there's lots of inbreeding and everyone talks in grunts. She has a clerical family background, of course."

"How suitable. But Mrs. Cobden-Smith, one thing does puzzle me about Miss Christie: why has she never married?"

"Ah!" said Mrs. Cobden-Smith. "That's what we'd all like to know! There's a rumour that she was once badly jilted, but I think she put that story in circulation to cover up a far less respectable reason for staying single."

"Oh?" I said. "And what would that be?"

"I strongly suspect," said Mrs. Cobden-Smith, lowering her voice confidentially, "that Miss Christie has a lust for power."

4

THE sense of an absurd anti-climax was so strong that I had to fight a desire to laugh, but fortunately Mrs. Cobden-Smith was more anxious to explain her theory than to see if I kept a straight face.

"Of course the popular rumour," she was saying, "is that Miss Christie's secretly in love with Alex, but that's nonsense because I can't see her being such a fool as to waste ten of the best years of her life being hopelessly in love with a married man. No, you mark my words, Dr. Ashworth, she's mad about power. Some women are. Not all women want to marry, and I think Miss Christie simply loves being in charge here, running the palace, looking after Carrie, helping the Bishop, meeting all the Church dignitaries and all the aristocratic guests like the Starmouths. In my opinion," said Mrs. Cobden-Smith decisively, "Miss Christie's merely an unusual example of a modern woman who's wedded to her career."

Having conquered my "fou rire" I could see now that Mrs. Cobden-Smith's theory was not so absurd as I had supposed; it was certainly more attractive than Lady Starmouth's wild assertion of lesbianism. However, before I could make any comment Mrs. Cobden-Smith exclaimed: "Ah, there's Carrie—downstairs in time for luncheon, thank God! And there's Willy with George. Will you excuse me, Dr. Ashworth? I must see George eats his horse-meat."

She set off briskly across the lawn, and as soon as I was alone I became aware that I was uncomfortably hot. I decided to cool off in my room before lunch while I reviewed the evidence produced in such profusion by my interviews.

By the time I reached the terrace Mrs. Cobden-Smith had disappeared with the Colonel and George, but Mrs. Jardine was waiting for me with her warmest smile. Now that I knew more about her the smile seemed poignant, and again I was aware of reality submerging itself beneath illusion in the heat of that Starbridge noon.

"How are you, Mrs. Jardine?" I said as I mounted the steps to the terrace. "I was sorry to hear you were feeling so tired."

"Oh, I'm much better now, thank you! So stupid about my insomnia, I must have had too much coffee by mistake last night, and then after I'd gone to bed I started thinking about your poor wife and the baby and . . . Well, you know how it is, I dare say, when one's thoughts go round and round, especially in the early hours of the morning, and suddenly I felt so frightened, I don't know why, I do get moments of panic sometimes, especially when the weather's so hot. Do you think there might be a storm coming, Dr. Ashworth? The air's very sultry, so close and threatening, and I feel as if something dreadful's going to happen."

The sky was cloudless and although the air was hot there was little humidity. I said gently: "I agree it's very warm—shall we go inside?" and I gestured to indicate she should precede me into the house, but Mrs. Jardine hesitated, looking uncertainly up and down the terrace. "I was wondering if we should have drinks out here," she said, "but I can't make up my mind. Alex never drinks at mid-day but my brother and sister-in-law do and so do the Starmouths. Do you drink at mid-day, Dr. Ashworth?"

"Not usually, no." Beyond the open French windows Miss Christie and the butler were entering the drawing-room. I heard Miss Christie say: "No, it's too hot outside, Shipton," and the butler set down his tray of glasses on a side-table.

"Lyle says it's too hot out here," said Mrs. Jardine, relieved that the decision had been taken out of her hands. She called to Miss Christie: "Dr. Ashworth doesn't drink cocktails at mid-day either, dear, so we'll be one extra for lemonade."

"Yes, I'd anticipated that," said Miss Christie, coming out onto the terrace to join us. "Good morning again, Dr. Ashworth. I hope you've been enjoying sunbathing in a clerical suit."

"I have indeed," I said. "In fact the morning's been so enjoyable that I'm resolved to have an equally enjoyable afternoon. Will you come for a drive with me after lunch?"

Miss Christie had given an inch and I had taken a yard. At least no one could accuse me of wasting my opportunities, but Miss Christie showed signs of regretting the conceded inch. Without hesitation she said: "I'm not a free agent, Dr. Ashworth. I have my duties here at the palace."

"Oh, but I shall only be resting this afternoon!" protested Mrs. Jardine. "Do go for a drive with Dr. Ashworth, dearest—why not!"

"Why not indeed?" said a familiar harsh voice, and swinging round I found that Dr. Jardine was watching me from the threshold of the drawing-room.

5

THERE was a pause. I glanced back at Miss Christie but she had already reached the practical decision that it was now less awkward to accept the invitation than to refuse it. She said politely: "Thank you. A drive would be very pleasant," and then she escaped past the Bishop into the drawing-room where the butler had just deposited a large jug of lemonade.

"It's abominably hot, isn't it?" said Jardine as I watched both the butler and Miss Christie disappear into the hall. "Carrie, you look on the verge of sun-stroke. Come in at once."

"I feel so odd, Alex—"

"I propose we launch an immediate assault on the iced lemonade."

The shade of the drawing-room came as an exquisite relief, but as Mrs. Jardine sat down on the edge of the sofa I noticed the nervous movements of her hands and sensed her tension more strongly than ever.

"Well, Dr. Ashworth!" said Jardine, passing a glass of lemonade to his wife and holding out a second glass to me. "Do I assume that the glories of the Cathedral Library left you cold? As far as I can gather you've spent the morning talking to one attractive woman and you now propose to spend the afternoon talking to another."

I said with a smile: "Having spent well over an hour admiring the glories of the Cathedral Library I felt entitled to spend far less than an hour—"

"—admiring the glories of Lady Starmouth. Quite." The Bishop was taking care to sound amused but I sensed his amusement was wafer-thin and I began to feel uneasy.

"But I thought you were talking to Amy, not Lady Starmouth!" said Mrs. Jardine to me. She sounded abnormally confused.

"Oh, Dr. Ashworth's been talking to just about everyone!" said the Bishop, and I could now clearly hear the acid note in his voice. "He seems to be suffering from an ungovernable urge to display the gregarious side of his nature!"

"He hasn't been talking to me," said Colonel Cobden-Smith, entering the room as I began to wonder if Lady Starmouth had lodged a complaint about my interrogation.

"That's because you've been exercising that unfortunate hound in this appalling heat and offering yourself as a candidate for a heart attack—and now I suppose you'll say you want a pink gin!"

"The heat's so bad for everyone," said Mrs. Jardine in an agony of anxiety before the Colonel could reply. "I'm sure there's going to be a storm, but according to the weather forecast—"

"Oh, for heaven's sake, Carrie!" exclaimed the Bishop in a paroxysm of irritability. "Stop talking about the weather!"

Mrs. Jardine began to cry.

"Ye gods and little fishes," muttered Jardine as the Colonel and I stood transfixed, and yelled at the top of his voice: "Lyle!"

In walked Miss Christie. It was almost as if she had been waiting in the wings for her cue.

"Lyle, Carrie can't take this heat. Do something, would you," said the Bishop, and stooping awkwardly over his wife he kissed her before murmuring: "I'm sorry."

"Darling," said Miss Christie to Mrs. Jardine, "you must drink all your lemonade at once and then you'll feel better. It's very important to take lots of liquid in hot weather."

Jardine remarked: "Maybe I should take lemonade regularly to prevent irascibility after an arid morning in my study. I've just been reading the latest crop of letters on the Marriage Bill from people who think I was the clergyman in charge of Edward VIII's wedding, and I'm now wishing more fervently than ever that my deplorable namesake had been called by any name other than Jardine."

This was a skilful attempt to manipulate the conversation back within the bounds of normality, but before a more relaxed atmosphere could be established Mrs. Cobden-Smith swept in. "Willy, George won't eat that horse-meat. Do you suppose—oh my goodness, what's going on? Carrie dear, you simply must make more effort! I know the heat's trying, but—"

"Amy," said the Bishop, "would you kindly stop addressing my wife as if she were an Indian peasant ripe for civilisation by the British Raj?"

"Well, *really,* Alex!"

"Mrs. Cobden-Smith," said Miss Christie with unprecedented charm, "I wonder if you'd be terribly kind and help me take Carrie upstairs to lie down? You must have had such a broad experience of heat-stroke in India and I'd so value your advice—should we call the doctor?"

"Quite unnecessary," said Mrs. Cobden-Smith, greatly mollified, "but perhaps she does need to lie down. Come along, Carrie."

The chaplain then chose an unfortunate moment to rush into the room with bad news. "Bishop, the Archdeacon's on the phone again and he's in a frightful panic!"

"Oh, hang the Archdeacon!" exploded the Bishop. "And hang that abominable instrument the telephone!" But he seized the chance to make a swift exit from the chaos caused by his irritability.

6

I WAS surprised how quickly order was restored. Coaxed by Miss Christie, Mrs. Jardine drank all her lemonade and said she felt better. The Starmouths arrived, and while they debated what to drink I could hear the Cobden-Smiths discussing George who presently made a lacklustre entrance. Miss Christie summoned the butler to replenish the lemonade jug, but before I had the chance to speak to her about our outing four guests appeared from various corners of the diocese and all opportunity for private conversation was curtailed.

Lunch passed smoothly if tediously. I busied myself by being sociable with a large matron whose favourite topic of conversation was the Mothers' Union, and although Miss Christie never looked in my direction I occasionally caught Lady Starmouth's sympathetic glance across the table.

However by half-past two the party had dispersed and I was preparing in my bedroom for a country excursion far removed from a clerical duty. Off came my clergyman's uniform. Having pulled on my coolest informal clothes I unbuttoned my shirt at the neck, adjusted the angle of my hat and once more turned to survey my image in the long glass. Immediately I wondered if I had gone too far with the informality; I fancied I looked like a commercial traveller taking a rest from hawking some dubious product, but when I decided to wear a tie I felt much too hot. Shoving the tie back in the drawer I undid the top button of my shirt again and made up my mind that I looked exactly what I was: an off-duty clergyman about to take a pretty woman for a drive in the country.

But then I looked in the glass and saw the spy beyond the clergyman, the image beyond the image, and beyond the spy was yet another man, the image beyond the image beyond the image. Reality blurred; fantasy and truth became inextricably intertwined. I told myself I had imagined the distant stranger but as I felt my personality begin to divide I covered my face with my hands.

Sinking to my knees by the bed, I whispered: "Lord, forgive me my sins. Deliver me from evil. Help me to serve you as well as I can." After that I felt calmer, and when I glanced again in the glass I found that the off-duty clergyman was now the only visible image. He was wearing a severe expression as if to stress that I had no business to let the heat addle my brain, and immediately, erasing all morbid thoughts from my mind, I set off to meet Miss Christie.

V

"Experience has made it certain that the clergyman's wife must either throw in her lot unreservedly with her husband's difficult and distinctive career, and reap her reward with a range and depth of personal influence which are unequalled in the case of any other married woman, or she must separate herself from his work and life with consequences ruinous both to his success and to her own credit, and, we must add, to the happiness of both."

HERBERT HENSLEY HENSON,
THE BISHOPRICK PAPERS

I

MISS CHRISTIE was wearing a pale green short-sleeved frock, which exposed her slim arms, and flat white sandals, which emphasised her slender ankles. Other fleshier curves were erotically concealed beneath the prim cut of her frock. She was sheltering beneath a wide-brimmed straw hat.

"Trying not to be recognised?" I said as we met in the hall.

"I might ask you the same question!"

"Well, at least you haven't said—"

"—'Oh, how different you look out of your clericals!' "

We laughed, and as I led the way outside to my car it occurred to me that if Miss Christie could cope with every conceivable crisis in an episcopal household, she could cope with a doctor of divinity who was mad enough to be afraid of his own reflection. Conscious of relief, happiness, nervous anticipation and sexual desire in pleasantly stimulating proportions, I decided the afternoon was going to be a success.

Miss Christie suggested that we might drive to Starbury Ring, a megalithic stone circle high on the Downs, and after she had directed me out of the city we headed up the valley to the north. The surrounding hills curved with a voluptuous smoothness in the limpid afternoon light. Leaving the main road we passed some farms and once were trapped behind a slow-moving cart, but otherwise nothing deflected our attention from the steadily unfolding views.

Suddenly Miss Christie said: "I ought to take Mrs. Jardine for a drive like this. It would do her good. We could even take a picnic and disappear for an entire afternoon."

"What about the Bishop?"

"Oh, I'd leave him behind. He hates eating 'al fresco.' His idea of relaxation is to write a letter to *The Times.*"

"I hear that was how he made his name before he became Vicar of St. Mary's Mayfair."

"Yes, he didn't have much else to do when he was a chaplain in North London."

I saw the chance to pursue my investigation. "No one's yet explained to me," I said, "why he was living in such obscurity before the translation to Mayfair. What happened to him after he was ordained?"

"He was given a parish in this diocese—in the slums of Starmouth. He stayed there for seven years and made a success of it, but it was desperately hard work and in the end his health broke down."

"That often happens to clergymen in sordid parishes," I said, and the next moment I was remembering my friend Philip's accusation that I lived in an ivory tower. Some guilty impulse drove me to add: "However, you mustn't think I speak from experience. I'm afraid my ministry's always been among the affluent."

"Christ preached to the rich as well as the poor, didn't he?" Miss Christie said composed. "And Dr. Jardine says that spiritually the rich can be just as impoverished as any family on the dole."

I glanced at her with gratitude but she was looking out of the side window at the curving hills. After a pause I said: "Tell me more about Dr. Jardine—what happened when his health broke down?"

"On the doctor's advice he resigned his living and borrowed the money to take a long holiday. The rest helped but he still didn't think his health could stand the strain of another parish, so he decided to do some writing and research at Oxford. I expect you know he's a Fellow of All Souls. However, his financial difficulties in those days were so acute that he had to have some sort of benefice, and finally the Warden of All Souls got him this obscure hospital chaplaincy in North London—the living was in the gift of the College."

"I gather Dr. Jardine had considerable family obligations in Putney."

"He was supporting his father, his stepmother and his two sisters," said Miss Christie dryly. "Although he didn't starve, he was hardly well-nourished. However, the chaplaincy suited him—the hospital was very small, no more than a large alms-house, and as there wasn't much work to do he used to spend the days in the middle of the week up at Oxford. He wrote some articles, preached various guest sermons—he already had a reputation as a preacher—and sent letters regularly to *The Times.*

Eventually, without Dr. Jardine's knowledge, the Warden of All Souls approached Mr. Asquith, who was then Prime Minister, and asked him if something could be done to improve the situation since it was obvious that Dr. Jardine's health was quite restored. Mr. Asquith had been enjoying the letters to *The Times* and he immediately remembered that the new vacancy at St. Mary's was in the gift of the Crown."

"That's what we clergymen call an edifying story," I said. "After many vicissitudes the good get their reward."

"I can't see why you should sound so envious," said Miss Christie, as if she felt she had been too friendly and was now obliged to redress the balance. "You're obviously in line for the choicest of bishoprics."

"You think so?" I said. "I'm flattered. But do you honestly believe I'm fit to be a bishop just because I've published a book on the Early Church and can survive at Cambridge Cathedral without quarrelling with the Dean?"

"Oh, I wouldn't presume to judge your fitness, Dr. Ashworth. I leave that to God and Dr. Lang."

I knew I had to demonstrate that I was not prepared to tolerate an asperity drummed up by a guilt that we should be getting on so well. Grinding the car to a halt I switched off the engine, swivelled to face her and demanded: "Why the hostility?"

She went white. At first I thought she was white with anger but then I realised she was white with alarm. When she protested: "I'm not hostile!" I said at once: "No—so why pretend?" and leaning forward I kissed her on the mouth.

This was fast behaviour for a gentleman on a sedate afternoon drive with a lady he had known less than twenty-four hours, and for a clergyman the behaviour was so fast that I felt I was travelling at the speed of light. Indeed my speed so stunned Miss Christie that for the first five seconds after our lips touched she behaved as if she were paralysed. Five seconds is a long time when two mouths are joined in a kiss. However, on the sixth second the response came, and contrary to my expectations the response was far from hostile. Her mouth opened beneath mine. At once I pulled her closer, but the next moment she was shoving me aside and with reluctance I let her go. Her face was no longer white but a pale pink. I had no idea what colour my face was but I felt as if I had run a hundred yards at high speed, and my mind was swirling not only with thoughts of empty champagne glasses but with images of bright swords, dark tunnels and other ambiguous objects blighted for all time by Freud.

Miss Christie smoothed her skirt—which I had not touched—and as she did so I noticed that she wore a signet-ring on the third finger of her left hand. Finally she said: "We met yesterday for the first time. We're not even on Christian-name terms. Aren't you behaving a little curiously for a clergyman?"

"At least I now know you well enough to call you Lyle."

"Dr. Ashworth—"

"My name's Charles. Yes, of course I'm behaving curiously for a clergyman, but whenever someone makes a remark which implies a clergyman should be some sort of stainless-steel saint I want to quote Shylock's speech from *The Merchant of Venice,* you know the one, the speech where he says he bleeds and suffers just as other people do—"

"Well, I wasn't implying—"

"Weren't you?"

"Dr. Ashworth—"

"Charles."

"—I'm afraid I'm simply not a candidate for a whirlwind romance—"

"No, don't pretend you're not interested in me! I saw you listening with bated breath last night when Lady Starmouth asked if I had a wife!"

"I—"

"Look." I adopted my calmest, most rational manner. "I could proceed in the conventional way. I could pay you nice safe little compliments and write you harmless little billets-doux and send you flowers and come down to Starbridge every fortnight to take you out to tea—I could do all that. I'm perfectly capable of behaving like a gentleman and playing the game according to the rules, but where would it get me? Absolutely nowhere. I found that out last night when I made that mild approach and you dodged away around the coffee-cups. Well, dodging around the coffee-cups may be great fun for you, but frankly I'm not prepared to be treated as a minor inconvenience. I want to get to know you very much better as soon as possible—which is why I suggested this drive—"

"Then why aren't we driving? I don't want to spend all afternoon in front of this five-barred gate while you regale me with impassioned nonsense!"

I started the engine and we drove on.

2

WITHIN minutes we had emerged onto a broad plateau, and ahead I could see a track leading away from the road towards the ridge which marked the summit of the Downs.

"Stop the car on the verge by that path," said Lyle. "This is where we begin the trek to the Ring."

"There's no need to sound as if you wished you were chaperoned!"

I said lightly as I halted the car once more. "Now that I've defined exactly where I stand, I promise I'll behave like a stainless-steel saint for a couple of hours."

"What happens after a couple of hours?"

"We'll be back at the palace and you can hide behind the Bishop."

As I opened the passenger door, she said: "You're very interested in the Bishop, aren't you?"

"Is there anyone in the Church of England who isn't?"

We set off up the track. I wanted to hold her hand but I exercised an immaculate self-discipline and kept my fists shoved deep in my pockets. However, I was not dissatisfied with my progress. At least she had neither slapped my face nor called me a cad nor demanded to be returned immediately to Starbridge.

"If you want to know me better," she said at last, "why don't you set the pace by helping me to know more about you? Most men usually can't wait to recite their life histories, but you seem peculiarly reticent."

"I didn't intend this to be a history lesson. I'd rather talk about the present."

"What's wrong with your past?"

"It's boring. I was born in the right county in the right residential neighbourhood of one of the right towns. My father has the right sort of profession and my mother indulges in the right sort of hobbies. I went to the right schools and the right university, got myself ordained at the right age, and began my right career at the right time with the right man. Then I taught at the right places, wrote the right book and eventually became a canon of the right cathedral. It's all very dull, isn't it? Dr. Jardine's past is so much more interesting than mine."

All Lyle said was: "You've left out the right marriage to the right wife."

"So I have. Careless of me. I suppose that was because she did the wrong thing and died."

We walked on. The sun blazed on the grassy hills dotted with sheep, and as we moved towards the summit of the ridge the view began to expand in every direction. It was uncannily quiet.

At last Lyle said: "You don't give much away."

"Does anyone, even the people who rush to recite the carefully selected facts of their life at tedious length?" I was trying to establish a line of conversation which would tempt her to rebut my argument with disclosures about herself, but she merely said with detachment: "I agree that the exact truth about people is usually impossible to know, but I think most of the time one can make an accurate guess about what goes on." She paused to look back across the valley behind us. "Take the Starmouths, for example," she said. "The Earl's a good decent Englishman of the old school who takes a conscientious interest in his estates, does his bit for the country by a regular attendance at the House of Lords, and is devoted to his wife and children. Lady Starmouth probably gets a bit bored with him but she's fundamentally good and decent too so she doesn't rattle around like a society hostess but instead amuses herself with the safest class of men—clergymen, who have a strong stake in sticking to the proprieties. Now, I'm not saying this is the exact truth about either of the Starmouths, but I think the odds are I've given you an accurate thumbnail sketch. I mean, I don't seriously believe, do you, that Lady Starmouth is a secret drug-fiend while the Earl keeps a mistress in St. John's Wood?"

"Lady Starmouth is certainly not a secret drug-fiend. But"—I thought of the Earl's candid admiration of Loretta—" I don't think I'm as sure as you are about that mistress in St. John's Wood. Over the years I've come to the conclusion that it's impossible to make reliable guesses about anyone's intimate life." Without looking at her directly I was nevertheless poised to analyse her reaction.

But she merely said: "Isn't the Earl a little old for fun and games in St. John's Wood?"

"He might consider a mistress rejuvenating. But no," I said with a smile as we moved on again towards the summit of the ridge, "I confess I don't really believe the Earl has a secret love-life any more than I believe Lady Starmouth is burning to seduce the Bishop."

She laughed. "Lady Starmouth's whole success with the Bishop lies in the fact that she at least would never play the over-passionate female in his company!"

"Are there so many over-passionate females besieging Dr. Jardine?"

Lyle suddenly chose to treat the subject seriously. "Not now," she said. "A bishop's more on a pedestal than an ordinary clergyman, but there were one or two very tricky women when he was Dean of Radbury, and apparently when he was Vicar of St. Mary's he was forever fending off society women who were far less principled than Lady Starmouth."

I said equally seriously, to show that I understood the problems which could exist for certain clergymen: "But surely troublesome women reserve their most ardent attentions for bachelors?"

"Oh, no doubt life became fractionally less hectic once he was married, but unfortunately many women even today are tempted to write Mrs. Jardine off as insignificant and imagine that the Bishop's languishing in an unhappy marriage. That's rubbish, of course. The Jardines may seem to a stranger to be ill-assorted but anyone who knows them well will tell you they're devoted to each other. It's an attraction of opposites."

We had reached the top of the ridge while she was speaking, and as we paused to survey the view we found that the outlines of the landscape soon faded into the heat-haze. Abandoning the obscure prospect across the valley, I turned my attention to Starbury Ring which was now visible less than fifty yards away. The Ring consisted of two dozen tall rocks, planted several thousand years ago for purposes which were no longer known but which at once conjured up images in my mind of human sacrifices and other horrors of heathen worship. I thought how comforting it would be to believe that all blood-stained idolatory in Europe now lay sealed in the past, and for a moment I wished I were a Victorian who still had faith in the doctrine of progress. How delightful it must have been to look forward with confidence to the time when mankind would have achieved its inevitable perfection! How soothing to be able to picture an immanent, cosily accessible God who could be known with the aid of reason and a good education! But now the War had destroyed the illusion of progress, blood-stained idolatory was once more invading Europe, and the powerful mind of Karl Barth had perceived that God was remote, utterly transcendent, capable of being known only by revelation.

"I'm sorry," I said suddenly to Lyle. "The sight of pagan stones sent me off at a theological tangent. You were saying the Jardines were devoted to each other—"

"Yes, Mrs. Jardine adores the Bishop, and the Bishop, like all men, adores being adored. Of course she gets on his nerves occasionally—well, you saw that this morning, didn't you?—but on the whole he considers a little irritation a small price to pay for a wife who's genuinely good, very popular and thoroughly loyal to him in every way."

"The Bishop seems to have a most remarkable talent for surrounding himself with adoring women!"

"The talent's probably developed in reaction to his bleak childhood. Adoration was in short supply then."

"I thought he had a devoted stepmother?"

"She wasn't demonstrative. Until he was eighteen he hadn't a clue how she felt."

"What happened when he was eighteen?"

"He went up to Oxford, and when he said goodbye to her she cried. It was her supreme moment of triumph, you see. She'd singled him out as the best of the bunch and put him on the road to Oxford, but he'd always thought he was just a hobby for her as she had no children of her own." Lyle paused before adding: "I think probably in the beginning he really was just a hobby for her, but after a while she found that her ambition for him gave her the determination to endure a difficult marriage. 'It was worth it all for Adam,' she said to me at the end of her life. She used to call him Adam. She hated the name Alex, thought it was frivolous, a nasty affectation of the Cobden-Smiths. 'Adam's not really Alex,' she said to me once. 'Alex is just a mask, and beyond the mask there's the Adam nobody knows except me.' That was a sinister thing to say, wasn't it? I look at the Bishop sometimes and think: there's an Adam in there somewhere! What a mysterious thing personality is, how eerie, how unfathomable . . ."

We were now standing in the middle of the stone circle. The stones themselves, stark and dark beneath their green-brown lichen, heightened the mystery of the Ring as it stood in that empty landscape, and seemed to bring the remote past deep into the present. I felt as if the Druids were brushing shoulders with Karl Barth as one blood-stained century merged into another in defiance of any conventional conception of time.

"This seems an appropriate place to discuss mysteries," I said, "and particularly the mystery of personality. Let's sit down for a moment."

When we were chastely settled two feet apart in the shadow of one of the stones, I offered her a cigarette. "Do you smoke?"

"Only in my bedroom. But if you're going to have a treat I don't see why I shouldn't have one too."

"You look like the kind of woman who smokes Craven A."

"Oh, so you see me as an adventuress!"

"Let's just say I have trouble seeing you as a companion in a clerical household." As I lit our cigarettes I noticed that her hands were small and that the large signet-ring emphasised the delicate curve of her finger. The skin on the inside of her wrist was very white.

"Are you sure you're not going to pounce on me again?" she said after her first puff. "You've got a pounce-ish look."

"That's because you're so pounceworthy. Now stop egging me on by putting impure thoughts in my head and tell me more about this Swedish stepmother. I'm interested in the influence she must have had on Dr. Jardine."

3

"*I FIRST* met her at Radbury," said Lyle. "She visited the Jardines there a couple of times, but then travel became too difficult because of her arthritis. The Bishop used to visit her in Putney whenever he could, but I myself never saw her again until she came to live with us in Starbridge at the end of her life."

"It's nice to think she ended her days with her Adam in his palace."

"Another edifying tale? Yes, I suppose it was, although the situation wasn't entirely a bed of roses because poor Carrie was terrified of her stepmother-in-law. However," said Lyle, effortlessly glossing over the crisis which had shaken the palace to its foundations, "we all got on very well in the end. Old Mrs. J. had decided that God was giving her a chance to redeem her previous coldness towards Carrie."

"She was religious?"

"Yes, she'd been a Lutheran originally, like so many Swedes, but she'd been married to a man who thought institutional religion was rubbish, so she hadn't been a regular churchgoer."

"But I thought Dr. Jardine's father was a religious fanatic!"

"The fanaticism took an anti-clerical form. He thought all clergymen were instruments of the Devil."

"How extraordinarily difficult for Dr. Jardine!"

"Being married to a religious crank was hardly easy for old Mrs. J.!"

"Did she confide in you? It sounds as if she did."

"Yes, she enjoyed telling a sympathetic stranger about all the ghastliness she'd endured in the old days so that 'her Adam,' as you called him, should survive his appalling home. Her first big battle was to get him to school. Old Mr. J. thought schools were sinks of iniquity."

"He certainly sounds the most tiresome husband. Did she never consider abandoning Putney and bolting for Sweden? Or did her religious beliefs, such as they were, make an escape out of the question?"

"There's no doubt religious belief played a large part in her decision to stay—she became convinced she'd been sent into the family in order to save that child. 'I felt it was a call from God,' she said. 'I felt no other action was possible.' "

"But surely once Dr. Jardine was grown up—once he'd got to Oxford—"

"Then the really ghastly problems began. The scholarship only covered his fees, and the beastly old father wouldn't give him any money for his keep. Old Mrs. J. used to starve herself so that she could send money from her housekeeping allowance—the old man only climbed down when she was half-dead with hunger."

I said amazed: "But wasn't the old man pleased that his son was up at Oxford?"

"He thought all universities were dens of vice. However, the Bishop survived and was awarded not only a first but a fellowship of All Souls—"

"Happy ending!"

"Good heavens, no—quite the reverse! Old Mr. J. then said: 'I've kept you all these years—now it's time for you to keep me!' and it turned out that as he'd been living beyond his means for years while he pursued a life of gentlemanly idleness, his capital was now exhausted."

"What an old scoundrel! So Dr. Jardine had to keep the family on the income from his fellowship?"

"Yes, for a time he didn't think he could afford to go into the Church, but eventually he made the decision to be ordained—"

"—and of course the old man disapproved."

"I gather the two of them nearly killed each other."

I said appalled: "But couldn't the old man see his son was opting for a good straight decent life?"

"Oh, he never thought his son would succeed in living decently, no matter what profession he chose. The old man saw him sinking inevitably into corruption."

"But this must have been terrible for Dr. Jardine!" I was now having trouble finding the words to express my horror, and Lyle was looking at me in surprise. "Terrible—monstrous—intolerable—"

"It got worse. The Bishop became vicar of the slum parish in Starmouth, and as he was unable to afford to marry and as he desperately needed a housekeeper he turned for help to his father, who was sitting in Putney being waited on hand and foot by a wife and two unmarried daughters. However, old Mr. J. refused to let either of the girls go to look after their brother. He had an obsession with female purity and thought they'd be ravished the moment they left his household."

"But surely if the Bishop was supporting them all he had the whip-hand?"

"The old man still wouldn't budge. Said he'd rather starve than risk his daughters becoming fallen women."

"Didn't the girls have any say in the matter?"

"Don't be silly, this was well before the War and he'd ruled them with a rod of iron for years!"

"No wonder one sister went mad!"

"Mrs. J. thought she'd go mad herself, but of course she came to the rescue. She said to the old villain: 'If you won't let either of those girls go, *I'll* go,' and when he still clung to the girls she went."

I dropped my cigarette and scuffled to retrieve it before it could burn a hole in my trousers. "But how could Dr. Jardine, as a clergyman, justify depriving a husband of his wife?"

"Oh, the old man wasn't too deprived—she used to go home for a visit every fortnight. Besides, neither she nor Dr. Jardine believed, when she originally went to Starmouth, that the arrangement would be other than temporary. They thought the old man would eventually release one of the girls, but as he wasn't rational on the subject, he didn't."

"So she stayed on?"

"Yes, she loved it after the gloom and doom of Putney. She involved herself in parish work, met new people—"

"But what happened—"

"—in the end? She went back. The elder sister began to go insane, and Mrs. J. felt morally bound to go home since her husband's need for her had become acute. However, once she'd gone, Dr. Jardine couldn't cope; he was already exhausted by the parish and he couldn't withstand the loss of her help."

"So when he lost her he broke down!"

"What an extremely ambiguous statement! All I meant was—"

"What happened next in Putney?"

"I've no idea. Mrs. J. skated over that, but a year later the sister died in an asylum and the old man went senile. Old Mrs. J. told me placidly it was the judgement of God."

"How did the Bishop deal with the new crisis?"

"By that time he was in North London. The house allocated to the hospital chaplain was small but he rescued his father, stepmother and surviving sister and squeezed them in somehow. The father died six months later. Then old Mrs. J. and the sister lived with the Bishop till his marriage."

I decided it would be politic to prove to her that my mind did not always leap to the most dubious conclusions. "I can't quite see why old Mrs. J. made such a fuss about that marriage," I said innocently. "Surely she wanted her stepson to make a good marriage as soon as he could afford to do so?"

"She didn't look upon it as a good marriage. Carrie only had a hundred a year. Also Carrie was a bit old—thirty-two. Mrs. J. thought that was suspicious, wanted to know why she hadn't got off the shelf earlier . . . But of course the real truth was that although Mrs. J. wanted her stepson to marry, no girl was ever going to be good enough in her estimation."

"Obviously it was for the best that she decided not to live with them after the marriage. But wasn't she tempted to move closer to Dr. Jardine once he left Mayfair? Radbury's a long way from Putney."

"She was afraid of quarrelling with Carrie. That was why she stayed away until she was too infirm to stay away any more."

"I see now," I said, unable to resist angling for an indiscretion by using a suggestive remark as bait, "that the Starbridge finale isn't just an edifying resolution of the problem of old Mrs. Jardine—it even qualifies as a romantic ending."

Lyle immediately looked annoyed. "It was a happy ending, certainly," she said in the tone of voice of someone who considers romance a breach of taste. "But romantic? That makes a complex and remarkable relationship seem banal."

"Have you got some grudge against romance?"

"Of course—it's the road to illusion, isn't it?" said Lyle carelessly. "Any realist knows that." She stubbed out her cigarette. "I think it's time we went back to the car—you've got that pounce-ish look again."

"I suppose you do realise, don't you," I said, extinguishing my own cigarette, "that you're pushing me back with one hand yet beckoning me on with the other?" And before she had time to protest I had taken her in my arms.

4

THIS time I did not have the advantage of surprise and she had her defences firmly in place. As I pulled her towards me she said: "No!" in a voice which precluded argument and shoved me aside as she scrambled to her feet.

I caught up with her halfway across the Ring but before I could speak she swung to face me and demanded: "What exactly are you up to? You take me for a drive so that you can get to know me better and yet all you do is ask questions about the Bishop!"

"But I do now know you better! I know you smoke cigarettes in your bedroom, think romance is the invention of the Devil and have a profound admiration for that formidable lady, the late Mrs. Jardine!"

"I wish I'd never told you about her!" said Lyle furiously. "It's obvious you think she had some sort of obscene passion for her stepson—"

"Wouldn't 'romantic affection' be a more accurate description?"

"It was not a romance!"

"Not in a tawdry conventional sense, no. But she sacrificed her life for his, didn't she, and isn't that really the unsurpassable romantic gesture? Dickens certainly thought so when he wrote *A Tale of Two Cities,* but no one's yet accused Sydney Carton of an obscene passion for Charles Darnay."

"I thought Carton sacrificed himself for Lucie's sake, not just for Darnay's. Maybe you should start rereading Dickens!"

"Maybe you should start redefining romance. Cigarette?"

"Thanks. I feel I need one after that exchange."

When our cigarettes were alight we wandered on across the ridge. The Ring disappeared behind us as the track led over the brow of the hill, and in the distance we could see my car, crouched like a black beetle beside the dusty ribbon of the road.

"I did admire old Mrs. J.," said Lyle, "because I knew what hell she'd been through for the Bishop, but I have to admit she could be an awful old battle-axe. During her two visits to Radbury she reduced Carrie to pulp, and what was worse she used to enjoy it. Poor Carrie!"

"You're very fond of Mrs. Jardine, aren't you?"

"She's the sort of mother I always wanted. My own mother was an invalid—she had a weak heart—and it made her very querulous and self-absorbed."

"And your father?"

"He was a soldier, one of the clever ones, very quick and bright and tough. He was killed in the War, of course, like all the best soldiers, and when my mother died in sympathy I went to Norfolk to live with my great-uncle. He was an ancient vicar who took me in out of Christian charity because no one else wanted me."

"How old were you?"

"Twelve. It was 1914. You were wondering about my present age, weren't you?"

"Now that I know you're thirty-five, allow me to tell you that I'm thirty-seven. How did you find Norfolk?"

"Dreadfully dull. I ended up writing my great-uncle's sermons just to stave off the boredom."

"You don't write Dr. Jardine's sermons, do you, by any chance?"

She laughed. "Not yet!"

We strolled on down the track. "Nevertheless," I said, "you've been described to me as the real power at the palace. How would the Jardines get on if you left?"

"Oh, but I'm not leaving," she said. "Didn't you know?"

"How lucky for the Jardines! But where does that leave you?"

"Exactly where I want to be—looking after my adopted mother and running the palace for the Bishop. I'm not interested in doing anything else."

"No, obviously there's no time for other interests," I said. "Keeping that marriage glued together must be a very all-consuming occupation."

She stopped dead. I stopped too, and as we faced each other I knew I had caught her off her guard.

"Don't misunderstand," I said swiftly. "I'm not calling you a liar. Earlier you made it plain that the marriage, despite its surface irritations, was a happy one involving that well-known phenomenon the attraction of opposites, and I see no reason to disbelieve that. Lady Starmouth also told me she thought the marriage was a success. But its success depends on you, doesn't it? If you weren't there to do all the things Mrs. Jardine can't do, the marriage would go to pieces along with Mrs. Jardine—just as it did at Radbury before you arrived with your jar of glue to stick the pieces together again. Well, it's always gratifying to one's self-esteem to feel that one's indispensable, but do you really think that once the Jardines are dead and you're on your own at last you won't look back and regret a lifetime of missed opportunities? Or are you simply going to say, as old Mrs. Jardine said at the end of her life: 'It was worth it all for Adam'?"

She was so pale that for the first time I noticed the faint freckles across her cheekbones. It was impossible not to conclude that I had shot an arrow into the dark and scored a bull's eye, but all she said in the end was a stony: "I don't call him Adam."

"Well, I should hope you don't call him Alex either," I said, "or my imagination would really run riot. I've noticed he calls you Lyle whenever he isn't referring to you as Miss Christie and I suppose it's natural enough after ten years that he should follow his wife's example in treating you as a highly favoured employee, but I'd certainly raise an eyebrow if you started calling him by his Christian name."

"Oh, shut up! You've made quite enough snide remarks for one afternoon!"

"I thought I was making some intelligent observations in an attempt to solve the mystery!"

"What mystery?"

"The mystery you present to any man who admires you, the mystery of why you're content to go through life as a mere companion—"

"I'm beginning to think *you're* the real mystery here, Charles Ashworth, with your interest in the Bishop and your Don Juan manners and the wife you won't talk about and the past you gloss over so smoothly! Why are you going through this elaborate charade of making torrid passes at me?"

"It's no charade. I knew as soon as we met yesterday that I was deeply attracted to you—"

"That's the most unreal opening a sentence could have! You know nothing about me. You're obviously deep in a romantic fantasy!"

"Why don't you tell me about this broken engagement of yours which has given you such a horror of romance?"

"I'm telling you nothing more!" She was taut with anger. "Take me home at once, please—I find this entire conversation deeply offensive!"

We walked on in silence, she hurrying as fast as she could without breaking into a run, I lengthening my stride to keep pace with her. At the car I said: "I'm extremely sorry if I've given you offence, but please believe me when I say my admiration for you is genuine."

"I don't want your admiration." Wrenching open the door she collapsed in a heap on the passenger seat; evidently I had shocked her to the core.

5

WE did not speak throughout the journey back to Starbridge, but as I halted my car in the palace drive I said: "Please give my apologies to Mrs. Jardine and say I won't be making an appearance at tea. I must do some work in my room on my St. Anselm notes."

"Very well." She had regained her composure and although she was still pale her voice was calm.

I wondered how long it would take her to decide—greatly against her better judgement, of course—that she wanted me to make another pounce.

6

UPSTAIRS in the cavernous Victorian bathroom I filled the bath to the halfway mark with cold water and sat in it for a while as I sluiced away both the sweat of my afternoon's exertions and my very carnal thoughts on the subject of Miss Lyle Christie. Then I returned to my room, pulled on some underclothes and cast an eye over my St. Anselm notes, but the glance was a mere formality. I wanted only to give a veneer of truth to my statement that I was missing tea in order to work, and eventually, my conscience assuaged, I began to imagine what I would have said to the Archbishop if he had appeared beside me and demanded a progress report.

I now knew very much more about Jardine than I had known before my arrival and I was certainly well on my way to building up a psychological portrait which would enable Lang to decide whether his enemy was the kind of man who could be disastrously exploited by Fleet Street, but I had still elicited no information about Lang's chief worries, the journal and the possible existence of indiscreet correspondence. I myself was now convinced that Jardine was far too shrewd to commit epistolary indiscretions, but the journal remained an unknown quantity. No one had mentioned it to me yet, but this silence was hardly surprising if the journal was a long-standing hobby which everyone took for granted.

I meditated on the subject for a while but came to the conclusion that Jardine would have been unlikely to use the journal as a confessional during the lifetime of his stepmother. Why confide in an impersonal notebook when one had a confidante who provided limitless sympathy and understanding? I could imagine him tossing off some lines in a frenzy if his stepmother had been inaccessible, but I was sure that a ruthless censorship would have taken place once the sympathetic understanding had been obtained.

I then asked myself if he might have used the journal as a confessional since his stepmother's death, but all my witnesses had testified that after the upheaval surrounding old Mrs. Jardine's arrival in Starbridge Jardine's life had been unpunctuated by crises; possibly no confessional had been required. The chaplain had said Jardine had been getting on better with Lyle; Lady Starmouth had remarked that a spacious palace made it easier for a married couple to live in close proximity to a third party; Mrs. Cobden-Smith had implied that by this time Lyle had been at her zenith as a miracle-worker. I suddenly remembered my friend Philip saying that Jardine had seemed "distrait" during the first year of his episcopate, and this observation from a stranger harmonised with the facts I now knew: the rocky start to the Starbridge career followed by years when Jardine was able to pursue his calling against a background of tranquillity. I decided that the journal was probably as dull as sackcloth and quite unworthy of a reduction to ashes.

At this point I paused in my meditations to light a cigarette, but as I shook out the match my thoughts once more turned to the Lovely Ladies. I had already decided that because of the Bishop's psychological constraint on the subject of class I could tell Lang with confidence that there was no risk of any scandal with an aristocratic Englishwoman, and although the incident with the foreigner Loretta Staviski could certainly be regarded with suspicion, I had believed Lady Starmouth when she had vouched for Jardine's good behaviour. Jardine was popular with the ladies; that sort of clergyman always risked fatally attracting a parishioner, but in the vast majority of cases the clergyman was innocent of misconduct and I was sure that Jardine, newly married and no doubt burning to make a success of his splendid preferment, had had powerful reasons for treating Loretta with propriety.

I had almost argued myself to the conclusion that Jardine was as pure as driven snow, but I had left the most sinister possibility to the last.

I began to think about Lyle.

I had noticed that although she had admitted she regarded Mrs. Jardine as a mother, she had not said she regarded the Bishop as a father. Yet she had described her own father as "clever," "bright," "quick" and "tough," all adjectives which could be applied to Jardine. Obviously she was fond of the Bishop; obviously she respected and admired him; but there was no hint in her manner of a schoolgirl's crush or a spinster's frustrated passion, and I was driven to suspect that her feelings here too were filial. In fact I now found I shared Mrs. Cobden-Smith's conviction that Lyle stayed with the Jardines not because of a passion for the Bishop but because of a passion for power—and not merely the power of running the palace but the power of keeping that marriage glued together, the power springing from the fact that she made it possible for the Bishop to continue his ministry. What happened to a bishop whose marriage went to the wall? It was a spine-chilling thought, and I thought it was a chill to which Jardine's spine had become well accustomed.

I did speculate about the possible ill-effects on Lyle of a broken engagement, but on this point I could form no more than the tentative conclusion that some adverse romantic experience seemed likely. Her response to my kiss indicated she was sexually normal; her repudiation of it indicated an abnormal fear of romantic involvement. Ignorance prevented me from expanding my theory further, but nevertheless I felt I could say to Lang that Lyle's aversion to marriage was more likely to spring from a broken engagement than from any inappropriate feelings towards the Bishop.

Having summed up Lyle's probable attitude to Jardine I turned the relationship around and began to consider Jardine's probable attitude to Lyle. This was easier because as a clergyman I could mentally put myself in Jardine's shoes without any undue strain on my imagination. I had married in haste but had almost certainly repented at leisure, and as the result of my rashness I now had a wife who was capable of being a crippling liability. I was an eminent cleric beyond hope of divorce so the most nerve-racking question in such nerve-racking circumstances inevitably became: how did I survive my marriage? Lyle was the Heaven-sent answer, and because Lyle was so vital not only for the welfare of my marriage but for the welfare of my increasingly illustrious career, I would take no risks whatsoever and exercise an iron control over any insane but pardonable desire to flirt. I would, of course, find Lyle immensely attractive, and that would make it difficult to adjust to her presence in the household—I would even tell Lady Starmouth I found the presence of a third party an intrusion on my marriage—but with prayer and will-power and plenty of deliciously risqué chats with my safe Lovely Ladies I would control myself, diverting the emotion into harmless channels whenever possible and suppressing the emotion which could not be diverted. I was Adam Alexander Jardine, a mature survivor trained in the hardest of schools, and I was neither weak nor a fool.

That left only one more vital question to be answered before I stepped out of Jardine's shoes. I was a man of volatile temperament with plenty of physical energy and a strong liking for women; did I or did I not live like a monk? I did not. I slept with my wife, who was still pretty, still adoring, still mildly lovable in her own maddening way and—most important of all—still available. Certainly no one else was, and married clergymen, like beggars, can't be choosers.

I decided this was not merely a plausible interpretation of the Jardine ménage but the only interpretation which made sense. I felt I could now say confidently to Lang: "The girl, who probably has strong psychological reasons for not marrying, regards the woman as her mother and regards the man as satisfying her hankering for power. The woman regards the girl as her daughter and regards her husband with adoration. The husband regards his wife as a liability but as a source of sexual satisfaction, and regards the girl as a Godsend but as sexually taboo. The marriage is entirely safe so long as this triangle is maintained and I see no sign of any approaching catastrophe."

But of course this last statement would be untrue. I knew now that *I* was the approaching catastrophe bent on breaking up the triangle, and once the triangle disintegrated the marital disaster would be poised to unfold.

I was still contemplating this prospect with appalled fascination seconds later when someone rapped loudly on my door.

I jumped, sprang to my feet and pulled on my dressing-gown. "Come in!" I called, assuming I was addressing a servant sent to deliver either a telephone message or perhaps a letter which had arrived by the afternoon post, and turned aside to extinguish my cigarette in the ashtray.

The door banged open and the Bishop blazed across the threshold.

"Now Dr. Ashworth," he said abruptly as I spun round in shock, "I think it's time you told me the truth—and when I say the truth I mean the truth, the whole truth and nothing but the truth. Exactly why did you come to Starbridge and what the deuce do you think you're playing at?"

VI

"The sexual appetite (which is the most insistent and the most important of our bodily desires) presses for satisfaction. . . . So we start with the certainty that sexual indulgence will be popular and that Christianity will be most difficult precisely at that point."

More Letters of
HERBERT HENSLEY HENSON,
ed. E. F. Braley

I

IN the second which followed I saw the Bishop with photographic clarity and noticed that his brown eyes were no longer brilliant but opaque. His mouth was set in a tight line, his hands were clasped behind his back as if to conceal clenched fists and his whole stance radiated pugnacity. "Well, Dr. Ashworth?" he demanded, and his pugnacity was formidable indeed. "Speak up! What do you have to say for yourself?"

I knew at once that I had to stop him thinking I could be intimidated, but unfortunately I was far from being completely unperturbed. Some form of defensive action was clearly called for. "I'm sorry, Dr. Jardine," I said, "but I refuse to conduct an interview with a bishop while I'm wearing only my underclothes and a dressing-gown. You must allow me a moment to dress."

There was a short tense silence. Then Jardine laughed, exclaimed: "I admire your nerve!" and sat himself down at the table by the window.

Scrambling into my clerical uniform I found I could all too easily deduce what had happened. Lady Starmouth had complained about my interrogation, the chaplain had revealed my interest in the palace ménage, Mrs. Cobden-Smith had disclosed what an excellent listener I was and Lyle had reported my episcopal obsession. I was about to be exposed as a deplorably unsuccessful espionage agent, but on the other hand my findings were all in Jardine's favour. If I allowed his rage to run its course, I might have a chance of pacifying him when he subsided into mere indignation. It seemed the best I could hope for. However, meanwhile I had to cope with his rage.

"Thank you," I said, when fully dressed at last I sat down opposite him at the table. "Now I feel more civilised. First of all, Bishop, let me apologise from the bottom of my heart—"

"Spare me the apologies. Give me the truth. Why are you here?"

"Dr. Lang sent me."

Jardine showed no surprise. "The Archbishop should take care," was his acid comment. "He's showing a talent for ecclesiastical skulduggery unmatched since the days of the Borgia Popes. And what was his objective—or rather, what did he tell you was his objective?"

"He's acting to protect you, Bishop. He's afraid his enemies in Fleet Street might use you in an attempt to smear the Church, and he sent me here to estimate how vulnerable you are to scandal."

"That may indeed be what he told you—but of course the real truth is that he's sent you here to spy on my private life in the hope that you'll find evidence which he can use to compel my resignation!"

"Bishop—"

"Monstrous! Archbishops have been executed for less!"

I felt I had no choice but to attempt my patron's defence. "Bishop, His Grace doesn't suspect you of any gross failure or even of any serious indiscretion, and I must absolutely insist that he's not trying to get rid of you—"

"No? It sounds to me as if he's recently travelled incognito to the Old Vic to see a performance of *Murder in the Cathedral*—with the result that he's now declaiming, in the manner of Henry II, 'Who will rid me of this turbulent priest!' "

"Dr. Lang," I said firmly, ignoring this shaft, "is worried primarily about the existence of a minor indiscretion which an unscrupulous journalist could distort. He's also worried in case your unusual domestic situation should be misunderstood. Bearing in mind the enormous amount of attention you've been receiving from the press lately, do you really think it's so reprehensible that Dr. Lang should send someone he trusts to survey the landscape to make sure you're not vulnerable to the worst form of exploitation by Fleet Street?"

Jardine controlled himself sufficiently to say in an even voice: "You're making heroic efforts to defend the Archbishop for his inexcusable trespass on my privacy, and I respect your loyalty to him, but didn't it occur to His Grace that I'm perfectly capable of constructing my own defences against any assault from the press?"

"The Archbishop merely wanted to make sure you hadn't accidentally left a chink in your armour."

"And dare I ask what kind of chink His Grace had in mind?"

"He was concerned in particular about the existence of unwise entries in your journal and the existence of indiscreet correspondence."

Jardine burst out laughing. Then he exclaimed with the most withering scorn: "What kind of a fool does he think I am?"

"I know it sounds preposterous, but, Dr. Jardine, it's a fact that men of your age—even brilliant men of your age—do sometimes go off the rails, and His Grace felt he had to make absolutely sure—not only for the sake of the Church but for your own sake—"

"Quite. Very well, I take your point. I suppose if one's Archbishop of Canterbury one should always allow for the possibility of a bishop going stark staring mad, and His Grace no doubt interpreted my attack on him in the Lords as the onset of lunacy. However, let me try to allay His Grace's melodramatic fears as swiftly as possible." Jardine leant forward, placing his forearms on the table, and clasped his hands purposefully. "First: my journal. It's not an adolescent's diary reeking of carnal allusions. I comment on the books I've read, record my travels, note the themes of my sermons, remark on whom I've met and generally try to reflect what it means to serve God as a churchman. I won't say I've never used the journal to record personal difficulties because I have, but as I've always excised the pages later and burnt them, you can tell the Archbishop that my journal in its present state would send any reporter from *The News of the World* straight to sleep . . . Or do you find that impossible to believe?"

I said truthfully: "No, I'd already reached the conclusion that you'd edit your work. I was only wondering—" I broke off.

"Well?"

"No, my next question would have been impertinent."

"You may as well ask it. Since I'm apparently surviving the Archbishop's monstrous assault on my privacy without suffering a stroke, one little piece of impertinence from you is hardly likely to dent my miraculous sang-froid. What's the question?"

"I was wondering when you last felt impelled to excise entries from your journal."

Jardine raised an eyebrow, gave me a searching glance, but concluded I was anxious only about the possibility of recent difficulties in his private life. "You needn't worry," he said dryly. "My life's been singularly uneventful for some time now. It's been five years since any pages from my journal were consigned to the library fire."

"Was that when you were still at Radbury?" I said, certain that the answer was no but hoping to egg him on to a further revelation.

"No, I'd just moved to Starbridge—and I trust, Dr. Ashworth, you won't graduate from a minor to a major impertinence by asking me what was going on in my life at the time."

"No, of course not, Bishop." I thought of Mrs. Jardine drifting again towards a nervous breakdown as she grappled not only with the arrival of her stepmother-in-law but also with what Mrs. Cobden-Smith had described as "an awkward time"—a euphemism I had translated as the menopause. I could well imagine the Bishop relieving his feelings in his journal as he waited for the arrival of his confidante.

"I had a difficult decision to make," said the Bishop unexpectedly, "and I needed to set down the situation on paper in order to clarify my mind."

That did surprise me. I could not immediately see what decision had had to be made. Possibly he had been debating with himself whether in view of his wife's mental health he had a duty to instal his stepmother not at the palace but in the best Starbridge nursing home.

"Very well, so much for the journal," Jardine was saying briskly. "Let's turn now to my correspondence. There are four women to whom I write regularly. First and foremost: my wife. Whenever we're apart I try to write her a line every day. I'd say that was fairly normal behaviour for a man of my generation who detests the telephone, although a young man like you might think it rather an extravagant use of writing paper. After my wife, the next woman on my list would be the incomparable Lady Starmouth, to whom I pen a line about twice a week. Our chief topic is clerical gossip, but we also discuss literature and politics—topics which interest Mrs. Welbeck and Lady Markhampton to whom I write regularly but less frequently than I write to Lady Starmouth. Am I making myself clear? My correspondence with all three of these delightful ladies, stimulating as it is, can't possibly be described as the kind which would encourage a husband to challenge me to pistols at dawn. You may assure His Grace he has no cause for alarm."

"May I risk another minor impertinence?"

"You're a brave man, Dr. Ashworth. But continue."

"Do you ever write to Miss Christie?"

"Only when I have essential information to impart. For example, the last time I wrote to her was in May when my wife and I were in London for the Coronation. I sent Miss Christie a line to say that Carrie and I would be staying up in town an extra day in order to dine with some old friends from Radbury."

"Why didn't Miss Christie go to London with you?"

"That's not an impertinent question, Dr. Ashworth, but as far as I can see it's an irrelevant one. I had a part to play in the Coronation ceremony and my wife had a seat in the Abbey. Rather than risk being crushed to death by the multitudes lining the processional route, Miss Christie sensibly decided to stay at home and 'listen in' to the proceedings on the wireless. Do you have any other irrelevant questions, or am I now allowed to inquire what kind of report you intend to present to Dr. Lang?"

I smiled at him before I said: "I shall tell His Grace that in my opinion every chink in your armour's sealed."

"Splendid! And are you also going to inform His Grace that in addition to entering my household under false pretences you've been further abusing my hospitality by playing fast and loose with my wife's companion?"

I felt as if I had been felled on the rugger field by an unexpected tackle. It took a considerable effort to look him straight in the eyes and say strongly: "I may be playing fast but I'm not playing loose."

"No? Miss Christie thinks your behavior lacked stability, and I must say I agree with her. Don't you think you were a little rash to subject a respectable woman to passionate advances less than twenty-four hours after your first meeting with her?"

"No more rash than you were at my age," I said, "when you proposed to your future wife on the strength of a four-day acquaintance."

There was a silence. We stared at each other. Jardine's amber eyes were dangerously bright.

"That was a major impertinence, Dr. Ashworth."

"And so, with all due respect, was your last remark, Dr. Jardine. No man, not even a bishop, tells me how to run my private life."

"What an extraordinarily arrogant statement! Are you saying you're never in need of spiritual direction?"

"I—"

"Who's your spiritual director? Or are you so adrift as to believe you don't need one?"

Beneath the table my fists were clenched. Somehow keeping my voice level I said: "My spiritual director is Father James Reid of the Fordite monks at Grantchester."

"Oh, I know the Grantchester Fordites from my days at Radbury—and of course I remember Father Reid, the best kind of cosy old monk, very gentle and saintly and kind. But don't you need someone rather tougher than a cosy old monk to advise you on your spiritual life, Dr. Ashworth?"

I said nothing, and when Jardine realised I had no intention of replying, he said in a voice which was unexpectedly compassionate: "Don't think I can't remember what it's like to be thirty-seven and unmarried. But impulsive romantic action isn't the answer, Dr. Ashworth, and you're quite intelligent enough to know that for those of us not called to celibacy the pressures of a celibate life can lead to emotional instability unless there's regular and effective counselling by someone who knows exactly what problems are involved."

Again he paused and again I remained silent. Finally he said: "Have a word with your Bishop. See if he can recommend someone more suitable than dear old Father Reid, who's been celibate so long that he's probably forgotten the male organ has a purpose other than urination. Cambridge is a good man, even if he does spend too much time writing theses about whether Ezra came before or after Nehemiah, and I'm sure he'd do his best to help you."

Once more the silence lengthened but eventually I was able to say: "Thank you, Dr. Jardine. And now, of course, since I've so thoroughly abused your hospitality, you'll want me to leave your house at the earliest opportunity."

Jardine leant back in his chair and regarded me as if I presented some difficult but fascinating problem. "My dear Dr. Ashworth," he said as he rose to his feet, "if you cut short your visit and leave the palace under a cloud, you're going to trigger exactly the kind of gossip Dr. Lang is so anxious to avoid. Can't you imagine the report in the gutter-press? 'We have it on good authority' (that would be the eavesdropping second housemaid) 'that a storm erupted in the Cathedral Close at Starbridge when Canon Charles Ashworth was expelled from the palace after an assault on the virtue of the Bishop's attractive young companion, Miss Lyle Christie.' (Naturally they would omit all mention of my wife.) 'We are reliably informed that the ravishing Miss Christie returned from a motor drive à deux with the handsome Canon only to rush sobbing to the Bishop: "He unleashed his passion at Starbury Ring!" whereupon the Bishop stormed to the Canon shouting: "Never darken my door again!" And so on and so on. Oh no, Dr. Ashworth! I'm not falling into the trap of asking you to leave! We do, after all, have a duty to the Archbishop to keep up appearances, even if he does insult us both by treating you as a spy and me as a fool."

During this speech the Bishop had crossed the room. He now opened the door and looked back. "You will complete your visit, you will behave like a gentleman and you will consider my advice on the subject of spiritual direction," he said, "and meanwhile I look forward to resuming our theological discussions over the port tonight. I should very much like to hear your views on the Virgin Birth." And he walked out, banging the door abruptly behind him.

2

I HAD been warned off.

I began to wonder how far the Bishop had interfered with Lyle's other romances. Most clerical suitors would have backed away in fright if the Bishop had bared his teeth, but I was far from being a vulnerable young cleric and I was not prepared to be intimidated. Anyone who had Lang's patronage was not obliged to worry about the approval of the Bishop of Starbridge, and I saw no chance of Jardine ever moving into a position which could affect my career; he had too many enemies among the politicians to receive either of the two most exalted preferments, the archbishoprics of Canterbury and York.

Having removed my collar I lit a cigarette to steady my nerves. I was wondering if I could place a sinister interpretation on the fact that Lyle had run straight to the Bishop, but I could only conclude that I should have predicted such a response. Obviously a close partnership between Lyle and the Bishop had developed over the years, and once I had accused her of providing the glue which prevented the Bishop's marriage from disintegrating, her natural reaction would have been to warn him that I was bent on rattling the skeleton in his cupboard. In these circumstances it was small wonder that Jardine had decided to rattle his sabre in return, particularly if Lyle had also considered it her duty as a loyal employee to warn the Bishop that I showed signs of wanting to demolish his ménage à trois. If the welfare of his marriage and career depended on Lyle, he not only had to rattle his sabre; he had to lunge straight for my jugular vein.

However, although I was willing to concede that the Bishop's belligerence was understandable, I thought his attitude was from a spiritual point of view unhealthy. I had a very Christian desire to remarry. He seemed bent on foiling my current attempt to attain that goal. Moreover Lyle's welfare as well as mine could be adversely affected, and after prolonged reflection I found myself unable to resist the conclusion that he was in the wrong.

I suddenly realised I had missed Choral Evensong again, and with an exclamation of annoyance I stubbed out my cigarette, replaced my collar and sat down to read the evening office.

Halfway through the *Nunc Dimittis* it occurred to me that Jardine must often have faced the possibility that Lyle would leave one day; he had not employed a woman who was so unattractive that her future was entirely predictable. I decided that if I were Jardine I would long since have formed a contingency plan which I could put into operation if Lyle handed in her notice, and the contingency plan would revolve around the fact that I would always have a suitable replacement in mind. Large numbers of companions were drawn from clerical homes where there was little money to support girls trained only to be ladies, and as a bishop I would be in a good position to survey the available candidates. Of course it would be difficult to find someone who equalled Lyle's ability to be a Godsend, but since an acceptably pleasant, competent woman could probably be tracked down without too much trouble, it could be argued that Jardine was now only fighting to save himself some inconvenience. Lyle's departure would certainly represent an earthquake in the episcopal household, but people do recover from earthquakes; life does eventually return to normal.

Yet anyone would imagine, from Jardine's pugilistic behaviour towards me, that if the earthquake happened at Starbridge all life at the palace would cease.

I told myself I was still smarting from the assault on my jugular vein, and returning to my prayer book I made a new effort to concentrate on the office, but long before I reached the end the inevitable possibility was seeping into my mind. I told myself to suppose, for the sake of argument, that my plausible explanation of the ménage à trois was in fact entirely wrong; I told myself to suppose, again for the sake of argument, that I suspended belief and started to think the unthinkable. If Lyle were Jardine's mistress it would explain both her reluctance to marry and Jardine's pugilism towards a dangerous suitor.

The only trouble with this theory, which seemed at first glance preposterous and at second glance so unpleasantly plausible, was that it fell apart as soon as it was submitted to a close examination. For a start I could not imagine that Mrs. Jardine would continue to treat as a daughter the woman who was sleeping with her adored husband. Mrs. Jardine was not the cleverest of women, but I thought she would be sufficiently intuitive to know if the two most important people in her life were having an affair. However, the real difficulty with the theory remained that I could not see a man of Jardine's integrity leading a spiritual double-life. I was still willing to bet heavily that he was not an apostate, and unless he was an apostate adultery was inconceivable.

Somehow I reached the end of the office and began to prepare myself for dinner. All things were possible, even the unlikeliest of apostasies, but it was a waste of time for me to think the unthinkable unless I found some indication, however small, that Jardine was capable of unthinkable behaviour.

I stopped flattening my hair and stared into the glass.

Other clergymen fell into error. Why not Jardine? Suddenly, for clouded reasons beyond my comprehension, I felt an urge to prove that Jardine had at least once since his ordination been guilty of a serious moral failure—and that was the moment when I first started speculating seriously on the subject of Loretta Staviski.

3

JARDINE'S threat to discuss the Virgin Birth with me over the port was never realised. One of the lay dinner guests, Starbridge's most distinguished architect, proved to be a non-smoker who could not be dispatched to the smoking-room, and out of courtesy Jardine at first avoided splitting theological hairs. However, after a discussion of the arrests which had recently taken place in the German Evangelical Church, the architect said deferentially: "Talking of clerical matters, Bishop, I hope you won't mind me mentioning the A. P. Herbert Bill. I'm interested in your opinion of it, particularly as I too think that the grounds for divorce should be extended, but I'm still not sure how you justify your views theologically. What makes you so sure that Christ wasn't laying down the law on this particular subject but only stating an ethical guideline?"

This was clearly an intelligent, sympathetic layman who deserved to be encouraged. Jardine said kindly: "Well, the first thing you must remember is that Our Lord wasn't a twentieth-century Englishman brought up in a culture which glorifies the modest understatement. He came from the Middle East and in the culture of his day people communicated important truths by the use of striking word-pictures, statements which we would call exaggerations. A well-known example of this is when Christ says: 'It is easier for a camel to go through the eye of a needle, than for a rich man to enter into the kingdom of God.' A modern Englishman would merely say: 'He can't do it.' "

"So in other words what you're saying is—" But the architect could not quite relate this warning about the un-Englishness of Christ to the teaching on divorce.

"The next thing you should remember," said Jardine, paying no attention to the interruption as he busily laid the foundations of his argument, "is that one should always try to see Christ against the background in which he lived. At the time of his ministry there were in fact two opposing attitudes to divorce within Judaism. One group, the Hillel Jews, thought that divorce could be granted even for the most trivial reasons—if the wife burnt the dinner, for instance. The other group held that divorce should be granted only for adultery and only to men—in fact divorce was actually required when a man had an adulterous wife; he had no choice."

"Good heavens!" said the layman, fascinated by the thought of compulsory divorce. I sensed he had almost said: "Good God!" but had remembered just in time that he was at the Bishop's table.

"Now," said Jardine, reassured that the layman was still conscious, "we come to Our Lord. What he was really doing was criticising the lax attitude of the Hillel Jews by a heavy underlining of the teaching of the stricter school of thought. And the way he phrased this criticism was in the Middle-Eastern way: 'fortissimo' by Semitic overstatement, not 'pianissimo' by British understatement. He said: 'What therefore God hath joined together, let not man put asunder.' Of course he was aware that both schools of thought permitted divorce, but he wasn't talking as a lawyer and he wasn't talking about the law. He was attacking the morality of divorce sought for trivial reasons, and he did this by emphasising the sanctity of marriage."

"Ah!" said the architect, recognising a familiar phrase. "Sanctity of marriage—yes—"

"Let me give you a twentieth-century parallel," said Jardine, helping him along. "If I were to tell you that recently in Reno, Nevada, a woman divorced her husband because he squeezed the marital toothpaste tube from the top instead of the bottom, you might well react by saying: 'Disgraceful! Marriage should be for life! Shocking debasement of the institution!' But you don't really think that marriage should always be for life; if it breaks down in such a way that its spiritual core is destroyed—if the marriage ceases to be a marriage in any meaningful sense of the word—then you and I and many thousands of others believe that the marriage is spiritually null and should be legally terminated. And *that* in my opinion is the compassionate teaching which must inevitably lie beyond Our Lord's statements stressing the sanctity of marriage."

"So what you're saying is," said the layman, who was now, like a promising infant, "coming along nicely," "Christ would have disapproved of the divorce law of Nevada but approved of the new divorce law proposed by Mr. A. P. Herbert."

"Precisely!" said Jardine. "Herbert's Bill has two main purposes: one is to relieve suffering—and do you suppose that Christ, with all his compassion, would have objected to that?—and the second is to reinforce the sanctity of marriage by permitting the dissolution of the marital travesties, the cases where the spiritual core of the marriage has been destroyed not just by adultery but by cruelty, desertion or insanity as well—and do you suppose that Our Lord, who recoiled from the debasement of marriage, would have objected to the elimination of the marriages which had become a mockery? I think not."

"How clear it all seems!" said the architect, delighted that his personal views, reached by moral inclination, could be justified theologically. "And how jolly to think of Christ approving of the A. P. Herbert Bill—although I suppose one might deduce that from the fact that the Bill's now certain to become law. Bishop, do we dare say that the success of the Bill's second reading in the House of Lords last month was God's will?"

"Well, it certainly wasn't the Archbishop of Canterbury's will," said Jardine, "but then as far as I know His Grace hasn't yet claimed to be God. Dr. Ashworth, I'm beginning to think your prolonged silence has an ominous quality. I hope you're not thinking I should be burnt at the stake."

"No, we'll acquit you of heresy today, Bishop!" I said smiling at him, and at once saw the amusement flare in his eyes.

When one considered all the adverse circumstances, it was most bizarre how much we both liked each other.

4

WAS he an apostate? I still could not believe it, and although his views might be startling to a layman I knew he was only treading a well-worn theological path; an examination of Christ's words in the light of conditions prevailing in first-century Palestine was nowadays considered a thoroughly respectable endeavour in the attempt to look beyond the glittering image of Christ in the Gospels to the historical figure about whom so little was known. Jardine's views on divorce were certainly open to criticism, particularly by the conservative wing of the Church, but he was a long way from a suspect Christianity, and the ardour of his conviction that compassion should be shown to the victims of hopeless marriages indicated a man who believed whole-heartedly in the reality of Christ, not an apostate who was covering up his lost belief with a few clever phrases.

Moreover on this issue Jardine was in distinguished company. Martin Luther had gone even further than A. P. Herbert in urging new grounds for divorce where the spiritual core of the marriage had been destroyed, but the trouble with such liberal views, I always thought, was that once one had embraced them it was hard to know where to stop. Unless one was careful one could so easily reason oneself into claiming that the compassion of Christ justified even divorce on the grounds of a careless squeeze of a toothpaste tube.

"You're looking very pensive, Dr. Ashworth!" called Lady Starmouth after my return to the drawing-room.

"I'm still recovering from Dr. Jardine's post-prandial wisdom . . ."

My own views on divorce were complex. Despite my public support of Lang, who regarded Herbert's Bill with antipathy, I privately approved the Bill on humanitarian grounds—which meant, in other words, that I was citing the compassion of Christ in order to approve extending the grounds for dissolving shattered marriages. However, I did think that theologically it was difficult to argue that Christ would ever have approved of extending the grounds for divorce beyond adultery. Jardine had had a good shot at the argument, but the architect's enthusiastic acceptance of it indicated not the strength of the thesis but the strength of Jardine's gift for manipulating a receptive audience. In my opinion Christ had been a good Jew, not "liberal" in the modern sense of extending a credo to its outer limits in the name of freedom, but "radical" in the original sense of cutting back the credo to its roots to rediscover its true spirit. This radicalism was illustrated by his opposition to the Pharisees and his determination to respond not merely to the letter but to the spirit of Judaism, a spirit which encompassed a far stricter view of divorce than that envisaged by Mr. A. P. Herbert.

I suddenly realised that Lady Starmouth was saying to me: ". . . and I do hope you'll call on us when you're next up in town!"

"How kind of you, Lady Starmouth! Thank you," I said, and at once remembered the Earl's information that Loretta was due to arrive in London that weekend.

Across the room Lyle was watching us. She had been avoiding me all evening but now she impulsively stepped forward, and as Lady Starmouth turned away from me to respond to a question from the architect, I eased myself around the back of the sofa to a spot out of sight of the terrace where the Bishop was enjoying a stroll with the architect's good-looking wife.

Lyle reached me a second later. "I'm sorry this afternoon ended in a mess," she said rapidly. "I enjoyed myself up at the Ring. Thanks for the outing."

So she had decided she was ready for another pounce.

"Have lunch with me tomorrow."

"Oh, that's quite impossible—the Starmouths are leaving, more guests are arriving and Mrs. Jardine will need me all day," she said without hesitation, but as she nerved herself to look at me directly I thought her eyes were communicating a very different message. At last she added in a low voice: "I'm sorry. It would have been nice. But I can't."

"Don't worry, I'll ask you again," I said. "Bishop or no Bishop."

For a moment she was motionless. Then she said in her politest voice: "Will you please excuse me?" and slipped away before the Bishop could return to the room to make sure nothing subversive was occurring in his absence.

5

I WAS quite unable to sleep that night. I tossed and turned, I read the most boring genaeologies of the Old Testament, I dowsed myself with cold water, I prayed, counted sheep and went to the lavatory. Finally at two o'clock I padded downstairs to the Bishop's library in pursuit of some light reading. Jardine's taste in literature was a varied one and we had already discovered a shared weakness for detective stories.

Reaching the library I switched on the light and began to prowl around the shelves. I was just thinking that the Bishop's book collection was less eclectic than I had anticipated when I discovered a shelf devoted to nineteenth-century novels, including a battered group by Sir Walter Scott. I was delighted. The novels of Scott never failed to lull me into a state of somnolence, and pulling out *Ivanhoe* I idly opened the cover.

To my surprise I found myself confronting a much-inscribed fly-leaf. At the top of the page someone had written INGRID ASHLEY, 1885, and below this signature another hand, bold and upright, had added: "My stepmother gave me this book to keep me quiet, but I solemnly swear I shall never read it because I know that novels are the invention of the Devil. ADAM ALEXANDER JARDINE, 1888 (aged 9)." But this was not the last entry on the fly-leaf. Further down the page the bold upright hand, now imbued with an elegant maturity, had written: "My dearest, just look at this inscription which I wrote to protect myself in case Father found a novel in my room! What a pathetic little horror I was and what a wonderful thing you did, introducing me to *Ivanhoe,* to English literature and to civilisation. Let me now return this book to its original owner and say: Welcome to Starbridge! All my love always, ADAM (ADAM ALEXANDER STARO, 1932—aged 53!)."

A footfall sounded behind me, and as I spun round *Ivanhoe* slipped through my hands to thud upon the floor.

"Can I help you, Dr. Ashworth?" inquired Jardine in his most sardonic voice. "Is there perhaps some information you still require?"

6

I SOMEHOW managed to say: "I assure you my espionage has its limits, Bishop. I wasn't making a secret assault on your journal." To hide my confusion I stooped to pick up *Ivanhoe* as I added: "I was looking for some light reading to ease the boredom of insomnia."

"In that case we're driven here by a common goal, but personally I'm about to fight my own insomnia with a detective story." He bent to extract a volume from the bottom shelf. "Have you read *The Murder of Roger Ackroyd* by the other, more famous Miss Christie?"

"Yes. That's the one where one has to watch the narrator."

"Precisely. I always find that the more I read that story, the more intrigued I become by the narrator's omissions and evasions." He glanced at the book in my hands as he added: "However, perhaps you're better off with Sir Walter Scott. That volume in particular has sentimental memories for me."

"I was just reading the inscription. Your stepmother must have been a remarkable woman, Dr. Jardine."

"She needed to be remarkable. It's a catastrophe for any family when the mother dies young, and by the time Ingrid entered our lives we were all deeply disordered . . . I suppose your own mother didn't die young, by any chance?"

I was surprised by the question but I answered easily: "No, she and my father are both still flourishing in Surrey." Setting aside the copy of *Ivanhoe,* I selected Dorothy Sayers's *The Nine Tailors* from the bottom shelf.

"What sort of man is your father?"

This time I was no longer merely surprised but astonished. I said abruptly: "Why do you ask?" but Jardine only laughed.

"Since you've been making various deductions about me," he said, "I've decided to make a deduction or two about you. Lady Starmouth remarked on your evasiveness about your family. Miss Christie commented how profoundly you seemed to sympathise with me when she touched on my difficulties with my father. Naturally I've been wondering if you too have a parent who's a heavy cross to bear."

"My father did disapprove of my ordination," I said, "but we get on very well now."

"I used to say that when people asked me about my father," said Jardine. "It was less painful. However, perhaps your father's a great deal less incomprehensible than mine was."

"Incomprehensible?"

"Isn't lack of understanding responsible for much of the misery in family relationships? I spent years trying to understand my father, but it was only at the end of his life that I finally realised what had been going on."

I said before I could stop myself: "Did that make a difference?"

"Of course. With understanding, forgiveness becomes possible . . . You do have trouble with your father, don't you," said Jardine, but I only answered: "No, we got over all the trouble a long time ago."

We were silent, locked in an enigmatic curiosity which lay beyond my powers of analysis, but at last Jardine said unexpectedly: "Sit down for a moment, Dr. Ashworth. I'm going to do something I never normally do. I'm going to talk about my father, because despite all you've said I think you may find my story relevant to that private life which you seem so determined to conceal."

7

"MY father was the son of an impecunious Cheshire farmer," said Jardine. "He ran away to London when he was sixteen with the idea of training to become a clergyman, but he soon discovered that neither the Church of England nor the respectable Non-Conformist churches wanted to know a penniless working-class boy with ideas above his station. Finally my father said to himself in a disillusioned rage: to hell with all ecclesiastical organisations and to hell with the priesthood.

"To assuage his sense of rejection he joined an obscure sect where there was no formal priesthood and everyone took it in turns to preach hellfire and damnation. That was when he discovered he had a God-given talent for preaching. Before long he was preaching in the open air on summer evenings, and eventually a rich widow offered to build him a chapel. Later he managed to marry her for her money. My poor father! Since his arrival in London he had been earning his living as a porter in a Putney warehouse but he knew he had no prospect of promotion; in those circumstances was it any wonder that he came to see his gift for preaching as the passport to the gentleman's life which he felt so strongly that a man of his intelligence deserved?

"I wonder if you've ever read *Elmer Gantry*. It's a novel about an American itinerant preacher who . . . well, it's a study of the seamy side of evangelism, the side we orthodox churchmen are ashamed of. It's the story of a preacher who uses his power over women to raise money not for God but for himself . . .

"No doubt you can imagine what happened. My father was without spiritual counselling and of course he fell into the grossest errors. He had this gift from God, the ability to preach, but you know as well as I do, Dr. Ashworth, what a dangerous charism that can be. That's why I myself never, never preach 'ex tempore.' The moment one departs from the written word, one's tempted to sway one's audience by playing on the most dubious emotions.

"My father never wrote down a word and he knew just how to keep the richest women fainting with excitement in their pews—and he also, I regret to say, knew exactly how to revive them afterwards in the vestry. Sir Thomas More has a word for it in *Utopia:* waywardness. My father was intolerably wayward with women. His first wife was an infirm old woman who could satisfy only his financial needs, and I'm afraid he convinced himself that all things would be forgiven him so long as he preached the word of God as fervently as possible.

"However, when his wife died, he did turn away in shame from his old life; he felt he could well afford to retire on the money she'd left, and he decided to devote himself to the study of theology. By that time too he had an additional motive for turning over a new leaf because he'd just met my mother, who was a young girl from a very respectable family, and he knew he'd never be allowed to marry her unless he could offer her a life of absolute propriety.

"I'm sure the marriage was a success, not only because I can remember the happy home my mother created but because I can so clearly remember how he went straight to pieces after she died. He'd seen my mother as a reward from God for good behaviour, poor man, and that was why he felt her death was a judgement; he was at once convinced that he hadn't been forgiven for his past sins after all.

"His guilt now began to crucify him. Is there any guilt worse than that of a man who has used a gift from God in the Devil's service? For a long while he shut himself up in his house and wouldn't go out. He wouldn't speak. He spent the whole time praying. He became wholly obsessed with his past sins, and from there it was but a short step to becoming obsessed with the sins of the world—the world which by rejecting him had set him on the road to corruption.

"You can imagine the effect on eight children of such behaviour. Eventually things came to such a pass that even my father, mentally ill as he undoubtedly was, realised that something would have to be done. By that time he had begun to preach again—though not for money; he thought the least he could do to appease God was to serve Him as honestly as he could in the pulpit, so he returned to the chapel of the obscure sect where he had first made his name, and one Sunday he noticed a newcomer, someone who had attended the service out of curiosity, someone who was apparently quite unmoved by his sermon, someone utterly different from all the women who fawned on him afterwards in admiration.

"It was my stepmother. She was employed as a companion to an old lady. She'd taken the position after her husband, a commercial traveller named Ashley, had been so inconsiderate as to die leaving her penniless. She hadn't the money to go home to Sweden but she was saving up for the fare.

"My father persuaded her to remain in England, but Heaven only knows how she found the strength to stay once the initial attraction to him had worn off. My father was very, very difficult, far too difficult for any of my brothers to endure. They all left home as soon as they could to earn their living across the river in London, and I was all set to go too—when I was thirteen my favourite brother found me a position as an office-boy in the firm where he was a clerk, but the position fell through and as soon as the news reached us my stepmother turned to my father—I can see her now—and said: 'You always said you needed a sign from God before you could allow that boy to go to school. Well, there's your sign, and either that boy goes to school or I walk out of this house and never come back!'

"I went to school. I hated it. I wanted to leave but she wouldn't let me. She was very tough, very ruthless. She said: 'Do you want to end up like your father or don't you?' and of course there was only one answer to that. She said: 'You're going to lead the life your father never had. You're going to open all the doors which were slammed in his face and you're going to be what he was never allowed to be. And then all the suffering will be redeemed,' she said—she was a deeply religious woman—'and all the pain will be smoothed away, and everything will make sense and he'll look at you and be so proud and happy at last.'

"It was a magnificent dream, wasn't it? But I couldn't see how it was ever going to come true. My father soon became extremely jealous of me—he couldn't bear to think I was leading the life he hadn't been allowed to lead. He was hostile and belligerent. What rows we used to have! How unhappy we made each other! Yet every time I wanted to give up and emigrate to Australia, my stepmother would say fiercely: *'You've got to go on!'* and I knew I could never walk away. Besides, by that time I'd seen the truth—I'd seen I was locked up in a dark room and my stepmother was trying to drag me out into the light. So I endured all the appalling scenes, all the endless unpleasantness, and I clawed my way to freedom, but I certainly didn't do it so that his suffering could be redeemed. Oh no! I did it for myself, I did it for her, but as for my father he could have rotted in Hell for all I cared. Towards him I was rude, unkind, contemptuous, impatient, angry, bitter, resentful, unloving and once or twice downright cruel. Could any son with a mentally ill father have been more un-Christian? I think not. And even after I was ordained I merely covered up my unacceptable emotions with a pious expression and observed my filial duties with gritted teeth.

"So when at the end of his life my father went senile, my first reaction was to hope he died quickly. In fact I couldn't understand why God was letting him live. It seemed quite pointless.

"But then he became a little better. He became lucid, lucid enough to know he was near the end, and then he began to talk to me. At first he would only talk about theology, but at last he began to review his life and suddenly I sensed his great urge to tell me every detail of his past—all the pathos, all the futility, all the waste—so that my present would take on a new meaning. And at last as my father talked to me with such painful honesty the miracle of communication occurred and I was able to understand the full dimensions of his tragedy. Then forgiveness was easy, and once I'd forgiven him I no longer saw him as a monster but as the father who had given me a Christian upbringing, no matter how bizarre, and who now wanted to heal our long and terrible estrangement before it was too late.

"He had a favourite text. It was 'I am not come to call the righteous, but sinners to repentance.' He kept urging me to preach on that text but I didn't care for it; I thought it was so typical of my father with his immense preoccupation with sin, but he was so insistent that at last, to keep him happy, I assured him I'd do as he wished. But I didn't. The next Sunday I preached on another text, and then when I came home I knew he was dead because I saw the blind had been drawn across the window of his room.

"Immediately I felt guilty. I thought: if only I'd preached on that text! And then before I knew where I was I was feeling guilty about all my cruel words in the past, all my unfilial behaviour, all my appalling lack of understanding and love—indeed I felt so absolutely pulverised with guilt then that I hardly knew how to bear the burden, but what I did know beyond any shadow of doubt was that I had to preach on that text which now seemed to speak directly to me. I felt that *I* was the sinner called to repent, and that a true repentance, a true turning away from my past errors, lay in struggling to become a far better clergyman than my ingrained rage against my father had ever allowed me to be before.

"So that became my own special text, and over the years I preached on it again and again—until when I finally stood as a bishop in Starbridge Cathedral and said: 'I am not come to call the righteous, but sinners to repentance!' I knew my stepmother's dream had come true at last. I knew the past had been redeemed, and that although my father had died when I was an obscure chaplain, he lived again whenever I said those words as the vicar, the Dean and the Bishop he had never managed to become. The most moving aspect of that entire ceremony at Starbridge was that my stepmother was still alive to see me sit on my episcopal throne. But there were no hugs and kisses afterwards, no gush of sentiment, no emotional tears. She wasn't that kind of woman. She just said casually to me: 'I knew it would be worth it all in the end,' and I said equally casually: 'Thank God you could never afford the fare home to Sweden.'

"Now, Charles Ashworth, this isn't a sermon and half-past two in the morning is hardly the hour to embark on heavy moralising, so I shall say only one sentence more: put your relationship with your father right because the longer you let it remain wrong, the more guilty you're going to feel when he dies . . ."

8

JARDINE stopped speaking. We were sitting facing each other across his desk, and behind him the books rose in well-ordered tiers from floor to ceiling. The surface of his desk was crowded but not muddled; on either side of the blotter piles of papers lay neatly pinned beneath glass weights while beside the silver inkstand pens and pencils were arranged with precision in a tray.

"Thank you, Bishop," I said. "It was extremely good of you to take me into your confidence like that and I regard it as the highest possible compliment." I suddenly realised that in my inspection of his desk I had been looking for an item I had failed to find, and the next moment I was unable to resist inquiring: "Do you have a photograph of your father and stepmother?"

"Of course. Every respectable couple in Putney had their picture taken to mark their engagement." Opening the bottom drawer of his desk he extracted a photograph and handed it to me. It was a studio portrait of a middle-aged man, bearded but still recognisable as a Victorian version of the Bishop, and a young woman of about thirty, good-looking and sultry with blonde hair, pale eyes and a resolute mouth.

"How attractive she was!" I said, startled. "Somehow I'd expected someone plainer."

"Oh, she didn't keep her looks. Shortly before I moved to Mayfair she put on weight—thyroid trouble—and became rather withdrawn, but I never cared what she looked like. I said to her once: 'Whether you're six stone or sixteen stone you'll still be Ingrid,' and she said: 'Whether you're nine or ninety you'll still be Adam.' Nobody calls me Adam any more," said the Bishop, replacing the photograph in its envelope, "but that doesn't mean Adam no longer exists. I sometimes think that having two names is like having a split personality. Alex is the Bishop, the famous man in public life—"

"The glittering image," I said.

"—but beyond Alex there's Adam, still staggering around beneath the burden of that difficult past, still haunted by so many fearful memories, still battling with that filial guilt which can never be completely assuaged—"

"Sometimes I too feel as if I've got a split personality," I said, "but my other self doesn't have a separate name."

Understanding flared in Jardine's eyes. He said abruptly: "Cut yourself loose from Lang and give your other self room to breathe. Being His Grace's lackey is doing you absolutely no good at all." He did not wait for a reply but moved to the door with his detective story in his hand. "I suggest we now make renewed assaults on our insomnia," he added over his shoulder. "I apologise for detaining you so long with my unsolicited bedtime story."

"I've no complaints, Bishop. Quite the reverse. Thank you again."

We retired in silence to our bedrooms.

9

I THOUGHT of that bearded Victorian version of Jardine with the sultry young woman who had restored order to a chaotic household. Then I thought of that woman, middle-aged but possibly still sultry, leaving her husband to keep house for the stepson twenty years her junior, the stepson who could not afford to marry.

"She said: 'It was worth it all for Adam,' " I could hear Lyle murmuring in my memory.

"He really is the most wonderful man, believe me," said the young chaplain Gerald Harvey as I slipped over the edge of consciousness and my mind was released from all constraint.

"You don't give much away, do you?" said Lyle to me in a vast church as we waited in vain for the Bishop to marry us. "You're the real mystery here."

"Karl Barth has solved the mystery of the historical Jesus," said Jardine to me as we stood in the centre of Starbury Ring. "He says you have to watch the narrator in *The Murder of Roger Ackroyd.*"

"I'm so glad I found you, Dr. Ashworth," said Mrs. Jardine, the present Mrs. Jardine, smiling up at me as we stood by the river at the bottom of the garden, "because I wanted to tell you that I've found out who killed Roger Ackroyd. It was Mr. A. P. Herbert. Isn't it wonderful that Our Lord's approved of the A. P. Herbert Bill? Divorce is always so interesting, isn't it, especially in hot weather."

"Loretta was divorced," said the Earl to me over his shoulder as he landed a huge fish. "Of course she'd been Jardine's mistress for years."

"No, no, no, Henry!" exclaimed Lady Starmouth who was swimming naked in the river. "She was never Alex's mistress! He always behaved with propriety!"

"That's what *you* say, Lady Starmouth!" said Mrs. Cobden-Smith, appearing with the St. Bernard. "But why should we believe you?"

"I'll tell you what I believe," said Lady Starmouth, climbing out of the river and revealing a pair of intriguingly spherical breasts. "I believe Dr. Ashworth wants to go to bed with me."

"I'm so sorry, Lady Starmouth," I said, "but I'm afraid I can't. I'm waiting to go to bed with Loretta."

"I'm your passport to Loretta," said Lady Starmouth, dressed in a white ball-gown as she led me out of the mortuary where my wife lay dead. "But I shan't introduce you unless you go to bed with me first."

Lyle said behind me: "I really do want to go to bed with you. But I'm afraid of the Bishop."

"Did you go to bed with the Bishop?" I said to the sultry Swedish girl who was waiting for me at the end of a dark corridor, but she said: "I have to take you to church because I'm such a deeply religious woman."

"Charles is so religious," said my mother, who was playing bridge in the nave as Ingrid and I walked into Starbridge Cathedral, "but despite that he's tremendously successful. His father's so proud of him."

"I never usually talk about my father," said Jardine as he mounted the steps to the pulpit. "My family was deeply disordered."

"We're such a wonderfully happy family!" said my mother, laughing as she dealt the cards. "We never exchange a single cross word!"

"You bloody young fool!" cried my father as he broke down the door and burst into the nave.

"I am not come to call the righteous," said Jardine from the pulpit, "but sinners to repentance."

"You narrow-minded bastard!" I shouted at my father.

"I am not come to call the *righteous,*" proclaimed Jardine in a louder voice, "but *sinners* to *repentance.*"

"No, Charles, no!" screamed my mother.

"I am not come to call the righteous, but sinners to repentance!" bawled the Bishop.

"You'll never make a clergyman!" yelled my father at me. "Who the devil do you think you're fooling?"

"I AM NOT COME TO CALL THE RIGHTEOUS, BUT SINNERS—SINNERS—*SINNERS*—"

"Father!" I shouted, sitting bolt upright in bed with the sweat streaming down my face. "*Father!* FATHER—"

Silence fell.

The bedroom was very dark. With a shaking hand I switched on the light. Then I slid out of bed onto my knees and began to pray.

10

THE Starmouths departed after breakfast the next morning and after we had waved goodbye I asked the Bishop if he could spare the time later for a word in private.

"Of course," he said, "but it had better be now before I start work on my sermon."

"You're preaching on Sunday?"

"At Matins, yes. I'm standing in for the Dean who's been called away to the north to conduct a cousin's funeral. Are you going to extend your visit to assist me at Early Communion?"

I was considerably surprised. "I'm sure," I said, "that you'd prefer to withdraw that invitation you made in your letter, Bishop."

"I can't think why. I'm a Christian, Dr. Ashworth, not a heathen politician anxious to blackball you from some exclusive club! Reconsider the invitation and let me know your decision later," he said, and as we entered his library he changed the subject by adding with a smile: "I trust I vanquished your insomnia last night!"

"I'm glad to say I was asleep within ten minutes." I paused before saying with care: "You were very frank with me then and now I'm going to be very frank with you. I suspect the Archbishop may well be pursuing a personal vendetta, but he never actually commissioned me to find the evidence which would cut your throat, and even if I did find it I'd never give it to him. I don't believe cutting throats should be part of my clerical duties. Nor do I believe that a bishop of your calibre deserves to be smeared by the press just because Lang made an exceptionally pompous exhibition of himself over the Abdication. Can you believe me when I say I'm entirely on your side? And if you believe me, will you allow me to ask a very impertinent question in order to confirm that you're absolutely impregnable from scandal?"

"Well, you're obviously working yourself up to some truly monstrous piece of impudence, Dr. Ashworth, but luckily for you I'm beginning to find your impudence entertaining. What's the question?"

"Is there any communication at present between you and Professor Loretta Staviski?"

VII

"Your treatment of women is a matter of the utmost concern."

More Letters of
HERBERT HENSLEY HENSON,
ed. E. F. Braley

I

THANKS to my elaborate warning Jardine took this new assault on his privacy remarkably well; perhaps, since Lady Starmouth had obviously reported to him every detail of my interrogation, he had even been expecting a question about Loretta. Showing neither surprise nor anger, he merely heaved a sigh of resignation.

"My dear Canon, I'm touched by your zeal on my behalf," he said dryly, "and I hardly like to sound ungrateful since you've been so generous as to assure me of your unqualified support, but isn't your zeal becoming a trifle excessive?"

"Not when one considers that the professor is arriving in England soon and that any Sunday rag in search of scandal is quite capable of having you watched. If you were to meet Professor Staviski in London—"

"I shan't. I haven't communicated with her for nineteen years, and anyway even back in 1918 there was no scandal. All that happened was that one of my parishioners fell in love with me and I was fool enough not to realise it for some time."

"Bishop, may I just ask how many people knew about this incident?"

"Only Lady Starmouth."

"But are you saying," I said astonished, "that no one else knew—no one else at all? What about your wife?"

"She was away from home when my friendship with Mrs. Staviski reached its unfortunate end. Our child had been born dead, the doctor had recommended country air for Carrie and she was spending a month with her parents."

"But did no one suspect what had happened? After all, you could hardly have been living in a vacuum in Mayfair!"

"Obviously the essence of the incident's eluded you. Mrs. Staviski was flawlessly concealing her true feelings and I merely regarded her as another good friend like Lady Starmouth. Neither of us was generating gossip."

"But wasn't your wife surprised when Mrs. Staviski suddenly vanished from Mayfair?"

"Yes, but it was war-time and a lot of people were coming and going. Also my wife was far from well and too preoccupied with her own troubles to pay much attention to the troubles of others. That was why I never confided in her, of course. It would have been selfish to add to her burdens at that time."

"How did Lady Starmouth find out?"

Jardine paused, considering the question. Then he said abruptly: "I'll tell you exactly what happened. Bearing in mind all the circumstances I see no point in keeping you in the dark, and as a clergyman you might even find it instructive to see where I went wrong. This is not a story of moral failure, Dr. Ashworth, but of extreme pastoral inadequacy—in other words, this is where we look beyond Alex the Bishop's 'glittering image,' as you put it last night, and see poor old Adam, struggling to be a good vicar and really making a very great hash of it indeed . . ."

2

"IT was surprising how many people called her by her Christian name," said Jardine. "I could never make up my mind whether it was because she was a foreigner and thus outside the English social structure with all its petty conventions, or whether it was because the xenophobic British merely balked at the alien surname. However, as a clergyman bound hand and foot by the proprieties I always called her Mrs. Staviski until the day our friendship ended. If I call her Loretta now it's not because I was accustomed to do so at the time but because 'Professor Staviski' (as she now is) makes her sound like some mad disciple of the Russian Revolution.

"I met her in 1917 when she left her husband and Lady Starmouth enlisted my help. I quickly realised that the marriage had broken down beyond hope of repair—the husband was homosexual—so I decided my duty as a pastor lay not in trying to preserve the marriage but in trying to salvage Loretta, who had been treated so abominably that her self-confidence had been wrecked. Her husband had made her feel she was an object of revulsion to the opposite sex, and I concluded that if she were ever to be restored to a normal life some other man had to repair the damage which had been done. This, I think, was a perfectly rational conclusion, but the trouble was that I then elected myself to do the repairs.

"Yes, you may well look at me with amazement, but I wasn't quite so stupid as this statement may lead you to believe. I only met her at Lady Starmouth's house—or at my own in the presence of my wife—and even when Loretta acquired a flat I never went there without a curate in attendance. I had three curates, and I'd learnt always to take one with me when I paid pastoral calls on lonely ladies in Mayfair.

"But of course I was making a big mistake. I should have realised Loretta wasn't stable enough to cope with platonic friendship. Men and women aren't, after all, intended by God for asexual intimacies, and in fact there's a sexual element in all my three long-standing platonic friendships, but the point about Lady Starmouth, Lady Markhampton and Mrs. Welbeck is that they're all married, well-balanced and happy; their friendship with me is essentially just a decoration on an already satisfying cake. But with Loretta I wasn't merely a decoration. I was the icing, the marzipan, the currants, the raisins—everything. She was a foreigner in London, her separation from her husband cut her off from many people who might have befriended her and she was very much alone. Did I allow for her extreme vulnerability? No, I did not. I called on her more often than I should have done; in an effort to divert her from her troubles I lent her numerous books—but all novels, nothing of spiritual value—and in an effort to restore her self-esteem I paid her numerous compliments. Naturally such folly could have only one conclusion.

"It all ended on a Saturday in September 1918. After breakfast I was just starting work on Sunday's sermon when a wire arrived to say that Lady Starmouth's favourite brother had been killed in action and could I go down to Leatherhead immediately. As you must have discovered by now, that's where the Starmouths have their country home; they have no connection with the city of Starmouth in this diocese beyond the fact that the first Earl's mother was born there and when he was offered his earldom he decided it would be less embarrassing to be called Lord Starmouth than Lord Leatherhead. Loretta used to like that story—Americans are always so ingenuously intrigued by titles . . . She was there, of course, with her friend when I arrived at Starmouth Court later that morning. She'd caught an earlier train from London.

"I talked to Lady Starmouth on her own for a while and then we all lunched together. The Earl wasn't there; he was on his way back from Scotland and wasn't expected until much later. After luncheon Lady

Starmouth decided to rest and I was about to consider my return to London when Loretta said she had something to tell me and I fell in with her suggestion that we should go for a walk down into the valley. The Starmouths' house is built on a hillside overlooking the River Mole—but perhaps you know that? I've just remembered that you come from that part of Surrey, don't you, and so you've probably often passed the house—it's visible from the main road between Leatherhead and Dorking."

Jardine paused, his eyes dark with memory, his hands clasped tightly as he leaned forward on his desk. "We walked to the river," he said. "We walked back. It was the first time we'd ever been alone together far from other people. There was traffic on the road—pony-traps, cyclists, even a motor—but we were alone. Then she told me everything and the friendship ended." He paused again before adding abruptly: "She cried a lot. When we got back, Lady Starmouth was downstairs. She took one look at Loretta and guessed everything—which in a way was a good thing because she was able to help us both. She helped Loretta get a passage to America, an almost impossible feat in war-time, and she helped me by never once offering a word of reproach. But of course by that time I could see how deeply I'd failed Loretta as a pastor, and so I knew far better than Lady Starmouth how very, very much I was to blame . . ."

3

I ALLOWED a moment of sympathetic silence to elapse before venturing the comment: "I can certainly understand why you made no further experiments in platonic friendship."

"I realise that you find the whole concept of platonic friendship fantastic, but then you're a member of the sex-obsessed post-war generation. In my young day a wider range of male-female relationships was possible . . . But I don't mean to make excuses for myself. I did make terrible mistakes with Loretta."

"But not scandalous ones. There were no letters, I suppose, Bishop?"

"Not after she'd declared her feelings, no. We'd had some harmless correspondence earlier but I burnt it."

"No entries in the journal?"

"Fortunately I had no pressing need to pour out my remorse on paper because I was able to pour it out to Lady Starmouth instead."

A thought struck me. "Did you confide in your stepmother?"

"Ah!" Jardine gave a wry smile. "I did tell her much later at the end of her life, but in 1918 I said nothing. My stepmother had made such a fuss when I married that I avoided talking to her about my women friends . . . Dear me, how possessive that makes her sound! Let me at once correct that unfortunate impression by saying that she always wanted me to marry, but unfortunately her idea of a suitable wife for me was quite different from my own. That's not an uncommon dilemma for mothers and sons to find themselves in, I believe." He leant back in his chair with another smile. "Well, Dr. Ashworth? Is the last chink in my armour finally sealed?"

"I think that as far as the press are concerned you really must be impregnable."

"And apart from the press?"

"Oh, you have your Achilles' heel, of course," I said, rising to my feet, "but fortunately the way to protect yourself there is very simple. May I suggest you start looking around without delay for a new companion to replace Miss Christie?" And as the smile vanished from his face I made a swift exit into the hall.

4

SO now I knew the story of Loretta. Or, to be accurate, I now knew Jardine's version of the story of Loretta, an account which harmonised dutifully with the account of Lady Starmouth. Of course he had not told me everything; I was prepared to bet there had been a kiss or two by the river in the intervals between the passing pony-traps which he had mentioned so carefully, but nevertheless I suspected he had been reasonably honest with me. A kiss between a married clergyman and a passionate young woman certainly represented the sort of indiscretion Lang had feared, but as far as I could see there could be no conceivable danger to Jardine now, nineteen years later, particularly since no one but Lady Starmouth and old Mrs. Jardine had ever known the friendship had gone so wrong.

I was genuinely pleased that Jardine was impregnable from scandal yet at the same time I was unforgivably disappointed that I still had no excuse to think the unthinkable; a minor indiscretion, even though reprehensible, was a long way from a major moral error. My disappointment baffled me. I felt it was irrational that I should want to unmask as an apostate a man I so much admired, and I began to wonder if my two personalities were subtly at war with each other. However, that was a mad thought which could not be entertained for more than the briefest of moments, and thrusting it aside I retired to my room to plot my next move.

It was now Friday. I had assumed I would have to leave on the following morning, but since Jardine had been gentleman enough to stand by the invitation in his letter I thought it would be churlish of me not to stay on. Besides, I was never a man who wasted his opportunities, and the extension of my visit would give me the chance to see more of Lyle.

Taking a sheet of the palace notepaper from the drawer of the table, I sat down and wrote: "My dear Bishop, Of course I'd consider it a great honour to assist you at Holy Communion and a great pleasure to remain at the palace. Thank you for your continuing hospitality which in the circumstances I find impressively generous. Yours most sincerely, CHARLES ASHWORTH."

But I wondered if he were already regretting his invitation.

5

THE day proved frustrating because I had no chance to see Lyle on her own. After leaving the Bishop's letter on the hall table, I made another nominal attempt to work in the Cathedral Library, but when I returned to the palace I was informed that Lyle had accompanied Mrs. Jardine to the station to meet the new guests who were arriving to replace the Starmouths.

There were hordes of people at lunch. I counted eighteen places laid at the extended dining-room table and soon discovered, to my disgust, that Lyle and I had been placed six seats apart. Moreover, as soon as the last visitor had departed, she and Mrs. Jardine drove off to open a church bazaar and I was left still debating whether I had been the victim of a conspiracy. Wandering moodily around the town to pass the time, I browsed in the antiquarian bookshops and finally succeeded in attending Choral Evensong.

The guests at dinner were confined to those who were staying at the palace. The new arrivals, four cousins of Mrs. Jardine, seemed incapable of talking about anything except fox-hunting, and I could see Jardine was missing Lady Starmouth's sophisticated glamour. However, after the cloth was drawn the lay guests were successfully dispatched to the smoking-room and he was able to cheer himself up by discussing the Virgin Birth with me. As I had suspected, he believed in the creed "ex animo" and in his own Modernist way was thoroughly orthodox.

We returned to the drawing-room. Lyle was on duty by the coffee-pot but the Bishop came with me to collect his cup and obstinately refused to take a turn on the terrace with any of the ladies. Possibly he felt all the female guests were too plain to be worthy of such attention, but possibly too he was determined to keep me from enjoying a private word with Lyle.

"Come and sit down, Dr. Ashworth!" called Mrs. Jardine, patting the vacant space on the sofa beside her as she presided among her elderly female cousins. "We all want to hear more about Dr. Lang!"

I suddenly decided I was the victim of a conspiracy. "I'm just coming!" I called back, and said swiftly to Lyle as the Bishop looked on: "What are you doing tomorrow?"

"I'm going out for the day with Mrs. Jardine. She wants to take her cousins to the sea."

"Dine with me when you get back."

She hesitated but the Bishop said briskly: "Give yourself an evening off, Lyle, and accept the invitation—unless, of course, you feel Dr. Ashworth so blotted his copybook at Starbury Ring that you don't wish to go out with him again. If that's the case then you'd do much better to be frank and tell him so."

"Thank you, Bishop," I said. I turned to Lyle. "Think about it," I said, "and let me know." And leaving her still sheltering behind the coffee-pot I joined Mrs. Jardine to recall my most flattering memories of Dr. Lang.

6

THE next morning I awoke after another turbulent night to find that a note had been slipped under my door.

"I shall be free from seven-thirty onwards this evening," Lyle had written in a small precise hand. "If you're uncertain where to dine, may I recommend the Staro Arms in Eternity Street? L.C."

I decided I had imagined the conspiracy.

Or had I?

I wondered what the Bishop was thinking.

7

I SPENT the day forcing myself to work on my St. Anselm notes until I reached the point where I could conclude my researches in the University Library at Cambridge. Afterwards, relieved to the point of frivolity, I scribbled experimentally on my notepad, and having produced three absurd verses I returned from the Cathedral to the palace, where I copied my lines onto a sheet of notepaper:

> There was a young lady named Lyle *(I wrote)*
> Who wanted to run half a mile

Whenever Charles A
Said: "Is there a way
You can care for me more, dearest Lyle?"

There was a smart bishop named Jardine
Whose name only rhymes with a sardine.
He said: "Go far away,
You bad Dr. A,
And leave Lyle to serve Mrs. Jardine!"

There was a canon called Ashworth from Laud's
Who aspired to the best life affords.
He knew to win Lyle
He must exercise guile,
So he tried hard to lure her to Laud's.

Underneath this last line I wrote: "Sorry this isn't a sonnet, but unfortunately not all clergymen can rival John Donne. Why don't you take a few days' holiday and visit Cambridge soon? Have you ever been punting on the Cam? Have you ever seen King's College Chapel? Have you ever watched the sun set over the Backs? There's a world beyond Starbridge, and I think it's time someone reminded you of it." Signing my Christian name I added my telephone number before concluding: "P.S. Bring Mrs. Jardine too, if you feel you can't leave her. Why not? The change would do her good."

Having demolished her most obvious excuse for refusing my invitation, I raided the garden for a rose and retired once more to the house. It was mid-afternoon. Jardine was out and Mrs. Jardine's party had not yet returned from the excursion to the sea. The butler was probably much surprised when someone rang the bell in the drawing-room, but when he appeared he had his sepulchral expression firmly in place and never even faltered at the sight of the rose in my hand.

"I want to leave this in Miss Christie's room, Shipton," I said, watching for any sign that might indicate the servants regarded Lyle as hopelessly out of bounds to all admirers. "How do I get there?"

However, Shipton seemed delighted by the prospect of a romance and possibly even more delighted by the prospect of a romance which was inevitably doomed. His sepulchral expression softened; his voice became confidential. "Miss Christie's room is a little difficult to find, sir. Allow me to show you the way."

We made a dignified journey upstairs, I bearing the rose, Shipton bearing his modified sepulchral expression, and I was led through a labyrinth of Gothic corridors to a remote room high in the south turret.

"New servants must need a map to get here!" I remarked as he opened the door.

"Miss Christie likes to give the Bishop and Mrs. Bishop every privacy, sir, as befits a lady in her position who lives as one of the family. Will that be all, sir, or shall I wait to show you the way back?"

"No, I'll find my own way back, thank you, Shipton, but if I don't return within twelve hours you can organise a search-party."

"Very good, sir." He padded away with his gravity intact, and I walked into the room.

It was a high bright octagon adorned sparingly with an unremarkable collection of furniture. Among the collection was a single bed, covered with a blue counterpane, and on the bedside table was the Penguin edition of Hemingway's *A Farewell to Arms* together with a faded photograph of a bright-eyed soldier in uniform. There was something unbearably poignant about his air of hope and vigour. On the dressing-table stood some silver brushes, a modest tray of make-up and a jam-jar of honeysuckle from the garden. Three pictures hung on the walls, a water-colour of a lake which could have been one of the Norfolk Broads, a framed sketch of a large Georgian townhouse which I suspected was the Deanery at Radbury, and a first-class engraving of the matchless Starbridge Cathedral. I stood there absorbing the scene so that I would be able to picture her in her seclusion when I was far away in Cambridge, and then I laid the rose on her pillow, took the verses from my pocket and left the folded paper beneath the rose's long stem.

On my way out I paused to look at her bookshelves and discovered in addition to the intelligent modern novels the controversial *The Quest of the Historical Jesus,* Albert Schweitzer's attempt to reconstruct the career of Christ within an eschatological framework. It was the only theological volume in the collection apart from her inevitable set of Jardine's books, but it made me wonder if she borrowed other works of theology from the library downstairs. I cast my eye over the Jardine volumes, the anthologies of sermons, his polemic on the doomed Prayer Book reform of the twenties and his notorious attack on the Malines Conversations, but I found no book which I had not already read. I was interested to see that beyond the Jardine collection there was a copy of A. P. Herbert's *Holy Deadlock* in which the author of the famous Bill had satirised the law on divorce.

I found the tone of her books vaguely worrying. Apart from the novels her collection suggested a mild preoccupation with religion but not, as far as I could see, with personal piety. There was no copy of the Bible visible in the room.

I began to wonder if Lyle were the apostate.

However, I knew I could discover at dinner the exact nature of her religious belief. Taking one last look at that deeply private room I opened the door again and began the convoluted journey back to the main part of the house.

8

HER first words to me as we met in the hall that evening were: "How did you find my room?"

"I took a map, a compass, a week's supply of rations and Shipton."

"I don't like to think of anyone prowling around my room," she said. "In fact I hate to think of it."

"Oh? That must make life awkward for the servants!" I said, smiling at her, and the next moment she was answering rapidly: "I'm making a fool of myself, aren't I, and being abominably rude as well. Thank you for the rose. It was beautiful. And thanks for the limericks. I'm glad you didn't write a sonnet because I happen to find sonnets a bore."

We set off for the short walk to Eternity Street where the Staro Arms, a former coaching inn dating from the fourteenth century, was built around a cobbled courtyard. In the garden beyond, wrought-iron tables shaded by scarlet sun-umbrellas dotted the lawn which sloped to the river, and along the low wall which divided the bank from the garden a row of geraniums stirred in the faint evening breeze. We chose a table which enabled us to see the reflection in the water of the medieval houses on the opposite bank, and soon the waiter arrived with our drinks. Lyle had ordered a Schweppes sparkling lime garnished with gin and ice, while I had requested a half-pint of Whitbread's pale ale.

"Don't you drink spirits?" Lyle asked.

I did not answer directly but said: "I think clergymen do better to avoid drinking spirits, just as they should always avoid smoking when they're wearing their clerical collar. Such habits project the wrong image on the ecclesiastical screen."

"Well, I'm glad you're keen to project the right one tonight. I was afraid you might be feeling pounce-ish again."

"What a stimulating thought!" I said promptly, but when she gave an exasperated laugh I added to soothe her: "We're going to have a civilised dinner. We're not even going to mention the Jardines, not unless you want to. We're going to talk about novels and theology and whatever else we find we have in common, and then I can tell you more—if you're interested—about my life in Cambridge, and you can tell me more—if you wish—about life in rural Norfolk where, so Mrs. Cobden-Smith tells me, everyone talks in grunts. In other words we're going to enjoy each other's company and relax with no thought for the morrow."

"That all sounds much too good to be true," said Lyle dryly, but she was already relaxing, and as we exchanged smiles again I decided I was finally on the brink of making substantial progress.

9

I MYSELF did not relax until halfway through the meal when I discovered she was not an apostate. She had an unmistakably genuine faith and an intelligent layman's interest in expanding its intellectual perimeter; as I had suspected, she often borrowed books from the Bishop's library. I did say with reluctance: "I noticed there was no Bible in your room," but she replied tartly: "Well, at least I now know you didn't open the drawer of my bedside table!"

I was deeply relieved. No matter how strongly I felt that Lyle was right for me I would have had no choice but to accept that she was wrong if I had uncovered evidence that she was not devout. How could one live with a woman in the closest intimacy unless she was able to understand the fundamental force in one's life? An attraction of spiritual opposites was a disaster for any clergyman.

This hint of my more private spiritual concerns evidently aroused Lyle's curiosity, and at the end of the meal she gave in to the temptation to inquire how I had reached my decision to be ordained. "And don't just say you were called," she said. "Obviously God called you but how did He do it?"

I said easily: "I'd been a regular churchgoer since my last year at school when Dr. Lang had given the prizes and made a speech which had caught my imagination, but although I did toy then with the idea of being a clergyman I knew my father wanted me to follow in his footsteps by becoming a solicitor in the family firm. However, after a year up at Cambridge I found the law had no message for me and soon I was feeling so miserable and confused that I wrote to Dr. Lang for advice. I decided that if he replied encouragingly, it would mean I should consider going into the Church, but if he merely replied politely through a chaplain, it would mean I'd have to think again."

"And he replied encouragingly."

"He wrote a letter in his own hand and asked to see me. He wasn't Archbishop of Canterbury then; he was Archbishop of York, and he invited me to Bishopthorpe for the weekend. Naturally I was overwhelmed. He was so very kind and understanding." I paused. The contrast between my past and present feelings for Lang was unexpectedly painful.

"So of course you felt you were being called."

"I knew it. My father was livid but he mellowed later and now he's very proud of my success." I signalled for the bill and said lightly: "So much for my calling. I'm afraid it's not very dramatic, is it? No blinding white light on the road to Damascus, no voice speaking from the clouds!"

"I should think it was very dramatic," said Lyle, "but on a human, not a divine level. However, I suppose it was only natural that your father should have been disappointed when you chose not to follow in his footsteps."

"Oh, it was no great tragedy," I said as the waiter brought the bill. "He got what he wanted in the end. My brother Peter took my place in the family firm and everyone lived happily ever after."

"Honestly? Or is that another of your extravagant romantic statements?"

"What extravagant romantic statements?"

"Never mind. That was a lovely dinner, Charles, and I enjoyed every mouthful. Many thanks."

Five minutes later we were walking back along Eternity Street in the moonlight. I had offered to take her to the Staro Arms in my car but she had evidently decided that a drive à deux was best avoided—or perhaps the Jardines had only let her out of their sight on condition that she abstained from travelling in my chariot of sin. I had learnt no more about her relationship with them, but I had not forgotten my impression that they were conspiring to chaperone her, and no matter how often I told myself the idea was absurd I was unable to convince myself I was being irrational.

At the antiquarian bookship which marked the end of Eternity Street we turned right and saw ahead the Cathedral Close's gateway illuminated by the pale light of the street-lamps. The Cathedral itself, massive against the moonlit sky, loomed in the distance and assumed an eerie shadowed beauty as we began to cross the sward of the churchyard.

We were silent. It was almost eleven o'clock and the lights in the windows of the houses around us were beginning to be extinguished. At the east end of the Cathedral we reached the white gate in the churchyard wall, and before I raised the latch I hesitated. Simultaneously we moved towards each other and simultaneously we held out our arms for an embrace. The resulting kiss was full, mutual, perfect, and I felt that old delectable satisfaction that the feminine flesh could be so entirely other yet so entirely complementary to the flesh in which I myself lived and moved and had my being. I was once more aware how small she was, how delicately made, and beyond this awareness I was conscious how densely my desire was spreading through my body as it drove away all doubt, all difficulty and all despair. I wanted to go on kissing her. I wanted to go on generating the heat which fired that exquisite force beyond description, but she broke away, dragging open the gate in the wall and running off along the East Walk.

I caught up with her halfway down the palace drive.

"My God, what a fool I am!" she gasped, pausing to scrabble frantically in her bag for her latch-key. "What a fool!"

"You're only a fool to say you're a fool! When are you coming to Cambridge to visit me?"

"Never." She finally found the key. "I'm sorry, I shouldn't have kissed you like that, I despise myself, I absolutely vowed I wouldn't lead you on—"

"What on earth's going on in this house?"

"Nothing!" As she succeeded in opening the door I saw her eyes were bright with tears.

I grabbed her for another kiss and although she tried to push me away I held her tightly. "Are you in love with him?"

"Oh, for God's sake! No, of course not!"

"Are you in love with her?"

"What?" She was so appalled that she even forgot to struggle.

"Then there's absolutely no reason why you can't be in love with me. Look, darling—"

Voices echoed in the distance, and as the grip of my arms automatically slackened she broke away, rushing over the threshold to safety. I paused to wipe her lipstick from my mouth, and by the time I entered the hall she was already vanishing upstairs.

I closed the door just as the Bishop's departing dinner guests began to stream out of the drawing-room, and when Mrs. Jardine made a confused attempt to introduce me I was obliged to linger in the hall. Eventually the last guest departed but Mrs. Jardine, smiling brightly, forestalled my attempt to slip away up the staircase.

"Did you have a nice evening, Dr. Ashworth? It's such a good thing for Lyle to get out and about with someone her own age, and I'm sure the outing cheered her up tremendously! She was so depressed about the Coronation."

The Bishop's harsh voice immediately exclaimed: "Carrie!"

Mrs. Jardine jumped. "Oh Alex, I'm sorry, I—"

"Lyle's quite recovered from all that now."

"Yes, of course she has—dearest Lyle, she's always so contented—well, we all are, aren't we, and Dr. Ashworth, what a mercy the weather stayed fine for you this evening! It must have been so delightful in the river-garden of the Staro Arms!"

I told myself I was going to solve the mystery of Lyle Christie even if it proved to be my last accomplishment on earth.

10

AS I walked to the Cathedral the next morning with the Bishop to assist him at the early service I was not expecting to be engaged in conversation. Silence is preferable before a profound act of worship, but on leaving the house Jardine said casually: "I'm glad you enjoyed your dinner at the Staro Arms. Rather an attractive example of a medieval inn, I've always thought."

"Yes, very."

"And as my wife said last night, it's good for Lyle to get out and about with someone her own age." As we passed through the palace gateway he fidgeted for a moment with his pectoral cross before adding: "Why my wife chose to bring up the subject of the Coronation I can't think. It's true Lyle was depressed at the time because she couldn't participate in the event as Carrie and I did, but she stayed at home by her own choice. I offered to get her a ticket for one of the stands in Parliament Square, but she was absolutely resolute in declining . . . Were you yourself in London for the Coronation?"

"I had a seat in the Haymarket."

"It was a magnificent ceremony," said the Bishop, "but I was infernally hot in my cope and the hours of standing about were hard on the older bishops." He paused but as we reached the Dean's door, the private entrance for the clergy, he said very courteously: "Well, Canon, I'm delighted to have you with me this morning—welcome once more to the Cathedral!"

I murmured my thanks, but on my way to the vestry I found myself wondering what—if anything—these casual comments on the Coronation had been designed to hide.

11

LYLE was absent from Communion, and as I helped the Bishop administer the sacrament I felt more bewildered than ever. A kiss with an unmarried man hardly constituted a sin serious enough to remove her from a state of grace. I decided she must have overslept but I remained worried, particularly since I knew she was a regular Sunday communicant, and later I realised that Jardine was worried too. I heard him say to his wife who was waiting for us after the service: "What's happened to Lyle?"

"She said she was feeling a little frail, poor dear. I told her to go back to bed."

"But Lyle never feels frail!" In his concern the Bishop sounded outraged.

"Well no, dearest, not usually, but any woman can have a frail day once in a while."

"Oh, I see," said the Bishop blankly.

I stepped closer to them. "Should we take her the sacrament, Bishop?"

"No, a state of frailty is hardly the equivalent of a state of prostration," said the Bishop severely, and at once I sensed he disapproved of the reserved sacrament in all but the most extreme cases. As we moved outside I murmured: "I suppose you're a long way from favouring perpetual reservation, Bishop."

"Perpetual reservation? Certainly not! I'll have no Popish practices here!" declared the Bishop, and as I realised he was probably behaving exactly like his Non-Conformist father I thought what a mysterious force heredity was, spreading like a stain across the texture of the personality.

We returned in silence to the palace.

12

LYLE missed breakfast but appeared later as we all gathered in the hall to go to Matins.

"I'm all right now," she said in response to the Bishop's abrupt inquiry. "It was just a passing malaise." And when she smiled at me I knew she was anxious to conceal the new tension in our relationship. "Thanks again for last night, Charles."

I said: "I was worried in case the dinner had disagreed with you."

"I admit those heavenly mushrooms gave me some interesting dreams!"

"I had some interesting dreams too," I said, keeping an eye on the Bishop who seemed to be abnormally restless. "Remind me to tell you about them sometime."

"Are we all ready," said the Bishop irritably, "or am I to deliver my sermon by a series of stentorian shouts from the palace doorstep?"

We set off once more to the Cathedral.

13

I HAD been hoping for a first-class sermon and Jardine did not disappoint me. His text was: "For what shall it profit a man, if he shall gain the whole world, and lose his own soul?" and as I watched, knowing he had written out every word even though he often gave the impression of speaking off the cuff, I admired him for keeping his God-given talent on such a tightly disciplined rein.

The sermon, perfectly constructed, immaculately delivered, unfolded itself like a complex flower opening its petals before the sun. I always found it arresting to see an expert in any field doing his work well, and Jardine was an expert in homiletics, selecting his intellectual strands sparingly but weaving them with stark skill into a rapier-sharp exposition of Christian teaching. Finally, reaching his peroration, he knotted the intellectual strands into a single dazzling sentence, heightened the power of his delivery and drove home his message with the full force of his oratorical sledgehammer.

I thought: I'll give up my ivory tower. I'll go to Africa as a missionary. Or I'll become a slum-priest.

Then I knew I had been hypnotised by those lambent amber eyes.

On my knees during the blessing I found my thoughts were becoming more rational but remaining revolutionary. I was telling myself that instead of passing the remainder of the Long Vacation at Laud's while I worked on my new book I should instead offer to do a locum so that some overworked country parson could have a holiday. But then the sinner's thought entered my head: the parish experience would look well on my curriculum vitae, and I despised myself.

During the silence following the blessing I prayed urgently: deliver me from temptation; show me the way; let thy will, not mine, be done.

Then the organist launched into a final toccata, and rising to my feet I began to wonder anew about Lyle.

14

LATER as we all assembled in the palace drawing-room prior to the mid-day Sunday dinner, I congratulated the Bishop on his sermon and added on an impulse: "I was hoping to visit a clergyman in your diocese before I left Starbridge, but it turns out he's away on holiday. His name's Philip Wetherall and he's an old friend of mine."

"Wetherall," said the Bishop. "Ah yes. The parish of Starrington Magna. An excellent wife, two well-behaved small children and a very vocal infant."

"I haven't met the offspring but the wife's splendid, I agree, and Philip himself is so hard-working and conscientious that I was most relieved to hear he was finally having a holiday." I had no intention of saying more but the other half of my personality evidently felt there was more to be said. Rapidly I murmured: "I feel guilty about my privileged ministry sometimes."

Jardine regarded me without expression. When he made no immediate reply I thought he might be considering my intercession an impertinence and my guilt an affectation, but suddenly he said: "I assure you Wetherall hasn't escaped either the eagle eye of my Archdeacon or my own keen interest. But I'm glad you spoke up for your friend, Dr. Ashworth; I'm glad to know you're not solely preoccupied with the seamy side of Church politics."

I managed to say: "It was a great sermon. It made me think. I want to change course, but . . . not so easy . . . sort of trapped . . . not sure I fully understand—"

"Go to your Bishop," said Jardine. "Ask him to help you find a new spiritual director in the Cambridge area. And do it soon."

The butler announced that dinner was served. Across the room the Colonel was finishing his pink gin and Mrs. Cobden-Smith was declaring that refrigerators ran more efficiently on electricity than on gas and Mrs. Jardine was telling her cousins what wonderful servants she had at the palace and Lyle was glancing at her watch and everyone was rising to their feet.

"But I don't want to go to my Bishop," my voice said to Jardine. "I don't want him thinking I'm in any sort of muddle—and anyway I'm fine, everything's fine, there's absolutely no need to bother my Bishop, no need at all."

"Come along, Alex!" called Mrs. Cobden-Smith. "The meal will get cold if we have to wait for you to say grace!"

Jardine ignored her. He said in a voice which would have been inaudible to the other people in the room: "The Fordite monks have a house in my diocese, as I'm sure you know. I'll have a word with the Abbot and ask him to recommend their best counsellor at Grantchester."

"That's very good of you, Bishop, but—"

"No buts. You absolutely must have proper counselling. Now let's make a speedy move to the table before Amy starts complaining about cold soup."

I followed him in silence to the dining-room.

15

I LEFT the palace an hour later. After the round of farewells had been smoothly accomplished and the words of gratitude warmly expressed to my hosts, all I said to Lyle in the porch was: "I'll be back."

Glancing into the driving mirror for a final view of the palace I saw she was still standing where I had left her, a small tense figure, enigmatic to the last, disturbingly alone.

16

WHEN I reached London some time later I steered my way through the stifling streets to my club in St. James's where I reserved a room for the night. Then leaving my car parked nearby I walked the short distance to the Starmouths' house in Curzon Street.

I was now more determined than ever to see Loretta Staviski in my quest for the evidence which would allow me to think the unthinkable. Rationally I still could not believe that Jardine had fallen into a gross moral error either with her or with anyone else, but I was beyond mere reason. I had sensed the bizarre in Lyle's distress the previous night, the inexplicable in her absence from Communion, the weird in the Bishop's attempt to gloss over her depression at the time of the Coronation and the sinister in his irritability as she and I had exchanged light-hearted remarks before Matins. I was now convinced that some very odd situation indeed existed at the palace at Starbridge, and although the mystery appeared increasingly intractable this only made me more determined to solve it. Taking a deep breath I sallied up the steps to the black front door of the Starmouths' tall, cream-coloured house and rang the bell.

However, I was destined to be disappointed; Lord and Lady Starmouth, I was told, had departed with their guest for their country home and were not expected back in London until the following Thursday. Retiring to my club I plotted an assault on Leatherhead, read the evening office and supped well off cold mutton and claret.

17

STARMOUTH COURT, slumbering in seclusion on its wooded hillside, overlooked a stretch of the Mole Valley which was attractively pastoral. Fields framed the water-meadows by the river, and beyond the fields the hills climbed steeply to give the landscape its balance and grace. It was hard to believe, as I approached the house on the morning after my arrival in London, that I was less than twenty miles from my club in the heart of the West End.

I showed my card to the keeper at the lodge, and when he opened the gates I drove up the steep winding drive. I was intrigued to see the house at close quarters after so many years of distant glimpses; the Queen Anne mansion was handsome, serene and well-preserved, like a wealthy dowager who had lived an uneventful life. Having parked the car I looked back towards the valley but the trees hid the view at ground level and the atmosphere of seclusion was heightened.

A modest young footman opened the door, and introducing myself I asked for Lady Starmouth.

"I'm sorry, sir," came the response, "but Lady Starmouth went into Leatherhead this morning and she isn't expected back until lunch-time."

I suddenly knew fortune was going to favour me.

"Then perhaps," I said, "I could see Professor Staviski if she's at home."

"I'll inquire, sir. Please come in."

He took my card and showed me into a small morning-room which faced the drive. I waited. For a long time nothing happened, and I was just wondering if the Professor had gone into hiding in order to preserve her guilty secret when high heels tapped across the hall, the door opened abruptly and at last I saw the woman who had proved such a pastoral disaster for Jardine.

VIII

"I was much interested and not a little surprised at her confidence, lack of reticence, and complete detachment from conventional sex-morality. . . ."

More Letters of
HERBERT HENSLEY HENSON,
ed. E. F. Braley

I

I HAD forgotten Lady Starmouth's estimate that Loretta was not much older than I was. I had been expecting a woman in her early fifties, a contemporary of Lady Starmouth and Mrs. Jardine, so it came as a considerable surprise when I found myself confronted by a woman barely past forty who looked younger; evidently the disastrous husband had been acquired in her teens. I had also been expecting someone plain, partly because of Lady Starmouth's remark that Loretta failed to conform to fashionable standards of beauty and partly because Jardine had portrayed her as a woman lacking in self-esteem, but this woman was smart, well-groomed, striking. She had dark hair, swept smoothly into a knot on top of her head, a suntanned complexion and an hour-glass figure which I immediately noted and fancied. Behind her stylish glasses her eyes were a vivid blue.

She looked me up and down with that unabashed curiosity which I had found before in American women oblivious of English constraint, and I sensed that she too was noting what she saw and fancying it. I smiled. She smiled back, and at once I knew we had travelled a long way before a word had been spoken.

"Dr. Ashworth?" she said in a slightly husky voice as she held out her hand. "What a coincidence! Evelyn's been telling me all about you."

This hardly surprised me; Lady Starmouth would have been quick to inform her that someone was taking much too keen an interest in that old friendship with Jardine, but as far as I could tell Loretta seemed quite unconcerned by my questionable invasion of her privacy.

"How do you do, Professor," I began formally, but she immediately set all formality aside.

"Call me Loretta," she said. "Everyone else over here does. Can I call you Charles or will you think I'm a scarlet woman out to vamp you?"

After the straitlaced atmosphere of Starbridge this was heady stuff indeed. "Please do call me Charles," I said, "and if you want to vamp me I'm sure I can give you the appropriate pastoral attention."

She laughed. "That's pretty good," she said, "for an Englishman. Well, Charles—is it too early for a drink? Yes, I guess it is. But how about some coffee?"

We decided there was nothing wrong with drinking coffee at eleven o'clock in the morning. The servant was summoned, the order given, and in response to my polite inquiry about her journey Loretta began to talk about her voyage across the Atlantic. I was soon so intrigued by her story about a Roman Catholic priest whom she had taught to dance the Black Bottom that I almost forgot to inquire after Lady Starmouth.

"She's calling on the local vicar," said Loretta, lighting a cigarette, "but I didn't feel in the mood for inspecting some dusty exhibit in Evelyn's clerical collection—with the result that here I am, entertaining the Archbishop of Canterbury's private eye!"

"And of course you're thinking my visit's the most monstrous piece of impertinence—"

"Not in the least! I'm enthralled . . . Sorry, I should have offered you a cigarette—do you smoke?"

"Not in my clerical collar."

"Maybe I should start wearing a clerical collar—I smoke far too much . . . Ah, here's the coffee." Our conversation was briefly suspended, but as soon as the servant had gone she added, amused: "Does old Lang truly think my infatuation with the local vicar twenty years ago could rock the Church of England?"

"I promise you that if Dr. Lang ever learns of your existence it certainly won't be from me. He merely dispatched me to Starbridge to make certain Dr. Jardine's impregnable from scandal, but I've come to the conclusion that although Dr. Jardine's made the occasional pastoral mistake there's no question of any serious moral error."

"Then why are you here? I mean, don't get me wrong—I'm delighted to meet you, but I can't quite see—"

"This is where I make my confession," I said smiling at her. "I've come here out of sheer curiosity because I've become an admirer of the Bishop and I'd like to hear more about those days in Mayfair when he was the same age as I am now. Are you by any chance free for lunch? There's an attractive hotel at Box Hill with a reputation for good food."

She was intrigued. "Will you produce a curate to preserve the proprieties?"

I laughed. "I don't have a curate!"

"In that case, yes, lunch would be wonderful—many thanks!" She laughed too. "Alex used to bring a curate whenever he called at my apartment," she said, shedding ash from her cigarette with a casual flick of her wrist. "Mr. Jardine, I used to call him in those days—how we didn't all die of respectability I'll never know, but I didn't call him Alex until right at the end when I put my cards on the table and found I'd overplayed my hand."

I said uneasily: "Perhaps you'd rather not talk about him."

"Charles, it's twenty years since I met Alex Jardine and nineteen years since I last saw him. A lot of water's flowed under the bridge since then."

"Nevertheless—"

"I'm the reassuring proof that contrary to all the sentimental nineteenth-century novels, frustrated romantic love needn't prove fatal. In fact if you want to talk about him I'd enjoy a reminiscence. What a man he was! Of course I can see why I fell for him and it wasn't just because I was lonely after a broken marriage. It was because he didn't regard it as an inexcusable breach of good taste for a woman to be born with brains. Oh, he was such fun! We used to laugh and laugh, even with the curate in attendance . . . But we can talk more about Alex at lunch. Tell me about you. Evelyn said you'd written a book which had mesmerised all the theologians . . ."

Time slipped lissomly away as the conversation glided from my book to a survey of academic life on both sides of the Atlantic. I forgot Jardine. I even forgot lunch until somewhere a clock struck twelve and Loretta said: "I'd better throw on some rags suitable for a country outing." And as she rose to her feet, she added: "Maybe I'll follow in Evelyn's footsteps after all and start collecting clergymen! They're obviously much more fun than stamps or antiques."

I laughed, just as she had intended that I should, but all the time I was wondering if in her lavish use of that casual American charm she was making a determined effort to annihilate those suspicions of mine which so obstinately refused to die.

2

THREE quarters of an hour later I broke my rule of abstinence from mid-day drinking and took a sip of a very dry Chablis. We were sitting in the dining-room of the hotel two miles away, and beyond the window of our alcove the garden stretched to the river which wound beneath the densely wooded slopes of Box Hill. I had been tempted to order champagne, but no clergyman had any business to be offering champagne to a lady he had known less than two hours. Merely by taking her out to lunch I was once more travelling at the speed of light, and I was well aware that I now had to be careful. I had not misinterpreted Loretta's un-English informality. I knew she could never have maintained her friendship with Lady Starmouth if her reputation had been other than exemplary, but her personality was so conducive to unguarded friendship that it would have been easy to make the mistake of assuming she was an adventuress. I suddenly remembered Lyle talking of the mystery of personality during our visit to Starbury Ring, and I thought that although Loretta was emanating an aura of gregariousness the reality beyond this mask was almost certainly more complex than I could at present perceive.

"Is this the moment when I embark on my journey into nostalgia?" she inquired when Jardine's name inevitably recurred in our conversation. "What a wonderful opportunity to be self-indulgent!"

"Well, if you're absolutely sure you don't mind—"

"A couple more glasses of this beautiful wine and you'll be wondering how to stop the tidal flow of my reminiscences! But let me just ask you this: how much do you already know?"

That was an awkward question. Since I wanted to see how closely her account tallied with the official version, the less I revealed the better. With care I said: "Dr. Jardine mentioned your sad circumstances in 1917 and how he'd tried to help you."

"I hope he stressed how ruthlessly he observed the proprieties. I don't want you to think he played Edward VIII to my Mrs. Simpson."

"But I've already told you I don't suspect him of any serious error."

"True. But I still have this nasty feeling," she said lightly, looking me straight in the eyes, "that you think we had a swing together from those Mayfair chandeliers."

"Dr. Jardine was newly married and had just received a dazzling preferment," I said, looking straight back. "I don't find it so difficult to believe he ruthlessly observed the proprieties."

The waiter arrived with our soup but as soon as he had departed she said: "Alex's hands weren't just tied by the marriage and preferment. He had to be particularly careful where I was concerned because in those days a woman who left her husband was socially as dead as a dodo. It's true that the War was hammering away at the conventions, but of course as a clergyman Alex had to keep up the good old prewar standards and so I wasn't surprised when his wife at first refused to receive me . . .

However, eventually he persuaded her to invite me to tea in the name of Christian charity."

"What was your verdict?"

"On Carrie? I thought she was pathetic. There she was with this husband who was just plain dynamite, and all she could do was simper around in a tea-gown and talk about the weather! My first reaction was: how does he stand it? I was bored to tears inside of five minutes. However, I should have realised that no stranger really knows what goes on in any marriage—God knows, no one had a clue what was going on in mine—and the truth was that Carrie suited Alex down to the ground. He didn't want to be married to a brain-box. He wanted to be married to an ornament who always went to bed looking sizzling in her latest Parisian nightgown. But it didn't occur to me then that Carrie could have her sexy side. I was very young, only twenty-one in 1917, and although I'd learnt a thing or two from my awful husband—whom you British would call a sod—I was still hopelessly ingenuous when it came to interpreting human relationships. I just jumped to the conclusion that the marriage was a failure and that Alex was longing for some extramarital entertainment."

"But no devout clergyman could even consider adultery, let alone commit it!"

"Sure, but I was very ignorant and I just thought clergymen were laymen in fancy dress. I didn't realise that a clergyman really does see life a little differently from the average boring old layman who's only interested in chasing sex and money."

"You weren't religious?"

"Not in the least, and certainly not after a hellish marriage. The War was another reason too why I misread the situation. I'd become quite used to the idea of everybody surreptitiously sleeping with everyone else whenever they could snatch a few days' leave from the horror of the Front—not that I was ever promiscuous; my husband had made me feel no man could possibly do other than throw up in my presence, but when Alex showed no signs of throwing up I naturally started to hope."

"But you concealed your feelings."

"Of course. Evelyn would have been shocked if she'd known how I felt, and Evelyn was my lifeline—I'd have gone to pieces without her. But in fact concealment wasn't so difficult—one can conceal almost anything if one lives in the hope that eventually one's dreams are going to come true, and my dream was that Alex would have an affair even if there was no possibility of divorce and remarriage. My God, how naive I was! It truly is the most crippling handicap not to have a religious upbringing. I thought I was so smart but suddenly I found out that a complete dimension of my mind lay undeveloped and that spiritually I was on a par with an imbecile."

"And now?"

"Now I'm old enough to be less arrogant and more humble . . . Maybe religion comes with age. I don't believe in the Incarnation—sorry, Charles!—so I guess I'm not a real Christian, am I, but I do believe in God now and I certainly admire Christ as a great man so I shan't feel too much of a hypocrite when I go to church with Evelyn next Sunday."

"Did Jardine try to talk about Christianity to you?"

"Oh sure, and when *he* talked about it I believed the whole story—Incarnation, Virgin Birth, the lot. But then Alex could make you believe anything—and not just because he could mesmerise you with those amazing golden eyes. He had tremendous powers of logic and reason. In fact I always thought he'd have made a good lawyer—the kind who can argue that black really is white and that if you keep seeing black you have some grave defect in your vision."

I laughed before saying: "But if you were learning about Christianity from the most persuasive of instructors, why didn't you see that you were wasting your time being in love with a clergyman?"

"How could I see? Love's blind, and my love was blind until one day in 1918 when . . . Has Alex told you about this?"

"About Lady Starmouth's brother being killed in action? Yes. Dr. Jardine said he came down to Starmouth Court to call on her, and after lunch when she was resting you suggested a walk so that you could reveal your feelings."

"That's right," she said. "That's the way it was." She took another sip of her wine. "We walked down to the bridge over the river . . . How lovely it was—such pretty country! There's a railroad track running parallel to the river in this valley but it's cleverly constructed on an embankment so it somehow avoids being a blot on the landscape. I remember I was just admiring the view when this little train appeared like a clockwork toy below us and huffed and puffed its way into the woods. We both laughed and said how cute it was—and that was the moment when he realised exactly how I felt about him . . . Why, Charles, how bemused you look! What's the problem?"

"I was trying to work out how you looked down on the railway line from that bridge over the river."

"Well, we—" She stopped. "You know the location?"

"Yes, I do. I was brought up near here at Epsom."

"Ah." She sipped her wine composedly. "Well, then it'll be easier for you to understand what I'm talking about. When we left Starmouth Court we walked along the road to the bridge and then turned off along a path which followed the river-bank. But after a few minutes we turned off that path too and followed a track which led under a second bridge—the railroad bridge—and into a steep field which had a clump of trees in the middle of it. You'll recall the field I mean—it's clearly visible from the main highway."

"I remember it well, yes," I said, but I was thinking of Jardine's statement with its massive omission: "We walked to the river. We walked back." I heard myself add: "I remember picnicking in that field when I was a boy and waving at the passing trains."

"Alex and I waved at our train, too. How we laughed! But then the next moment the train was gone and I finally began to understand what being a clergyman was all about." She paused before saying abruptly: "Alex said he couldn't abandon the vows he'd made at his ordination. He quoted the Bible, something about how once you'd put your hand to the plough you couldn't turn back, and finally he just said: 'I'm not going to end up like my father.' "

"Ah!"

"Freudian, wasn't it? But in fact God left Freud far behind in the end. Alex said: 'Try to understand. God's not a fairy tale. He's real, He's there and I have to serve Him as a clergyman, but I won't be able to serve Him if I break His rules.' Then he put it in another way. He said: 'If I broke the rules I'd be damaging myself, sliding into a divided life which induces a cancer of the soul. It would be the end of my life as I know it and the beginning of a new life where I'd wind up in a hell of guilt, mentally ill and cut off from God.' He made it all seem so blindingly obvious—and of course I just couldn't take it. A man who not only had principles but lived up to them! I felt as if my cynicism had been blasted to bits; I felt not only rejected but defenceless, annihilated . . . Poor Alex! I sobbed and sobbed and the scene was—oh, indescribably harrowing! But Alex, from a clerical point of view, was perfect. No wonder he's a bishop now. He deserves to be."

We had both finished our soup and again conversation ceased as the waiter removed our plates. Then I said: "I think Dr. Jardine deserves to be a bishop, too. But then I never seriously thought that anything you said would make me think otherwise."

I sensed rather than saw her relief.

We settled down to enjoy the remainder of our meal.

3

ALL I could think was how much she must have loved him not only to defend him to the hilt nineteen years after the disaster but to defend him at such cost to her self-esteem. In fact the most suspicious aspect of the present situation was Loretta's frankness. Even after allowing for her American informality I thought it highly unlikely that she would welcome the opportunity to talk to a stranger about a painful episode which showed her in such a pitiable light.

My imagination accelerated. I pictured Lady Starmouth saying to her: "My dear, the most frightful thing's happened—a young clergyman's found out about you and Alex, and to make matters worse he's not just any young clergyman, he's the Archbishop of Canterbury's spy!" And I felt I could understand all too clearly why there had been such a long delay before Loretta had come to the morning-room to meet me. As soon as she had seen the name on my card she had feared the worst and paused to work out the best way to defuse the danger. I could almost hear her saying to herself: "Charm him and disarm him. Make him think I have nothing to hide."

Putting a brake on my imagination I reminded myself that still nothing had been proved. Jardine had certainly made a large omission from his narrative, but in the circumstances that was natural; he would never have wanted me to know that he and Loretta had walked deep into the countryside far from all those passing pony-traps. He could still be guilty of nothing worse than a minor indiscretion, but nevertheless my suspicions were now thoroughly roused. I reminded myself that he had been under acute domestic strain in 1918 following the stillborn birth of his child and his wife's nervous breakdown. I reminded myself that Loretta was an attractive woman who had been deeply in love with him. Was it really possible that Jardine, despite his faith in the concept of platonic friendship, had had no perception of the strong undercurrent of sexuality which must have inevitably permeated their encounters?

I thought not. I was now sure he had known of her feelings long before that September day in 1918 and I was sure too that he must have been strongly tempted to reciprocate them. Yet I was unable to see how I could prove these convictions were true. Loretta had clearly reached the limit of all she was prepared to tell me about the incident, and she was quite shrewd enough to sidestep any attempt I might make at cross-examination.

I thought of Jardine, and suddenly I remembered him stooping to pluck *The Murder of Roger Ackroyd* from the bookshelf in his library. Inspiration dawned. I remembered the mystery novels I had read. When a detective wanted to test a theory he was unable to prove, he returned to the scene of the crime and staged a reconstruction.

4

"... *SO* the Bishop of London shouted out: 'I say to you that the streets of Hell are paved with champagne, fast cars and loose women!' whereupon an innocent voice from the audience called back: 'O Death, where is thy sting?' "

Loretta shook with laughter. "Is that a true story?"

"If it's not, it ought to be. Look, I've just had an idea—that was a large lunch and I fancy some exercise. Would you like to come for a walk with me down by the river?"

"That sounds an attractive proposition, but unless you want me to get bogged down in the meadows I'll have to go back to Starmouth Court to change out of these high heels."

I had anticipated this. "We'll call at the house, then drive to the river and leave the car at the bridge."

"The bridge where—"

"I'm sorry, am I being insensitive? If you'd rather not go near that spot again—"

"Oh, for heaven's sake!" she exclaimed. "Why make a big deal over a love affair that never happened? Let's go and wave at another cute little train!"

I was now sure she was bending over backwards to allay my suspicions.

We went outside to my car.

5

I WAS not looking forward to meeting Lady Starmouth, but to my relief the footman told us she was having a siesta. I thought she would decide I was behaving in a very questionable manner for a clergyman, and I was sure she would be deeply suspicious, even deeply annoyed, by my interest in her guest.

Loretta kept me waiting ten minutes in the morning-room. I was just wondering why it was taking her so long to slip out of her high heels when she reappeared not only in different shoes but in an informal sunfrock with a large matching hat. She looked foreign, exotic. The sunfrock had a neckline which was well within the bounds of decency but which nobody could have described as high.

"This is the coolest dress I have," she said as we stepped outside, and casting me a sympathetic glance she added: "It's a pity you can't strip off that hot uniform of yours."

"What a delectably improper suggestion!"

She laughed. "Relax!" she said. "I haven't forgotten you're a clergyman!"

"I'm glad at least one of us remembers." We were both laughing by that time but I knew I had to apply an emotional brake. "I'm sorry," I said abruptly as I held open the door of the car for her. "My tongue's running away with me."

"Is that a sin?"

"No, just a mistake. Like smoking in a clerical collar."

"A breach of self-discipline?"

"Yes." I was surprised by her understanding. "Exactly." I said no more and seconds later we were on our way down the drive. On the main road, Loretta said unexpectedly: "God's at the centre of your life too, isn't He? He doesn't just fade away when things are going well, as He does with most people. He's there all the time—and like Alex you *know* He's there."

I said obliquely: "The sun's not a mere disc in the sky which you can see whenever you bother to look up. The warmth of the sun permeates the world even on a clouded day, and that's not mere wishful thinking or sensual illusion. You can see the plants reacting to the warmth. It's real."

"I wouldn't quarrel with that. But I still think the ability to be religious—to keep God constantly in view—is a gift. It's like playing the piano well. A lot of people long to be accomplished pianists but if they've insufficient talent they fail, no matter how hard they practise and how many lessons they take."

"I agree we're not all born with supreme mystical powers, but on the other hand a certain level of spirituality is within everyone's reach. It's a question of . . . But no," I said, smiling at her, "I really mustn't lecture you as if you were one of my undergraduates."

She smiled back. "Aren't you going to try to convert me to Christianity?"

"The best way to convert someone like you is probably not to adopt an intellectual approach. You'd find the doctrinal arguments mentally stimulating but your soul would remain untouched."

"Then how would you go about converting me?"

"I'd say you'd be more impressed by action than by words. For instance, back in 1918 what was it that impressed you most about Christianity? Was it Dr. Jardine talking hypnotically about the Incarnation—or was it Dr. Jardine rejecting you in the face of a very great temptation?"

The car was approaching the river. I could see the bridge ahead of us, but as I glanced sideways at Loretta I sensed her thoughts were far away.

"Christianity did make an impact on me when he ended our friendship," she said at last. "I thought that all men—real men—ever thought about was chasing money and women. To find a man—a real man—who thought there was more to life than that . . . Yes. It made me feel I had to try to understand."

"But understanding proved elusive?"

"Not entirely. I see Christianity as a beautiful dream. But that's what being human's all about, isn't it? That's what sets us apart from the apes. We have beautiful dreams and the finest lives are spent trying to make those dreams come true."

"To think of Christianity as a dream is to ignore its reality, although perhaps what you're really saying is that the finest lives express man's yearning for transcendent values. That's real enough—but just listen to me! Trust a theologian to make the nobler aspirations of humanity sound dry as dust!"

We laughed, and driving across the bridge I halted the car on the verge. But then some unexpected impulse made me add: "I agree that a lot of men appear to be interested only in money and sex but I think too that a lot of men would secretly like to believe there's more to life than the materialist's treadmill. However, society forces them to chase worldly success in order to be esteemed, and then they chase women either to forget how unhappy they are chasing success or because they see women as boosting their value in the eyes of the world."

"So all men's troubles arise from the pursuit of worldly success? That's an interesting theory, Charles! I wonder if I'm beginning to learn a little about you at last!"

I said lightly: "Am I such a mystery?"

"We're all mysteries," said Loretta. "That's what makes life so fascinating."

I could not deny it.

We left the car and set out on our walk.

6

THE ground sloped from the road to the river which meandered lazily beneath the bridge, and when we reached the path by the bank I paused to shade my eyes with my hand. On either side of the valley the wooded hills shimmered in a heat-haze and on my left the water sparkled hotly in the brilliant light.

Loretta paused too, and as I saw the stillness of her face I said suddenly: "Are you sure you want to go through with this?"

"That sounds as if we're on our way to get married. Yes, sure I'm sure! Let's exorcise all the past horrors . . . Do they still perform exorcisms in the Church of England?"

"Nowadays it's generally regarded as a somewhat unsavoury superstition."

"How odd! Is it wise for the Church to abandon exorcism to laymen?"

"What laymen?"

"They're called psycho-analysts," she said dryly. "Maybe you've heard of them. They have this cute little god called Freud and a very well-paid priesthood and the faithful go weekly to worship on couches—"

"Ever tried it?"

"Sure. My analyst told me that the reason why I kept trying to marry impossible men was because deep down I didn't want to get married at all—and after two years of lying on his couch and reviewing my past I came to the reluctant conclusion that he was right."

"What extraordinary things go on in America!"

"Maybe. But the fact remains that the analyst exorcised my demon of despair when I was spiritually sick."

"Well, of course the Church provides counselling for the spiritually sick, but *exorcism!* That's a different matter altogether!"

"But is it? Isn't it all one? If no one finds you when you're spiritually sick, don't the demons eventually possess you to such an extent that you end up climbing the walls and screaming for help?"

"But is it really appropriate, in this scientific twentieth century, to call a nervous breakdown demonic possession?"

"I don't see why not. Personally I find it a lot easier to believe in demons and the Devil—especially in this scientific twentieth century—than in God and the angels. If the world's fundamentally evil, I'd say the difference between a nervous breakdown and demonic possession is purely a matter of semantics."

"I'd deny the world's fundamentally evil, no matter how prevalent evil may be. I see you have dangerous tendencies," I said, smiling at her, "towards the Gnostic heresy!"

"The most dangerous tendency I have is to talk too much. Why on earth did I tell you about my analyst? Now you'll be thinking I'm crazy."

"My dear Loretta—"

"Maybe it's time I kept quiet for a while."

The path forked ahead of us, and leaving the river we turned uphill towards the bridge which carried the railway line over a gap in the embankment. I did make attempts to renew the conversation but her replies were monosyllabic, and by the time we reached the bridge we had once more relapsed into silence. Beyond the bridge rose the steep field she had described, the field in which I had picnicked as a boy with my parents and my brother Peter.

"It's odd how close the past seems sometimes," I said as we paused for breath. Out of respect for the severity of the gradient we had avoided struggling directly uphill and were cutting a diagonal path across the field, but the way was still steep. Ahead of us the spinney, a dark cluster of trees clinging to the hillside, once more stirred my memories; I had retired there to sulk after squabbling with Peter and arousing my father's irritation. "I feel I've only to look back now over my shoulder," I said, "and I'll see myself as a child long ago on that family picnic."

She made no reply. She was standing motionless, listening, and as I listened too I heard the distant murmur which had caught her attention.

It was the train.

"We were farther up the hillside last time—nearer the trees—oh, I must get there, I must, I want it to be just the same . . ." She dashed forward, I hurried after her and all the time the noise was increasing as the train thundered down the valley towards us.

Below the spinney she halted. We could see the train now. It was approaching from the left, and beyond the railway line, beyond the river, beyond the water-meadows I could see the main road and the miniature cars and the Starmouths' house on the hill. The train, looking curiously like an over-sized toy against a painted backdrop, roared closer.

"We must wave!" cried Loretta. "Wave, Charles, wave!"

We waved. The engine driver saluted gamely, and as the train swept past, assorted children waved back at us from their window-seats. Then in a flash the episode ended. The train disappeared from sight beyond the far corner of the field, the noise died away and all was quiet again. I turned to Loretta, but my amused comment was never spoken for I saw her cheeks were wet with tears. The next moment she was stumbling across the few yards which separated us from the spinney, and as I stared after her she disappeared among the trees.

I allowed her time to compose herself, but when she showed no sign of reappearing I followed her. The trees were guarded by dense undergrowth; it took me longer than I had anticipated to find a gap in that barrier of bramble-bushes, but once I had stepped into the shadows I saw her at once. She had retreated to a secluded spot on the far side of the spinney and was sitting amidst a patch of bracken. I glimpsed the strained lines of her red sunfrock as she clasped her knees in a foetal position, and as I drew nearer I could see her shoulders shaking as she wept. She had taken off her glasses but when she heard me coming she scrabbled to retrieve them.

I knelt down, covering her hands with mine, and the glasses remained unworn. "Forgive me," I said. "I should never have brought you here."

"I thought I could take it, but . . ." She began to cry again.

I put my arm around her. It was an instinctive gesture born of guilt and I withdrew almost immediately as prudence triumphed over sympathy, but the message had been communicated; she looked up.

"My God, this is strange!" she said in a shaking voice. "It's just as if you're him and it's happening all over again."

We stared at each other. Then as I slowly put my arm around her once more I knew beyond doubt that it was not she who had suggested that walk to the river nineteen years ago and not she who had made the first move beyond the bounds of convention.

7

I SAID: "I think I'm going to do something very stupid," and I kissed her on the mouth. Then I said: "Of course I'm crazy but I'll think about that later," and I kissed her again.

All she said when I eventually eased aside the straps of her sunfrock was: "I don't want you to suffer the torment Alex suffered. Oh God, Charles, if only you knew what we went through—"

"It's different this time. I'm not married."

"Yes, but—"

I interrupted her with a kiss. More time passed and when at last I paused to slip off my jacket she said no more about suffering but merely reached out to touch my collar.

She whispered: "I remember the way it fastens at the back."

And then I knew I could begin to think the unthinkable.

IX

"I am grieved that you also have to sustain the shock and shame of clerical scandals . . . how much clerical failure and scandal I have witnessed. I am sure our way is far more difficult than most men realise: and that of all men we have most need to remember: 'Let he that thinketh he standeth take heed lest he fall.' "

More Letters of
HERBERT HENSLEY HENSON,
ed. E. F. Braley

I

THE bracken was cool against my hot skin. I was aware of that coolness as I fought and won the initial battle for control over my excitement which was very deep and very powerful. There was only one awkward moment. It came when I sensed she was ready and moved myself into position between her thighs. She said suddenly: "You're going in."

I halted. "It's too soon?"

"No, no—" She pulled me close and kissed me with such fervour that disaster nearly intervened. I had to twist my mouth away to regain my control.

When I could speak again I said: "It's safe? Will I have to withdraw?" but again she said: "No, no—" and again she pulled me close until at last I began to penetrate her.

The first ninety seconds were marred by my dread of an early finish, but once I was inside she seemed more aware of that danger and I was conscious of her sensitivity as she matched her response to mine. Gradually the disadvantages stemming from abstinence faded and the rewards became predominant; once the battle for control had been won I knew I could sustain myself for a long time.

"Are you all right?"

"Dumb question!"

"The bracken's hardly a well-sprung mattress."

"I wouldn't even care if it was concrete." She raised her mouth to mine and later I heard her murmur: "It's been such a long time."

"How long?"

"Three years. I was so tired of the pain of nothing working out . . . And you?"

But I merely drew her into a different position and thrust myself deeper into her hot curving flesh.

2

WHEN we had finished we were too exhausted to do more than lie in silence and watch the blue sky beyond the overhanging branches of the tree above us. My mind was empty. I knew the pain would begin later but meanwhile I was anaesthetised, every fibre of my body satiated and every ache of tension smoothed away. I longed again, as I had longed so often before, for the intimacy of married life, but that reminded me of Lyle and immediately my mind began to divide. I squeezed my eyes shut as if I could erase the present by refusing to look at it, but still my two personalities struggled to separate in a battle which lay beyond my understanding.

"Cigarette?" said Loretta, retrieving a packet from her handbag.

"Thanks." I was diverted. My mind emptied itself again and the battle was suspended.

After we had smoked in idleness for a time she said: "How the hell do you manage, not being married?"

"Contrary to popular belief no one ever dies of chastity." I began to trace the outline of her breasts with one finger.

"True, but let's be honest—chastity can be pretty damned uncomfortable. Why haven't you remarried?"

"Why haven't you?"

"Oh, I'm an easy case to explain." She too started tracing. I felt her finger slowly circle my chest. "My analyst and I figured out that (a) most men can't cope with my brains, (b) most men can't cope with my success, (c) I don't like playing second fiddle, (d) I'm not domestic, (e) my husband was enough to put anyone off marriage for life, and (f) I've never really got over Alex. I kept waiting to meet someone who could match him, and by the time I realised that wasn't going to happen I was past the age when I felt inclined to compromise."

"You must have loved him very much."

"Well, of course we'd have married if it hadn't been for that dumb wife. My husband wouldn't have been a problem because by the end of 1918 he'd drunk himself to death, but you know, Charles, I often wonder how Alex and I would have got along. I'm not fundamentally a religious person and I've got an independent streak which might have made marital life difficult. In fact I think I'd have been a very unsatisfactory wife for a bishop."

"But if you'd married Jardine at that stage of your life when your mature personality still wasn't completely formed—"

"Yes, I might have adapted, but we'll never know, will we? It's the world of might-have-been . . . like that second marriage you've never made. Why don't you want to remarry?"

"I do." I stubbed out our cigarettes and began to caress her again.

"Then why haven't you done so years ago? Maybe you're like me. Maybe deep down you don't want to get married at all."

"But I do! I must! I—oh, don't let's talk about it any more, I hate even thinking of my baffling and intractable problems—"

"But maybe you should. Some problems don't just go away by themselves. They're like demons and they have to be exorcised."

"Well, I don't know any exorcists and I've got my demons under control," I said, but as soon as the words left my mouth I panicked. "Oh my God, what am I doing, what's happening to me—"

"Charles—darling—"

"I'm all right," I said, ramming myself so deep inside her that she gasped. "I'm all right, I'm all right, I'm all right—"

I had anaesthetised myself again.

The panic faded.

I settled down to saturate myself in sex.

3

THIS time the experience began differently. It was darker, more disjointed, but I knew it reflected my inner disorder and she knew it too for she sought in various subtle ways to soothe me. I responded. Slowly I relaxed until at last I was the one on my back in the bracken and her soft flesh above me was a delicious contrast to the hard ground beneath my spine. The only unsuccessful moment came when I guided us into different positions in an attempt to share her finish; we slipped apart and the climax came when I was outside her.

"Damn."

"It's okay." She held me tightly in her arms while we recovered and only released me when I reached again for the cigarettes. Eventually I said after meditating on her present pleasure and her past abstinence: "I suppose it's easier for a woman to cope with chastity."

"Thanks. I'll think of that next time I'm dying of frustration. I'm sure it'll be a great comfort."

"I'm sorry, that was appallingly insensitive of me—"

"Funnily enough Alex made a remark like that, too. He spoke as if no woman could possible imagine what hell the celibate life could be."

"How did *he* manage before he married at thirty-seven?"

"I don't know and later I always wished I'd asked. In the old days Evelyn and I often used to speculate about his early life, but we never reached any firm conclusions."

"Tell me, how much does Lady Starmouth actually know about you and Jardine?"

"Well, she knew at the end that Alex was just as much in love with me as I was with him—I mean, she saw us, we couldn't have kept it from her, we were in pieces. However, there was no question of her not standing by us and doing all she could to cover up the mess. She'd made up her mind that Alex was going to go right to the top of the Church of England."

"Wasn't she angry with you for jeopardising him?"

"Livid. But she forgave me. You might not think it, but Evelyn's another of those rare people who really do make an effort to live up to their religious beliefs."

"How appalled she must have been when I found out about you!"

"She said she nearly died. She apologised to me because she had explained the incident away by depicting me as a tiresome neurotic female and Alex as purity personified, but what choice did she have? I took the same line just now at lunch, but of course . . . the truth was very different."

"The love was always reciprocated?"

"Always. We fell in love right away when we met in 1917, but my God, how he fought against it! That awful curate whom he used to bring along as a chaperone! And those awful minutes alone at the Starmouths' house whenever Evelyn was called away to the phone—but he never kissed me, not even then. It would have been too dangerous; anyone could have walked in . . . But the worst part was visiting him at home with his wife. I didn't want to go, but he felt the fact that his wife had received me would kill any gossip which might be simmering."

"What were his feelings about his wife by that time?"

"When we were here he said he'd realised on his honeymoon that he'd made a frightful mistake but he was sure the situation would be redeemed when they had a family. Well, the kids didn't happen, did they, though back in 1918 she'd just had a baby and no one knew she'd never conceive again. Alex said it had been a terrible year, the child arriving stillborn, Carrie having a nervous breakdown, he getting no sex for months on end . . . He didn't exactly mention sex in the same breath as Carrie and the baby, but I had no trouble getting the message that sex was important to him. In fact in the end he said: 'The marriage could be worse. When Carrie's well she's very dutiful.' Dutiful—ugh! What a repulsive Victorian euphemism! That was one of the moments when I remembered he was seventeen years older than I was. Anyway I was vilely jealous to think of her having him several times a week and I became more jealous than ever when he told me he'd be happy to make love every night. However, he said he thought that would be selfish—probably he was frightened in case she developed a dislike for it. It meant so much to him that he was prepared to exercise a moderate amount of restraint."

"I simply can't understand how he could have stayed chaste from his ordination till the age of thirty-seven. Surely he must have had lapses!"

"Maybe—but maybe not. Remember Freud. Sex can so often be affected by what's going on in the mind."

"You think there could be psychological as well as religious reasons for Jardine's chastity during those years?"

"Where sex is concerned," said Loretta, "anything's possible. For instance, his father was one of the hellfire-and-damnation school and that kind of guy can make his children feel guilty about sex, particularly if he feels guilty about it himself. Alex might have taken some time to get over that. Then when he was ordained he was so violently Anglo-Catholic (reacting against Dad the Fundamentalist) that he even vowed himself to celibacy, so obviously it took him some time to get over *that*. Then he was given some terrible parish where he slaved himself into a physical if not a nervous breakdown, and *that* must have sublimated his sexual energy nicely. But the most important factor of all was that he was never deprived of female companionship for long, and personally I believe that loneliness, rather than lack of sex, is often the reason why celibacy becomes intolerable. He had this stepmother—"

"Here we go again. I keep hearing about this stepmother. I've even wondered if they were having an affair."

"I'd doubt that."

"Why?"

"Because I don't think Alex would ever enter into a continuing illicit relationship," said Loretta, voicing my own insuperable objection to this theory. "He proved that when he rejected me. It would have been easy for us to have had an affair—after all, I was living apart from my husband in my own apartment—but he wouldn't do it even though he was crazy about me."

"That's certainly very significant."

"Any clergyman can have an isolated lapse which he can atone for afterwards," said Loretta. "Clergymen are human beings, not angels. But how can a devout clergyman pursue his calling if he continuously lives in sin?"

"He either ends the sin or becomes an apostate."

"Well, Alex certainly wasn't an apostate when I knew him. He was a believer through and through."

The ménage à trois at the palace was beginning to look innocent again, but the thought of Lyle was still too difficult to endure. Stubbing out my cigarette I turned once more to Loretta, and in the manner of a patient begging his nurse for a pain-killing injection I whispered: "Love me."

4

THE strength came as soon as I touched her but she made me wait as she kissed my body and drew her hands over my thighs. At last when I was too strong to bear further delay she yielded; our positions changed; I linked us again and felt her flesh enclose mine as she expelled her breath in pleasure. I clung to her. She stroked my hair and for some seconds I did not move but remained in that position of extreme intimacy. At last I said: "I want to confide in you." I had realised I could fuse my two personalities by drawing the past into the present and bringing together within the same boundary of time and space the Charles of Starbridge and the Charles who was lying naked on that Surrey hillside.

"Then go ahead," she said, still stroking my hair. "I promise you can trust me."

The sexual strength slackened as if the power had been switched to other channels. Slipping out I buried my face for a second in her breasts before embarking on the full story of my visit to Starbridge.

The tale took some time to tell but finally I heard myself say: "You must be appalled by the idea of me making love to you while I'm in love with someone else. I'm appalled myself. I don't understand what's going on, but I'm beginning to think there are two mysteries here, the mystery of what's going on at the palace and the mystery of what's going on in my head—and the most peculiar thing of all is that these two mysteries seem somehow to be connected . . . Or does that make me sound completely crazy in addition to being thoroughly immoral?"

Loretta did not respond with a quick reassurance as a lesser woman might have done. Nor did she make any tart comment about Lyle. Instead after careful thought she said: "No, I don't think you're crazy. And I don't think you're fundamentally immoral either. But I do think you could be fundamentally confused."

"That's a very generous judgement—"

"I'm not interested in being generous, just in being accurate. Charles, are you sure you're in love with this girl? If one's confused it becomes harder to distinguish between truth and illusion, and in my opinion your instantaneous attraction to Lyle does suggest there might be some degree of illusion going on."

"I'm quite certain my feelings are genuine."

"Yes, but . . . Okay, let's leave Lyle and turn to Alex because this is where you seem to be very confused indeed. Your interest in his past borders on the obsessive—it's as if you're seeing him as some kind of symbol impregnated with hidden meanings—"

"What on earth do you mean?"

"I only wish I knew. I feel I'm groping around in the dark, but Charles, I'm sure you ought to discuss this with someone who's a great deal more competent than I am to sort out what's going on. Do you have an adviser you can consult? Clergymen usually have someone, don't they—what do you call them?—confessors, counsellors, directors—"

"I go to the Fordite Abbot of Grantchester, near Cambridge. The Fordites are Anglican Benedictines, not Roman Catholic monks, but monks within the Church of England."

"Fine. See your Abbot and tell him everything."

"Maybe I should make a short retreat." I thought about it, but the prospect of any spiritual exercise which included confession was so appalling that I could only shudder and press my face against her breasts again. However, when I realised I could only divert myself from the horror of confession by dwelling on the Starbridge mystery I withdrew from her and propped myself up on one elbow. "In your opinion," I said, "what's going on in that ménage à trois?"

"My guess would be absolutely nothing—I think you got it right the first time. Lyle keeps the marriage glued together and her presence satisfies the different needs of all three of them: her need for power, Carrie's need for a daughter and Alex's need for an orderly home."

"I agree that's the only answer which makes sense, but the fact is that the atmosphere just doesn't tally with that explanation. I'm sure there's something going on between Lyle and Jardine, although now you've confirmed my opinion that he'd never enter into a continuing illicit liaison I don't see how they can be having an affair."

"Okay," said Loretta briskly, sitting up. "Let's try and cut through some of this confusion of yours by running through the various possibilities. Possibility number one: Lyle's in love with Carrie."

"Out of the question."

"Is it? Very feminine helpless women like Carrie often do wind up in lesbian situations, and you should remember there's always the chance that your feelings for Lyle could be an illusion."

"Yes, but—"

"The biggest argument against the existence of lesbianism," interrupted

Loretta, taking my side before I could dispute the idea further, "is that I can't see Alex ever tolerating it. I think we can assume that whatever's going on must somehow succeed in satisfying all three of them. Okay, let's move on to possibility number two: Lyle's crazy about Alex but Alex isn't crazy about her; he's kept the situation in control and nothing's ever happened between them."

"I can't see any clergyman in his right mind tolerating an infatuated woman in his household," I said. "The situation would be much too inflammable. He'd have got rid of her straight away."

"But supposing he wasn't in his right mind? This is possibility number three. Supposing he's crazy about her but his religious beliefs are keeping him in check?"

"From a clerical point of view that would be even worse than the previous situation—it'd be disastrous for his spiritual health to have such a temptation constantly on his doorstep."

"So that leaves the final possibility: Alex has lost his mind, thrown all scruples to the winds and is deeply involved in a fully consummated love affair."

"And that," I said, "is impossible for two reasons. The first is that I'm sure Mrs. Jardine wouldn't tolerate it, and the second is that he couldn't remain a bishop in those circumstances unless he's an apostate—which we're both sure he's not."

"I agree that last difficulty seems to be the eternal stumbling block," said Loretta, "but I think I can visualise a situation where Carrie would be complaisant. According to Evelyn, Alex and Carrie never gave up hope of having a family—a hope which would give each of them a powerful motive for continuing to have sex. But supposing, once Carrie reached the menopause, she turned against sex on the grounds that it had become pointless. It's not an uncommon thing to happen, and when it does, the marriage usually reaches a crisis. That's the point where the husband, if he's a layman, takes a mistress and the wife looks the other way."

I stared at her. "I think you've hit the nail on the head," I said. "I think that's what happened. From something Mrs. Cobden-Smith said I deduced the menopause was going on five years ago, and that was exactly the time when Mrs. Jardine was once more on the brink of breakdown."

"But that was because the old stepmother turned up."

"Yes, but supposing there was more to the crisis than that. Jardine told me that this was the last occasion on which he recorded personal difficulties in his journal—and he admitted that he'd had an important decision to make. Supposing he was trying to decide whether or not to—"

"I agree it's suggestive. If anything happened, I'll bet it happened then, but the big question is: did anything happen? And if it did, how did Alex square his conscience?"

"I'm going to find out. I've got to, *got to*—"

"I know. It's worrying me. Charles, you're much too obsessed about this—"

"How can I not be obsessed with it if I want to marry Lyle?"

"Yes, but . . . Okay, let's have another shot at putting the situation in some sort of rational perspective. The plain truth is that you don't know whether you're in love with Lyle or not. However, you think you are and this makes you ultra-sensitive to this mysterious ménage à trois. The most likely explanation of the ménage is that there really is nothing going on, but because you're not perceiving reality properly you're sliding deeper and deeper into illusion by devising this theory which will explain Lyle's coolness without damaging your own ego. In other words you're saying subconsciously to yourself: she and Jardine are having an affair and that's why she's not responding to me properly. But I think you ought to face the possibility that by reading too much into people's innocent reactions you're winding up imagining this sinister atmosphere at the palace. In fact in my opinion the really relevant question here is not what's going on in the ménage but what's going on in your subconscious; for example, why are you so sure Lyle's right for you?"

"She can cope with anything."

"But that makes you sound like a lunatic in need of a keeper!"

"Does it?" I pulled her into my arms again. "One more time," I said. "Just once more."

She parted her legs and put her hand gently on my body to guide me in.

5

THE knowledge that this was to be my last chance for some unknown time of satisfying myself sexually made me urgent as I gave physical expression to my despair. My misery was compounded by exhaustion and soon I felt the power fading. Loretta moved to restore it but my flesh was already contracting and seconds later I was closing my eyes against the light as I slumped back upon the bracken.

I slept. Then waking suddenly, just as one so often does after a short deep sleep, I sat up and said: "Jane." Loretta kissed me on the cheek. In confusion I saw she was dressed.

"I've been asleep," I said dazed.

"Only for ten minutes. I thought you needed it . . . Who's Jane?"

"My wife." Absurdly my eyes filled with tears, and terrified by this fresh evidence that I was on the point of disintegration I grabbed the lighted cigarette Loretta was offering me and turned my back on her. As I dressed I was able to say: "I've proved Jardine was capable of a single lapse. Now I've got to prove he was capable of a continuing illicit liaison. If I knew he'd been sleeping with that stepmother before his marriage—"

"I'm sure he wasn't. Look, Charles, you've just got to get this obsession in perspective—"

"I suppose he might have fought shy of taking his father's wife. After all, even though there was no blood relationship between them the legal relationship would have brought them within the prohibited degrees—"

"Well, that wouldn't apply in this case, would it?" said Loretta, taking her glasses from her handbag.

I stared at her. "What do you mean?"

She stared back. "My God!" she exclaimed. "Don't tell me you didn't find out!"

"Find out what?"

"Alex's father never married her, Charles. She lived for twenty-five years as his mistress. There was neither a blood-tie nor a legal relationship between Alex and Ingrid Jardine."

6

"ALEX told me and Evelyn about it once," said Loretta. "He was trying to establish a better relationship between Carrie and his stepmother but he wasn't making much progress and he confided in us out of sheer exasperation. Apparently Carrie was taking the line that she wasn't obliged to receive anyone who had lived in sin for twenty-five years."

"But the father was a religious fanatic! Why on earth didn't he marry her?"

"He hated all formal religion and he hated all clergymen so he kidded himself into believing he didn't need a clergyman reciting the wedding service over him in order to be married before God. He had to marry Alex's mother in church—she was a girl from a very respectable family—but Ingrid was on her own and apparently quite prepared to humour his crankiness; probably there was a very strong sexual attraction going on. Anyway old Jardine summoned her to his bedroom one night, and after they'd said some prayers together and exchanged a few vows he put his signet-ring on her finger, took her to bed and consummated what he was pleased to call his new marriage."

"Wait," I said. "Wait." My heart was thudding hard. "Just a moment."

"God, what is it, Charles? You're as white as a ghost!"

"Did you say a signet-ring?"

"Yes, maybe he thought a real wedding ring was as unnecessary as a clergyman reciting the wedding service—or maybe the marriage was unplanned and he used the only ring available at that moment . . . Charles, what the hell is it? What's the matter?"

I said: "Lyle wears a large signet-ring on the third finger of her left hand."

7

EVENTUALLY Loretta said: "No. I know what you're thinking but it's impossible."

"It's the only explanation that fits. Jardine married Lyle informally before God and they now think of each other as husband and wife. They believe they're not living in sin, and that means they can go on receiving the sacrament regularly."

"No." Loretta shook her head. "That definitely has to be a fantasy. Old Jardine had no education and didn't know any better, but Alex would know that kind of marriage had no validity. And anyway, damn it, he wasn't free to marry!"

"Obviously before he talked himself into an informal marriage he talked himself into an informal divorce. Have you heard of the A. P. Herbert Bill? Parliament's about to extend the grounds for divorce but I think Jardine's views go far further than the new law. He believes that a prima facie case for divorce exists whenever the spiritual core of the marriage is destroyed—in fact I'd say he was well in step with Martin Luther who believed that refusal of marital rights should be a ground for divorce. If Mrs. Jardine was refusing to have sex—"

"Charles, you're in the stratosphere—for God's sake come down to earth!"

"But I know I'm right!"

"And I know you're wrong! Alex couldn't possibly get himself in such a mess—"

"Didn't you say that where sex is concerned, anything's possible?"

"You're out of your mind!" shouted Loretta, but added at once in a calmer voice: "Okay, I can see the theory's plausible, but try to keep one truth nailed up in front of you: it hasn't been proved."

"It soon will be—all I've got to do now is go back to Starbridge and talk to Lyle!"

"But even if your theory's true, she'll never admit it!"

"Oh yes she will! I'm going to rescue her."

"Charles, you're just not in touch with reality! If your theory's true—and I don't think for one moment that it is—then that girl's besotted with Alex. I say that because no woman who wasn't besotted would ever acquiesce in the humiliation of a secret marriage."

"I think the marriage is breaking up."

"Oh my God . . . Look, Charles, before you rush off to Starbridge to make some horrific exhibition of yourself, please, *please* go and see that Abbot of yours—"

"Oh, I have to see him first, I agree. I can't go on serving God as I should until I've made my confession. I'll go back to Cambridge tonight and call on the Fordites tomorrow morning."

"Promise?"

I promised. She sagged in relief, and taking her in my arms I held her for a long moment.

At last she said: "Charles, I know we can't meet again; I know you'll have to put things right with God by promising there'll be no repeat performance of this afternoon's drama, but could you write to me? Just once? Otherwise I'll go out of my mind wondering what on earth happened in the end."

"I'll write."

We left the spinney. It seemed a long way back to the bridge over the river. We walked in silence as I planned my next assault on Starbridge and she no doubt wondered how to convince me of its futility, but when we were within sight of the car she said: "Alex began to hurt here—it was terrible. He kept saying he wanted to leave his wife but he knew he'd never survive the guilt which would cut him off from God—and that was the moment when he said: 'I don't want to end up like my father.' Charles, I'm just so sure he'd never follow in the old man's footsteps—"

"I agree he'd never want to end up mentally unstable and spiritually wrecked, but how far can one exercise control over one's heredity? Of course with God's help anything's possible, but if one turns away from God—"

"I don't think Alex could turn away from Freud. He had a psychological as well as a spiritual horror of immorality."

"But that's exactly why he'd feel compelled to convert adultery into marriage!"

"I give up. Let's agree to differ," said Loretta, kissing me as we reached the car, but when we eventually opened the doors we found the interior was so hot that there was no temptation to linger for further embraces, and with reluctance we embarked on our return journey to Starmouth Court.

8

OUTSIDE the house our hands clasped and on an impulse she said: "Never think I don't understand how difficult your calling is. Never think I believe you're a bad clergyman just because for once you couldn't live up to your ideals."

But I only said: "I've failed you."

"No," she persisted, "you dream the dream. That's all that matters. It's just that in an imperfect world no dream can come true all the time."

"How comforting life must be for you soft-hearted liberal Deists! But Christianity's much tougher and more virile than that. I ignored the care of your soul in order to exploit you for my own selfish purposes. That's acting without love and compassion. That's sin. That's failure."

But still she struggled to comfort me. "You're the one who's hurt here. I exploited you every bit as much as you exploited me."

"That wasn't exploitation. Your action was a cry for help as you sought an end to loneliness—a loneliness which I've completely failed to alleviate." I saw her expression change as she realised I had seen much further than she had ever intended, but I was unable to stop myself saying: "The psycho-analyst helped you. The Christian priest rejected you. What a travesty, what an unforgivable debasement, of the way things ought to be!"

For a moment I thought she would be unable to reply, but at last she said unsteadily: "It's such a beautiful dream!" Then she struggled out of the car and ran into the house without looking back.

I drove down the dark winding drive into the valley.

9

IT was late at night when I reached my rooms in Cambridge, and I was very tired. After a bath I drank some whisky and slid into bed.

I had not read the evening office. I had made no attempt to pray. For a long time I lay still, as if I could retain my equilibrium in the spiritual void by aping unconsciousness, but when I felt the void deepening I left the bed to pour myself another drink. In panic I focused my mind on the Starbridge mystery, that proven distraction from my problems, and later—it was around one in the morning—it began to dawn on me that

I had to solve the Starbridge mystery before I could make my confession to Father Reid.

Yet I had promised Loretta I would go to the Fordites before I returned to Starbridge, and I had to keep my promise to Loretta.

I drank some more whisky.

Eventually I decided that I would call on Father Reid but only to arrange a retreat at the end of the week. Then I could go back to Starbridge, and once the mystery had been solved I could concentrate on putting my soul in order in time for the Cathedral services on Sunday.

Happy ending.

I drank another whisky as if I needed help in believing that such happiness was within my reach, and gradually as I thought of Starbridge, radiant ravishing Starbridge, that shining city which contained the key to all my secrets, I knew how deeply I was compelled to prise apart that glittering image in order to confront the stark dark truths beyond. Then in my mind's eye I saw Jardine, not the Adam who hid behind Alex, but the Bishop empowered with the "charismata," the corruscating churchman, just the kind of churchman I wanted to be, but of course I *was* Jardine, I knew that now, and that was why I had to see him again as soon as possible.

"I've got to talk to Jardine," I said aloud to the whisky bottle as I turned it upside down to shake the last drops into my glass. "He understands me. No one else does." And as soon as those words were uttered I knew I could never confide in Father Reid. Seeing Father Reid would be a waste of time, but I had made my promise to Loretta and like all good clergymen I never broke a promise. I would see Father Reid for a brief social visit before I departed for Starbridge because I was such a good clergyman, such a brilliant success, and my father was so proud of me and yes, I'd definitely go to see Father Reid and that was final.

In the name of the Father, the Son and the Holy Ghost. Amen.

10

THE next morning I took some Alka-Seltzer, brewed some strong coffee and made myself read the office. I had made up my mind not to go to pieces. The bout of panic had been aggravated by my foolish lapse with the whisky, but now I had regained my equilibrium all would be well.

I drove to Grantchester, the village near Cambridge where the Fordites had their house. I had decided to pass the time with Father Reid by telling him about the St. Anselm manuscript; I still intended to arrange a retreat, but now that I was sober I remained more convinced than ever that my confession could be made only to Jardine.

So difficult was it for me to face the painful reality of my situation that I was halfway to Grantchester before I perceived the obvious objection to my plan. Jardine would inevitably decide that our lives had become so entangled that he was disqualified from acting as my confessor. Indeed, if he considered himself married to Lyle he was quite unfit to offer me spiritual counselling.

At this point I felt so confused that I stopped the car. I felt unable to speak of Loretta to anyone but Jardine because it seemed to me that only someone who had made an identical error would be able to summon the compassionate understanding necessary for granting absolution. At the thought of Loretta my body stirred restlessly, and that small movement which my mind failed to control at once emphasised the overwhelming nature of my problems. Devoid of effective counselling, confronted by the utter breakdown of my celibate life, knowing myself temporarily cut off from God, I had my back to the spiritual wall.

Panic flooded through me again but I conquered it by bombarding my mind with images of Starbridge. Lyle, Jardine, Carrie—Jardine, Carrie, Lyle—Carrie, Lyle, Jardine—

Driving the last mile to Grantchester I reached the monks' house and turned through the gateway.

II

THE Fordite Order of St. Benedict and St. Bernard had been founded in the last century when an old rogue named Ford, who had made a fortune in the slave trade, came under the influence of John Henry Newman and suffered a startling conversion to Anglo-Catholicism. Shortly before Newman seceded to Rome Ford died, leaving all his wealth to the Church of England for the purpose of founding a monastic order. His incensed widow eventually acquired a fraction of her husband's estate, but the Fordite monks had begun as a rich community and the careful management of their resources had ensured that the community became richer still. In this prosperity they formed a striking contrast to attempts by others to lead a cenobitic life within the Church of England, attempts which usually ran into financial difficulty.

There were four houses, all granted the status of Abbey by various benign Archbishops of Canterbury, but with one exception—the boys' school where the title had been retained to impress the parents—the word "Abbey" was not used by the Order. This was because the Fordites liked to stress their separation from the Roman Catholic orders and considered that the word conjured up unfortunate images of the religious climate in England before the Reformation. Indeed, although the Fordites lived a Benedictine way of life, their English idiosyncrasies set them apart from traditional Benedictine communities. The title "Dom" was never used either; people outside the Order were encouraged to address those monks who were ordained as if they were still Anglo-Catholic priests in the world, and apart from the London headquarters, where the Abbot-General lived in disconcerting luxury, there was a notable lack of pomp and pretentiousness in the communities.

The headquarters had once been old Ford's townhouse, the school Starwater Abbey had been his country seat and the Ruydale estate in Yorkshire had formed part of his extensive property investments, but the house at Grantchester had been acquired long after his death for the purpose of specialising in retreats for theological students, and I had stayed there on a number of occasions both before and after my ordination. The house lay on the outskirts of the village made famous by Rupert Brooke's poem, and was set in secluded grounds of five acres where the monks grew vegetables and kept bees. The Fordites' Grantchester honey, recalling the poem by Brooke, was much in demand by visitors to Cambridge.

When I rang the bell that morning, the front door opened so swiftly that I jumped. I had an immediate impression of improved efficiency, and the impression was strengthened by the young doorkeeper himself who was exceptionally clean and neat in his appearance. The Fordite habit, with its vague resemblance to the habit of the Trappists, underlines the idiosyncratic nature of the Order; the over-tunic is black and sleeveless but the under-tunic is white with long sleeves which tend inevitably to grubbiness. However, this monk's sleeves were sparkling white, as if he were advertising some new soap powder, and his little brass crucifix gleamed as it hung from his leather belt.

"Good morning!" he said cheerfully, an impressive illustration of the contented celibate life. "Can I help you?"

Despite all my troubles it was impossible not to smile at him. "I'm Dr. Ashworth from Laud's," I said. "I was hoping Father Reid might be free to see me for a moment."

The monk immediately became grave. "I'm afraid I must give you some sad news, Doctor—Father Abbot died last week and was buried on Friday."

I was nonplussed, not merely because my plans were flung into disarray but because I had been fond enough of Father Reid to feel a keen regret that he had been separated from me. "I'm very sorry," I managed to say.

"I shall miss him. He was my spiritual director." I tried to collect my thoughts. Obviously as a canon of the Cathedral I had a duty to see the new authority, express my condolences and offer him my good wishes for the future. "Perhaps I could see Father Andrews," I said tentatively, naming the officer whom I assumed had taken Father Reid's place.

"I'm sorry, sir, but Father Prior's been transferred to London."

The young monk's face was now expressionless and suddenly I sensed that a massive upheaval had taken place within those closed community walls. As I recalled my earlier impression of an improved efficiency it occurred to me that a new broom had begun to sweep the house very clean.

"Well, if Father Reid's dead," I said, "and Father Andrews has been transferred, who's now in charge?"

"Father Abbot-General has appointed someone from outside our community, sir—Father Jonathan Darrow from our house in Yorkshire." He opened the door wide. "Please do come in, Dr. Ashworth—our new Abbot wishes to meet everyone who came under Father Reid's direction, and I'm sure he'll see you straight away."

That settled that.

I crossed the threshold, and although I did not know it I was crossing my private Rubicon.

I was about to meet my exorcist.

X

"There is no part of my duty as bishop that perplexes and distresses me so much as the treatment of clergymen who have fallen into some gross impurity."

Letters of
HERBERT HENSLEY HENSON,
ed. E. F. Braley

I

I SAT down in the Visitors' Parlour, which was a large plain room containing a table and several chairs. Above the fireplace a crucifix hung on the wall but there were no pictures. A glass panel had been inserted in the door so that no monk could have an unobserved conversation with a female visitor.

It was past the hour of Mass which concluded the early services, and I knew the monks would be engaged in their private tasks before they reassembled for the next service at noon. The house was quiet. The Fordites are not bound to observe a strict rule of silence but conversation is discouraged except during the weekly recreation hour on Saturdays.

Three minutes passed. I was continually rephrasing my words of condolence, and I was still searching for the most appropriate formula when swift footsteps echoed in the hall and the new Abbot strode into the room.

He was very tall, even taller than I was, and had a lean but powerful frame. His iron-grey hair was cut very short, his iron-grey eyes saw, I knew, everything there was to see, and the strong striking bone structure of his face was impressive but intimidating in its austerity. It was an irony that the lavish pectoral cross and heavy ring which symbolised his office succeeded in underlining this austerity rather than negating it. An abbot was usually considered the equal in rank of a bishop within the Church of England, and although a bishop had a pastoral duty towards any monks in his diocese, a duty acquired when he was appointed "visitor" to their cloister, a Fordite abbot was answerable only to his Abbot-General in London and to the Archbishop of the province.

"Dr. Ashworth?" said the stranger as he paused on the threshold of the room, and added much as the chairman of the board might have addressed a young director who interested him: "Good morning—I'm Jon Darrow, the new Abbot here."

He somehow managed to be formal and informal at the same time. The use of the abbreviated first name was striking and led me to assume he had kept his original name on entering the Order. Monks were supposed to choose a new name to symbolise their new life in God's service, but the Fordites regarded this cenobitic tradition as optional.

He closed the door and we shook hands. His clasp was firm, brief, confident. Mine was cautious, uncertain, perhaps even unnerved.

"I'm extremely sorry that you weren't informed of Father Reid's death," he said, "but unfortunately he kept no list of those he counselled so it was impossible for me to write to you." He made the omission of a list sound like evidence of an unpardonably inefficient administration, and I began to wonder if he had ever served in the Army. The authority he exuded had a certain "spit-and-polish" quality; as I tentatively embarked on my set speech I found myself remembering the young doorkeeper's dazzling crucifix.

"I was very surprised—and greatly saddened—to hear the news—it must have been a shock to you all—"

"It was, yes," said Father Darrow, crisply terminating my unimpressive attempt to express my condolences. "Father Reid was held in considerable affection by the community and will be much missed."

That disposed of Father Reid. Still trying to find my bearings, I said uncertainly: "I understand you've been brought in from outside—isn't that rather unusual? I thought that normally the community elected an abbot from among their own number."

"It's very unusual, yes, and a stimulating challenge both for me and for my Grantchester brethren." That disposed equally crisply of the unusual appointment. "Please sit down, Dr. Ashworth. I presume you came to see Father Reid about a spiritual matter?"

Uncertainty continued to grip me. I hesitated.

"Let me tell you a little about myself," said Darrow, sitting down opposite me at the table. "I think it's often difficult to confide in someone new and untried; spiritual directors are not, after all, something one acquires without thought at the local shop, like a sack of potatoes. I'm fifty-seven years old and I entered the Order when I was forty-three. Before that I was a chaplain in the prison service, and before that I was a chaplain in the Navy—in which, incidentally, I served during the War.

I obtained my theology degree at Laud's. For nine years of my life I was a married man and I have a son and daughter, now grown up." He paused. "That, I fear, is very much of a thumbnail sketch, but I hope perhaps you may find it illuminating."

I did. A former Naval chaplain who knew what sex was all about and had even got as far as fathering two children might well be an acceptable alternative to Jardine, and spurred on by the knowledge that I had my back to the spiritual wall, I said cautiously: "Thank you, Father. Yes, that's very helpful. I'm sorry I was so hesitant." I tried to dispense with hesitancy. "I came here this morning in the hope of arranging a retreat," I said, attempting a passable imitation of my usual self-confidence. "I thought I might return here on Friday, have a talk with you—at your convenience, naturally—and make my confession. Then I'd like to spend some time in prayer and meditation under your direction before leaving early on Sunday morning in order to attend the services in the Cathedral."

Father Darrow was looking straight at me with his very clear grey eyes. My nerve failed. "Well, I mustn't take up any more of your time," I said rapidly, rising to my feet. "If you have no objection to my plans, I'll—"

"Sit down, Dr. Ashworth."

I sank back in my chair.

"When did you last make your confession?"

In the circumstances it was a conventional question but that did not make it easier to answer. However, I thought that with luck he would accept my information without questioning it. "Last April," I said.

"And you made your confession to Father Reid."

Damn. "No," I said casually, trying to pretend there was nothing unusual about such an evasion of one's spiritual director.

"To whom did you make your confession?"

Double-damn. This was very awkward. I cleared my throat and rubbed my nose to give myself time to think. "I was in France," I said at last, "on holiday. I made my confession to a priest in a Paris church."

"A Roman Catholic?"

"Yes."

There was a pause. "You discussed the matter with Father Reid, of course," said Darrow, "on your return."

"Well, as a matter of fact," I said, "no, I didn't."

"When did you last make your confession to Father Reid?"

"Last March, before Easter."

"How often do you make confession?"

In my confusion I was so preoccupied that my normal practise of confession might be judged inadequate that I failed to realise he was bent on exposing the abnormality of two confessions made in rapid succession. "Well, I'm not really an Anglo-Catholic, Father, not nowadays, and since confession isn't compulsory in the Church of England—"

"Once a year? Twice? Three times?"

"Once a year. During Lent."

"I see." There followed a pause as I belatedly realised I had revealed a situation I would have preferred to conceal. Darrow waited, but when I remained silent he said with perfect courtesy: "Today is Tuesday. May I ask why you wish to postpone your confession till the weekend?"

Triple-damn. I had no wish to start discussing my need to return to Starbridge. "There's a very important matter," I said firmly, "which I have to attend to."

"A worldly matter?"

I was caught. If I said yes, he would accuse me of putting worldly interests before my spiritual welfare. If I said no, he would want to know why I was clearly reluctant to discuss a matter which was part of my spiritual life. I stared at him, and as he stared back, grave and uncompromising, I realized with the most profound uneasiness that he was formidable.

"When did you last receive the sacrament?" he said while I was still floundering over his last question.

This was easier. With relief I said: "Sunday." And driven by the compulsion to polish away the tarnish which he had perceived on my glittering image I added: "I was staying at Starbridge—at the palace—and the Bishop asked me to assist him at Communion." This sounded reassuringly impressive, and I was just relaxing in my chair when he said: "And if your own Bishop were to telephone you today with the same request how would you answer him?"

In the silence that followed I felt my face grow hot as I shifted in my chair and stared down at my clasped hands. No reply was possible. I felt humiliated, angry and gripped by a violent desire to walk out. Yet I stayed—and not only because I knew I had my back to the spiritual wall. I stayed because he was mentally pinning me there and I was quite unable to wriggle away.

"What is your Christian name?" said Darrow.

"Charles."

"Then since you've put yourself under my direction I shall call you by your Christian name—you have put yourself under my direction, haven't you," said Darrow in a voice which made it clear he expected no argument, and I nodded. At that point I was incapable of shaking my head.

"Very well. Now, Charles, let me summarise the situation for you as you seem to be too confused to see it clearly. You come here and tell me that you wish to make confession. Because you normally make confession only once a year during Lent it would appear that some abnormal difficulty has overtaken you since you attended Holy Communion last Sunday. Moreover since your confession during Lent another abnormal difficulty apparently overtook you last April which necessitated a confession to a Roman Catholic priest, a most unusual step for an Anglican clergyman to take and a step which you apparently felt unable to discuss with your confessor Father Reid. These abnormal difficulties suggest you need help and obviously you're not unaware of this, but you come here this morning and suggest that you put your spiritual life in abeyance for a few days while you attend to some matter which you insist is of great importance. I put it to you that nothing is more important than that you should make your confession and return to a state of grace at the very earliest opportunity, and I do beg you most earnestly to rearrange your plans so that you can return here either today or—at the very latest—tomorrow morning."

He stopped speaking. I stared at my clasped hands and as I watched, my fingers began to twist together, interlocking until the knuckles shone white.

At last I said: "I do realise how odd my behaviour must seem, but there's a mystery I have to solve and until it's solved I can't understand the mystery beyond the mystery, which is the mystery in my mind, and until I solve the mystery beyond the mystery, how can I hope to achieve any real understanding of what's going on?"

I was mouthing gibberish. I broke off in despair but Darrow said: "What you're saying is that you can't make your confession because your errors are shrouded in mystery; you're saying that until you unravel this mystery, you're unable to achieve the understanding which must necessarily precede any truly meaningful repentance."

"Exactly." I was impressed as well as deeply relieved by his grasp of the situation. "Once I solve the mystery in the foreground," I said with more confidence, "then the mystery in the background—that is, the mystery in my mind which is driving me into error—will become clear and I'll be able to make an effective confession."

"But what makes you so sure that this first mystery, the mystery in the foreground, is solvable?"

"Well, it must be." I stared at him. "Of course it must be."

"Must it? In my experience the puzzles of life can seldom be unravelled easily into clear-cut solutions. Suppose you fail to solve the mystery. What then?"

"But there's no possibility I'll fail! All I have to do is to go back to Starbridge and talk to a certain person."

"But what makes you so sure that the mystery in the background will then be triumphantly illuminated? Supposing, on the contrary, the solution of the first mystery results not in light but in darkness?"

I continued to stare at him. "How could that happen?"

"What you're really saying is this: you're saying you need a light to illuminate the dark corners of your soul. But one has to be very careful with dark corners of the soul. Too much light too suddenly can be dangerous. The dark corners can hit back and put the light out."

There was a long silence. Then Darrow rose to his feet. "I'll take you to the guest-wing," he said, "and assign you a room. You shouldn't leave here now. It's too dangerous."

"Dangerous!"

"You're like a yachtsman with a high fever who insists on steering straight for the rocks. Drop anchor, lie down and get well enough to plot a better course."

"I can't. I want to but I can't." I leant forward in a last desperate effort to explain. "I've got to go back to Starbridge—I can think of nothing but Starbridge—it's as if Starbridge is a huge magnet pulling me so hard that I can't escape, and although I don't want to put my spiritual life in abeyance I must, I can't help myself, I can't do anything until I've solved the Starbridge mystery—but once the mystery's solved and I return to Cambridge—"

"Come straight here, no matter what time of the day or night it is."

I could not reply, but as I looked again into those grave grey eyes I had the uncanny dread that he was clairvoyant.

I said sharply: "I'll be all right." I tried not to make it sound like a question.

I shall always remember what he said next. He spoke his biblical paraphrase as if it were a famous quotation. "High and wide is the gate which leads to self-deception and illusion," he said, "but for those seeking truth strait is the gate and narrow the way and brave is the man who can journey there. How profound is your courage, Charles? And how deep are your reserves of spiritual strength?"

I could not answer. I knew what a weak spiritual state I was in, and unable to meet his eyes I retreated, more confused than ever, to the hall.

All he said as he opened the front door was: "I'll pray for you."

I wanted to linger. I could feel the power of his mind pulling me back, but by that time I was being driven by a compulsion which was quite beyond my control, and hurrying to my car I set out on the road to disaster.

2

WHEN I returned to my rooms to pack a bag for the journey I found a letter from Jardine had arrived by the second post. Recognising his handwriting at once, I ripped open the envelope.

"My dear Dr. Ashworth," I read,

> I have spoken on the telephone today to the Abbot of Starwater, and he told me that the man you should see at the Fordites' Grantchester house is without question Father Jonathan Darrow. Father Reid, I'm sad to say, is no longer with us and the Grantchester community has only just acquired this new Abbot who has a first-class reputation as a director of souls. He comes from the Fordites' Yorkshire house where he was Master of Novices, but apparently his work has extended far beyond the training of monks. I have also spoken on the telephone today to one of the bishops of the Northern Province who told me he has sent troubled clergymen to Darrow on several occasions and always with the very best results. I do urge you not to delay your next visit to Grantchester, and in trusting that this letter will be of help to you in your difficulty, I remain yours very sincerely,
>
> ADAM ALEXANDER STARO

I remembered Jardine saying how much he hated the telephone. I was impressed by his evident concern for my welfare, but I was intrigued too.

I wondered how far he identified with me.

3

SO I came once more to Starbridge, radiant glittering Starbridge, and as I approached the city through the pass in the hills I saw again the spire of the Cathedral appearing and disappearing as the road twisted and turned, the vision of truth fleetingly glimpsed but continually erased in the mirrors of fantasy and illusion.

I was again too late for Evensong, but after I had taken a room overlooking the river-garden at the Staro Arms I made myself read the office. Then I extracted the bottle of whisky from my bag, poured myself a stiff drink and lit a cigarette. I was wearing grey trousers with a sports jacket and an open-necked shirt, and as I glanced in the glass I thought

I no longer looked like a salesman hawking a dubious product but like an actor who was having trouble remembering his lines.

I had a second stiff whisky. Then I went downstairs to the telephone kiosk in the hall.

At the palace the chaplain picked up the receiver and after the necessary exchange of pleasantries I asked for Lyle. A long delay followed, and I was just wondering if she was trying to invent an excuse for avoiding a conversation with me when her voice said sharply: "Charles?"

"Darling"—in my relief that she had made no attempt to evade the call I allowed myself the luxury of an endearment—"I'm back in Starbridge and I must see you. Can you dine this evening?"

"You're in *Starbridge?*" She sounded dazed.

"I could collect you in half an hour—"

"Just a moment." As she put the receiver aside I heard her say to Gerald Harvey: "Where's the Bishop?"

"Lyle!" I shouted but she was gone. I nearly hung up in rage but sheer obstinacy made me stand my ground and seconds later Jardine was exclaiming: "My dear Canon, why didn't you let us know you were returning? You could have stayed at the palace!"

This confused me. I had been expecting hostility, not hospitality.

"I felt I couldn't possibly impose—after the awkward aspects of my last visit—"

"Nonsense! Come and dine!"

"Tonight?"

"Why not? We'll expect you at seven-thirty. I shall be so interested to hear about your long luncheon with Loretta," said Jardine, and rang off without waiting for a reply.

4

HAVING consumed a third whisky I changed into my clerical clothes and set off on foot up Eternity Street towards the Close. After my long drive it was a relief to forsake the car, but as I reached the palace gates the rain began to fall and I was obliged to sprint the last yards to the front door.

The butler seemed pleased to see me. The unexpected revival of last week's doomed romance would no doubt provoke further enjoyable speculation over the teacups in the servants' hall.

"Are there many guests expected tonight, Shipton?"

"None at all, sir. The Bishop and Mrs. Bishop were due to go to London with Miss Christie today but unfortunately their host was unwell and the visit had to be cancelled."

"So there'll be no one here tonight except—"

"—except the three of them and yourself, sir. Mr. Harvey's dining out." And opening the door of the drawing-room he announced in his most melancholy voice: "Dr. Ashworth, my Lord."

Jardine was alone by the window, his hands in his pockets, his slim frame emanating his characteristic restless energy, his eyes watching the rain as it streamed against the glass. As I walked in he turned to face me, but I saw no hint of distaste or disapproval in his expression.

"Ah, there you are!" he said, moving towards me with his hand outstretched. "Welcome back to Starbridge. Did you get my letter?"

"Yes—thank you, Bishop. It was extremely good of you to go to so much trouble." We shook hands. "I did in fact meet Father Darrow this morning and I've arranged to begin a retreat under his direction this weekend."

"I'm very glad to hear it, although surprised you saw fit to delay the retreat in order to return here."

I made no reply but picked up a copy of *Country Life* which was lying on a nearby chair and embarked on a detailed examination of the cover.

"I was of course much disturbed when Lady Starmouth telephoned yesterday to say that you'd abducted Loretta for an excessively long luncheon," said Jardine, "but I think it would be best if we avoided discussing your continuing obsession with my past until we're alone together with the port."

"What a pity," I said, flicking through the pages of *Country Life*. "I was hoping for another theological discussion once the ladies had retired. I thought we might debate Luther's view that the refusal of marital rights should constitute a ground for divorce." And I tossed aside the magazine.

The door opened and in fluttered Mrs. Jardine. "Dr. Ashworth!" she exclaimed, as Jardine and I continued to stare at each other. "How nice to see you again—although you seem to have brought some very tiresome rain with you from Cambridge!"

"Yes, I'm afraid that storm you feared has finally arrived, Mrs. Jardine," I said, taking her hand in mine, and as I glanced beyond her I saw Lyle watching tensely from the doorway.

5

OF the three of them Mrs. Jardine alone behaved as if my swift return to Starbridge were unremarkable, and during dinner she maintained the burden of the conversation by chatting about subjects of an almost intolerable banality. Lyle was polite but withdrawn; we exchanged only a few stilted sentences, and once the dinner-table lay between us I had no opportunity to take a close look at her ring, which she was as usual wearing on the wedding finger of her left hand. Meanwhile with a sublime disregard for the tension in the room Mrs. Jardine was telling me some long story about how she had forgotten to go to a charity committee meeting because the third child of the Canon in Residence had contracted mumps. She then asked me what kind of charity work my mother did—an awkward question since my mother led an idle life drinking too many cocktails and getting on my father's nerves. However, I had only to mention my mother's fondness for fashion magazines and Mrs. Jardine was telling me about the fashion show she had organised to raise money for the children of the unemployed dockers in Starmouth.

"Lyle organised it," said the Bishop, who appeared sunk in boredom at the far end of the table, and suddenly as I remembered Loretta saying that I might be reading too much into people's innocent reactions, I wondered if this tension existed only in my mind; I wondered if this unusually private glimpse of the ménage was revealing not the sinister undercurrents I had anticipated but merely the blameless tedium of a well-worn regime.

"No, Carrie did the organising!" Lyle was insisting to the Bishop. "I merely hired the hall, instructed the caterers and sent out the invitations."

I was just wondering what had been left for Mrs. Jardine to do when Mrs. Jardine herself exclaimed warmly: "You were wonderful, Lyle!" She turned to me with enthusiasm. "Does your mother have a companion to help her, Dr. Ashworth?"

"Only my father."

"Maybe we can discuss your father over the port," said the Bishop, finally unable to resist livening up the dinner by shooting a provocative verbal arrow into the conversation. "That could prove an interesting debate."

"More interesting than Luther on divorce?"

Lyle glanced up from her food. I was looking straight at her. Immediately she glanced away and began to dissect her potato.

"Talking of fathers, did I ever tell you about my own father, Dr. Ashworth?" inquired Mrs. Jardine, swiftly terminating the silence, and no further pause was allowed to develop in the conversation until the end of the meal, when she felt obliged to refresh her voice with a sip of water.

At once I said to Lyle: "When am I going to see you tomorrow?"

Lyle's eyes seemed to darken. I glanced instinctively at the Bishop, but to my surprise it was Mrs. Jardine who spoke first.

"I'm terribly sorry, Dr. Ashworth," she said, "but I'm afraid I'll be needing Lyle all day tomorrow, and then on Thursday we go off to Bath and Wells—well, it's Wells actually, but we're staying with the *Bishop* of Bath and Wells because Alex has been invited to preach a special commemorative sermon—what exactly are they commemorating, Alex?"

"I've forgotten," said Jardine, and instantly laughed at the absurdity. Lyle and Mrs. Jardine laughed too, and suddenly I longed to smash the innocuous facade of the conversation. I said abruptly to Lyle: "In that case I'd like to see you alone this evening before I leave. I want to talk to you about your signet-ring."

I thought I saw Lyle turn a shade paler but it was impossible to be sure.

"Oh, isn't it a lovely ring!" exclaimed Mrs. Jardine, innocence personified, but as she succeeded once more in cloaking the tension with banality I wondered if she were deliberately checking every abnormal turn in the conversation. "People often remark on it! I remember I had a ring once—"

"Will you tell me later how you acquired that ring?" I said to Lyle.

"Of course she'll tell you!" exclaimed the Bishop with impatience. "But why wait till later? The subject hardly merits a private interview! Tell him now, Lyle."

Lyle said composed: "The Bishop's stepmother gave it to me. It had great sentimental memories for her but she could no longer wear it because the joints of her fingers were swollen with arthritis. I was touched because I admired her very much, and I wear the ring in memory of her."

"Ah, how interesting!" I said, pouring myself a fourth glass of claret from the decanter. "That must be the ring the Bishop's father gave her during their highly unusual wedding ceremony."

Jardine said at once: "That'll be all, Shipton," and both butler and footman withdrew.

As soon as the door closed, I said to Lyle: "I was wondering if the ring meant that you too had been through a highly unusual wedding ceremony."

"If that's a joke," said Lyle in a low voice, "I don't think it's funny."

"It's no joke and I didn't come here to be amusing." Draining my glass, I reached for the decanter again.

"Dr. Ashworth," said Mrs. Jardine with surprising strength, "I'm very distressed to see you not behaving as a gentleman should. I think you forget yourself."

"Mrs. Jardine," I said equally firmly as I poured myself a fifth glass of claret, "I came down to Starbridge to see Lyle, but you and your husband are clearly conspiring to prevent me from having any conversation with her alone. In the circumstances can you wonder that my annoyance is verging on anger and that my good manners are becoming frayed at the edges?"

"I don't want to have any conversation with you alone," said Lyle, immediately responding to the challenge.

"Why not? Because you're afraid you'll give me another adulterous kiss—like last Saturday's kiss which kept you from Communion the next morning because you felt you'd betrayed your husband?"

Lyle was speechless but the Bishop at once leant forward to address his wife. "It's all right, Carrie," he said. "Don't be alarmed. I'm afraid Dr. Ashworth is mentally very disturbed indeed."

"You're damn right I'm disturbed!" I said, tossing the "damn" into the conversation to smash its normality beyond repair. "What's happening here would disturb anyone!"

"You're drunk!" said Lyle in contempt, and before I could reply Jardine said curtly: "Of course he's drunk. He reeked of whisky when he arrived and he's been drinking claret as if it were lemonade. Carrie—"

"Yes, of course, dearest." She rose with perfect dignity to her feet. "Lyle—shall we?"

We all stood up, I resting my hands lightly on the table to steady myself, Jardine opening the door for the ladies. As Lyle walked away I shouted after her: "He's in error! The divorce is a fantasy, the marriage a lie!"

Lyle swept out, followed by Mrs. Jardine. Neither of them looked back.

The door closed.

"Sit down, Dr. Ashworth," said Jardine abruptly. "It's time you and I had a very serious talk together."

6

I NEVER hesitated. I said in fury: "You 'married' Lyle five years ago just as your father 'married' your stepmother. Well, that sort of behaviour might have been excusable in your father, an eccentric uneducated widower who no doubt sincerely believed he was marrying before God, but *you!* You're well-educated, subtle, sophisticated—all the things your father never was—and *you were already married!* How can you sit on your episcopal throne and believe that what you've done could ever have God's blessing? You've cut off a young woman from a normal married life, you've perverted the vows you made at your ordination—no, don't try to tell *me* she's your wife! She's your mistress—and don't try to tell me you're divorced either. You're not divorced, not by the law and not in the eyes of God! You've just wrecked Lyle's life in order to satisfy your own selfish needs!"

I stopped speaking. I was trembling. Grabbing my glass of claret I drained it and reached for the decanter.

"Sit down, Charles," said Jardine in his calmest voice, and as he used my Christian name I knew that like Father Darrow he was using it because he was a senior churchman trying to help one of his younger brethren in distress.

I sat down abruptly. The claret was smooth in my throat. Overcome with emotion I knocked over my glass accidentally as I replaced it on the table, and as the dregs spread in a red stain across the undrawn cloth I had the bizarre impression that although I was the one who had launched the attack I was the one who was now bleeding.

Jardine said, deeply concerned: "Did Father Darrow make no attempt to detain you this morning?"

"Yes, but I knew I had to come back here to solve the mystery—and I've solved it, haven't I? I've finally worked out the truth!"

"My dear Charles, I'm afraid your truth is a fantasy and you've solved absolutely nothing."

"That's a lie!" I shouted.

"Try to keep calm. I can't help you if you persist in being truculent—and believe me, I'm most anxious to help you extricate yourself from this distressing muddle. I presume it was Loretta who told you about my father's marriage?"

"How can you call it a marriage! Your stepmother just cohabited with him and then left him to cohabit with you!"

"I'm sorry, but I can't permit such a gross distortion of the facts. My stepmother," said Jardine, "was in a very real sense my father's wife; certainly they both believed themselves married in the sight of God. It's true that when I finally found out there had been no legal marriage, I took a priggish line—I was at the height of my narrow-minded Anglo-Catholic phase—and I did encourage her to leave him; I thought I was saving her from a life of sin by sanctioning her decision to come to Starmouth to keep house for me. But years later when she decided she had to go back, I realised she'd always been as good a wife—as dutiful a wife—to my father as any woman who had been married in church. However, since most people find it impossible to regard an informal marriage with charity, I strongly object to the facts being circulated. I'm most distressed that Loretta was so indiscreet—and naturally it makes me wonder what on earth went on between the two of you yesterday—"

"I followed in your footsteps." I was having trouble emptying the claret decanter into my glass. "We went to the steep field to watch the train go by."

"Oh, so you found out about that! Yes, I did go a little farther with her than I admitted to you—"

"In every sense of the phrase!"

Jardine looked at me carefully. Then he fetched the port decanter from the sideboard and said: "I'm not going to offer you this because you've had quite enough to drink already, but I don't see why I shouldn't take a glass to fortify myself against your fantasies. Now about this sad little incident in the field—"

" 'Sad little incident'? My God, what a way to describe adultery!"

"Adultery?"

"Don't you try to deny it!" I shouted. "I had her myself in the same corner of that spinney where she had you!"

Jardine stared at me. Then he walked to the door, glanced out into the hall to make sure no one was listening and closed the door again. "Charles," he said in his gentlest voice as he returned to the table, "I want you to recall Loretta's words with great care because although people can change very much during the course of two decades I can't believe she would have changed enough to lie to you on this point. Did she actually say that I'd committed adultery?"

I tried to think. My mind was in chaos, but I had a sickening memory of Loretta saying: "You're going in," and suddenly I knew she had been neither apprehensive nor dubious but surprised.

"Of course," said Jardine in the voice of one who states the obvious, "I never penetrated her. The adultery exists only in your mind, Charles."

7

"I ADMIT some embraces took place," said Jardine. "I admit my behaviour was thoroughly reprehensible for a clergyman. But there was no consummation. How could there have been? How could I have gone on as a clergyman if adultery had taken place?"

All I managed to say was: "I don't believe you." But I did.

"I wonder how I can make you see that it's the truth. Perhaps I can make my abstinence more credible if I admit it was due not so much to virtue as to fear, the fear which reflected my horror of waywardness, my horror of ending up like my father. Can't you see? I was incapable of consummating an adulterous union, Charles, psychologically incapable of it."

I covered my face with my hands.

At last Jardine said, again using his gentlest voice: "And now let me talk about Lyle. I admit that when she entered my house at Radbury ten years ago I was attracted to her—in that tiresome inconvenient manner which is so common among middle-aged men whose marriages have entered an awkward phase. Naturally I told my wife that Lyle would have to go, but Carrie's nerves were so bad at that time that when she objected I gave way—and not only because I shrank from any course which might have tilted her into a full-scale nervous breakdown. I gave way because I felt Carrie's objection reinforced my own opinion that Lyle was the heaven-sent solution to our troubles. The situation was desperate. I was spending so much time trying to cope with my wife that I could barely cope with my duties as Dean, but when Lyle came I was set free to serve God properly at last."

He paused. I had uncovered my eyes but could only stare at the red stain on the table-cloth.

"I'm sure you see how inevitable my next decision was," said Jardine. "I realised that if Lyle were to remain in my house, I could on no account permit even the faintest trace of impropriety in my manner to her. Impropriety wouldn't merely have been stupid; it would have been ungrateful to God, who had sent Lyle to us to ease so much of our sadness and difficulty. You may be thinking that this attitude of extreme propriety towards Lyle was hard for me to adopt, and you'd be right; it was. But curiously enough once the attitude had been adopted it was easy to maintain because my marriage became so much more tolerable. Carrie greatly improved, thanks to Lyle's care, and the result was that we were able to resume our marital relationship after a long interval. That disposed of my last doubts. I knew then it was right that Lyle should stay."

Again he paused, and as I raised my eyes from the table-cloth to the empty claret decanter I was aware of him sipping his port. "However," he said, "you mustn't think I haven't spent a lot of time worrying about Lyle's welfare. Our triangle would hardly be morally acceptable, would it, if Lyle were unhappy and unfulfilled? But Charles, the point here is that if Lyle really were unhappy and unfulfilled, she wouldn't stay. It's impossible for me to explain her aversion to matrimony without breaching her confidence so all I can say is that a psychological aversion, rooted in her past, does exist, but nevertheless Carrie and I have both made great efforts to help her overcome this difficulty—for instance, we've always encouraged her to go out with young men, and I'm sure you'll remember that it was I who urged her to dine with you at the Staro Arms. Of course Lyle's sometimes tempted to indulge in a romantic flutter or two, but the rock-bottom truth is that she likes her life exactly as it is, and if she wishes to remain single she has a perfect right to do so. I quite see that this must be highly frustrating for you, but—"

"I'm going to marry her!" I was struggling to overcome the terrifying conviction that every word he said was true. "You're telling me all these lies because you're jealous, possessive and deeply in love with her yourself!"

"My dear Charles—"

"If your wife died, you'd marry Lyle tomorrow!"

"Let's try to keep this conversation rational, shall we? I admit," said Jardine, "that when I first met Lyle, I told myself I'd marry her if ever I became a widower, but I soon realised one can hardly spend one's life waiting for one's wife to die! That way insanity lies. The truth was—and still is—that I'm a married man, I'm a clergyman and I'm stuck with the status quo, but at least it's a status quo that enables me to serve God to the best of my ability with the support of a loving dutiful wife of whom I'm extremely fond. As I remind myself daily I'm very lucky to have any workable status quo at all, and need I stress that it would be quite unworkable if I hadn't so far recovered from my initial attraction that I can now regard Lyle with a healthy affection and respect? I think not. The facts speak for themselves. Be reasonable, Charles! I know you're far from being in a rational frame of mind, but isn't it patently obvious that there's nothing improper going on here?"

It was. Yet I found myself quite unable to admit it. I began stubbornly. "I think—" but he interrupted me.

"Yes," he said, "this is where we get to you and what you think—and this is where we meet two intractable problems. The first is that you're at present too drunk even to face your difficulties, let alone grapple with them, and the second is that although you urgently need counselling, I'm quite the wrong person to give it to you. I'm part of the crisis, aren't I?"

I was so incensed that he should call me drunk merely because I had had a little extra claret that I shouted: "I don't want your damned counselling!" I tried to grab the port decanter but he whipped it away.

"No," he said severely. "No more."

I waited till he had replaced it on the table and then I lunged forward, swiped the decanter from under his nose, and began to pour the port into my empty glass.

"You're being very foolish," said Jardine, "but you want attention, don't you? You're like a little child who misbehaves in order to get noticed. You say you don't want my counselling, but in fact I suspect that's exactly what you're angling for. You're deep in some private fantasy, and—"

"*You're* the one who's deep in some private fantasy if you think you're deceiving me!" I was now so enraged that I hardly knew what I said. "Do you think I can't see exactly what's going on? You're just fighting tooth and nail to stop your glittering image coming apart at the seams!"

"No," said Jardine, "you're the one who's fighting that particular battle, and the glittering image is falling apart before my eyes." He rose to his feet. "Let me call my chauffeur and ask him to drive us over to the monks at Starwater."

"I'm not leaving this bloody room," I said, "until you bloody well admit you've been sleeping with Lyle!"

"Charles, you need help. I can't give it to you and you absolutely must let me take you to someone who—"

"You're not washing your hands of me!" I shouted. "I'm not going to be brushed off, I'm not going to be kicked out, I'm not going to be treated as if—"

"All right! All right, all right, all right . . ." Jardine cast a quick glance at the door to reassure himself it was still closed. "You want me to be the one who helps you. Very well. I'll do what you want, but I do it greatly against my better judgement and only because you're giving me no choice. Now"—he drew up his chair in order to sit down at my side—"let me try to bring you closer to what I fear will be a very unpalatable reality . . ."

8

"FOR some reason," said Jardine, "you've picked me to be the central figure in your life at present. We won't call this a fantasy because you evidently find that word hurtful, so we'll just say that you were experiencing certain difficulties in your private life and when you met me, I seemed in some mysterious way to provide you with a solution. Obviously you liked the idea—which that old fool Lang had put into your head—that I was an eminent churchman who led a double life. No, that's an understatement. You didn't just like the idea—you were enrapt by it.

"So you arrive in Starbridge and soon you've far exceeded your brief from Lang—after all, it must have quickly become very clear to you that I'm not the sort of man who compromises himself by dabbling in foolish love-letters or keeping an uncensored journal. However, you're not interested in Lang's brief, not any more. What you're now interested in is the possibility that behind the glittering image of my ecclesiastical success lies a life steeped in the kind of error which would make even Lang's senile speculations look pale. You embrace this theory with such zest that it becomes necessary for you to prove it, but the interesting part is that the more obsessed you become with proving my guilt, the more fervently you swear you're on my side. By this time, of course, you've parted company with reality altogether. By this time you're acting out the most elaborate and fantastic of delusions—"

I had levered myself to my feet. My voice said trembling: "I refuse to listen to this."

"But you will. You will, Charles, you will." The lambent eyes were suddenly so bright that I could not look away. "Sit down, Charles," said Jardine, and at once I sank back in my chair. "Charles, listen to me—listen to me, Charles, because I say you can't afford to go on with this fantasy any longer, you must try to face reality, and the reality is that you're ill, mentally ill—"

"No—*no*—"

"Yes, Charles, yes—how could any normal man have misinterpreted my situation in such an extraordinary and bizarre manner? The truth is that the man I am has nothing to do with the man you think I am. You've invented me. I exist only in your imagination. You think you know me so well that you can see numerous resemblances between us, but every one of them's an illusion, an illusion which is necessary to support your longing to believe we're identical. And why do you want to believe that we're identical? Because you think you can justify your own unfortunate behaviour by saying you're only following my example—you feel you can escape from your problems by projecting them onto me. So you place me in front of you as if I were a blank screen and your mind the magic-lantern projector, but in fact it's *your* image, not mine, which you're seeing reflected. The real mystery here, Charles, is not what's going on at Starbridge—that's just a drama you've invented to divert yourself from your problems. The real mystery is what's going on in your soul. Why does an extremely able and successful young clergyman with a brilliant future and an unclouded past suddenly, for no apparent reason, start mentally falling apart?"

I jumped up, knocking over my chair, and as he too sprang to his feet, I said: "You can't talk to me like that, you can't." I was so dizzy that I had to grab the edge of the table.

"I'm sorry—I've taken a risk in speaking so plainly, but I could see no other way of convincing you that you simply must have help. I myself can now do no more but I'm sure the monks at Starwater—"

"You're rejecting me!" I shouted. "You keep rejecting me! You've rejected me over and over again!"

"My God," said Jardine, suddenly ashen, "this is what happened with your father, isn't it? You poor boy, I didn't realise—oh, what a hash I've made of this, I'm so damnably sorry—"

I shoved him aside and rushed from the room.

9

I HAVE no clear recollection of my journey back to the Staro Arms. All I remember is the hotel receptionist's disapproving stare as she gave me the change for the telephone call. Then I shut myself in the hall kiosk again and asked the operator to connect the line to Starmouth Court.

By the time Loretta came to the telephone I was almost beyond speech, but I managed to say: "Why didn't you tell me the whole truth?"

"What do you mean?"

"He didn't do it, did he? He didn't go in."

"Wait," she said. "Wait. I understand what you're saying and I'm willing to talk, but not on the phone. Where are you?"

"Starbridge."

"Okay, obviously I can't see you tonight, but tomorrow—"

"I'm coming tonight."

"But, Charles—"

"I've got to see you. If he lied about you I'll know he lied about everything," I said, and rang off before she could reply.

10

IN my room I changed back into my grey trousers, sports jacket and open-necked shirt. I also drank two glasses of water in pursuit of sobriety. Then I packed my bag, paid my bill and left the hotel.

The drive took less time than I had anticipated for there was little traffic at that time of night. Beyond the Surrey border on the ridge called the Hog's Back I felt tired but I cured that by stopping the car and drinking from my bottle of whisky. Staring at the lights which stretched north to London in the valley below me, I thought of Starbridge, its radiance masking unutterable horrors, but that memory was too painful to bear, and taking another shot from the bottle I drove on into the dark.

It was after midnight when I reached Starmouth Court, but a light was shining in the little morning-room where Loretta and I had first met. I glimpsed her figure silhouetted against the window, and a moment later I was stumbling into her arms.

"Everyone's gone to bed," she said. "Come and have a drink. You look shot to pieces."

In the morning-room she passed me a glass of brandy and I drank half of it straight off. Then I said: "Just what the devil did go on in that bloody spinney nineteen years ago?"

"We made love."

"Completely?"

"No."

"But why the *hell* didn't you make that clear?"

"Oh, for God's sake, Charles, give me credit for at least the minimum of good manners! You were panting to make love to me. How could I say: 'Wait a minute!' and regale you with a blow-by-blow description of what had happened with Alex?"

"But I only went ahead because I thought he'd gone ahead too!"

"My God, that's a bizarre remark!"

"But if I'd known there'd been no penetration—"

"The way he made love that hardly mattered. Alex did tell me that without penetration there was no adultery according to the law of England—remember me saying he'd have made a good lawyer?—but when one's busy having an orgasm, the legal niceties don't seem very important. As far as I was concerned I'd made love to him and he'd made love to me and—"

"But he told me the truth." I could think of nothing else. " 'I never penetrated her,' he said. So if he told me the truth about you, then he must have told me the truth about Lyle—"

"What did he say?"

I started drinking my brandy rapidly again. "He called my theory a fantasy."

"I'm not surprised."

"Shut up!" I shouted.

She jumped. "Charles—darling—take it easy—"

I tried to apologise by kissing her, but she was unresponsive, and the next moment she was removing the brandy bottle to the far side of the room.

"Maybe this is where I start to dream the dream," she said dryly. "You're obviously incapable of dreaming anything at the moment so I'll have to do the dreaming for you to help you along." She glanced at her watch. "How long would it take to get to Cambridge at this time of night?"

"Less than three hours. Perhaps less than two and a half. Petrol will be a problem but there's an all-night garage on the Great North Road." I swallowed the rest of my brandy. "Well, if you're washing your hands of me I may as well go."

"Don't be dumb, I'm coming with you."

"What!"

"Well, someone's got to look after you, haven't they, and there doesn't seem to be anyone else volunteering for the job!"

"But I wouldn't dream of dragging you all the way to Cambridge!"

"And I wouldn't dream of letting you go alone when you've obviously been hitting the bottle. I'm going to drive you home."

"But you're an American! You'll drive on the wrong side of the road!"

"Don't be ridiculous! I may have my faults but I'm not incompetent. Excuse me while I just scribble a line to Evelyn—and I'd better call a hotel to let them know I'll be arriving in the middle of the night. Which hotel should I stay at?"

"The Blue Boar. But, Loretta—"

"I'll use the phone in the hall. Just a minute, Charles."

I sank back on the couch, but as soon as I was alone the pain began to pound me and seconds later I was retrieving the brandy bottle.

II

SOMEWHERE north of Hatfield she said: "Where does that Abbot live—the one you told me about?"

"Heaven. He died and changed his address. Found that out this morning."

"Is there a new abbot yet?"

"You bet there's a new abbot—as you Yankees would say. He's an ex–Naval chaplain called Darrow who knows all about sex. Married nine years. Became a monk. Amazing." I took another sip of whisky. I had stopped having drinks now, of course. I just had little sips occasionally.

"He sounds like the kind of guy who could cope with anything. How do I get to the Abbey to deliver you?"

"Keep going to Cambridge. Turn off just before you get there. Little village. Grantchester. Like the poem by Rupert Brooke. My wife used to like his poetry . . . Did I ever tell you about my wife?"

"You said her name once. Jane."

"Jane, yes. I loved her very much. She was so pretty, so sweet, so good, and I was so unfit, so unworthy, so . . . But Father Darrow will be able to cope. Did I tell you he'd even fathered two children? Extraordinary. How could such a man become a monk, you ask. How could any man become a monk, you ask. Well, I'll tell you. It's a special gift—a 'charism,' as we say in the Church. In fact Father Darrow is what we in the Church would call 'charismatic.' He's six foot three and looks as if he practises telepathy in his spare time."

"Well, start exercising your telepathy, Father Darrow," said Loretta, "and lay out the welcome-mat for Charles."

I took another sip of whisky to help me face the thought of Darrow waiting beyond the welcome-mat, and the car sped steadily on through the night towards Grantchester.

12

THE porch light was shining at the Fordite mansion but the rest of the house was in darkness. Halting the car, Loretta switched off the engine and turned to face me.

"I'll leave the car keys with the bell-hop at the Blue Boar," she said. "Have you got that, Charles?"

"Car keys. Blue Boar. Porter. What funny words you Americans use!"

"Do you have a suitcase in the trunk?"

"No, I have a bag in the boot." Opening the door I levered myself from the passenger seat and leant against the car as I gazed up at the stars. "Beautiful," I said. "Reminds me of God. Utterly transcendent. Says Karl Barth."

Loretta was moving swiftly up the steps to ring the bell. Leaving my bag by the front door, she ran back to the car.

"Come along, darling. This way."

"I love you, Loretta. Marry me."

"No, you're going to marry Lyle. Remember?" She was steadying me as I cautiously navigated the steps.

"But you could cope. You're coping. I love you. That wonderful sex—if I could have you every night—"

"—you'd get tired of me. Look, someone's opening the door. Come on, darling, just another couple of steps. Nearly there."

A little white-haired monk appeared on the threshold. I had never seen him before but he said: "It's Dr. Ashworth, isn't it? Father Abbot's been expecting you."

Then I knew Darrow was already exercising his charism.

13

LORETTA kissed me and said: "Good luck."

"I'll never forget you, never," I said, but she was already on her way back to the car. The engine started, she waved goodbye and seconds later I could see only a pair of red lights vanishing beyond the gateway.

"This way, Doctor," said the little monk, steering me firmly over the threshold with one hand while he carried my bag with the other. He closed the door by a gentle push of his foot. "This way."

I was guided through a door which led into the guest-wing, and manoeuvred with skill to the corridor of bedrooms on the floor above. We finally stopped outside a door where the numeral four was painted on the panel, and the little monk, never relaxing his grip on me for a moment, set down my bag to turn the handle.

"Four's my lucky number," I said. "I'm so lucky, so privileged, so successful, it's really amazing how lucky I've always been. Did you know I was one of the Archbishop of Canterbury's chaplains when he was Archbishop of York? My parents were so proud. I come from a wonderful home—I've got wonderful parents, a wonderful brother, everything's always been so wonderful—I've had every possible advantage and yet I don't deserve it, don't deserve it at all because I'm so unworthy, so unfit." I sat down very suddenly on the bed. The room was small and neat, the bed placed in the corner, the table and chair by the window, the wardrobe against the inner wall, the basin in another corner by the unlit gas fire. There were no curtains, only a black blind, and no pictures. On the bedside table stood a lamp and a Bible.

"Now take a little rest on your bed," said the monk, speaking to me as if I were an exhausted child who had been thoroughly overstimulated by too much excitement, "and I'll tell Father Abbot you're here."

"He already knows," I said, kicking off my shoes and slumping back against the pillows.

The little monk smiled and disappeared.

The room began to revolve.

Closing my eyes I at last escaped into oblivion.

14

SOMEONE came into the room not long afterwards but I never saw him. Someone unpacked my bag and put it away on top of the wardrobe, someone put my prayer book by the Bible, someone put two aspirins and a glass of water on the bedside table. Someone, without doubt, paused to say a prayer for us both.

Then the light was turned out, the door was closed, and I was left to sleep dreamlessly in the dark.

15

I AWOKE in excruciating pain. My head was hurting, my stomach was hurting, my intestines were hurting, and beyond them my mind was hurting, every grain of it, and my soul was screaming steadily but soundlessly for relief.

But relief was absent and meanwhile I had to grapple with physical humiliation. I got my eyes open. They were aching. I struggled upright but had to bend over low to keep conscious. I crawled to the basin. I vomited. And all the time my soul was screaming steadily but soundlessly for relief.

I crawled back to the bed, saw the aspirins and somehow managed to swallow them, but I was too ill to be helped by pills and the next moment I was vomiting again. I only just managed to reach the basin in time. I levered myself upright, shuddering, shivering, stupefied with the pain, and when I looked in the mirror above the basin I saw myself as if in a distorted glass and recognised the stranger I was too afraid to know.

I backed away, nearly fainted, crashed into the table, slid down by the bed. "Oh God . . ." The pain was overwhelming me. I wanted to die. I knew it was a sin to pray for death but the pain was beyond all endurance and the never-ending scream of my soul, as if it surveyed the enormity of my shattering failures, was finally finding expression in the agonised words which streamed from my mouth like a haemorrhage. "My God, my God—forgive me, don't leave me, help me, *help me,* HELP ME—"

The door of the room opened and in walked Father Darrow.

PART TWO

THE MYSTERY BEYOND THE MYSTERY

"I am only facing the two quite general, but quite sufficiently rousing facts: that we all of us have 'selves' (the enemies of our good true selves) to fight, and that only so fighting are we adult, fruitful and happy."

Spiritual Counsels and Letters of
BARON FRIEDRICH VON HÜGEL,
ed. Douglas V. Steere

XI

"You will realise that the care of your health is a religious duty."

More Letters of
HERBERT HENSLEY HENSON,
ed. E. F. Braley

I

I GASPED: "I'm cut off from God." I was in terror. I was shuddering from head to foot. Tears were streaming down my face. "He's gone. He's rejected me. He's not here—"

"He's here but you can't see Him. You've been blinded."

"Blinded—"

"It's only temporary but meanwhile you must do exactly as I say. Let's try to get you up from the floor—and onto the bed—that's it—"

"I'm being invaded." I was shuddering again, gasping for breath. "Without God—all the demons—taking over—telling me I'm not fit to—"

"Take this." He shoved his pectoral cross hard into my hand. "The cross bars their path. No demon can withstand the power of Christ."

"But he's not here—"

"He's here. He's here whenever his followers are gathered together in his name. He's here."

I looked past the cross and saw the Spirit. It was there in his eyes, absolutely real, immediately recognisable. The demons retreated. I said not to Darrow but to the Spirit: "Don't leave me."

"There's no question of abandonment. When you're calmer you'll realise that, so your first duty to yourself—and to God—is to be calm. Keep holding the cross in your right hand and give me your left. That's it . . . And try to breathe better, take deep breaths . . . Good. Now I'm going to say a prayer for you, a silent prayer, and I want you to listen with your mind and try to hear what I'm saying."

Silence fell. I obediently listened but I heard nothing. However, after a while I became aware in my darkness of a strange heat. The cross slipped as my right hand began to sweat, and my left hand, enclosed between Darrow's palms, began to tingle. Thinking it was afflicted with cramp I tried to shift its position but he at once tightened his grip and the tingling continued. I was so fascinated that I made no further movement but sat docilely on the bed with my eyes closed. He had pulled up the chair from the table and was sitting within inches of me but on a higher level.

Slowly my hand was released. I opened my eyes to find he was watching me, and as our glances met, he said: "Did you hear the prayer?"

"No. But I remembered Our Lord saying: 'Lo, I am with you always, even unto the end of the world.' "

"And now you're calm." He smiled, quite unsurprised by my reply, and as I belatedly realised that the words of comfort without doubt reflected the essence of his prayer, I saw he was not only satisfied with my progress but pleased with his own uncanny skill. Slowly I said: "You're a healer. You helped me not only by prayer but by channelling power through your hands. That was the charism of healing."

"You're very flattering," he said, "but one could also say you healed yourself by breathing deeply, concentrating your mind on a fixed task and cutting off the supply of adrenalin which was drowning you."

I thought about that. He let me think about it. There was no attempt to hurry me. We continued to sit calmly together, I dirty and dishevelled in my grey trousers and crumpled shirt, he crisp and clean in his black habit with the white sleeves. As I continued to clutch his cross I became aware that life was, for the moment, bearable. My soul had stopped screaming. I was experiencing a remission of pain.

At last I said: "I suppose I'm having a nervous breakdown."

"Oh, I've always thought that a very unhelpful term—why don't we leave it to the medical gentlemen?" said Darrow carelessly, with that touch of confidence excusable in a healer who knows he may succeed where doctors fail, and suddenly he seemed so approachable, so compellingly easy to trust. Before I could stop myself I said: "I don't want to go to a lunatic asylum."

"There's no question of you going to a lunatic asylum."

"You don't think I'm—"

"Obviously you're going through some profound spiritual ordeal, but defining it in questionable medical terms is simply a waste of breath; it does nothing to solve the problem."

I managed to say: "How does the problem get solved?"

"If I may use the terms you employed so intriguingly yesterday, I'd say we have to examine the mystery and then look at the mystery beyond the mystery in order to locate the source of your pain and heal it. But first we must attend to practical matters. You're going to be here for some time. Are there any engagements you should cancel, any matters which have to be attended to?"

I remembered my car at the Blue Boar and gave him the telephone number of a friend who would remove it to Laud's. As he jotted down the information in a notebook I added that Lang would be expecting to hear from me, but before I could say more I found to my horror that my eyes were filling with tears. "I can't talk to him," I whispered. "I can't talk about—" But I was unable to finish the sentence.

"Leave him to me," said Darrow, as if the Archbishop were a troublesome schoolboy. "Is he expecting to hear from you this morning?"

"No, there's no great urgency, but—"

"We'll draft a message for him later. Now, Charles, your next duty to yourself—and to God—is to regain your physical fitness because as far as I know no one's yet tackled a spiritual ordeal successfully when they're worn out and hung over. How much did you drink yesterday?"

I tried to tot up the large drinks and the little sips but lost count.

"Was yesterday just a binge or have you been drinking heavily for some time?"

"A binge. But—" I hesitated before forcing myself to add: "I've been drinking more than I used to."

"How do you behave when you're drunk? Do you become the life and soul of the party, or do you merely fall asleep? Or do you perhaps become someone you most definitely don't want to know when you're sober?"

"The latter. I become angry and aggressive."

"The angry stranger . . . Yes, well, we'll take a look at him later, but meanwhile you must rest. I absolve you from reading the morning office because you're too sick to do it properly, but I'll bring you a book to look at if sleep proves difficult. Could you keep the aspirin down? No? Very well, I'll bring you some Alka-Seltzer."

"If I could have some black coffee—"

"No, I want you relaxed, not stimulated, and besides any liquid serves to flush out a hangover." Removing my glass, he refilled it from the basin. "Now I'm going to leave you for five minutes," he said, replacing the glass on the bedside table, "and while I'm gone you're to put on your pyjamas and get between the sheets."

I clutched the cross and fought my panic but panic won. "Don't go." Shame overwhelmed me. "I'm sorry—I'm being so stupid, so weak—"

"Michael, whom you met last night, will come at once if you call him. But I'll be holding you in my mind," said Darrow in the enigmatic language used by those who regard abnormal powers as merely a commonplace aspect of reality, "and I won't relax my grip. You won't need to call Michael."

I believed him. Mind triumphed over matter. Darrow was again exercising his charism.

2

ON his return he gave me another cross which I could wear instead of his own, and once the Alka-Seltzer had been consumed he produced the book he had brought from the library. It was *Mystics of the Church* by Evelyn Underhill.

"This is very light reading for a man of your background," he said, "and as it was published after you concluded your life as an undergraduate I doubt if you've ever troubled to read it. However, a glance at mysticism can often prove to be the shot of oxygen which revives a debilitated theological mountaineer, so if you can't sleep skim through a chapter or two, and when I return after the office at noon you can tell me whether or not you find the book mildly diverting . . ."

3

I WAS asleep when he returned. I had not even opened the book because sleep had overpowered me when I was still waiting for my headache to ease. I was woken at half-past one by the little white-haired monk who brought me a mug of soup, two hunks of bread, a plate of vegetables in a cheese sauce and a dish of plums. A glass of milk also stood on the tray.

"Father Abbot says you're to eat it all," said the little monk. "Remember your duty to God to be fit, he says. He says when you're finished you're to have a shower and get dressed and he'll come back and see you at three. The water won't be hot, Doctor, not in the middle of the day, I'm sorry, but Father Abbot says you're not going to be killed by a cold shower."

I was beginning to feel like an athlete in the hands of a ruthless trainer. Assuring Michael that I could well survive a cold shower I sat up, savouring the absence of nausea, and resumed the struggle to return to normality.

4

WHEN Darrow returned at three o'clock, I was dressed in my clerical suit and seated at the table as I read Miss Underhill's book. I had discovered that I could function normally so long as I did what I was told; no doubt this was why Darrow had given me such precise orders.

"That's better," he said as he saw me. He was carrying a chair which he placed opposite me at the table. "Did you forget to shave?" he asked as he sat down. "Or was there some difficulty—other than the lack of hot water—which made you feel shaving was best avoided?"

"You didn't tell me to shave."

"That's true, but nevertheless you must have considered the idea, if only out of habit . . . Was the difficulty centred on the razor? No, I knew there'd be no risk there. Then it was the mirror, wasn't it? You were frightened, perhaps, in case you saw the angry stranger, the one who takes you over when you're drunk."

I nodded but had to shade my eyes with my hand to conceal my distress.

"When you understand him better," said Darrow, "he won't seem so alarming, but before we concentrate on these problems of yours, let's dispose of the Archbishop of Canterbury. Since you became distressed when his name arose earlier, am I right in assuming he has some connection with the mystery which you went to Starbridge to solve?"

"Yes, he gave me this—this commission—"

"All I need at present is some short message such as: 'Commission completed, full details later.' Then I can telephone His Grace, give him the message and say that as you've been working very hard lately I've insisted that you make a lengthy retreat—in fact I can even say with perfect truth that I wanted you to begin the retreat earlier but you postponed it because you were so anxious to complete his commission."

I made a great effort. "You could say to him: 'All's well. Journal safe. No letters.' "

Darrow wrote down the message, snapped shut his notebook and said briskly: "Good. So much for the Archbishop. Now the next thing we have to decide is whether you're fit to begin discussing your problems today."

"I'm fine now."

"Fit enough to begin the task of confiding in me informally so that I can help you approach your formal confession before God?" said Darrow, clarifying the issue in case I was under the illusion that a talk between us would mean a mere sociable conversation. "Fit enough to talk about this commission in Starbridge?"

"Yes."

"Very well, go ahead and tell me about it."

There was a long silence. Eventually when the tears blurred my eyes again, I said in despair: "I must be mad because I can't stop crying and men never cry unless they're off their heads."

"That's a very powerful myth in our culture and a myth which can produce extremely unhealthy results. Which is better: to express grief and pain by using tear-ducts specially created for the purpose or to express grief and pain by enduring a silent secret haemorrhage of the soul?"

I said as the tears began to fall: "I feel so overwhelmed by the memory of all my unfitness."

"Very well, perhaps so far you haven't served God as well as you might have done. Perhaps you've even longed to put matters right—"

"I have, yes—oh, indeed I have, I've prayed and prayed for help but—"

"Then your prayers are being answered, aren't they?"

I stared at him. "Answered?" I looked around the room. I was barely able to speak. "I've broken down so utterly that I'm unable to continue as a clergyman, and you say *this* is God answering my prayers?"

"Of course. Do you think God's been unaware of your difficulties and the suffering you must inevitably have endured? And do you think He's incapable of reaching out at last to bring you face to face with your troubles so that you can surmount them and go on to serve Him far better than you ever served Him in the past?"

I understood but was unable to tell him so, and as I covered my face with my hands I heard him say: "God hasn't sent this ordeal to destroy you, Charles. He's come to your rescue at last, and here in this village, here in this house, here in this room where you've hit rock-bottom, here's where your new life finally begins."

5

HE cut short the interview at that point, but he rejoined me at five o'clock that afternoon as I was sitting on the wooden seat facing the herb-garden. The air was warm and scented, the sun was shining fitfully and a breeze was stirring the last pages of Miss Underhill's book in my hands.

"I telephoned the Archbishop," said Darrow, sitting at my side. "He thanked you for your message which he said was quite sufficient for the time being, and said he was delighted to hear you were making a retreat. He told me he always worried about young clergymen who were unusually successful by worldly standards, and he was sure a retreat could only prove beneficial. Finally he sent his good wishes along with his approval, and said he would be keeping a special place for you in his daily prayers."

Such affectionate sympathy triggered a guilt that I had rejected him. With great difficulty I said: "Dr. Lang's been very good to me in the past."

"And in the present?"

"He hasn't changed. But I have. I've drifted away from him. He's not a man I feel in tune with any more."

"Whom do you feel in tune with now?"

It was no use trying to hide my distress. I merely sat motionless, radiating misery, but when Darrow made no attempt to press me for a reply I became increasingly aware of my need to lance the misery by communicating with him. I said: "At Starbridge—" but no more words came, and I was just contemplating in despair the utter failure of my attempt at communication when he said idly: "I've never met the Bishop of Starbridge, but I heard him preach once when he was Vicar of St. Mary's Mayfair."

By a miracle of intuition he was transforming my failure into a triumph, and suddenly I sensed the line of communication, fragile but undeniably real, floating between us on the fragrant breeze from the herb-garden.

"That type of preaching is a special gift," reflected Darrow, "and like all charisms it can be dangerous if abused. I remember my spiritual director saying to me when I was a young man: 'Beware of those Glamorous Powers, Jon, the Powers which come from God but which can so easily be purloined by the Devil!' Dr. Jardine's a fine preacher and certainly when I heard him he had his gift immaculately disciplined, but I thought he was potentially a dangerous man."

I shuddered but the line of communication was no longer a fragile thread; it was a thick rope which was steadily hauling me out of the abyss of silence.

"A volatile temperament," mused Darrow, "a hypnotic edge to an attractive appearance, a brilliant mind, a God-given genius for homiletics—it's an explosive mixture, isn't it? In fact I've often wondered in recent weeks how I would feel if I were Archbishop of Canterbury and had to deal with a bishop whose latest hobby was creating havoc in the House of Lords."

My fingers closed on the cross below my neck and it was as if I grasped Darrow's hand at last after my long haul upwards on the end of the rope. I whispered: "I feel as if he annihilated me," and slowly, very slowly, I began to talk about my commission in Starbridge.

6

THE talk covered many sessions and was punctuated by periods of rest; later I realised that Darrow could judge with uncanny precision how much conversation I could tolerate without breaking down and how long

I needed afterwards for recuperation. However, as the days passed I became stronger, and by the time I had completed a detailed account of my first visit to Starbridge, I felt anxious to continue the story without further interruptions. It was an irony that I then encountered the formidable obstacle of my afternoon with Loretta. My narrative became disjointed; I lapsed into silence. It was late at night, and the only light in the room came from the bedside lamp which left Darrow's face in shadow as we sat facing each other at the table.

"Just say: 'There was an interval,' " he said at last, but when I remained unable to continue he commented not unsympathetically: " 'Strait is the gate and narrow is the way'—but perhaps a little too strait and narrow for you at present. Very well, we'll leave the story there for a while."

I realised then that I was being a coward, pointlessly holding my tongue when the nature of my error must by that time have been so obvious, and making a new effort I said: "You're using that quotation in the context of truth, just as you did when we first met. 'High and wide is the gate,' you said, 'which leads to self-deception and illusion, but for those seeking truth strait is the gate and narrow the way—' "

" '—and brave is the man who can journey there.' "

Crawling out from the shadow of my cowardice I told him what had happened in the spinney.

7

"... AND it was as if I was giving myself shot after shot of morphia. Every time the morphia wore off I had to give myself another shot because I was too frightened to face up to what was happening."

"And how would you define what was happening?" Darrow, who had registered no emotion during my confession, now permitted a note of interest to enter his voice as if I had made a statement which was worthy of a detached discussion, and I was so relieved by the absence of censure that I had no trouble replying: "My celibate life as a widower had utterly broken down and I couldn't see how I was going to go on."

"How old were you when you married?"

"Twenty-seven. Having no gift for celibacy I was tempted to marry immediately after my ordination, but since marriage then would have put me in a financial straitjacket and limited my opportunities—" I broke off in shame. "How calculating and ambitious that makes me sound!"

"It's not a sin to be prudent. It needn't necessarily be a sin either to be ambitious in God's service." He smiled at me. "But if you didn't rush to the altar in your early twenties, how did you solve the problem of chastity at that time?"

"More by luck than virtue. Not long after my ordination I became one of Dr. Lang's chaplains, and soon there I was, living at Bishopthorpe with the Archbishop watching over me like a lynx-eyed chaperon—"

"But surely if you had no call to celibacy, this role of secretarial monk must have become increasingly irksome?"

"Yes, I left the Archbishop eventually, returned to Laud's where I was a Fellow and began to teach. That was when I began to make a name for myself with my lectures on the Early Church."

"You were looking for a wife, of course."

"Yes, but I couldn't find anyone who was entirely right. Then I had the most astonishing piece of luck: Dr. Lang recommended me for the headmastership of St. Aidan's at Eastbourne, and soon there I was, twenty-seven years old, headmaster of a Church of England public school with a splendid salary—and a wife. She was the daughter of the retiring headmaster and I met her when I went down to St. Aidan's for the interview."

There was a pause but Darrow said nothing, and at last, driven by the need to terminate the silence, I said rapidly: "We were married three years and then she was killed in a car accident. She was pregnant. It would have been our first child. The shock was terrible. I . . . well, it took me a long time to get back to normal. I left the school and returned to Laud's to sink myself in research. I wrote a book—"

"I've read it. Very lucid. Arianism disembowelled with a chilling surgical skill."

"I wanted to disembowel something—it stopped me thinking about what had happened, so I worked and worked until my whole life revolved around that book to such an extent that I began to worry about what on earth I'd do when it was finished. However, in the end I didn't have to worry; there was no time. The book was a big success in academic circles and I was awarded my doctorate and suddenly I found myself being lionised—"

"—by the ladies, no doubt, as well as by the enthusiastic scholars."

"Yes, the celibacy got harder and harder, but somehow . . ." My voice trailed away. Again Darrow waited, and at last I was able to say: " . . . somehow I've never quite managed to remarry. Yet I do want to remarry—in fact I'm desperate to remarry, but . . . I don't."

"It sounds as if you're caught in some mysterious way between the Devil and the Deep Blue Sea. I can quite understand why you might regard the celibate life as the Devil if you've no call to celibacy, but why should you regard marriage as the Deep Blue Sea?"

"But I don't! I was very happy with my wife—my marriage was the most splendid success!"

"Then if the problem doesn't lie in marriage per se, where do you think it does lie?"

There was a long silence.

"Well, never mind," said Darrow at last. "That's not important for the moment. Now I suggest we call an end to the discussion at this point and—"

"The problem lies in me," my voice said. "*I'm* the problem. I'm so unfit and so unworthy that I feel no woman would ever be able to cope with me."

"And do the women you meet appear to share this view of you?"

"Oh no! But then they never meet the man I keep hidden. They just meet the man on public display." I hesitated but added: "I call him the glittering image because he looks so well in the mirror. But beyond him—"

"Beyond him," said Darrow, never batting an eyelid, "stands the angry stranger who appears in the mirror whenever the glittering image goes absent without leave."

"Yes. He's a destroyer. No woman could cope. Except Lyle. I think—yes, I really do think that Lyle could cope—"

"We'll stop there," said Darrow.

"She copes with everything, you see—everything—"

"We'll talk about her later but not now—you're exhausted. And anyway before we start discussing the dramatis personae, you must reach the end of your story. At present we're still with you and Loretta at Leatherhead."

I rubbed my eyes futilely at the thought of Loretta, but when I whispered in despair: "Stupid tears. Such a coward," Darrow said: "Nonsense! You've begun to squeeze through the narrow gate. You're being just as brave as you could be," and once again he gave me the strength to go on.

8

". . . AND then Jardine said: 'Let me try to bring you closer to what I'm afraid will prove a very unpalatable reality,' and he began to make this speech . . . I can't describe it—it was a nightmare—he tore up my glittering image and rejected my other self beyond—I'm sorry, that doesn't explain anything—"

"Oh yes it does," said Darrow.

"—but I can't find the words to convey the horror, the absolute *horror*—"

"You don't have to tell me any more than that for the moment. Just say: 'After Jardine had made his speech . . .' "

It was afternoon, that period of the day following the monks' dinner when there were no offices to be sung and they were free to attend to other work. Darrow and I were again sitting at the table in my room. We had hoped to hold the conversation in the herb-garden but the arrival of wet weather had made this impossible, and I was sorry to be confined to the house. At Darrow's suggestion I had been doing a little gardening in the afternoons; monks are always aware how much energy is required to sustain an adequate spiritual life and how much needs to be expended in physical labour.

There were other guests staying in my wing of the building, but Darrow thought it would be too arduous for me to be sociable, so to my relief I was told to avoid the common-room downstairs and see the other guests only at meal-times when the rule of silence ensured I could eat in peace. As a special privilege, providing me with an alternative to the seclusion of my room, I was allowed into the enclosed section of the house in order to read in the library, but I read only as Darrow directed; by that time my new examination of mysticism had advanced from Evelyn Underhill to Dean Inge and Baron Friedrich von Hügel, and as my reading progressed, I was both amazed and ashamed by the shallowness of my knowledge. Having long since decided that I preferred to work in the less spiritually demanding sphere of historical facts, I had tended to view mysticism merely as a recurring phenomenon which broke out, like a religious version of measles, whenever orthodox ecclesiastical life became sunk in abuse and inertia. Perhaps also I had felt that the morbid, aberrant aspects of mysticism made it suitable for study only by women, emotional adolescents, and eccentrics, and this prejudice had blinded me to the value of a true mysticism stripped of Oriental nihilism and Roman superstition.

However, I was at present too enfeebled to have much insight into this blindness which had undoubtedly sprung from spiritual arrogance as well as intellectual pride, and it was as much as I could do to read obediently, garden conscientiously and attend the services regularly in the chapel. I was forbidden to attend the night office of Matins because Darrow thought it was more important for my health that I should have an unbroken night's sleep, but I attended Prime at six in the morning, the combined service of Terce and Sext at noon, the combined service of None and Vespers at six in the evening, and Compline at eight. Mass was celebrated after Prime, and each morning I stayed to watch. I wanted above all to receive the sacrament, but I had accepted that I must abstain until my errors were fully understood and true repentance became possible. Darrow and I had discussed the situation once I had told him about Loretta.

"Of course you want to rush into a formal confession and wipe the slate clean without delay," he had said to me. "That's only natural. But I warn you, I'd ask some very searching questions before I gave you absolution, and quite frankly I doubt if at present you could begin to answer them. For instance, I'd want to know exactly why you made love to Loretta. Were you driven solely by what the melodramas call 'unbridled lust' or was there in fact very much more going on than the mere gratification of a passing whim? And whether or not the incident was merely the result of lust, I'd want to know what guarantee you could give me that such an incident wouldn't happen again—and that, of course, would bring us to the vexed question of your celibacy. How far do you really understand your problem about remarriage? It seems to me we have a lot of detective work to do here before you can view your situation with the degree of clarity necessary for any effective confession."

He paused as if he thought I might want to argue, but when I remained silent he said: "The point I'm making is that your behaviour with Loretta can't be confessed in isolation because such a confession would inevitably be inadequate. And can you in all conscience receive the sacrament after an inadequate confession of at least one very disabling sin?"

That question could only be answered in the negative, and I saw then how wrong I had been to hope that his absence of censure on the subject of Loretta meant that he intended to be lenient with me. I was used to benign elderly spiritual advisers who bathed me with sympathetic softheartedness; to encounter a director who was sympathetic but tough was unnerving. Yet it was also a relief. I knew a firm discipline was necessary as I struggled to regain my health, and because I could acknowledge this truth, I felt no desire to rebel against him; on the contrary, I found myself increasingly anxious to win his approval and had soon redoubled my efforts to complete the Starbridge narrative as truthfully as possible.

" . . . so Loretta said she'd drive me to Cambridge," I found myself saying at last. "I don't remember much about the journey but I do remember arriving here and seeing the stars and talking about the transcendence of God. I think I even mentioned Karl Barth."

"What an indestructible passion for theology!" said Darrow amused, but as I smiled, relieved beyond measure that my narrative was finally completed, I was unable to resist saying: "You must be thinking I've behaved like a lunatic."

"That's an emotional word and singularly unhelpful in this context. I think it would be more accurate to say that you're a normal man and like many normal men you have a set of personal problems which you're obliged to cart around with you wherever you go. However, you're also a strong man, strong enough to keep the hatches battened down on these problems, and you go on leading a normal life until one day you arrive in Starbridge. Then everything changes—and it changes because the Starbridge mystery somehow blasts aside those battened-down hatches and . . . Well, if I were still in the Navy, I'd say the Starbridge mystery had kicked you right in the balls."

I was so relieved by his stress on my normality that I was able to say at once: "The worst part of all is that I feel as if I'm still being kicked. I didn't solve the puzzle. I still don't know for certain what's going on. I do believe Jardine—I know that rationally I ought to believe him—I know that if I don't believe him I must be—" I broke off. "Yet I don't believe him," I said. "I can't believe him, I *won't* believe him—"

"Exactly. You're going round and round the mulberry bush in an emotional frenzy which is thoroughly exhausting for you and can serve no useful purpose." Darrow leant forward, resting his forearms on the table. "Charles, the first important truth to grasp is that neither you nor I, on the evidence so far available, can solve this mystery conclusively."

"But I've got to know—I've got to find out—"

"There you go again, burning to rush around the Starbridge mulberry bush in a dance which can only prove unproductive! You've got to break out of that circle, Charles, so let's approach the problem from another angle: why is it so important for you to solve this mystery?"

"It's because of Lyle, of course. I want to marry her, so I've got to know what's going on."

"Very well, let's take a closer look at your feelings for this woman who's at the heart of the mystery. I think this is the moment, Charles, when we finally begin to talk about Lyle."

XII

"I cannot honestly say that I think the adoption of celibacy would meet our present difficulties."

More Letters of
HERBERT HENSLEY HENSON,
ed. E. F. Braley

I

"IT'S easy to be sceptical about the idea that a lasting love can spring into being at first sight," said Darrow, "but one must always bear in mind that improbable things do happen and your feeling for Lyle might just be one of those improbabilities. In other words, Charles, I've resolved to keep an open mind on the subject. But can you make a similar resolution? Ideally I'd like you to prise your mind open an inch for the length of this discussion."

I regarded him warily. "You're asking me to admit I could be wrong about her."

"Don't feel threatened. I'm not out to undermine your feelings, only to clarify them, because I believe important consequences could flow from the clarification."

With reluctance I said: "Very well, I've got my mind prised open an inch. Go on."

"Let's suppose for a moment," said Darrow, "that your feelings are, in fact, an illusion. I think you'd agree that once you'd found out you were deluded, there'd be no question of marriage, and therefore the mystery of whether or not she's Jardine's mistress would become irrelevant."

With even deeper reluctance I said: "That's true. But nonetheless I'm sure—"

"Very well, let's now assume you're not deluded and that Lyle's the long-awaited Miss Right. Then obviously you must know the truth, but how likely is it that you've been able to see Lyle with such clarity so early in your acquaintance with her? Or to put it another way, we know that love at first sight's possible, but exactly how probable is it in this particular situation?"

"I just feel so certain that I can't be wholly mistaken—"

"Then let's consider a third theory. Supposing your feelings for Lyle are based neither wholly in illusion nor wholly in reality but in a mixture of the two. In other words there may well be some illusion going on but nevertheless you've recognised some quality in Lyle which you correctly believe will make her a good wife for you."

"But this is exactly what I feel!" I exclaimed. "I looked at her and knew she could cope with my problems!"

"The most important comment I can make about that statement," said Darrow, "is that probably no woman could cope satisfactorily with your problems before you've learnt how to cope with them yourself. The next most important comment I can make is that you've no way of knowing how true that statement is until you can perceive where the borderline between truth and illusion lies. Contrary to what you suppose, the real difficulty here is not what's going on between Lyle and Jardine but what's going on between you and Lyle. You've actually been going round and round in circles chasing the wrong problem."

"But surely it's vital to discover—"

"It's only vital to discover whether she's his mistress if you first discover that your feelings for her are solidly rooted in reality."

"But I can't be completely deluded! After all I'm a mature widower of thirty-seven—"

"I agree that's a powerful argument in your favour, but, Charles, no matter how undeniable your maturity and experience you should allow for the fact that these troubles of yours might be warping your judgement."

"You're leading me gently up the garden path," I said, "but I still can't see the front door. Are you saying—"

"I'm saying that this problem is all one and that we can't consider your feelings for Lyle in isolation from the remainder of your troubles any more than we could consider the incident with Loretta in that way. I'm saying that the best approach to the entire crisis is not to waste time speculating about what might or might not be going on at Starbridge, but to solve your private troubles, because then and only then will you be able to look at the Starbridge mystery with eyes clear enough to separate truth from fantasy and reality from illusion."

2

WE met again that evening. He took me for the first time to the parlour, not the Visitors' Parlour with its plain table and chairs but the Abbot's Parlour across the hall, and presently a monk brought us some tea and a plate of oatmeal biscuits.

"Is this a reward for good behaviour?" I inquired amused after the monk had departed.

"My intention was to give you a holiday before we embark on our voyage among your private problems."

The room was large and furnished with surprising lavishness in the style of the 1890s. I presumed that this decor had been inherited from the original owners of the house and preserved to impress any important visitors who might call on the Abbot. We were sitting on well-sprung armchairs which were upholstered in red velvet and placed on either side of a marble fireplace. Above the chimneypiece hung a passable painting, probably a Fordite investment, of Christ in the Garden of Gethsemane. A magnificent clock, its dial held aloft by two scantily-clad nymphs, ticked discreetly on the mantelshelf. The frieze below the shelf showed pagan hunting scenes containing more dubiously-clad females. I was surprised it had survived the Fordite invasion.

"It's an interesting room," I murmured politely as he passed me my cup of tea.

"That depends entirely on one's interests."

We laughed, and suddenly I wondered if he had ordained the holiday for himself as well as for me. I sensed he was glad of my company to relieve the strain of being a stranger in unfamiliar surroundings, and I was just about to ask him to tell me more about himself when he said: "How are you feeling now about the Starbridge mystery? Is it still revolving unceasingly in your mind or have you finally managed to encase it in a straitjacket?"

"I've got hold of the straitjacket; I do see that it's useless at present to expend further energy on speculation. But I can't quite get the straitjacket on the mystery. What I'd really like to know, Father, is what on earth you make of my story."

"My opinion isn't important," said Darrow at once. "My business is to illuminate the problem so that you can form a rational opinion of your own."

"I understand that. But—"

"It's also arguable that any opinion I had would be worthless. I wasn't a witness at Starbridge. All I have is your evidence, and your evidence must necessarily be influenced by many factors, some of which may distort the truth no matter how hard you've tried to be honest."

"Yes, I understand that too. But nevertheless—"

"I can certainly shine a spotlight into the dark corners. But will that help you get the mystery into the straitjacket or will it merely encourage you to go round and round the mulberry bush?"

I tried to put into words my need to have a yardstick against which I could measure my sanity. "I feel I need a reaction from you," I said. "Otherwise I'm going to spend my time wondering if you secretly think—" I could say no more but I had apparently said enough; at once Darrow made his decision.

"Very well," he said, "I'll turn on the spotlight. There are in fact a number of points about your story which I feel have a certain significance . . ."

3

"LET'S turn the spotlight first on Lyle," said Darrow. "Unless she's either a lesbian or else deeply involved with another man, it's hard to see why she should make such Herculean efforts to keep you at arm's length. After all, let's be frank; you're extremely eligible. I haven't forgotten that she may have profound psychological reasons for being set against marriage, but it seems to me that if she were completely frigid—to use the word in its psycho-analytical sense—you'd have deduced this during your more intimate moments with her."

"When I think of that sweltering kiss after our dinner at the Staro Arms—"

"Yes, if you feel she's sexually normal, your natural reaction would be to look around to identify the man who has the benefit of her normality; but, Charles, even if this man is Jardine, that still doesn't prove she's sleeping with him. She could well be in the grip of an unconsummated passion, and if we're wrong and she does indeed have some shadow on her psyche—a fear of sexual intercourse, perhaps, which could coexist with an apparently normal enjoyment of romantic attentions—then she might feel that an unconsummated passion suited her better than a passion which was consummated."

This unpleasantly plausible theory was not new to me but that did not make it less unpalatable. "In essence that was Jardine's explanation of Lyle's spinsterhood," I said with reluctance.

"Yes, but that proves nothing," said Darrow at once. "It could be true—but if he were obliged to invent a story to explain her abstention from marriage, he'd naturally pick the most plausible story available." And before I could comment, he added: "Let's shine the spotlight now on Jardine himself because the next significant point on my list is Jardine's attitude to you. I don't think you've quite realised how odd this is. Here you have a man who has a reputation for being fairly rude fairly often in his relentless crusade against hypocrisy. However, when your Machiavellian purposes are finally unmasked, does Jardine lose his temper with you? No, he doesn't. After a formal expression of outrage in which his anger is directed not against you but against Dr. Lang, he apparently makes strenuous efforts to be civil—indeed, he seems to pursue a policy of converting you into an episcopal pet. Now this is all very admirable but is it typical of Jardine? Not from what I've heard of him. Why didn't he kick you out of the palace? It's nonsense to say that your abrupt departure would have created unfortunate publicity. Jardine's always having rows with people. He'd just had a row with his Archbishop in the House of Lords. What newspaper would pay the slightest attention if he now had a row with a mere canon? His whole behaviour is most intriguing."

This was certainly an angle I had failed to perceive in the dimensions of the Starbridge mystery. "What's the explanation?" I asked.

"Let's hear your opinion, not mine."

"Jardine could have decided to tame me in order to allay my suspicions—and because he didn't want to worsen his relationship with Lang by throwing me out."

"True. Perhaps too he feared that if he threw you out, Lang would suspect the worst. Go on."

"I've run out of explanations."

"There's one other possibility," said Darrow, pouring me some more tea. "He might have given in to the urge to treat a promising young man as a son. It's a common syndrome among childless middle-aged men and would certainly explain his unusual benevolence towards you."

I suddenly found I could not drink my tea. I had to replace the cup in its saucer.

"All we can say with confidence here," said Darrow, watching me, "is that Jardine acted out of character, a fact which could be significant. And my next significant fact—"

"Yes," I said, "where does the spotlight go next?"

"Let's turn it on the signet-ring. Everyone so far, even Loretta, seems to have treated your theory of the informal marriage as if it were the last word in outrageous fantasy, but the fact remains that it's the one theory which explains how Jardine could enter into a liaison with Lyle and still believe he was avoiding apostasy. The fact that he would be grossly deluding himself is beside the point."

My relief was so great that I was unable to speak.

"The question I'd like to ask Lyle," said Darrow, when he saw I was beyond speech, "is this: why did old Mrs. Jardine—the stepmother—give her that particular ring? Most women of that generation would own several rings, not necessarily expensive ones but ornamental dress rings incorporating semi-precious stones. If Mrs. Jardine's hands were so afflicted by arthritis, she wouldn't have been able to wear any of her rings. Why not pick a pretty feminine ring for Lyle? Why choose this masculine signet-ring unless it had some special significance?"

"That's true." Excitement restored my power of speech.

"Don't get excited, Charles. The choice of ring proves nothing—old ladies can have strange whims. But nevertheless it's significant." He poured some more tea for himself. "I also find it significant," he said, "that when at the dinner-table you finally began to make statements implying the existence of an informal marriage, no one made any remark such as: 'Good heavens, what's he talking about?' or: 'I'm so sorry, Dr. Ashworth, but could you repeat that because I think I must have misheard you?' Your bizarre statements are received with a notable lack of astonishment—but this may merely have been because everyone was frozen with embarrassment by your lack of sobriety."

"So still nothing is proved!"

"No, but the next significant fact—Jardine's final explanation of his ménage—certainly makes one wonder what can be going on."

"Does it?" I said confused. "But he was so convincing! He destroyed my certainty that I knew the truth!"

"That says much for Dr. Jardine's powers of persuasion and he may indeed be innocent of wrong-doing, but there's an inconsistency in his story which appears to have eluded you. First of all he says he was attracted to Lyle but he appeased his wife by keeping Lyle in the household. It seems unlikely that any clergyman would decide to steer such a risky course unless he was deeply in love and not responsible for his actions, but let's concede he was at his wits' end about his wife's health; let's assume he spoke the truth when he implied his feelings for Lyle were a mere sexual inconvenience and that he had an overwhelmingly urgent reason for continuing to employ her. He then states that he mastered his feelings so that the ménage was able to function successfully. This too seems unlikely, but let's remember that middle-aged men do recover from tiresome minor infatuations, particularly if, like Jardine, they have powerful motives for recovering; in other words, let's once more give him the benefit of the doubt and assume this statement too is true. But then he brings out a really amazing piece of information: he admits that when he and Lyle first met, he wanted to marry her. Now, Charles, in my opinion that statement is incompatible with his earlier assertion that she was a mere sexual inconvenience. When a man wants to marry, deep passions are involved which can't conceivably be dismissed as an inconvenient middle-aged itch."

"So he was probably lying when he said he'd mastered his feelings!"

"No, don't jump to conclusions. This inconsistency certainly makes his story less plausible but implausible things do happen and we still have no evidence that he didn't succeed in controlling his feelings at Radbury. In fact his statement that Mrs. Jardine improved so much under Lyle's care that she was able to resume the marital relationship has the ring of truth and supports the idea that far from foundering further, the marriage took on a new lease of life."

"But what happened when they came to Starbridge and Mrs. Jardine's health deteriorated again? Couldn't Jardine's strong feelings towards Lyle have resurfaced?"

"It's impossible to know. And may I remind you, Charles, that we have no evidence whatsoever that Jardine and his wife aren't still enjoying marital intimacy."

"But according to Loretta—"

"Loretta submitted a plausible theory about what might have happened to the Jardines' marriage five years ago, but it remains a theory." Darrow paused to allow me to digest this before adding: "Charles, the significance of Jardine's disclosure that he once wanted to marry Lyle is *not* that it constitutes proof of gross misconduct. It doesn't. The significance lies in the fact that it reveals a situation which could hardly have been worse for Jardine's spiritual health. Even if there was no adultery in any physical sense, the scope for continuing adulterous thoughts is enough to make any confessor blanch."

This fact at once seemed so obvious that I exclaimed: "Why on earth didn't I see that at the time?"

"You were drunk and intolerably confused, but the truth is, of course, that any spiritual counsellor would have told Jardine to get rid of the girl even if the dismissal resulted in another breakdown for Mrs. Jardine. One's driven to conclude that Jardine sought no advice and merely went his own way—a very dangerous course for a clergyman to steer in such a very dangerous situation."

"So the stage would have been set for the kind of gross error represented by the unofficial marriage."

"Possibly, although there's still no proof that the gross error ever happened. Nevertheless the situation's significant—as significant as that final scene between you and Jardine, the scene which could justifiably be described as a nightmare in counselling."

I stared at him. Then I gave a convulsive shudder and looked away.

"We needn't talk about it now," said Darrow at once. "All I'm implying is that Jardine's gross mishandling of the scene suggests that he might have been shattered by the accuracy of your disclosures, but this again, like all our other theories, is non-proven. The innocent explanation is that he was shattered to see a young man whom he regarded as a son in such extreme distress, and his emotional involvement with you destroyed his ability to give effective counselling."

Still not looking at him I said carefully: "I want you to explain, please, why you're so sure he grossly mishandled the scene. After all, I haven't told you the details. How could you possibly know whether the disaster was his fault for being inept or my fault for being—" I gave another shudder.

Darrow said without hesitation: "Obviously you were in an extremely bad way and obviously something had to be done, but the solution was not to make a long speech which wound you up so tightly that in the end you snapped and rushed off on a journey you were quite unfit to undertake. What he should have done was calmed you down by letting you talk; he had absolutely no business to be making speeches when he should have been listening. Then the next mistake he made was to say what he did say, because whatever was said clearly proved unendurable to you. In that single comment you made earlier on Jardine's speech, you said: 'He tore up my glittering image and rejected my other self beyond.' Now we won't attempt an analysis of that sentence yet, but it seems clear to me that Jardine did something which is psychologically taboo: he dismantled defences which should have been left intact until you were strong enough to dismantle them yourself."

"Defences . . ."

"Don't worry about that now. Obviously we'll have to discuss the significance of your glittering image, just as we'll have to discuss your whole relationship with Jardine, but we won't discuss them until you're ready to do so, and when we do embark on a discussion I can promise you that the conclusions you draw will be your own, not conclusions which I've imposed on you during a long speech."

After a pause I said slowly: "He clearly thought—he made me believe—"

"We'll stop there," said Darrow, rising to his feet.

"—but in contrast you're treating me as if—"

"Come on, I'll take you back to your room."

"But tomorrow," I said, "I'll talk about him. I know I can talk about him now. You've got faith in me. You take my theories seriously. You don't think I'm—"

"Let's deal with tomorrow when we come to it—you're too tired to talk more at present," said Darrow, and sinking obediently into an exhausted silence I let him lead me back to my room.

4

"I WANT to talk about Jardine," I said the next day, to let him know my courage had not faded overnight.

"We can certainly talk about him if you wish, but I rather thought we might begin this examination of your private troubles by having another look at the vexed question of your celibacy. I'll tell you why: it's because it seems to me to be your most urgent problem. After all, you can probably live without Jardine, but can you live without a wife? The answer would appear to be no."

I relaxed as the ordeal of discussing Jardine was postponed. We were sitting at the table in my room again, and outside in the garden it was still raining.

"The situation is certainly confusing," Darrow was adding. "On the one hand you appear to have no doubt that you're not called to celibacy. But if we take celibacy in its strict sense—abstention from marriage—there's no denying that the celibate life is exactly what you've managed to achieve."

"But that's not in response to a call from God."

"You may well be right, but it's a very important point and we've got to be sure. I think you'd agree that as far as marriage is concerned, there are two types of churchmen. One set feels that marriage distracts them from serving God as well as they can, and the other set feels that as single men they can't serve God properly because they're continually distracted by loneliness and by wondering (as the naval ratings would say) where the next fuck was coming from."

"That's me," I said.

"Possibly, but don't rush to judgement. Now I think you'd also agree that sexual frustration can afflict even those called to celibacy because in both types of churchman the determining factor in their choice between a married and a celibate life isn't always the strength of the sexual drive."

"Think of St. Augustine," I murmured.

"Think indeed of St. Augustine, a celibate who admitted to a strong sexuality. The point I'm making, Charles, is that the urgency of your present sexual inclinations isn't necessarily an indication that you're not fundamentally called to celibacy, and the question I'd now like to ask you is why, at this particular stage of your life, are you having sex? Is it just to scratch the familiar itch or are there more complex reasons?"

"You're remembering that I likened the sex with Loretta to shots of morphia. You're thinking that I might be using sex merely to escape from my problems."

Darrow said: "If you are indeed using sex in that way, the danger is that marriage may not solve your problems but compound them. That's why we must be so cautious when considering your mysterious ambivalence about remarriage. Are you in truth suited for the domestic life? Might you be able to serve God better as an unmarried man? These are questions which should be carefully considered if we're to reach an accurate assessment of your difficulty here."

"I see the point you're making, Father, but the fact remains that I've been a married man and I know beyond doubt that marriage can help me to pray better, work harder and maintain a much steadier spiritual life. At present I'm hopelessly erratic and subject to distraction."

"All right, so be it; I accept that you're not abstaining from marriage because of a call to celibacy which your private problems are preventing you from recognising. Now having established that you do need a wife in order to serve God best, let's probe a little deeper into the mystery of why you can't reach the altar." He paused, and then looking straight at me with his very clear grey eyes, he said: "Tell me, Charles, who's the one who wants to get married?"

The question was so bizarre that I could only stare at him in silence.

"After all," said Darrow, "we mustn't forget, must we, that there are two of you."

I grappled with the implications of this statement for some time, but again he made no attempt to hurry me and at last I was able to say: "It's the glittering image who wants to get married."

"He's keen to marry the perfect wife and live happily ever after, just as a model clergyman should?"

"*I'm* keen to marry the perfect wife and live happily ever after, just as a model clergyman should."

"You're the glittering image?"

"Yes."

"Very well, but what about your other self? Let's hear again what he thinks about remarriage."

"Yes, I mentioned his attitude the other day, didn't I? He doubts that it's possible for him to marry and live happily ever after because he's so unfit and unworthy that no woman could cope with him. Except Lyle."

"Yet Lyle, in some mysterious way, is unavailable for marriage. Is it just a coincidence, do you think, that of the two women in your life at present, one is an independent woman uninterested in matrimony and the other seems determined not to become deeply involved with you?"

Again I had to take time to think but eventually I said: "It's no coincidence. It's part of a recurring pattern. For some years now I've only been attracted to women who aren't available for marriage to a clergyman." I was unable to stop myself adding: "Does that sound quite insane?"

"Not in the least," said Darrow serenely. "It's most sensible of your other self to take stringent precautions against remarriage if he feels such a step would be a disaster." He paused before adding: "It sounds as if he's very much afraid of this potential disaster."

After a long silence I managed to nod.

"This must be a great burden for your other self. Has he been carrying it long?"

"Seven years."

"He must be exhausted. Has he never been tempted to set down the burden by telling someone about it?"

"I can't," I said.

"Who's 'I'?" said Darrow.

"The glittering image."

"Ah yes," said Darrow, "and of course that's the only Charles Ashworth that the world's allowed to see, but you're out of the world now, aren't you, and I'm different from everyone else because I know there are two of you. I'm becoming interested in this other self of yours, the self nobody meets. I'd like to help him come out from behind that glittering image and set down this appalling burden which has been tormenting him for so long."

"He can't come out."

"Why not?"

"You wouldn't like him or approve of him."

"Charles, when a traveller's staggering along with a back-breaking amount of luggage he doesn't need someone to pat him on the head and tell him how wonderful he is. He needs someone who'll offer to share the load."

I considered this metaphor with care.

"Think of me as the porter," said Darrow, "and consider the possibility that life might be less exhausting if you unloaded some of your bags onto my empty trolley."

I considered this extension of the metaphor with even greater care. Finally I said: "Where do I start?"

"We need to go back seven years, I think, to that time when the burden claimed you. Can you say what happened seven years ago or is it too difficult? If it's too difficult at present we can leave it and talk of something else."

After a long moment I managed to say: "My wife died. Seven years ago. She died."

"Ah yes," murmured Darrow and waited, but my glittering image only said with composure: "I'm afraid there's nothing I can tell you that you don't already know."

"Nothing at all?"

"No, I've already told you, haven't I, how terrible it was when she died, and obviously I'm still affected by my grief. It's as if I don't want to risk involving myself with anyone else who might die and cause me so much pain."

"I can quite understand that," said Darrow, "but isn't the grief in any way alleviated by the memory of the years you had together before she died?"

"Yes, of course," I said at once. "We loved each other very much and had three years of perfect happiness."

"No clouds in the sky?"

"None at all."

Darrow merely said: "You mentioned your wife was pregnant when she died. Had she been pregnant long?"

"No, she'd only just found out."

"I see. And you'd been married three years. That must surely have been a considerable strain for you both."

"Strain?"

"Wondering month after month why no child came."

I got up and walked out of the room.

XIII

"Childless husbands and wives fall easily apart."
Letters of
HERBERT HENSLEY HENSON,
ed. E. F. Braley

I

I WENT to the bathroom and sat for a minute on the edge of the bath. When I had myself completely in control I returned to my room and found Darrow was still sitting at the table but I gave him no chance to speak. Immediately I said: "My marriage is of no significance in this context and I don't want to waste your time talking of matters which are of no significance. I know it's ridiculous that I haven't remarried, but all I have to do is to pull myself together and behave sensibly." As I spoke I was moving around the room, pausing by the bedside table, picking up the Bible, flicking through the pages. The various books streamed past my fingers: Genesis, Exodus, Leviticus, Numbers, Deuteronomy, Joshua—

"Obviously you'd prefer to resume this conversation later," said Darrow, rising to his feet. "I'll leave you to unwind."

"You completely misunderstand!" I said annoyed. "You're thinking I can't go on but I can—of course I can! And I don't need to unwind—I'm not wound up!"

"Then why are you pacing around like a lion at the Zoo?"

I bit back the exasperated blasphemy, smothered the impatient obscenity and flung myself down in my chair again. Darrow too resumed his place, but although I waited for his next question, he merely embarked on a minute examination of his Abbot's ring until at last I was driven to demand: "Why don't you say something?"

"I was waiting for you to talk to me."

"But I've nothing to say!"

"Very well, we'll sit in silence."

I leant forward and tugged at his sleeve to stop him examining the ring. Then I said: "I want to go on but I can't unless you ask questions."

Darrow immediately reverted to his usual close attentiveness. "Let's leave your wife for the moment," he said, "and talk about these ineligible women who have been attracting you since her death. In what way were they unsuitable for a clergyman?"

"They were divorced or separated or agnostic—or if they weren't agnostic they were vague Deists like Loretta."

Darrow said casually: "Did you sleep with any of them?"

I was appalled. "Good heavens, no, of course not! Word would have got around—it would have ruined my career, my whole future—I couldn't possibly have had sex with any of them!"

Darrow said: "Who's 'I'?"

I was silenced.

"We know for a fact," said Darrow, "that someone called Charles Ashworth has indeed had sex recently with one of these ineligible women, a vague Deist called Loretta Staviski."

"That wasn't me."

"So it was your other self who made love to Loretta. But how does he normally manage if he finds chastity difficult?"

After a pause I said: "He goes abroad. Holidays. Always abroad. Loretta was an exception because when I'm at home I usually succeed in keeping him locked up."

"And at the end of these holidays abroad there's always confession to a foreign priest?"

"Of course! Confession, repentance, absolution . . . well, I couldn't have gone on otherwise, could I, and I must go on because nothing must stand between me and my calling. Unless I serve God in the Church my life would be entirely meaningless so it would be quite wrong, wouldn't it, if my longing to serve Him was frustrated just because someone unfit and unworthy who isn't me at all commits an error every now and then."

"Tell me," said Darrow, "were you never able to discuss with Father Reid these difficulties caused by your other self?"

"Oh, but I couldn't! Dear old Father Reid, he liked me and approved of me so much and I couldn't bear the thought of disillusioning him." I hesitated but added firmly: "It would have been cruel."

Darrow said: "And what about Dr. Lang, who clearly also likes you and approves of you? Did you ever confide in him or did you decide that that too would have been cruel?"

I looked at him closely but saw no trace of an irony which would hint at either incredulity or condemnation. With care I said: "I was chaste when I worked for Lang."

"I realise that, but what about the time before your ordination when you were already very much Lang's protégé? Were there no wild oats sown during your Varsity years?"

"But I couldn't possibly have told Lang about that! It would have meant the end of his patronage—he wouldn't have liked and approved of me any more!"

"Charles, would I be reading too much into your remarks if I deduced that liking and approval are very important to you?"

That was an easy question to answer. "Well, of course they're important!" I exclaimed. "Aren't they important to everyone? Isn't that what life's all about? Success is people liking and approving of you. Failure is being rejected. Everyone knows that."

"We'll stop there," said Darrow.

"Success means happiness," I said, "and that's why I'm in fact such a happy person despite these little troubles which are bothering me at the moment. I've always been so successful—a wonderful career, a wonderful marriage—"

"We'll talk again this afternoon," said Darrow. "The weather looks as if it might clear up. We might talk in the herb-garden."

2

"I MUST apologise for making such a stupid exhibition of myself this morning," I said as the scent of the herbs floated towards us on the mild air. "Of course I realised as soon as you left that I'd behaved like a lunatic."

"You were a little irritable, certainly, but I saw no signs of lunacy."

"What about all that mad switching about between the two personalities?"

"You were speaking of very difficult matters and I was encouraging you." Darrow was quite unruffled. "It was I, not you, remember, who brought the concept of the two personalities into the conversation in the hope that it would bring us closer to the truth."

I relaxed. "Nevertheless," I said, "I was a fool to pretend my marriage was all sunlit perfection because I'm sure that aroused your scepticism. After all, you've been married yourself; you must know very well that even in the happiest of marriages there can occasionally be a dark corner or two."

There was a pause while I gripped the arm of the garden seat with my left hand and groped for my cross with my right. Then Darrow said idly: "When did the first dark corner appear in your marriage?"

"Straight away because there was a problem about money. I regret to say I'd been extravagant, keeping up with the people who mattered, and by the time I met Jane I was in debt. There was no real difficulty because I had the prospect of an excellent salary as headmaster, but starting out in married life is expensive and I didn't want Jane's father to think I couldn't afford to give his daughter the best."

"Her father approved of you?"

"Very much, yes, so of course I didn't want to upset him by confessing I was in financial difficulty. Well, after the wedding I said to Jane we'd have to be careful for a while—no radical reduction in our standard of living but merely an avoidance of any major expenditure."

"Sounds reasonable."

"Yes, but . . . no doubt you can imagine the dilemma that put us in, Father."

"I can still remember," said Darrow, "the heart attack I almost had when my wife bought the baby's perambulator and told me how much it had cost."

"Yes, I knew you'd understand, and you can see too, of course, what an awkward position I was in as a clergyman. When I married in 1927 the Church of England's official attitude to contraception was still negative."

"Very awkward."

"Jane was devout and when I suggested contraception, she was shocked. She'd have accepted it later, after we'd had four or five children and another pregnancy might have been detrimental to her health, but she didn't believe contraception was right for newly-weds. Well, neither did I, but . . . It was difficult, Father. It really was."

"Did this lead to quarrels?"

"Jane wasn't the sort of person who quarrelled. She just cried and then tried to be brave, but I was terrified she might confide in her father. The old boy was a clergyman of the Victorian school and he thought all contraception was the invention of the Devil."

"What effect did this difficulty have on your intimate life?"

"Well, Jane wanted to be a good wife so everything seemed on the surface to be all right, even when I began using French-letters, but . . . I knew she was unhappy about the situation and that made me feel guilty—and feeling guilty made me feel angry because I resented being made to feel guilty. Sex got a bit tense. Everything got a bit tense—"

"You were using French-letters all the time?"

"Yes, except occasionally when I ran out of my supply. I couldn't buy them locally because of the risk of being recognised, and I didn't always have the time to make the necessary expedition further afield so sometimes I had to practise withdrawal—but oh, how I hated that! I was always so afraid of an accident—"

"Profoundly afraid? Why? Were you still in financial trouble?"

"No, my financial affairs were much improved. By the time we celebrated our first wedding anniversary, I even had a balance in the bank."

"In that case I presume the subject of a baby again came up for discussion?"

"Yes. Jane wanted to abandon the contraception and I agreed. But then an awful thing happened, Father, every man's nightmare. I began to suffer from premature ejaculation. I'd ejaculate even before I'd penetrated her."

"How very distressing. What did your doctor say?"

"Oh, I couldn't go to my doctor! I knew him socially—he was a friend of my father-in-law's, and I didn't want anyone I knew thinking I was a sexual failure. Anyway I was all right so long as I was using the French-letters."

"You're saying you went back to the contraception?"

"Well, I had to, didn't I? Our sex-life had turned into a disaster without it. So I said to Jane: 'I'll have to keep on with the French-letters until I can get over this difficulty,' and she said: 'Just as you think best'—but then I heard her crying in our bedroom—"

"When did you confide in your spiritual director?"

"I didn't. This wasn't a spiritual problem."

"Are you telling me that this severe marital worry didn't impinge on your life of prayer and your service to God?"

"But I couldn't tell dear old Father Reid! He was so holy—so celibate—how on earth could I have talked to him about French-letters and premature ejaculation? It's just not the sort of thing one talks about to one's spiritual director, is it, and besides . . . I didn't want another churchman to know about the contraception."

"Thinking of your duties as a churchman, may I ask how you were faring as headmaster of St. Aidan's while this trouble was going on?"

"Oh Father, in a way that was the worst problem of all—I hated it! I was so bored with all those adolescent boys—I'd forgotten how tedious boarding-school life could be—"

"When did you realise you'd made a mistake?"

"Almost straight away but I felt I couldn't say anything because everyone—especially Lang—was expecting me to make a huge success of it and I couldn't bear the thought of disillusioning them. So I knew I'd have to endure the situation for a minimum of three years—if I'd left earlier people might have judged me a failure."

"What did Jane think of your unhappiness with your work? She must have been very upset."

"Oh, I never told her," I said. "No, of course I never told her. Like everyone else she was expecting me to be a great success, and anyway she was so upset already that I felt I couldn't bear to upset her further—"

"Where had your intimate life got to by this time?"

"It was all very awkward. Occasionally I dispensed with the French-letter but it never worked. However, we both tried very hard to pretend nothing was wrong, so—"

"But surely such a situation couldn't have gone on without some sort of crisis occurring?"

"Jane did become a little depressed. It wasn't a nervous breakdown, you understand—no one ever called it that—but she cried all the time and said she wanted to go and stay for a while with her father . . . I nearly had a fit when she said that, but then she screamed at me that I cared more about what her father thought than about what *she* thought, and I said no, I care terribly what you think, I love you, and she broke down and said how could I be content to go on without a baby, and I said I'm not, I want a child as much as you do . . . And then, Father, finally, the terrible truth dawned on me and I realised that was a lie. I didn't want a child. I didn't know why. I still don't know why. I just thought: I can't be a father, I can't cope. But I knew I couldn't tell Jane and I knew I couldn't tell anyone else. A Christian marriage is for the procreation of children, and I wasn't just a Christian, I was a clergyman. But this stranger, the one who lives behind the glittering image, he didn't want a child and he took over my marriage; I—I tried hard to keep him out, I tried so hard, Father, so hard—" I was breaking down but I dragged myself together. " 'Strait is the gate,' " I whispered, " 'and narrow is the way.' " I scrubbed my eyes with my cuff and somehow found the strength to go on.

"The odd thing was," I said, "that as soon as I'd admitted to myself that I didn't want a child, I had no more trouble with premature ejaculation. It was as if that just protected me from fatherhood while I couldn't face up to the truth, but once I'd faced the truth, I found I had almost limitless powers of control. I used to pretend with Jane. I'd pretend to reach a climax and somehow manage to hold back until I could get to the lavatory afterwards—"

"But Jane must surely have realised there was no seminal fluid."

"I don't know. I don't know what she thought, Father. We never talked about it."

"You were, in fact, by this time deeply estranged."

"Oh no, Father, everyone always remarked how happy Jane and I were, the ideal young couple—"

"How did the tragedy end?"

I opened my mouth to say: "It wasn't a tragedy!" but the words were never spoken. I was too overwhelmed with relief that at long last the pain had been correctly identified. I felt as if I had finally exchanged a pair of brutal clogs for a pair of handmade leather shoes. "Tragedy," I said. "Tragedy." I had to say the word aloud to make sure it was real. I said to Darrow: "It's the word 'success' which is unreal here, isn't it? But I always have to talk in terms of success because tragedy and failure are"—I groped for the right word but could only produce—"unacceptable."

Darrow said nothing.

"Tragedies and failures don't happen to me," I said. "They're not allowed to happen."

"Who's 'me'?" said Darrow.

"The glittering image."

"Then whom did this tragedy happen to?"

"My other self."

"He agrees now, does he, that it was a tragedy?"

"I think he always knew. The suffering seemed so undeserved."

"Made him feel angry, did it?"

I managed to nod.

"Good!" said Darrow astonishingly. "It's right that he should be angry if he's been locked up and forbidden to acknowledge his suffering! What could be more inhumane to a suffering man than to imprison him?"

I said confused: "But I've got to keep him locked up!"

"Yes, but I think," said Darrow to the glittering image, "that you need a rest. Being such a ruthless jailer must be the most exhausting occupation. I think the prisoner might be allowed out on parole here in this room—just for a minute or two—so that he can complete the story of the tragedy which he feels belongs to him and him alone. Or does he perhaps feel too angry to talk about it?"

"No, he wants to talk," I said, "because he knows you'll understand." Then I stepped out from behind the glittering image. I felt stark naked, terrifyingly vulnerable but not alone. I came out because Darrow was there to meet me and I trusted him not to recoil in horror.

"The tragedy ended when Jane got pregnant," I said, and *I* said it, my other self said it, and not just my other self but *my true self,* the real Charles Ashworth, said: "I don't know how it happened, but I suppose that for once the coitus interruptus wasn't so interrupted as I thought it was. Then one night I came back to the headmaster's house after an absolutely damnable staff meeting—oh, how I hated that school!—and Jane was waiting for me with shining eyes to tell me the good news. And then I—my other self—MY TRUE SELF—*I* took over from the glittering image. I said: 'My God, that's the last thing I need to hear after another bloody awful day at this bloody awful school,' and I poured myself a double whisky. Jane said: 'You're not the man I thought I was marrying.' Tears were streaming down her face, and immediately I was crucified with guilt. I went over to her, begged her to forgive me, but she shouted: 'Never!' and hit me and rushed out. I was so stupefied that I didn't at first rush after her—and when I did, it was too late. She'd gone to the garage and taken out the car. I couldn't catch her before she drove off and less than five minutes later she'd crashed into a tree—killed instantly—no other car was involved, and the coroner at the inquest said what a tragic accident it was, but of course I always wondered—I always wondered—"

"—if it was suicide," said Darrow.

I leant over the table, buried my face in my forearms and cried as I had not cried since I had learnt of Jane's death seven years before.

3

"IF she was devout," said Darrow, "suicide is unlikely." He had moved his chair around the table so that he could sit at my side.

"But I can never be certain of that and meanwhile I feel her death was entirely my fault—"

"I quite understand why you should feel that, Charles, but it's not a judgement you're qualified to make. We never know all the circumstances of a tragedy, and even if we did we might not have the wisdom to interpret them correctly."

"But the indisputable fact remains—"

"The only fact which is beyond dispute here is that your wife is dead. God saw fit, for reasons which are hidden from us, to claim her after only a short life in the world, and you must accept this. Your guilt is making you say that this shouldn't have happened, that God made a mistake, but this is arrogance. Say to yourself instead: 'Jane is now beyond all pain and this is God's will. I did make errors during my marriage but the best thing I can do now is not to wallow in guilt but to find out why I made these errors so that I can ensure they never happen again.' Then Jane's death will have meaning."

"I did love her," I whispered. "I really did."

"Of course. That's why you're not sitting back and saying: 'My marriage was a disaster but thank heaven I escaped!' And that's why you must, in memory of her, reconstruct your life so that you can make the right marriage to the right woman. Your first task, I think, is to understand exactly why your marriage ran into such painful difficulties."

"But I do understand! It was because my real self was so unfit, so unworthy—"

"Stop!" said Darrow so incisively that I jumped. "That statement contradicts every word you've just uttered!"

I stared at him. "I don't understand."

"In your narrative you made it quite clear that your true self didn't get a chance to speak his mind until that final scene. Who was really running that marriage of yours?"

I could not answer.

"Your marital difficulties didn't begin in that final scene, did they? They began before you were married when you ran into financial trouble—and who got you into financial trouble by luring you into keeping up expensive appearances? Who kept you from seeking help by demanding that no one should know your marriage was in difficulty? Who seduced you into that disastrous headmastership and then insisted that you stayed there? Who came between you and your wife and prevented you from being honest with her? Who initiated this tragedy and then left your real self bearing the burden of all the guilt and the shame?"

But still I could not speak. My emotion was beyond expression.

"You're not the villain of this story, Charles," said Darrow. "You're the victim. It's the glittering image who should be locked up in jail."

4

THERE was a long silence while I struggled to adjust to this new perspective on my identity, but eventually Darrow added: "I'm beginning to feel very, very sorry for this true self of yours. Terrible things happen to him but no one knows because he's not allowed to talk about them. He's cut off, isolated by that ruthless jailer. He only ever escapes when the jailer has too much to drink and then he's always so aggressive that he seems thoroughly beyond the pale, but no wonder he's so angry! He's been imprisoned on a false charge by a jailer who should himself be behind bars. Tell me, can you really feel no sympathy for him in his predicament?"

"Yes, but . . . what good would my sympathy do?"

"All the good in the world because if you regard him with sympathy instead of horror then a different image will begin to appear in the mirror. Love and compassion breed understanding and forgiveness, and once a man's understood himself sufficiently to forgive himself for his mistakes, the unfitness is made whole, the unworthiness is redeemed—and that's what we want, isn't it, Charles? We want to restore your belief in your own worth so that you can find the courage to set aside the glittering image and triumph over this tyrant who's tormented you for so long."

Once more the unwanted tears began to fall. I heard myself whisper: "Why do I feel so worthless? Why has all this happened?" and Darrow said: "That's the mystery beyond the mystery—and that's the mystery we've now got to solve."

5

WE met again that evening. The bedside lamp glowed behind Darrow as usual and gave his unremarkable grey hair a distinguished silver sheen. His ineradicable air of authority was heavily muted; I was conscious primarily of his serenity.

"Can you come out on parole again?" he said. "I'm anxious to hear what you think about that glittering image now that you've had the time to reflect on our last conversation."

"He's got to be locked up. I can see that. But I can't see how I'm ever going to do it."

"It's possible," said Darrow, "that if we can solve the mystery beyond the mystery, he may simply wither away."

I was intrigued but sceptical. "I can't imagine him not being there."

"Been around long, has he?" said Darrow casually.

"Always."

"He's always been there defining success in terms of winning everyone's liking and approval?"

"Yes."

"But what about you, Charles? How would your true self define success?"

"Well, of course I do realise," I said, "that there's more to life than winning everyone's liking and approval. Success is pursuing one's calling to the best of one's ability. In other words, one dedicates oneself to serving God, and—"

"Which self?"

"One's true self," I said automatically, and heard my sharp intake of breath. Still grappling with the insight which had been thrust upon me, I concluded: "One dedicates one's true self to serving God and one strives hard to do His will."

"Or to put it in non-theological terms," said Darrow, allowing me time to complete the struggle, "success involves realising the fullest potential for good of one's true self so that one's life is a harmonious expression of one's innate gifts. Now, Charles, how would you, your true self, define failure?"

"Locking up one's true self in order to live a lie," said my voice. "Living out of harmony with one's true self in order to pursue the wrong goals for the wrong reasons. Caring more about other people's opinions than about serving God and doing His will." I added in shame: "I can see I've been very much in error."

"Yes, but the point to note is that your errors haven't arisen because of any profoundly incapacitating unfitness on the part of your true self. He knows—*you* know—exactly what you should be doing with your life, but that glittering image has such a stranglehold over you that you have to devote an enormous amount of time and energy to keeping him happy."

I explored that summary and finally pronounced: "I'm like someone who's being blackmailed."

"Exactly. The glittering image insists that the right people won't like and approve of you unless you give him a luxurious home right in the forefront of your personality, and for some reason you're so addicted to liking and approval that you're willing to give in to this demand in order to satisfy your addiction."

I thought that over. "When I know people like and approve of me," I said tentatively, "I don't feel so unfit and unworthy any more."

Darrow looked pleased as if some inarticulate pupil had made an eloquent speech. "Excellent," he said. "And now perhaps you can see why, if we solve the mystery beyond the mystery, the glittering image may simply fade away."

"It must be a question of breaking the addiction. If I don't feel unfit and unworthy, then I won't be so dependent on people liking and approving of me and I won't need the glittering image to secure their liking and approval."

Darrow looked pleased again as if the inarticulate pupil had finally reached the top of the class, but before he could comment I said in despair: "I can see all this intellectually, but—"

"—but emotionally you still can't imagine how you could ever live without your glittering image systematically captivating the people who matter. But I think if we trace him back to his roots and find out how he came into existence, we'll begin to see why you feel too unfit and unworthy to go through life without him."

"But the glittering image doesn't have any roots," I said, baffled. "I told you—he's always been there."

"How very remarkable," said Darrow blandly. "I've never before heard of a baby who arrived in the world complete with a glittering image."

I smiled uncertainly at him before saying: "Supposing we can't find the roots?"

"I don't see why we shouldn't. It's just a question of knowing where to dig. Then once we reach the roots, we'll prise them out so that the entire noxious weed can be left to wither away in the sun while the half-strangled starving plant in the flower-bed will be able to flourish at last."

I considered this prospect in silence and the silence lasted a long time.

"However," said Darrow watching me, "digging's hard work and you may not be strong enough yet."

I said suddenly: "Is this where the gate gets even straiter and the way even narrower?"

"Yes, but we don't have to approach this new gate yet, Charles. We can just sit and look at it for a while."

But all I said was: "I want to go on."

XIV

"It is not quite easy to fix an autobiographical paragraph into such a composition as that which I am now addressing to you, but I think it will have to be attempted, for undoubtedly my personal religion has been strongly affected by the eccentric course of my early years."

HERBERT HENSLEY HENSON,
RETROSPECT OF AN UNIMPORTANT LIFE

I

IT was morning and the light of a clouded day illumined my room as we sat down again at the table. I had repeated my desire to begin the excavation which would lead to the root of my glittering image, but Darrow had made no immediate reply; I suspected he was calculating how far I spoke out of bravado.

"Well, we won't drill straight away to bedrock," he said at last. "Let's first scrape off a little topsoil by talking of Jardine."

My hand groped for my cross.

"We won't discuss him in detail," said Darrow quickly. "I'd just like you to clarify my mind on a single point: did Jardine like you straight away? He obviously liked you very much later or he wouldn't have told you about his father."

I could think of the early part of my visit to Starbridge without difficulty. "I don't think he did like me particularly at first," I said. "He thought I was just one of Lang's bright young men."

"Did you want him to like you?"

"Yes, of course."

"Why 'of course'? It could have been a matter of supreme indifference to you."

"Yes, but during our row at the dinner-table he gave the impression he strongly disapproved of everything I said—"

"—and you didn't like him disapproving of you."

I hesitated before saying abruptly: "I hated it."

"Yet it would be true to say, wouldn't it, that by the end of your visit you'd managed to win his approval despite all the friction caused by Lang's commission and your attraction to Lyle?"

I nodded.

"Very well," said Darrow, "we've established that here was an important man many years your senior who liked and approved of you. Now let's leave Jardine and go further back into the past—let's talk about your relationship with Dr. Lang. There seems to be a similar pattern here . . . but perhaps I'm mistaken."

"No," I said reluctantly. "Lang and Jardine are two very different men but I was equally successful in winning Lang's liking and approval."

"Can you describe the relationship with Lang in more specific terms?"

"I was his protégé."

"Yes, but is there one adjective, do you think, that we can use to describe the attitude of this distinguished man many years your senior who likes and approves of you?"

"Benign."

"There isn't another adjective you'd choose?"

"No," I said at once.

"Very well, let's go back a little further to Jane's father, another distinguished man many years your senior who regarded you benignly. When you were telling me about Jane, you made it clear how important his liking and approval were to you, and obviously you succeeded in getting on well with him. Did Jane have any brothers?"

"No. The old boy minded that very much, I think."

"In that case he must have been very pleased to have acquired such a first-class son-in-law."

I traced a mark on the table with my forefinger and said nothing.

"This is really quite a coincidence, isn't it?" said Darrow. "Three distinguished older men, all regarding you with exceptional approval! Would you say they had any striking feature in common?"

"The Church."

"Was that the only common denominator?"

"Yes," I said at once.

"And when you were up at Cambridge as an undergraduate—I expect there was someone special there too, wasn't there, who took a benign interest in you?"

"Well, as a matter of fact," I said, "yes. I became the protégé of the Master of Lauds."

"Did he have a family?"

"Both his sons were killed in the War."

"And before you went up to Cambridge I'm sure the headmaster of your school took a special interest, didn't he?"

"Yes, I was head-boy."

"And at prep school?"

"Yes, I was head-boy there too."

"And what happened before you went to prep school?" said Darrow. "Who was the important older man in your life then?"

I looked out of the window, I looked all the way down the garden, I looked far back into the past, and the silence closed around us as the memories stirred in my mind.

"Charles," said Darrow, "for some days now I've been watching all the characters in the drama of your life parade across the stage, but there's a very important person who hasn't yet appeared. Is this perhaps the moment when he makes his long-awaited entrance or are you going to save him up for a later scene?"

I laughed. "By all means let him make his entrance!" I said. "But in fact my father's not important in this context."

"If you'd prefer to say no more—"

"Oh, there's no question of that! What do you want to know?"

"Well, perhaps you could just mention in passing how you get on with him—"

"Exceptionally well," I said. "He's the most splendid chap and I have nothing but respect and admiration for him."

"You've always got on well with him, have you?"

"Always. Well . . . I admit there was a little difficulty when I went into the Church—no, let's call a spade a spade and say there was a big row—but we got over all that years ago and now he's proud of my success. I'm very fond of both my parents and I'm very good friends with my brother—in fact I'd say we were an unusually close, happy family."

All Darrow said was: "When did you last go home?"

2

I SAID: "I don't think I'll talk any more this morning. I'm all right, there's nothing wrong, but I think I'd like time to reflect on the extraordinary coincidence that I keep meeting these benign older churchmen!" I smiled to show him how amused I was, how detached, how absolutely in command of myself, and my self was the glittering image, threatened, fearful, prepared to fight hard to survive.

Darrow said to him politely: "Just as you like. Shall we hope for sunshine this afternoon in the herb-garden?"

3

"I SUPPOSE you now want me to admit," I said later as Darrow sat down beside me on the bench in the herb-garden, "that there are a bunch of terrible skeletons in the family cupboard."

"Charles, I'm just the porter with the trolley. I'm not here to criticise the quality of your luggage or to order which bag you should put down. My function is simply to offer you the chance to get rid of any bag which you don't want to carry any more, but the decision to keep or discard each bag must be yours and yours alone."

Having considered this I felt sufficiently reassured to say: "I'm not a fool. You wanted me to describe all this benign interest from the older men as paternal. You wanted me to admit that the one thing they all had in common was that they had no sons of their own. You wanted me to acknowledge that it's no amazing coincidence that I always seem to have this kind of older man in my life. You want me now to concede there's something wrong with my relationship with my father. But there isn't. There really isn't. We're very fond of each other."

"Very well," said Darrow serenely. "We won't bother to talk about your father. Let's talk instead about all these father-figures you've accumulated over the years."

"What a bloody awful word 'father-figure' is!" I exclaimed, and with the word "bloody" I felt the glittering image slip. A clergyman had a duty to avoid bad language. I suddenly realised my true self was trying to escape and I needed time to lock him up. I said to Darrow to divert him: "Are you a follower of Freud?"

"Let's just say I'm an interested observer."

"I think Freud's rubbish. I refuse to believe all men are in love with their mothers and searching continually for father-figures."

"Is that what Freud actually says? However, let's forget Freud—and let's forget that description 'father-figure' which I agree is absurdly lugubrious. How would you yourself describe all these benign older men in your life?"

"Well, obviously they're a substitute for my father, I can see that, but that can't be the whole explanation because my father's attitude towards me is benign too."

"Do you think it's possible," said Darrow, "that you simply enjoy being a son? If your relationship with your father is so good, you may be unable to resist the urge to repeat it at every opportunity."

This suggestion struck me as bizarre. Regarding him with suspicion, I said austerely: "I hardly collect fathers for pleasure."

"Well, as a matter of fact it did occur to me that being the ideal son must be a somewhat time-consuming and tiring occupation."

I laughed. "You'll be telling me next I was so exhausted being a son that I didn't have enough energy to face being a father!"

Darrow laughed too. "Sounds absurd, doesn't it?"

"Ridiculous!" I traced a pattern on the wooden arm of the bench.

"Perhaps it would be closer to the truth to say that your father didn't make fatherhood seem an attractive occupation."

"That's a ridiculous suggestion too. He's always been wonderful."

"The ideal father?"

"Well . . . He has his faults, of course, just as we all do, but by and large—"

"He's wonderful. I see. Now, Charles, there's a question I'd like to ask but you may not wish to answer it. If you don't—"

"I wish you'd stop treating me as a hopeless neurotic!" I said irritably. "Of course I'll answer any question you care to ask—what do you think I've been doing since this interview began?"

"It's been a glittering performance," said Darrow.

I at once picked up the Bible, which I had been reading before he had joined me, and began to flick through the pages. Again the books streamed past my fingers: Genesis, Exodus, Leviticus, Numbers, Deuteronomy, Joshua—

"What's this next question of yours?" I said casually.

"Are any of these benign older men like your father or is he in a class of his own?"

"He's nothing like them at all." I had reached the New Testament, and suddenly one verse rose straight from the page to meet me. "Strait is the gate," I read, "and narrow is the way, which leadeth unto life, and few there be that find it."

I closed the Bible carefully, very carefully, as if I feared it might shatter to pieces in my hands, and gently, very gently, I set the book down on the bench. Then I said to Darrow: "I'm not telling the truth. I'm sorry. Yes, there's a likeness, a common denominator."

"The Church?"

"No, my father's an atheist. He sent me to Church of England schools but that was only because he's so obsessed with what he calls 'a good straight decent life,' and he wanted schools which laid stress on morality. The common denominator between my father and the father-figures," I said, "is that they're all moral upright men."

"Your father's beginning to intrigue me very much," said Darrow.

"Do you think you could attempt a thumbnail sketch of his personality?"

This seemed a reasonable request and I thought I could grant it without difficulty. "Why not?" I said, looking him straight in the eyes to show I was undaunted, but I was setting out at last, although I did not realise it, on my harrowing journey to the heart of my glittering image.

4

"MY father's very truthful, very frank," I said. "He resembles Jardine in detesting hypocrisy but he doesn't have Jardine's intellect or sophistication. My father despises glamour; he thinks it's bad form, pretentious. He'd distrust that nouveau-riche aura of the fast social traveller which makes Jardine so interesting in his palace. My father hasn't the slightest desire to travel socially because he likes life exactly where he is; he thinks that to be a member of the English middle classes is to belong to the best caste in the world.

"At the same time, within that caste he's very ambitious. He founded his legal firm on his own and wound up thirty years later with sixteen partners and a first-class reputation. He's only just retired. Of course Peter and I went to the best schools and of course we all lived in the best part of Epsom. My parents still live there. My mother has higher social aspirations than my father, but although he's always scathing about anyone with a title, he wouldn't want the aristocracy abolished because he thinks England should remain quite unchanged. He despises the working classes en masse but he's kind to them as individuals—he's good to his servants, good to his employees at the office, because he thinks that's his duty.

"My father's very keen on duty. He thinks that's what being a middle-class English gentleman's all about; one has a duty to work hard, live a decent life, deal honestly in business, set an example to the community and stand by one's family. He despises inefficiency, sloth, slovenliness, disloyalty, crime, immorality and cruelty to animals. He keeps a black Labrador called Nelson and drives a black Rover. He could afford a Daimler but he'd think that was pretentious. My mother gets livid with him on that subject and compensates herself by making regular shopping expeditions to Harrods. 'What a nasty pretentious-looking piece of nonsense!' he said when she bought her new fur coat, but in fact he secretly likes her to look smart and expensive because that symbolises his success—which of course he'd never dream of bragging about; that wouldn't be the done thing at all.

"When I was appointed Lang's chaplain, my mother bragged about it to her friends and couldn't even complete a sentence without mentioning the word 'Archbishop,' but my father just said: 'My son's got an interesting post. He's a sort of private secretary. Useful start to his career.' But he was very pleased. He said to me: 'Better than wasting your time in a bloody vicarage somewhere in the back of beyond,' and then he said: 'For God's sake don't get drunk or fool around with some girl and get sacked.' When I got the headmastership of St. Aidan's, he said: 'A bit young, aren't you?' but he was thrilled. He said: 'Important step up the ladder. But don't let it go to your head—no airs and graces, no drinks you don't need, no stupid flirtations. Never forget that pride comes before a fall.'

"Later when I published my book, my mother was soon boasting away as usual and even told my aunt how much money I had been paid on the advance, but my father overheard her and was furious. He thinks any public talk about money is vulgar, but in private he likes to know every financial detail. He said to me: 'I suppose the book will only sell a few copies,' but when I told him it could make money as a textbook he lapped up all the figures. However, he wouldn't let my mother keep my book permanently displayed on the drawing-room table. 'Not the done thing,' he said. 'Flashy. I won't have it.' And he put the book away in the bookcase. My mother was so livid that they had a row—the first row they'd had over me for years—but she had to give in eventually.

"They used to have rows over me when I was small. He said she pampered me too much and she said he didn't pamper me enough. I don't mean they had rows in front of me when I was a child—that would have been bad form—but once or twice I listened at the key-hole.

"When they had the row over my book they had the row in front of me—rows are apparently permissible in the presence of adult offspring—and finally my mother called him a brute and burst into tears. My father said: 'Stupid woman. Storm in a teacup,' and stumped off to his study to read *The Daily Telegraph.* My father doesn't read *The Times.* He thinks it's pretentious. He likes the *Telegraph* for the sport and the business news. He doesn't read much, only the occasional biography. 'I shan't read that,' he said when I gave him a copy of my book. 'Not my cup of tea.' But late that night I went to his study and found him reading it. 'Can't think how anyone takes Christianity seriously,' he said. 'Amazing how those Early Church people survived. Personally I'd have thrown the whole damn lot to the lions.' He read the whole book and said: 'Quite interesting but a pity they couldn't have printed it on better paper.' That was high praise, coming from him.

"When I was awarded my doctorate, he said: 'Well, don't expect me to call you doctor. As far as I'm concerned doctors are rogues who charge too much for trying to put their patients in coffins, and thank God you never wanted to dabble in medicine.' My mother loved me being a doctor and she begged me not to mind about my father's attitude—she said his aversion to doctors had developed even before I was born and there was no hope of changing him. It was easier when I became a canon. 'Damn silly title!' said my father. 'How long do I have to wait before I can call you Bishop?' That was when I knew how pleased he was. Then he said: 'You're doing rather well, aren't you? Amazing! Well, if you've got to be a damn clergyman, at least I have the satisfaction of knowing you're a successful one. *Well done, Charles!*' he said, and smiled at me.

"I'll never forget that. I was so overcome I couldn't speak. But the next moment he was saying: 'Now don't make a mess of it. Keep your nose to the grindstone. Stick to the straight and narrow, watch your alcohol consumption and don't make a fool of yourself over some bloody woman. All your faults and weaknesses won't go away just because you've got some fancy clerical title and can put the letters D.D. after your name.' My mother overheard that last sentence and she was livid. She shouted: 'How dare you talk about faults and weaknesses when he's standing there good as gold in his clerical collar?' and my father lost his temper. He said: 'Stupid woman, treating him like a saint! Can't you see all that religious rubbish is just an act? He's only in it for the glamour and the play-acting!'

"Well, I wasn't going to let him get away with that, but I was in such a state that all I could do was shout: 'You bastard! You *bastard!*' and then my mother started to scream and I tried to hit him but she got herself between us and sobbed: 'No—please—I can't bear any more suffering—' and my father yelled: *'Shut up, you stupid woman!'* and slapped her, and I tried to hit him again but she flung her arms around me and I had to hold her because she was sobbing so violently, but I said to my father: 'That was the damndest thing you could possibly say to me and the damndest attitude you could possibly adopt to her and I'd like to take her right out of this house this instant!' And he said: 'Take her away and good riddance—at least I'll still have Peter.' And somehow that was the last straw. I shouted: 'I'm so bloody sick of bloody Peter always being your bloody favourite—*damn* bloody Peter!' and my mother started screaming again but my father just said: 'Disgraceful language to use in front of a woman. You're not much of a clergyman, are you, whenever you forget to put on that glamorous act! Well, you never take *me* in, not for a moment,' said my father, and slammed the door of his study in my face.

"I banged on the panels but he'd turned the key in the lock and although I begged him to let me in, he wouldn't. He wouldn't even reply and I felt absolutely rejected, utterly cut off—and I hadn't done anything except protest against his insults! I couldn't bear it, but I couldn't go on banging at the door because my mother was so upset, weeping and weeping, and so I tried to comfort her by saying I really would take her away, but that horrified her. She said: 'But I couldn't possibly leave! What would everyone think?' and she said: 'We've got to keep up appearances. Nobody must ever know.' Then she cried again but finally she said: 'We're really very happy—he's just a little difficult now and then, that's all, but you mustn't think he doesn't love us both and you must never think he's not terribly proud of your success.' I said: 'He's got a very funny way of showing it, and if he thinks I'm coming back here to be insulted in future he's made a big mistake.'

"That was last year, last September. I haven't been back. I asked my mother to visit Cambridge but she refused because she was afraid people might think it odd if she came without him, and she has this obsession with keeping up appearances. That's why there's been no divorce, of course. My mother would be too frightened of scandal ever to risk an affair, and my father . . . well, he's not the sort of man who plays around with women. He'd think that vulgar and cheap. Adultery's for cads and bounders, not for strict, strong-principled men like him. I can imagine him thinking to himself: I vowed to be faithful to that woman and I'll be faithful to her even if it kills me—and even if it kills her.

"He did write to me after the row. I can remember the letter word for word. He said: 'Of course the stupid woman got the wrong end of the stick. She didn't realise I'd praised you before I warned you about your faults and weaknesses. But praise should be sparing and I'm not here to flatter and pamper you to death. That's not what fathers are for. My duty as your father was to bring you up to be a good straight decent man and once I'd done that—and I did—my next duty was to make damned sure you stayed that way. That's why I regularly remind you of your faults and weaknesses. I'm not in this parenthood business to be loved and doted on. I'm in it to do my duty and be respected. You wouldn't respect me if I allowed you to go to the dogs and I wouldn't respect myself either.' Then he signed himself: 'Your affectionate Father,' and added: 'P.S. Visit us again soon if only to keep your mother happy.'

"There wasn't a word of apology. I wrote back and said I wasn't going to return unless he apologised for scoffing at my vocation and calling me a fraud. He wrote back and said he was waiting for me to apologise for using filthy language in front of my mother and trying to hit him. I didn't write back. So that was that. However, finally Lent arrived, and when I saw Father Reid—dear old Father Reid!—he said: 'I think you're a little bit in error here, Charles. I don't think calling Mr. Ashworth a bastard is compatible with the commandment "Honour thy father," and besides, if we're mocked for our vocation we must always turn the other cheek and accept the suffering.'

"Well, by that time I was feeling thoroughly miserable about my father so I hardly needed any extra pressure to coax me into writing to him again. I sent a friendly letter apologising, inviting him to bring my mother to Cambridge for a visit and offering to put them both up at the Blue Boar. He wrote back saying he'd come so long as I wasn't expecting him to attend any mumbo-jumbo in the Cathedral. That finished it. He was so damn rude. I didn't write back. I just tried to put him out of my mind, but that wasn't so difficult because I was very busy with my undergraduates, and even after they'd gone home for the Long Vacation I had yet another distraction because Lang arrived with his commission. And when I came at last to Starbridge . . . well, as soon as I met Jardine, my father ceased to be important any more.

"Jardine killed the pain. They all did, all those older men with no sons of their own who thought I was worthy of special attention. They killed the pain of knowing my father dislikes me. I'm just a duty as far as he's concerned. I thought that if I was a success I'd finally make him like me—I've worked and worked and worked at being a success because I know success is the only language he really understands—but even though I try to talk to him in his own language, he doesn't hear me. In fact, it's almost as if he refuses to hear me—oh, how unjust it is! How unfair! It makes me feel so angry, Father, so angry, so hurt, so resentful, and all that anger goes round and round in my mind until I feel I can't bear the pain of it any longer—and when the pain becomes unbearable I hate him, yes, I do—*I hate him*—oh God forgive me, I know it's wicked but I've so often been so unhappy—so often when I was growing up I found myself hating him, so often when I was growing up I found myself being vilely jealous of my brother for being the favourite, and all that hatred and jealousy made me feel so guilty—oh, how I despised myself, because of course I do love my father, I do—I love him all the time I'm hating him but the whole relationship's such a back-breaking burden and now I can't carry it a second longer, I've got to put it down, I *want* to put it down but I don't know how to do it, and that's why you've got to help me, Father, you've got to help me, *you've got to help me*—"

XV

"I think there is probably in most lives a point at which private confession is both natural and salutary, very largely because it is felt to be the fitting and almost inevitable beginning of a new spiritual chapter in personal life."

HERBERT HENSLEY HENSON,
RETROSPECT OF AN UNIMPORTANT LIFE

I

I WAS tugging at my cross and suddenly as the clasp snapped, the chain slid through my fingers. I gasped but Darrow scooped it up and thrust it back between my shaking hands. I could barely see. My throat seemed to be swelling so fast that my supply of air was impeded. I felt as if I were standing naked before an icy wind.

"I can't breathe—"

"Oh yes you can," said Darrow, and shoved me back hard against the bench to straighten my spine. Automatically I cried out, my windpipe relaxed its spasm and the air flowed again into my lungs. "And again," said Darrow. He gave me another shake to help the next breath along; I felt as if I were being resuscitated from drowning.

"Why am I so cold?" I had begun to shudder from head to toe.

"Shock. You opened the cupboard door and looked directly on the skeleton inside. Now, Charles"—he sat down again beside me—"keep holding the cross and give me your free hand. I'm going to say a silent prayer, just as I did on the morning after your arrival, and this time I want you not only to continue taking those deep breaths but to think of the heat of those Palestinian summers when Our Lord exercised the famous charisms—preaching, teaching, healing . . . and all in the heat, all in the warmth, all in the sun."

The silence fell, and gradually I found I could feel the sunlight on my face as I sat motionless on the bench. Behind my closed eyelids I saw the sun-baked Palestinian landscape, but then the scent of the herb-garden brought me back to England and for a brief moment I saw Jane smiling at me. I remembered I was working to give her death meaning by my own rebirth, and as I realised that all I now needed was courage, I felt the warmth begin. It seeped through my hands to my arms, through my arms to my heart, through my heart to my mind and through my mind to my soul.

I opened my eyes at exactly the same moment as Darrow opened his.

"You heard, didn't you?" he said.

"Yes. Courage. A new life. And Jane was there."

Darrow smiled but was silent and suddenly I was saying: "You saw her. You must have done. I know you did. Why don't you admit—"

"You mustn't tempt me, Charles. Do you remember me telling you of the spiritual director who said: 'Beware of those Glamorous Powers'? It's so easy to make a gift from God look like a charlatan's parlour trick . . . But now forget the parlour tricks and look around you. Do you know where you are?" And as I looked blankly at the herb-garden, he added: "No, look in your mind. The strait gate is behind you; you're in the middle of the narrow way at last."

I sat there, outwardly calm but inwardly still shattered by the aftermath of shock, and it was a full minute before I was able to say: "Will he start fading away now?"

"Not yet. We're looking on the roots but they're deeply embedded and we have to dig a little deeper before we can remove them successfully."

"But I'm going to be all right—you're going to sort everything out—"

"No, Charles, *you're* the one who's going to sort everything out. But only when you're rested and fit." He took off his Abbot's cross and gave it to me. "Put that on and let me take the one with the broken chain. I'll get that repaired and you can have it back tonight." He paused as I thanked him but then he said casually, as if he could no longer resist the temptation to help the healing process by a flash of unorthodoxy: "That was a pretty locket Jane was wearing." And rising to his feet with all the showmanship of a conjuror who had just produced a rabbit from a hat, he sauntered forward to inspect the nearest bed of the herb-garden.

2

THE effect—as no doubt he had anticipated—was to divert me entirely from my shock and to restore me at a stroke to normality. I jumped to my feet and evidently the rapid movement served to remind him that I might be liable to panic. At once he said: "I'll get someone to sit with you," and I realised that despite his flamboyant parlour trick he remained the careful priest, pleased with his healing skills but humble enough to realise that they should be supplemented by a more conventional care. "You shouldn't be alone at the moment."

"I'm all right." I was still so enrapt by the display of his Glamorous Powers that I barely heard him. "Father, she's happy, isn't she?" I said, but immediately I was overwhelmed with embarrassment. "I'm sorry, I know what happened. I wasn't seeing her as she is—I was remembering her as she was, and you looked across and saw my memory." In shame I added: "Forgive me for sinking into the error of superstition, but I suddenly had a great urge to communicate with her."

"That's a healthy sign." He showed no anger. "I suspect you've been suppressing all thought of her for years, so if you now seek to commune with her memory it suggests that the burden of guilt is beginning to lift."

"It's because I'm at last doing something to put matters right—wiping out the man who made her unhappy—"

"Yes, the glittering image has certainly taken a pounding today, but now you need time to recuperate. If you're strong enough—and only if you're strong enough—we'll resume the attack this evening."

3

THAT evening we exchanged crosses following the repair of the broken chain, and as he replaced the Abbot's cross on his chest I thought how ill its lavish splendour accorded with his austere, occluded, tightly disciplined personality.

"Well?" he said as we sat down at the table. "How are you feeling after this morning's haemorrhage?"

"Haemorrhage!"

"Is that an exaggeration? You lost a lot of emotional blood, and sometimes," said Darrow, embarking on another meticulous examination of his ring, "after an ordeal like that one can suffer a reaction. One can feel guilt and anger, guilt that one's betrayed one's most private secrets, anger that one's been lured into speaking the unspeakable."

We considered this possibility in silence but at last I said: "I do feel guilty—but not because I've told you my most private secrets. And I do feel angry—but not with you for luring me into self-revelation. I feel angry with myself because I wanted to give you a fair picture of my father yet I ended up by delivering that vile tirade. And I feel guilty because I failed to convey to you what a wonderful man he is and how much I admire and respect him."

"There was no failure," said Darrow. "You did convey those feelings clearly."

"I did? But at the end when I said I hated him—"

"If all you felt was hatred you wouldn't be here. You'd have walked away from him years ago and heaved a sigh of relief that you'd finally escaped from his clutches. But you can't walk away, can you? During the past year you've tried but you've merely made yourself thoroughly miserable."

"It's as if . . ." I strained to identify the elusive words and at last ventured: "It's as if he's got some colossal hold over me."

"Of course. We're very much at the mercy of those we love, and never more so than when those we love don't love us quite as we would wish in return."

"But he doesn't love me at all."

"Who's 'me'?" said Darrow.

"My true self. He doesn't love and approve of me as I am, and that's why—"

Darrow waited.

"—that's why I have to become someone else. But he doesn't even like the glittering image!"

"He respects him, though, doesn't he? And so long as you're slaving away fulfilling his definition of a successful man, you stand a hope of hearing him say once in a while: 'Well done, Charles!' "

"Yes, but he thinks it's all an act."

"This is where your father resembles Jardine. He has a knack of spotting a performance that doesn't quite ring true, and so there are inevitably times when he sees straight past your glittering image and starts disapproving of you all over again—as he did during that last terrible quarrel."

Shading my eyes with my hand I traced a line on the table and said: "He tore up my glittering image and rejected my other self beyond." Suddenly I could no longer see. I had to use both my hands to shade my eyes.

Darrow said: "That was a cruel thing to do, wasn't it?"

I nodded. "But it wasn't his fault."

"No?"

"No, it was my fault. If I hadn't been so unfit and unworthy, he wouldn't have needed to disapprove of me so strongly. You see, he's so straight, so upright, so decent—if only I could convey to you what a hero he is—"

"Charles," said Darrow, "your father may indeed be a remarkable man in many ways, but if he's at the root of your glittering image—if he consistently rejected your true self so that you were obliged to become someone else—if he was in any degree responsible for launching you on that road which finally resulted in you arriving here one night dead drunk and spiritually shattered—his status as a hero is very much open to debate."

It had never occurred to me before that my father's heroism could be debatable. I wrestled with this revolutionary idea for some time before saying firmly: "He can't be entirely to blame."

"That seems fair. I must say, I entirely disapprove of the Freudian tendency to blame all a child's troubles on his hapless parents . . . Very well, let's assume you should share at least some of the responsibility for arriving here wrecked in the middle of the night. But how much of the responsibility should you shoulder?"

I could only say in despair: "All of it—I can't blame my father for anything. If I wasn't so unfit and unworthy—"

"Who says you're unfit and unworthy?"

"I do. How else can one explain my father's attitude towards me?"

"That," said Darrow, "is the big question, Charles."

I stared at him. "But of course I'm unfit and unworthy!" I said. "And of course my father's right to despise me for it. When I think of my recent errors—that drinking bout—Loretta—"

"Never mind your recent errors for the moment. Let's concentrate on your more normal behaviour. You work hard, don't you—try to do what's right—aim to lead what your father would call a good straight decent life?"

"Yes, but—"

"Then is it realistic to treat you as a drunken wastrel who's perpetually poised to go straight to the dogs? And is it fair? You're not really such a bad chap as all that, are you?"

I tried to speak but nothing happened.

"Well, I mustn't put thoughts in your head," said Darrow. "If you want to believe you're a bad chap you have a perfect right to do so, but I'd like you to consider very carefully how far this belief chimes with the actual evidence provided by your life. I'd also like you to consider the indisputable fact that your father is not the Pope speaking ex cathedra; he's not infallible. No matter how heroic he is he's still capable of making mistakes, just like any other human being."

I managed to say: "I'd like to believe I'm not such a bad chap. Sometimes I do believe it."

"How do you feel about your father's judgement then?"

"Angry. But that's wrong, isn't it? I must turn the other cheek and forgive him."

"Yes, you must—eventually. But how can you possibly forgive him at present when his attitude towards you is so inexplicable?"

"It's not inexplicable. My father adopts this attitude towards me because I'm so unfit and unworthy," I persisted, but even as I spoke the words began to assume a curiously hollow ring.

"This is indeed how you've always explained your father's attitude," said Darrow, "but supposing, just for the sake of argument, this explanation's dead wrong?"

The psychological chain binding me to my self-hatred was suddenly wafer-thin. I said: "My father certainly *thinks* I'm unfit and unworthy. That's undeniable. But—"

"But?" said Darrow, coming to meet me as I struggled out of the dark into the light.

"It's just possible . . . it's not wholly out of the question . . . in fact it's within the bounds of probability—" I drew a deep breath and said: "He's made a mistake." The chain snapped apart as the truth overpowered me like an avalanche, but after the avalanche came the silence, and into the silence came the first faint whisper of the massive questions which I had never before been able to hear. Eventually I found I could say the questions aloud. "Why does he have this low opinion of me?" I said, baffled. "What have I done to deserve it?" and as I spoke, I felt as if I were turning some great psychological corner to confront a strange new landscape in my mind.

"And that," said Darrow, "is the mystery beyond the mystery beyond the mystery. Congratulations, Charles. Now we're indeed beginning to make progress."

4

"YOUR father certainly seems from your narrative to be strong and high-principled," said Darrow when we met later, "but he also seems to be dangerously proud. Pride is always dangerous. Pride coupled with a strong inflexible character can be lethal.

"Part of your father's pride, I think, would be manifested in the way he brought you up. Once he'd made a commitment, he'd stick to it through thick and thin, and he seems to have been saying to himself (if I may borrow the phraseology you yourself used): 'I'll bring Charles up to be a good straight decent man even if it kills me—and even if it kills him.' That sort of inflexible determination, though it can be admirable if riveted to a moral principle, is potentially destructive because it's incapable of adjusting to changing circumstances. Perhaps your father was justified in being strict with you when you were small—bright children often need a firm hand—but it seems he was incapable of modifying his attitude when you grew up.

"Now we come to the heart of the matter. There you are, clever, nice-looking, successful beyond any father's wildest dreams. Most fathers would be grovelling at your feet in sentimental adulation, so why should your father be sunk in this incorrigible pessimism? Of course one must make allowances for his character—his hatred of boasting, his natural English reserve, his admirable horror of spoiling you. One might suppose he's incapable of being demonstrative towards a son, but since you tell me your father displays an all-too-human paternal partiality towards your brother, one feels driven to wonder why he's so inhibited in showing paternal partiality towards you.

"Now let's see where we've got to. We've speculated that your father adopted this attitude towards you when you were very young; this is supported by your impression that the glittering image has always been there. We've deduced that because of his inflexibility he was later unable to change his attitude, even when you turned out well, but we still don't know why he was compelled to adopt it in the first place. We know he was a conscientious father who was consumed with the desire to bring you up to be a good man, but we don't know why he's apparently unable to believe his success here is permanent. We can assume, I think, that he would act with the best of motives, but we don't know why he's wound up treating you so unfairly. Perhaps the whole mystery can be summed up by asking: how has this particular road to Hell been paved with your father's good intentions?"

Darrow stopped speaking. We were sitting again in the herb-garden but I was by this time oblivious of my surroundings. I was too busy channelling my mental energy into the mystery as if it were a piece of research which demanded absolute concentration.

"How much clearer everything seems," I said, "but that means, paradoxically, how much more mysterious. I feel as if I'm seeing the outline of the mystery for the first time."

"Then let's now step past the outline to examine the mystery at close quarters. Tell me about your brother. Is he older than you?"

"No, he's two years my junior and I suppose one could describe him as a sunny-natured version of my father. He's married with three children and lives near my parents in Epsom."

"Is he clever? It's hard not to imagine you outshining him on every front."

"He's certainly no fool; he's a partner in my father's firm, but he's limited in his interests and we don't have much in common."

"How did his early career compare with yours?"

"I did outshine him. I often suspected my father felt driven to favour Peter in order to compensate him—in the same way as my mother felt driven to favour me in order to compensate me for my father's harshness." I hesitated before adding: "However, explaining the family relationships in terms of favouritism fails to convey their complexity. For instance, although I'm my mother's favourite, neither of us is comfortable with the other. She's much more relaxed with Peter."

"You're not close to her?"

"I hate to say it but I find her a strain. It's because she's very effusive—but not in a natural way. In fact she always makes me want to cringe and protest: 'For heaven's sake treat me normally instead of putting on this act!' Yet it's not an act. The emotion's genuine enough but she can't express it in a relaxed manner."

"Yet you said she was relaxed with Peter."

"He doesn't seem to affect her in the same way. In fact the atmosphere Peter generates with our parents is entirely different, but I suppose this must happen frequently in families where the two children are unalike."

"I agree this is a fairly common phenomenon, but has it ever struck you in your own case as seeming distinctly abnormal?"

"Well, I remember one instance in particular: I was visiting them soon after I was ordained—it was before Peter was married and he was still living at home. I was watching the three of them when they were in the garden and I was indoors. My father was laughing, Peter was sprawled happily in a deck-chair—even my mother was looking relaxed. Then I walked out of the house to join them and it was as if a curtain had come down over the scene. Peter didn't change. He went on sprawling in his deck-chair, but my father said 'Here comes the clergyman' in a typical sardonic voice and my mother said with that awful false brightness of hers: 'Let's all have cocktails!' and I felt—"

"Yes?" said Darrow. "How did you feel?"

"Like an unwanted guest." It was too difficult to go on.

"Odd man out? I'd been thinking," said Darrow, coming to my rescue, "how different you must be from the other members of your family and how awkward this must have been for you when you were growing up."

The knowledge that he understood enabled me to say: "When I was fifteen I even wondered . . . Well, Father, don't laugh, I know this sounds melodramatic and ridiculous, but I even wondered if I were adopted."

"That sounds rather a sensible explanation to me. Who said it was melodramatic and ridiculous?"

"My father."

"Ah!" said Darrow. "I see. Your father made you feel melodramatic and ridiculous, just as he made you feel unfit and unworthy."

There was a silence while I grappled with the huge implications of this statement, but at last I said, resigned: "No, this time there's no question of my father making a mistake. I really was being stupid. You see, what happened was this . . ."

5

"I'D BEEN wondering for some time if I were adopted," I said, "and finally I decided to inspect my birth certificate to see if there were any clues there. My father kept all the family documents in a file in his study so it was a simple matter to make a raid one night when everyone was asleep. I found no hint of any irregularity on my birth certificate, of course, but in the file I came across the certificate of my parents' marriage and then I did make a discovery which astonished me: my parents had married a year later than I'd thought. I knew the month and day of their wedding because they always celebrated their anniversary, but I thought they'd married in 1898. I'd never realised they were married in 1899 and that I'd arrived—in 1900—only seven months after the wedding."

"Premature?"

"That was my first reaction, but no one had ever mentioned me fighting for life in my cradle. Then I wondered if I'd been conceived out of wedlock with the result that my father had been forced to marry my mother, but somehow I couldn't see him seducing a girl from a respectable family. And at that point I remembered my father's sister mentioning cattily once that my mother had been considered fast when she was young, and immediately it occurred to me that I might have been fathered by someone else."

"Did you go back to your aunt for further information?"

"No, I didn't like my aunt. I might have gone to my mother, but I was in the throes of a sex-obsessed puberty and I balked at the prospect of asking her intimate questions. So in the end after much soul-searching I went to my father. I'd convinced myself he'd be relieved to tell me the whole truth at last."

"How did he respond?"

"He was livid. Mortally insulted. 'Never heard such melodramatic ridiculous nonsense in my life!' he said. 'How dare you doubt my paternity after I've been slaving away all these years to give you a decent upbringing!' Well, as you can imagine, Father, I was completely cowed."

"Of course you were, but did he deign to explain—"

"Yes, he had a thoroughly convincing explanation for my early arrival. He said that in 1899 everything was going wrong for him; it was before he founded his own firm, he was unhappy in his work, and although he wanted to marry my mother he'd given up hope of her accepting him. So on an impulse he volunteered for the Army—the Boer War was brewing all that summer—and when my mother realised he could be sent overseas to fight she became aware how much he meant to her and she finally agreed to marry him. Well, in the end the Army rejected him because of his eyesight, but for a time both he and my mother believed they were about to be separated so they rushed to the altar as soon as possible—and in all the drama the conventions slipped; he did have her for the first time before they were married. 'Very reprehensible,' he said, 'but I was so carried away that she'd agreed to marry me and so worried in case I had to leave before the wedding that I lost control and blotted my escutcheon.' "

"So what conclusions did you draw from this conversation?"

"I believed him. He was so dogmatic, so positive, so convincing—"

"Was he hurt?"

"Hurt!"

"Well, if my son had questioned his paternity in that way," said Darrow, "I certainly wouldn't have been dogmatic or positive. Neither would I have been livid or mortally insulted. I'd have been deeply upset and extremely worried about why he found our relationship so unsatisfactory that he was driven to search for painful explanations. Tell me, did you ever discuss this with your mother?"

"He absolutely forbade it. He said: 'Your mother's a very emotional woman, she feels guilty that you were conceived before the wedding, she suffered agonies of embarrassment when you arrived early, and you're never on any account to mention the subject to her.' "

"So his testimony is unsupported."

"Yes, but I'm sure he was telling the truth."

"What makes you so certain?"

I finally voiced the conclusion I had drawn years earlier after great pain and difficulty. "I'm certain," I said, "because I believe that if he wasn't my real father, the truth would have surfaced when I decided to go into the Church. I can't begin to describe the awfulness of the rows we had, but the one thing he never did was disown me."

Darrow was silent.

"I realise that illegitimacy is the obvious explanation of the mystery," I said, "but it can't be the right one."

Darrow remained silent for a moment before saying: "Very well, where have we got to? We've already established that your father's attitude to you doesn't arise from the fact that you're profoundly unfit and unworthy. We've now established that it doesn't arise from the fact that he's not your natural father. What, then, is your final explanation of the mystery?"

"Well, I suppose all one can say is that sometimes, even in the best of families, a parent has an antipathy towards one of his children and this creates tensions within the family."

"I agree such cases do happen," said Darrow, "but unless the parent is either mentally ill or sunk deep in poverty, there's always a reason for the antipathy. For example, sometimes the child reminds the parent of someone unpleasant—Great-Uncle Cuthbert who beat him when he was little, perhaps, or Great-Aunt Matilda who deprived him of chocolate in childhood. Do you perhaps remind your father of any such disagreeable antecedents in the family tree?"

"I don't see how I can. I'm not like anyone in our family. That's the point, isn't it? I'm such a stranger."

"How curious," said Darrow, "because your father seems to look at you, Charles, and see someone he knows."

I was astonished. "Does he?"

"It's all there in your narrative. Take a moment to think about it."

I reviewed my story with meticulous care. Then I said cautiously: "It's as if he's not seeing me—my true self—but a glittering image. Yet it's not *my* glittering image. It's a far more sinister glittering image than mine."

"Exactly. Your father's big aim in life—as he's always telling you—is to bring you up to be a good straight decent man, but his very insistence on this seems to suggest he's terrified he'll fail. He looks at you and can hardly believe you've turned out so well—in fact he daren't believe it, he behaves as if he's scared to death something could still go wrong. He thunders to you on the subject of drink. He exhorts you not to get in a mess with women. There you stand before him, a good straight decent man in a clerical collar—in fact you've been called to a profession which ensures that you're just about as good and straight and decent as you can get—but your father doesn't see the clerical collar, Charles, and he doesn't see you, either. He looks beyond you in his memory and he sees a wastrel, someone who drinks too much, someone who gets in a mess with women, someone who ruins himself, someone whom perhaps your father once resented and feared . . . And who do you think that is, Charles? If the description doesn't tally with any member of your family, whom do you think it fits?"

"My real father," I said, and saw a new world shudder loose from the chrysalis of the old.

XVI

"He impressed me as wise, patient, discerning, experienced and unquestionably sincere, a genuine pastor. His counsels were worth having and I have never forgotten them. I could not doubt that, if all clergymen were as well qualified as he, there would be few who would not benefit by 'opening their grief in private confession.' "

HERBERT HENSLEY HENSON,
RETROSPECT OF AN UNIMPORTANT LIFE

I

"WE could be entirely wrong," said Darrow. "The deduction seems obvious enough from the evidence but any evidence can be subject to misinterpretation."

My mind was so absorbed by the thought of the stranger who had been conjured up out of the most opaque corners of my narrative that I could only say: "I know we're right."

Darrow at once anchored me to reality. "You know no such thing. What you do know, on the other hand, is that you can go to your parents to demand the truth and the odds are that one of them's bound to reveal it. At this stage of your life they can't claim they're justified in lying to protect you."

"Do you suppose that was why my father lied to me when I was fifteen? But why should he have wanted to protect me? It would have been more in character if he'd leapt at the chance to tell me the truth once I'd voiced my suspicions!"

Darrow said nothing.

"And why did he marry my mother in such terrible circumstances?" I demanded, my incredulity mounting. "What a fantastic thing to do! And then to bring up the child as his own—and never to betray the secret despite considerable provocation . . . Why, I can't imagine how or why any man could do such a thing!"

"That's exactly the sort of remark people often make to a man who becomes a monk," said Darrow. "They entirely overlook the fact that where a call from God exists, any other course of action becomes unthinkable. Your father may have felt called to perform this unusual and difficult action—he may have believed, for reasons which seemed to him to be incontrovertible, that he had no choice but to marry your mother and assume responsibility for you."

"But my father's an atheist! He wouldn't even hear a call from God, let alone believe in one!"

"What a heretical statement! Are you saying an atheist can limit God's power to call men to do His will?"

"No, of course not, but—"

"What sort of an atheist is your father anyway? It sounds to me as if he's a man who's too proud to admit there could be more to the world than he can discern with the aid of his senses yet too honest to be entirely comfortable with his arrogance; his attacks on Christianity and the Church suggest he's trying to convince himself as well as others that religion has nothing to offer."

"I'd agree with that, but despite his secret ambivalence I still can't imagine him responding to a call from God. After all, a call can't take root and endure unless there are fertile conditions prevailing in the psyche, and I find myself quite unable to conceive what his motive was here."

"The answer's patently obvious. If you can somehow manage to discard your preconceived notions you'll find the facts permit only one conclusion."

I stared at him. "I can see he might have made the original decision because he loved my mother—although what an amazing gesture of love that would have been!—but why didn't he tell me the truth when I was fifteen? I can't see why on earth he should want me to go on believing he was my father if he didn't care about me."

"Precisely," said Darrow, rising to his feet. "Good. Well, we'll call a halt to the conversation there, and this evening we'll—"

I grabbed his sleeve. He sat down again. "But my father doesn't care about me," I said. "That's the point. He doesn't care."

"What evidence can you provide to support that statement?"

"Well, I told you . . . I explained . . ."

"You told me things which made me suspect he could be obstinate, pig-headed, misguided and rude, but I can't think of a single thing you said which made me think he was indifferent to you. Uncaring fathers don't lash themselves into a frenzy of anxiety every time they imagine their sons are going to the dogs." He stood up once more. "Think about it," he said over his shoulder, "and we'll talk again this evening."

2

"OF course," I said, when we met later in my room, "no matter what the solution of the mystery is, he *is* my father. Fatherhood is much more than initiating a process of reproduction."

"That sounds like a promising approach to a very difficult dilemma. But let's assume our theory's right and that somewhere in the world there's a man who could claim to have begotten you. How would you feel about him?"

"Hostile. He nearly ruined my mother and must have caused her enormous pain."

"True. Go on."

"He walked out on me when I was an embryo and has never made any attempt—so far as I know—to show the slightest interest in me."

"True again."

"However . . ." I hesitated before concluding carefully: "If he's alive I'd like to meet him, just once, for a quick look. Then I can put him aside and get on with my life, but if there's no meeting I suspect I'll always wonder what he was like and I might wind up being obsessed by him."

Darrow said neutrally: "Adopted children usually do have a psychological need to meet their natural parents. Very well, what do you think your next step should be?"

"I want to leave here as soon as possible in order to visit my parents and find out if our theory's true. But when do you think I'll be ready to make my formal confession and receive the sacrament again?"

"I'm already impressed by the realistic approach you're displaying to this new dilemma. Has the moment finally come, I wonder, when you can give me a realistic assessment of your relationships with Lyle, Loretta and Jardine? If you can accomplish that to my satisfaction, then I promise I'll hear your formal confession without delay . . ."

3

"LET'S start with Lyle," said Darrow, after I had assured him I now understood my errors well enough to profess a valid repentance. "Tell me what you think was actually going on beneath the storybook romance."

Without hesitation I said: "When I arrived in Starbridge I was in despair about my inability to lead a successful celibate life, and I was intent on discovering not just a woman I could marry but a woman who could cope with the worthless person I believed myself to be. I thought myself to be worthless in this context not merely because my father had a low opinion of me but because I'd made Jane unhappy; however, I couldn't think of Jane because that was too painful, so I told myself that everything would come right so long as I found a problem-solving miracle woman. Naturally I was indulging in fantasy—how obvious that seems now!—but I was so desperate to marry and put an end to my bouts of fornication that I had to believe I could make my fantasy come true."

"That's an excellent beginning," said Darrow. "Go on."

Much encouraged I said: "The odds were heavily against the possibility that Lyle was Jardine's mistress, but nevertheless I suspect that in my subconscious mind I'd pictured them in bed together and thought: a girl who could maintain a clandestine love affair with an eminent churchman is just about the only kind of woman who would have a hope of coping with me. Probably I thought this before I ever met Lyle, but when I saw her this wild deduction about her suitability was reinforced because I did find her exceedingly attractive. And to cap it all—to make the psychological situation perfect—she was in a mysterious way unavailable and for years I'd only been attracted to unavailable women."

"You can see clearly now, no doubt, why you chased the unavailable women despite your genuine desire to remarry?"

"I had an equally genuine desire not to remarry because I was terrified I might drive another woman to suicide. I hadn't come to terms with Jane's death at all, and the tragedy acted as a block in my mind."

"Good. Very well, so you fell for Lyle—"

"I fell for her hook, line and sinker, and whether or not this was all a huge illusion I still don't know. I'd like to believe my feelings are in some way rooted in reality, but I do concede now that I'll have to see her again when I'm in a much more stable frame of mind before I can finally decide whether she's right for me."

"That's most impressive, Charles—what an improvement on your earlier extravagant declarations! Now can you approach Loretta with a similar realism?"

I knew this would be harder. After a pause I said: "What a good friend she was to me at the end! I shall always remember that rescue of hers with gratitude, but apart from that . . ." My voice trailed away but Darrow made no attempt to intervene, and after another pause I was able to confess: "My afternoon with Loretta was a disaster—although I must be honest, mustn't I, and admit the sex was magnificent. However, that's just judging the incident from a physical point of view. Emotionally it was a disaster for me because it ploughed up my feelings for Lyle and put me in the biggest possible muddle. Mentally it was a disaster for me because the new muddle pushed me nearer the brink of breakdown and made me sink myself more obsessively than ever in the Starbridge mystery in order to divert myself from my problems. Spiritually it was a disaster for me because it cut me off from God and magnified my guilt as a clergyman to such an extent that I was unable to respond to your initial attempt to help me. And pastorally it was a disaster for me because I exploited a woman who was lonely and ignored a soul's unmistakable need for care. How can I do other than regret an incident which was an emotional, mental, spiritual and pastoral disaster? All physical gratification becomes sour and futile when isolated in such a wasteland."

Darrow said: "Can you put into words, do you think, why you were tempted to make love to her? Or are you implying this was solely an act of physical gratification?"

"That was the most obvious motive, but I can see now that I was driven by other forces too. For instance, I was in a state of extreme spiritual weakness brought on by my private troubles; I'd been working harder to preserve my glittering image than to serve God. Then I was also in a state of profound emotional turmoil and I used Loretta to anaesthetise myself from my problems. And finally . . . well, this is the crux of the matter, isn't it, Father? I thought she'd had full sexual intercourse with Jardine, and my identification with him at that point was so strong that I just thought: if he had her, I'll have her; if he can do it, then why on earth shouldn't I?"

Darrow leant back in his chair. "Very well, now can you tie up the last loose end and tell me how you view your relationship with Jardine as you look back through the strait gate from the narrow way?"

"Yes, of course," I said, and once more paused to collect my thoughts, but this time they proved uncollectable.

"Never mind," said Darrow. "I wasn't really expecting you to expound on Jardine tonight."

"I know what I want to say but I can't quite—"

"You've done extremely well, but now you need to rest. Get a good night's sleep, Charles, and tomorrow I think we'll finally succeed in putting the Bishop in his place."

4

"AS far as I can make out," I said after a sleepless night, "there are two aspects of my relationship with Jardine. First of all I seem to see him as an exceptionally compelling father-figure."

Darrow nodded. "Can you see why he should have this exceptional appeal?"

"I need older men to give me the approval my father withholds and Jardine entered my life at a time when I was completely estranged from my father."

"Yes, but what made Jardine more compelling than, for example, Dr. Lang?"

"Well, I can see now that as far as I'm concerned, Lang and Jardine aren't so unalike as they seem to be," I said with reluctance. "They're both eminent churchmen and they both have glamour."

"Ah, now we're progressing."

"Lang seems . . . well, it sounds unkind but he seems like a worn-out gramophone record now, a pompous stagey old bachelor who has no message for me any more. But certainly when we first met I thought he had great glamour. Jardine, on the other hand, not only has glamour but he's far from being a pompous old bachelor; he's a racy married man who has problems with women. I not only liked him but I came to identify with him—and that brings me to the second aspect of our relationship: I came to regard him as a double."

"Before we deal with that, tell me why you've chosen father-figures who are glamorous and clerical."

"I suppose I'm rebelling against my father, who hates clerics and despises glamour. He thinks Lang's hopelessly theatrical and if he were ever to meet Jardine he'd say: 'Fellow's not quite a gentleman. Bit too flashy with the vintage port. Bit of a bounder with the ladies.' "

"All right, so far so good. Now let's take a look at this curious doppelgänger situation. Can you explain how you came to regard Jardine as a double?"

"This is where I get into difficulties. As far as I can make out—" I stopped. Darrow waited. In front of me on the table my hands began to twist in their clasp. "As far as I can make out," I forced myself to say, "this is the part where I went stark staring mad."

"Oh yes?" said Darrow casually. "Were you violent—physically violent, not merely verbally abusive?"

"No."

"Were you performing bizarre acts, like taking off your clothes in public?"

"Good heavens, no!"

"Did you hear voices, see visions and think that little green men were out to kill you?"

"No, of course not!"

"Well, you could have been mad, I suppose," said Darrow, "but you certainly weren't stark staring mad, and personally I doubt whether we can convict you of anything worse than emotional stress. What I suggest is that we now put aside for a moment this thesis that you were stark staring mad and take a look at what was actually going on. Exactly when did you start doubting your sanity?"

"It was during that last scene with Jardine, the scene where he made his speech—"

"Ah yes, the speech he made when he should have been listening! However, I'm sure it was an oratorical masterpiece. After all," said Darrow expressionlessly, "if there's one thing we all know about the Bishop of Starbridge it's that he has a very powerful and persuasive tongue."

It was as if a spell had been broken. "He could make you believe black was white," I said, and suddenly I found I had the courage to look at the memory without flinching. As my hands stopped writhing in front of me I leant forward on the table and began to describe how Jardine had laid waste my equilibrium.

5

"... AND I know I'm not describing this well, Father—it's so hard to find the words—but Jardine made me feel my whole identification with him was a grand illusion."

"Obviously he was very convincing. But how did he raise the possibility that you were deluded?"

"He said I was using him as a mirror—only he didn't use the metaphor of the mirror. He talked of a blank screen and a magic-lantern. He said I was imposing on him—projecting onto the blank screen—feelings and situations which existed only in my mind."

"The Bishop seems to have been reading Feuerbach. But go on."

"He said that in my mind I'd picked him to be my hero and was justifying my own bizarre behaviour by saying I was only following his example." I shuddered at the thought of Loretta. "There was some sort of horrible truth in that—"

"Projection theories always seem difficult to rebut until one realises that the whole truth has failed to be projected. We know now that your behaviour, bizarre or otherwise, didn't arise solely from a desire to mirror Jardine; we know that you were driven by a variety of other factors including your estrangement from your father and your wife's death. However, let's go on with this thesis of Jardine's that you were the magic-lantern projector and he was the blank screen. Did he actually say that the resemblances between you were non-existent?"

"He said that I'd imagined him and that the man he was had nothing to do with the man I thought he was—and that's madness, isn't it, when one can no longer distinguish between reality and illusion? He made me feel as if I'd imagined the entire Starbridge mystery, he made me feel—"

"Yes, try to say it out loud—"

"—rejected. It was as if a door had slammed in my face. I felt as I'd felt during that last row with my father when he'd slammed the door of his study and locked it, but this was infinitely worse because in addition to feeling rejected I also felt stark staring—"

"Were you aware of his eyes while this was going on?"

I was abruptly diverted from the nightmare of insanity. *"His eyes?"*

"Think carefully. Were you looking directly at him?"

"Yes." I shuddered at the memory but managed to add: "His eyes are light brown but he can make them glow until they seem amber. They were amber then."

"And was there a point in the conversation when he repeated a phrase several times, a phrase such as 'listen to me'? Or was there a point when he repeated your name perhaps three times in one sentence to secure your attention?"

I said slowly: "Yes, there was. At one stage I said: 'I refuse to listen to this,' but he said: 'You will—you will, Charles, you will. Sit down, Charles—sit down and listen to me—listen to me, Charles—' "

"Ah yes," said Darrow nonchalantly, as if we were discussing behaviour which was commonplace. "I thought so. He was using a hypnotic technique to heighten the power of his charism—a technique which can occasionally be useful but which is always fraught with danger. I believe I now understand what happened. A charism which manifests itself in oratory can operate like a wireless, and Jardine had not only switched on this wireless but turned up the volume-knob as high as it would go. The effect would be unusually devastating because you were drunk and in a severely weakened state, but, Charles, now that you're stone-cold sober and in a far stronger frame of mind you should have no trouble turning down the volume-knob and finally switching the wireless off."

I was greatly intrigued but all I could say was: "I can't quite find the volume-knob."

"It's his assertion that you imagined the resemblances. All you have to do is explode it."

"But how?"

"Make a list of the apparent resemblances and we'll see whether or not they're valid."

I said cautiously but without difficulty: "The wife who got so depressed that she had to go back to her parents for a while—that was what Jane threatened to do and what Carrie Jardine actually did. The wife who was dutiful about sex—although this didn't stop the marriage from running into problems. The Jardines' period of childlessness followed by the birth of their dead baby, a period which corresponds to my years of contraception followed by the loss of the unborn child. Jardine's aversion to the celibate life, an aversion he confessed to Loretta, which corresponds to my own feelings about celibacy."

"Admirably put. There you have several genuine resemblances between you and Jardine. Can you see any more?"

I said with growing confidence: "Jardine comes from a lower social class than I do, but his long climb to the top of the social tree has resulted in him winding up with two personalities—a fact which suggests that like me he has trouble preserving a unified identity. He himself admitted to me that Alex is the glittering image and Adam is the man beyond, the man he likes to keep secret because Adam's made so many mistakes. Like me he normally doesn't talk about his past—and in particular he doesn't talk about—"

"Yes? Go on, Charles—"

"His father," I said. "His father."

"And there you have the most dramatic resemblance of all."

My confidence was now complete. "His father-problem was on the surface very different from mine," I said, "but in essence it was the same. Jardine had felt unloved and rejected by his father until the old man was near death." I paused as I remembered my nocturnal talk with Jardine in his library. "It was strange how Jardine sensed I had problems with my father," I said. "I merely pursued my usual policy of reticence, but unlike everyone else Jardine had the personal experience to know what that reticence meant."

"In other words he saw himself in you—the identification process was working in reverse."

"Yes, I'm sure now that this was why he didn't throw me out of the palace when he discovered I was Lang's spy—I intrigued him so much that he couldn't resist the urge to let me stay on so that he could get to know me better, and later after he had confided in me about his father, I became convinced that he was the only man I knew who had the experience to look beyond my glittering image and sympathise with the man I really was. That was why his rejection at the end was so terrible to me."

"In other words," said Darrow, "the psychological recognition was mutual and real. The resemblances between you were not only numerous but striking. So much for Jardine's accusation that you were projecting a fantasy."

The relief was so overwhelming that it was some time before I could say: "How could I have believed him?"

"You were hypnotised into believing you were mad and then you were too terrified to confront the memory to realise his thesis was false." There was a toughness in Darrow's voice but he eradicated it. Without expression he added: "Clearly the charism was abused."

Having finally faced my memory of the scene, I was able to voice the most sinister possibility of all. "Could he have deliberately sent me over the edge in order to protect himself?"

"He could," said Darrow, "but on the other hand if he saw himself in you, it seems unlikely that he would have been deliberately destructive. The most likely explanation is that in the distress caused by his involvement with you he lost control over the charism."

"But surely his use of hypnosis can only be sinister?"

"Not necessarily. He may well have resorted to hypnosis with the best of intentions—to calm you down. However, where he made his big mistake was to assume that if he confronted you with certain realities, you'd be able to pull yourself together. From a counselling point of view, as I told you earlier, this was quite the wrong approach, and the error was compounded by his lurid presentation of what he believed those realities to be. But, Charles, let me stress that despite the abysmal mess he made of the scene, there's still no proof that he was engaged in covering up an affair with Lyle. All the disaster proves is that even an experienced bishop should never attempt to counsel someone when all his better instincts caution him against it."

There was a silence while I digested this truth but finally I said: "At least I can now see the scene in its true colours. I can't tell you how much better I feel."

"I'm very glad, but don't start relaxing too soon because we're not quite home yet. We've established that you should on no account think you were mad just because you identified yourself with Jardine. But what happened when you pursued this identification to its limits? Can you take another look at that incident with Loretta?"

"I suppose this is where I convict myself of being emotionally disturbed even if I wasn't certifiably insane. I wanted him to be guilty of adultery. When I found he hadn't penetrated her, I felt cheated. And in the end I wanted him to be sleeping with Lyle—I wanted it even though the thought was unendurable."

"And why did you wish these sins upon him?"

"I felt that if he could be guilty and still be a brilliantly successful churchman, then I could too. I thought . . . I was so afraid . . ."

"Yes? You're almost there, Charles. One last hurdle—"

"I was so afraid my vocation was breaking down and I couldn't bear to think of it. All I want is to serve God in the Church, but everything seemed to be falling apart—my celibacy, my career, my whole life—and in those circumstances Jardine became—Jardine symbolised—"

"Symbolised—"

"—he was a symbol of hope—and in the end he was hope personified, my only hope, my last hope . . . I thought: if only he could be guilty, I'll be all right—if he can go on, I can go on . . . And that was why—that was why—"

"When he rejected your identification with him, he wasn't just rejecting you as a father, was he?"

"No, he was destroying my last hope of serving God in the Church, damning me to the hell of broken vows—and oh God, I couldn't bear it, Father, I couldn't bear it, I couldn't bear it, I couldn't bear it . . ."

6

"IT was very terrible for you," said Darrow, pulling his chair around the table so that he could sit beside me. "But you can see now, can't you, how you used this valid identification with Jardine to drum up defences which would keep your fears about your vocation at bay? You were afraid not of losing your faith in God, which I suppose is the commonest fear of clergymen with such beleaguered psyches, but of losing your ability to serve Him in the Church."

I was able to say: "I believe now that eventually I'll be able to go on in obedience to those vows I made at my ordination, but the past months have been such a nightmare of fear and doubt—"

"Of course they have. And of course you can now understand how that nightmare burgeoned in your mind until it reached intolerable proportions. It began not merely because your father had convinced you that you were unfit and unworthy, a man who was only acting the part of a clergyman, but because you felt your father's scepticism was to a frightening degree becoming justified. You *were* worried about your increasing need for alcohol, and you *were* finding yourself in increasing difficulties with women—but why was this happening? Not, contrary to what your father might think, because of some genetic curse. It was happening because you were under increasing psychological strain. The glittering image was becoming more and more of a burden—no wonder you wanted to drink to escape from him!—and you had this crucial problem, which you couldn't master, about your inability to face remarriage. The tension caused by this problem remorselessly drove you into errors—errors which only made you feel more unfit, more unworthy—and the inevitable result was that you became imprisoned in a downward spiral of despair. In the circumstances the wonder is not that you became emotionally disturbed but that you didn't do so much earlier, and in my opinion you must be absolutely dedicated to serving God. A lesser call would have disintegrated long ago."

When I was calmer, I said: "It was almost as if I knew I couldn't break down until I'd found someone who could be guaranteed to glue me together again."

"One of the saddest aspects of your story is undoubtedly that you felt unable to confide in anyone before you met me, but before either of us makes the mistake of becoming too self-satisfied with the results of our meeting let's remember that although your troubles have been clarified, they haven't yet been resolved. You have some hard work to do now on the home front, but we can discuss that later. At present there are more immediate matters to consider."

"My formal confession?"

"Yes. It can be brief, since we've already discussed your errors in such depth, but you must still approach the task with care; I'm going to make some suggestions about prayer and meditation. Then once your confession's been made, we can discuss what you're going to do on your return to the world. I think it's extremely important for you, both emotionally and spiritually, that we draw up a very meticulous battle plan."

7

I MADE my formal confession before God that evening, and Father Darrow, granting me absolution, assigned me a short penance which I performed in the chapel before I went to bed. I had expected a severe penance, possibly even a protracted one, but Darrow said that the severe protracted ordeal of my informal confession to him had formed a penance which now only required completion with prayer.

The next morning, for the first time since my arrival, I was able to participate in the Mass.

All the Fordite services were conducted in the vernacular, and although the form of worship represented the apex of the High Church wing of the Church of England, the language stressed that sharp division from Rome which formed the hallmark of the Fordite monks. The chapel was ornate, but the lack of emphasis on the Virgin set it apart from any church under the Pope's jurisdiction. I could not see the entire chapel because visitors were allowed only in a section of the transept, but the stained glass which was visible to me stressed the life of Christ and the single work of sculpture consisted of a crucifix.

I received the sacrament. I had been so buoyed up by my anticipation that it was a shock when after the first seconds of overwhelming comfort I experienced the panic of despair. I started fearing I might fall into error the moment I left my secure retreat; I began to worry that I would still be unable to face remarriage and fatherhood; I tormented myself with the dread that my feelings for Lyle were entirely illusory, that the liberating theory of my paternity was mistaken and that I was indeed utterly unfit to serve God as a clergyman.

My new hope shattered. My frail self-confidence crumbled. After the service I stumbled back to my room, pulled the blind, and lay face downwards on the bed with the cross pressed against my chest as I struggled to repel the demon despair. The demon and I wrestled for some time. He never entirely vanquished me but he made exhausting attacks. I was immobilised. I needed all my strength to bar his path to my soul.

Darrow found me after his chapter meeting. He walked in, took one look at my prostrate form, pulled up the blind and said: "On your feet, Charles. Kick the demon in the arse and let's get down to work."

The mood represented by the symbol of the demon immediately dissolved into the framework of my mind. I slunk to the table.

"I thought I'd be all right now," I said with shame. "I thought I'd be strong as an ox and brave as a lion and ready to stride out of your front door singing 'Onward Christian Soldiers.' "

Darrow laughed. "Some frightened citizen of Grantchester would undoubtedly have summoned an ambulance! No, Charles, I'd be most perturbed if at the present stage of your profound ordeal you were to stride out of here singing a militant hymn." And he added as we both sat down at the table: "In a way I'm glad you've had this setback because now you'll have no trouble believing me when I say I think you should stay here a few days longer. Spiritually you're still extremely weak, and since taking the sacrament isn't by itself going to restore you miraculously to full strength, I'm going to set you some spiritual exercises."

I tried not to look alarmed. Even in the most ardent days of my training for the priesthood I had never been keen on work which offered me no chance to excel with my academic gifts.

"You probably won't need to remain here longer than a week," said Darrow, "but for the next twenty-eight days I want you to rise at six in the morning and spend one hour in reading, prayer and meditation as I shall direct. You may have a cup of tea or coffee to wake you up but no food during this hour, please, and no cigarettes."

My heart sank. I was never at my best early in the morning and before approaching an hour of spiritual exercises I felt I needed a three-course dinner, several cigarettes and a stiff whisky. Laymen think clergymen have an inexhaustible ability to pray and meditate, but in fact unless one is a monk trained to spend a large portion of each day in worship few clergymen have either the time or the energy for a full hour of solitary spiritual hard labour. Every morning I said my prayers and read the office, but these activities resembled a short spiritual sprint; what I was now being required to do was to run a spiritual mile, and I knew very well that I was out of training.

However, my resolve to rebuild my life to give meaning to Jane's death compelled me to say to Darrow: "I want more than anything to get fit. I'll do whatever you say."

"Let me explain what I'm aiming for: I want to help you restore the balance to your spiritual life which your private problems have inevitably distorted. In your pursuit of a success which would impress your father you've probably tended to channel too much energy into your work as a scholar; I'm not saying you haven't been conscientious in your public worship and private prayer, but have you been more than merely conscientious? I feel you should now devote more time to cultivating your inner life so that you can achieve more than a mere outward semblance of your vocation."

"I'm beginning to see why you've been leading me through a course of reading on mysticism."

"There were two reasons for that. The first was that you seemed to be too much preoccupied with the transcendence of God—a common failing among admirers of Karl Barth, I fear—and I thought you needed to be reminded of the mystics' doctrine of synteresis, the idea that a divine spark exists in every human being—"

"—and that God's immanent as well as transcendent."

"Exactly. Mysticism provides a middle way between a Liberal Protestantism stressing the immanence of God and Barth's Crisis theology stressing the transcendence."

"And your second reason for directing me to the mystics?"

"I wanted to see how you reacted to a stress on the relationship between man and God which can exist beyond the rituals of formal worship, and during our subsequent discussions I began to suspect you weren't using your spiritual gifts, such as they are, to their full capacity—with the result that your misguided belief in your unworthiness had been reinforced. And that's another reason why you now need to spend time each day in training and rehabilitation. You need the boost to your self-esteem that the achievement of a balanced spiritual life will provide."

I was unable to stop myself saying: "I feel so depressed that I'm in such a weakened state."

"Then it's all the more important that we should build up your spiritual strength. Now, Charles, you clearly need some hard physical work if you're to avoid spending the morning moping on your bed—come into the garden with me and let's see if we can discover some small useful tree which is crying out to be cut down . . ."

8

THERE was no tree crying out to be cut down but there was a large patch of ground which was asking to be dug up. I dug and I dug and I dug. After a while I felt better, and later as I took a shower I remembered Lady Starmouth saying with a smile: "I adore Muscular Christianity!" Her remark seemed a terrible irony now that I could acknowledge what a debilitated Christian I had become, but when I looked in the glass and saw not my glittering image but my true self I thought that one day, a long way off in a future almost impossible to imagine, an approving reference to Muscular Christianity might not seem so misplaced.

It was an encouraging thought, and I knew then that I was starting to hope again, starting to rebuild my shattered confidence.

9

DARROW spent our afternoon session assigning me my books for the exercises and discussing the most effective techniques for meditative reading. "We'll start the meditations with the Synoptic Gospels," he said, "because I want you to focus your attention on Christ, and then we'll move on to St. John's Gospel so that you can focus on the Spirit. You're too theocentric, possibly because your psychological problems have made you preoccupied with God as Father. I've noticed a marked imbalance in your whole perception of the Trinity."

I began to feel alarmed again. I might be a doctor of divinity but now I felt like a student about to fail an examination, and suddenly I found myself desperate to pass. Supposing I were unmasked as a complete spiritual failure? The thought of abject failure was appalling enough, but the thought of disappointing Darrow was intolerable. In panic I cast around for a solution which would protect me in my vulnerability, and when Darrow returned to my room that evening, the glittering image said to him: "I do wish you'd tell me more about yourself, Father! There's so much I'd like to know."

As soon as the words were spoken I felt myself relaxing. This was an infallible technique for acquiring the good-will of older men; I would ask them about their past, I would listen with the ardent interest of the model disciple and I would be rewarded by a gratifying display of paternal benevolence which would be blind to all the faults and failings I was so desperately anxious to conceal. "Tell me about your days in the Navy!" I urged Darrow with all the warmth and charm I could muster, but although I waited with confidence for the response which would anaesthetise my fear of unfitness, Darrow was silent. At first I thought he was merely pausing to set aside his counsellor's mask, and when he smiled at me I was sure he was about to become confidential, but then he said gravely: "No, Charles. If I'm to help you best I must continue to be to a large extent impersonal. I can only be your spiritual director. Nothing less. And nothing more."

Another silence fell as I painfully perceived the machinations of my glittering image, but at last Darrow said with a firmness which enabled him to be gentle without sounding condescending: "This isn't a rejection, Charles. Quite the contrary. I'd be rejecting you if I allowed you to put our relationship on a footing which would merely reinforce these psychological difficulties which have plagued you for so long. One of my most vital tasks at present is not to prove to you that you need a father-figure; it's to prove to you that you can do without one."

I nodded. After a while my true self was able to say: "Don't think I'm unaware how absurd it is for a man of my age to need a father-figure constantly in the background."

"I'm sure that once you're at peace with your father, a great many difficulties are going to be resolved. But I'm equally sure, I'm afraid, that this peace isn't going to be easily attained."

In an effort to overcome my embarrassment by changing the subject, I said rapidly: "Is this where we start drawing up the battle plan for my return to the world?"

"Perhaps it is," said Darrow, who had of course gauged the exact depth of my distress and wanted to support my effort to counter it. "Very well, let's visualise your approaching visit to your parents in Epsom . . ."

10

"YOUR task here," said Darrow, "is to put your relationship with both your parents on a new basis. Establishing the facts about your paternity isn't just going to satisfy your very pardonable curiosity; it's going to provide an atmosphere of truth in which a new relationship with your parents can be created."

"Yes, Father."

"No, Charles, don't just sit back and say: 'Yes, Father,' like an obedient novice! Work hard, think hard, be constructive—"

"How do I approach this task of creating a new relationship?"

"That's better. Your task is to approach them as a good Christian, and that reminds me of something you said during your narration of the Starbridge story. Didn't you confess that you felt guilty about your lack of parish experience? Well, here's your chance to take over from the local vicar and minister to your parents' spiritual health."

"But my dear Father—"

He gave me a steely look. "You think your parents aren't worth ministering to? You think that just because they don't go to church, they're unworthy of your rarefied spiritual attention?"

"No, of course not, but—"

"Is being a priest just a matter of letting off the occasional homiletic firework and writing books on the Early Church?"

"No, Father. One preaches the Gospel by living one's calling."

"Precisely. Go down to Epsom and live your Christian message. You need never mention God. You needn't even wear your clerical collar. Just turn up on your parents' doorstep and show them by your actions what you believe in."

"Yes, but Father, whenever I visit them I do always try so hard—"

"To do what? To be the perfect son, doing his duty to those two cardboard figures labelled 'Father' and 'Mother'? Put aside that glittering image, Charles—and put aside their glittering images too! Look beyond the cardboard facade and discover those two strangers who have kept themselves hidden from you even as you've kept yourself hidden from them. What's really going on in your parents' lives? How's your father coping with retirement—always a great hurdle for any successful man? How is he, the atheist, facing the prospect of imminent extinction? And your mother—how's she facing old age and the prospect of a declining appearance? How's *she* coping with your father's retirement—always a disturbing change for any wife? How lonely is she? How much does she miss you and how much does she long to confide in you? Charles, you have this challenging pastoral situation on your hands. Are you going to spend your summer at Laud's, comfortably insulating yourself from your twentieth-century problems by seeking exile once more in the remote academic past, or are you going to come down from your ivory tower at last and serve God in a place where you may well be needed more than you've ever been needed in your life?"

I felt as if God had called me not with a whisper but by a blast on the trumpet, and I hung my head in shame to think that I could have been so deaf for so long.

XVII

"The marks of Jesus are silently impressed on His true disciples in the normal procedure of life in society as well as in the crises of suffering and martyrdom."

HERBERT HENSLEY HENSON,
RETROSPECT OF AN UNIMPORTANT LIFE

I

"IT won't be easy," said Darrow. "Your father will no doubt be objectionable as usual and your mother will probably make you cringe, just as she always does, but keep calling on them, Charles. Devote your summer to it. Then in the end caring may generate understanding, understanding may generate forgiveness and once you've forgiven them you'll be at peace with them both at last."

I said abruptly: "That reminds me of Jardine. When he was talking about his father, he said: 'With understanding, forgiveness becomes possible.' "

Darrow relaxed his professional neutrality far enough to say: "My rock-bottom opinion of the Bishop's spiritual perception goes up a notch," but at once he looked as though he regretted his frankness, and before I could comment he was adding swiftly: "And now, no doubt, you're anxious to extend the battle plan from Epsom to Starbridge."

I tried to choose the words which would show him I understood my position. "I do realise," I said, "that my parents must come first. I must sort out Epsom in order to gain the equilibrium which will enable me to sort out Starbridge. However"—I hesitated but could only confess—"I hate the thought of putting Lyle in abeyance."

"I agree this is a most difficult point," said Darrow at once, and encouraged by his sympathy I made a new effort to express my feelings.

"I think I'd find it easier to put Lyle in abeyance if there was a limit set to the time I had to wait," I said. "Assuming I do well with my parents—"

"They'll probably still need the lion's share of the remainder of the Long Vacation. Why don't you pick a date at the end of September for your reinspection of Lyle?"

Six weeks seemed a long time to wait but I said without hesitation: "Very well, but meanwhile could I write to her to re-establish contact?"

"That's a fair question, but I don't see why you should assume I can answer it better than you can. Let me ask you some further questions to help you make up your mind. For instance, what would a letter achieve beyond re-establishing contact? How would you feel if she failed to respond? Would you feel more frustrated than ever? Might this anxiety deflect you from your parents who should now be your first consideration? Might you be tempted to rush off to Starbridge for another bruising encounter with the Bishop?"

I was obliged to admit these were all disturbing questions. "Perhaps I should do nothing for the moment," I said with reluctance.

"We'll keep the matter open and discuss it regularly. Then I'm sure a satisfactory solution will evolve . . . And talking of evolution, Charles, I think you're fit enough now to hear some information I've been keeping from you about the evolving situation at Starbridge. On the morning after your arrival here, Jardine telephoned me."

I was shocked by the nervousness of my reaction. "Did he tell you I was mad?"

"He was much more anxious that I should tell him you were safe. Of course he was frightened in case you'd smashed yourself up in your motor; if you had, part of the responsibility would undoubtedly have been his."

"Did he phone again?"

"Three days later, yes. He wanted to know how you were getting on. I said: 'How kind of you to inquire, Bishop—Charles is in better health and benefiting from a quiet time with us.' I was curious to see if he'd press me for further information."

"And did he?"

"He certainly went fishing. He said: 'Charles was in a very distressed state when he left us. I was most concerned because he seemed to be dabbling in some incredible fantasies.' I then made some mild noise such as 'Hm' and inflected it so that it could mean almost anything—whereupon he lost his nerve, changed course and asked me how I was settling down in Cambridgeshire."

"So he did try to convince you I was mad!"

"I don't think so," said Darrow with that serenity which never failed to reassure me. "If that had been his aim I think he'd have tried a direct approach by insisting you'd been raving, but he was clearly more concerned to get information than to make slanderous accusations."

"But of course he's scared you'll believe me!"

"Of course, but that would apply whether he was guilty or innocent, wouldn't it? Even the holiest of bishops would blanch at the thought of a canon spreading a story of episcopal adultery through the hallowed cloisters of the Fordite monks!"

Gradually I felt myself relax. "I'm sorry," I said. "I'm behaving stupidly."

"Not at all. It's just as natural for you to worry about Jardine convincing me that you're mad as it's natural for Jardine to worry about whether you're convincing me he's an adulterer. But, Charles, my purpose in relaying this news of Jardine was not to make you anxious; I was trying to make the important point that time hasn't stood still at Starbridge since you rushed away from the Bishop's dinner-table. I think you're tending to see Lyle and Jardine and their relationship—whatever that may be—as frozen in time, but the situation at the palace will be constantly evolving, just as your situation here has been evolving, and that's another reason why I think you should wait a little longer before you make your final circuit of the Starbridge mulberry bush. You flung a big stone into that particular pond, Charles; stand back now until the ripples reach the edge of the pond and you can see what's been washed up at your feet. I think you may well find that the wait will pay significant dividends later . . ."

2

MY first attempt at the spiritual exercises went entirely wrong. The opening half hour had been allocated to reading at a normal pace passages from St. Augustine's *Confessions* and *The Imitation of Christ* by Thomas à Kempis, two famous works which naturally I had studied earlier in my career but which had for some time remained unopened in my library. This task seemed simple enough, but when I finished in fifteen minutes I realised belatedly that I had been reading at the abnormal speed developed by my academic work, and to make matters worse I found on rereading the pages that some of the paragraphs were unfamiliar. I felt disconcerted by this proof of poor concentration, but it was not until I moved on to my assignment of meditative reading that my problems began in earnest. I had been given a short passage from St. Mark's Gospel to consider, not an interesting section like the Little Apocalypse which would have involved me in some challenging scholarly thoughts on Jewish eschatology, but the few verses which described the healing of Jairus's daughter. The story was excruciatingly familiar, and after five minutes I found all my attempts at meditation had run aground on the rocks of boredom.

To pass the allotted time I translated the verses first into New Testament Greek and then into medieval Latin, but I was acutely aware that I was not supposed to be exercising my scholarship, and it was with mortification that I approached the last quarter of an hour which had been allocated to prayer. This section was easier, as I was in the habit of praying, but I was so upset by my failure to meditate competently that I found my concentration was wandering again and my prayers lacked depth.

I saw then how adrift I was unless the scholarly side of my intellect was engaged, and although I was no stranger to a broader religious awareness I realised that over the years my experience had narrowed instead of expanded. I liked my religion to take a cool, hard, analytical form and then I was capable of feeling very devout indeed, but without the prop of my intellectual power I was lost. I told myself I was not temperamentally suited to meditation; my gift was for studying and teaching, not for sitting around brooding over the spiritual resonances of one tiny section of St. Mark's Gospel.

However, I knew I could never utter such unacceptable thoughts to my mentor, and after prolonged anxiety I decided that the only course I could take was to concede my failure but to stress that a vast improvement was both imminent and inevitable.

We met after his chapter meeting.

"Someone suffering from malnutrition often has trouble taking normal food at first," he said mildly after I had admitted my difficulties, "but the important thing is that you had the desire and the will to stay at the dinner-table and confront your plate for the duration of the meal. Let's take a detailed look at what happened so that I can adjust the diet for you."

After a post-mortem of the entire ill-fated hour he extended the time allocated to simple reading, kept the time of prayer unchanged but reduced the meditative reading to eight minutes. However, the length of the material remained the same. "If you were in training," he said, "you could take twenty-five minutes over that passage—which is about as long as most people can profitably spend on this sort of reading—but don't get discouraged. I don't expect too much from you yet."

However, I found I could not bear this oblique confirmation of my failure. At once the glittering image said before I could stop him: "Don't worry, Father—I'm sure I'll soon master these little difficulties!" and at once I knew I was making the same mistake as I had made when I had tried to reduce my relationship with Darrow to a purely personal level. I tried to find the words to retract the remark in all its false absurdity, but in the end it was Darrow who spoke first.

"Charles," he said, "you don't have to be a huge success in order to win my liking and approval. So long as you do your best—no matter how mediocre your best is—my liking and approval are guaranteed."

There was a silence as the glittering image, battered but not yet dead, subsided once more into my subconscious, but still I was too shaken to reply.

"Let's face the truth here," said Darrow, and again his firmness allowed him to be gentle without sounding condescending. "You are in many ways a very ordinary young clergyman. You have a certain modest spiritual gift which you've neglected, and you now have to pay it attention by developing it as far as you can. But I'm not looking for any glamorous success here, Charles—I don't expect you to transform yourself into St. Ignatius Loyola in order that I may pat you on the head and say: 'Well done!' What I'm hoping is that you, the real Charles Ashworth, will struggle doggedly on at this task which is so very far from easy for you, and eventually achieve a possibly small but nevertheless solid improvement in your spiritual life. *Then* I shall say: 'Well done, Charles!' but I won't be setting the seal of approval on any glamorous play-acting; I'll be demonstrating my faith in your true self. Keep smashing that glittering image, Charles. It's the enemy within. Keep smashing it until you can finally excavate the roots by remaking your relationship with your father."

Deeply ashamed of my dishonesty I promised him I wanted only to live in the truth.

3

I SPENT another five days with the Fordites before I felt confident enough of my strength to risk returning to the world. My second attempt at the exercises proved equally humiliating, but now that I was relieved of the burden of trying to become a latter-day St. Ignatius Loyola I found I could concentrate better; I was no longer distracted by the worry of what Darrow would think of my failure.

Day by day Darrow made further adjustments to my spiritual diet, and gradually I stopped being nervous of the post-mortem and welcomed it instead. His questions clarified my thoughts, pinpointed my weaknesses and gave me an additional incentive to concentrate when the exercises were in progress. It soon became evident that he always knew when I was trying as hard as I could and when I was unwittingly drifting into inertia, and once I trusted him never to underestimate my efforts or to overestimate my ability I was able to surrender myself willingly to his discipline and bend my whole will towards achieving the balanced spiritual life which my problems had so effectively prohibited.

We only discussed the Starbridge situation once more before I left Grantchester. On the evening before my departure I said to him: "I've been thinking again about whether I should write to Lyle, and I've come to the conclusion that if I want to do the normal thing here, I should write not to Lyle but to Mrs. Jardine. After all, she was my hostess at that terrible dinner and the least I can do now I'm better is to apologise for my drunken behaviour."

Darrow merely said: "What would you expect such a letter to achieve beyond reassuring them of your good manners?"

"It would reassure them of my stability. It seems to me that if I shoot off a passionate polemic to Lyle now, she'd simply dismiss it as further evidence that I'm round the bend."

"Very well, by all means write to Mrs. Jardine, but tell me, Charles, are you still disturbed by the need to put Lyle in abeyance?"

"Disturbed but resigned. I do accept that my parents must come first."

"I'm sure they'll prove a substantial diversion . . . And how do you feel now as you prepare to face the world again?"

"Nervous. But hopeful because I know I'm taking positive action, working for my own rebirth. I won't let you down, Father, I promise."

"It's not I whom you mustn't let down."

"I realise that. But aren't I allowed to see you as a symbol?"

Darrow said lightly: "It's dangerous to see people as symbols. I think you'll be on much safer ground if you simply regard me as a priest doing the work God's assigned to him." He stood up, added: "Come to the Abbot's Parlour after breakfast so that I can give you my blessing," and then before I could reply he was moving swiftly from the room.

4

THE next day we parted in plain style in that lavish parlour. I knelt to receive his blessing, and as I stood to shake his hand he said: "This is where a new phase of your ordeal begins, Charles. I'll be praying hard for you until we meet again."

It was difficult to thank him adequately but I tried to imbue the conventional phrases with the gratitude no words could ever have expressed. I also tried to give him back the borrowed cross but he waved it aside. "No," he said, escorting me to the front door, "you'll need that a little longer, I think."

I thanked him again, slipped the cross around my neck and walked away from him into the world.

5

AFTER taking a bus into the city I entered my rooms at Laud's as the Cathedral clock was striking eleven. For one long moment I stared at those familiar but curiously alien surroundings where my glittering image had toiled so arduously to promote the myth of his perfection, but at last I closed the door, set down my bag and walked to the desk to telephone my parents.

Before I lifted the receiver I removed my clerical collar and opened my newly-purchased packet of cigarettes. The first taste of the cigarette evoked an image of the proverbial nectar of the gods, and leaning forward in my chair with my elbows on my desk I inhaled in a trance of satisfaction as I flicked through the pile of correspondence which had accumulated. As usual there were too many bills, but several undergraduates had sent me diverting postcards from places scattered throughout Europe and an unknown American professor had written a friendly letter about my book. Ignoring the pile of theological journals and Church newspapers, I embarked on my call to Epsom before glancing at the copy of *The Times* which I had just bought. China was still fighting Japan. The Spanish were still fighting each other. The Devil was still stalking Germany. So much for the world. I was just thinking that life in the cloister, despite the lack of women, did have a great deal to offer, when the telephone bell stopped ringing in Epsom as my parents' long-suffering adenoidal parlourmaid finally picked up the receiver.

"Hullo, Ada," I said, after she had announced herself as the Ashworth residence. "You sound in good form."

"Mr. Charles—well, what a lovely surprise! Just a minute, your mother's out having her hair done but your father's at home—I'll get him out of the greenhouse."

I inhaled deeply from my cigarette. Minutes passed, and I was about to transfer the receiver to my other hand to relieve the muscles which had begun to ache with tension when a series of noises at the other end of the line culminated in my father saying abruptly: "Charles?"

"Good morning, Father. I—"

"What's all this? Are you in some sort of trouble?"

My heart began to thud at a brisk pace. "I can't imagine why you should say that," I said, and somehow succeeded in burning a hole with my cigarette in the front page of *The Times.*

"And I can't imagine why else you'd telephone when we're apparently quite beneath your notice these days! Well, I don't suppose you want to speak to me. Your mother said she'd be back by twelve. That means one. I'll tell her you telephoned."

"Wait!" I was dimly aware that for some reason I was grinding out my half-smoked cigarette. "Father, I want to come down to Epsom for lunch tomorrow—I was planning to arrive around noon with a bottle of champagne—"

"Champagne?"

"Yes, I want to bury the hatchet"—I was now shredding the cigarette to pieces in the ashtray—"and I thought the burial would be worth celebrating."

"Nasty pretentious drink, champagne, except at weddings. No need to waste your money. Just turn up tomorrow at noon with a civil tongue in your head and you can be sure the hatchet will be buried six feet deep. Then we can drink a glass of my best sherry and that'll be that."

"Yes, Father."

"You should guard against extravagance, Charles. No need to behave as if you're a member of the fastest set in town."

"No, Father."

"Tomorrow at noon, then. Your mother will be very pleased. But make sure you drive carefully and don't wreck your car pretending you're a motor-racing hero," said my father severely, and hung up the receiver before I could grope for a reply.

6

I THOUGHT of Darrow and took several deep breaths as I held my cross. Then shrinking from all thought of my parents I embarked on the task of attending to the many mundane matters which had accumulated in my absence. Later, on my way to the bank, I paid my respects to my car which was standing safely in the Laud's forecourt. I felt as if I had come back from the dead; the sense of beginning a new life was becoming stronger.

That evening I wrote Lang a long friendly letter apologising for my delay in reporting to him, and padded the pages with some carefully selected details of my retreat. That gave me the opportunity to praise Darrow and compose a scholarly paragraph on mysticism. Sandwiched between the irrelevant paragraphs I wrote: "In respect of your commission I found no evidence that all was not currently as it should be, and Your Grace will be reassured to know that the complete absence of any proof must render our man safe from hostile forces east of Temple Bar." I also added on a less dramatic note: "Of course if you wish to see me to discuss this matter further I'll come to Lambeth immediately, but I fear there's little I can add beyond the fact that I encountered a most generous hospitality during my visit which passed, in many respects, far more pleasantly than I had anticipated."

I had now finally escaped from my role of archiepiscopal spy. Sealing the envelope I left my rooms, posted the letter in the pillar-box by the Cathedral and still savouring my liberation from the burden which had triggered the onset of my great ordeal, I returned thankfully to College to dine.

7

AT the end of the evening I poured myself a small whisky to help me sleep but it tasted so vile that I threw it away. The result was that for hours sleep proved elusive, and when my alarm clock rang at six, I could hardly open my eyes. However, before I could sink back into unconsciousness I remembered Darrow, and seconds later I was struggling out of bed to make coffee.

The exercises seemed bafflingly difficult again, the texts remote, my meditations arid, and as I struggled to concentrate I could think only how odd it was that I should be groping my way so clumsily towards my new life in that room where the glittering image had so adroitly displayed his techniques for acquiring his shallow success. And suddenly in my despair that I should now be so slow and awkward I longed more fiercely than ever for my new life. The longing had no words but I knew I was praying for a strength which had to be granted from without, not dredged up from within where my resources were so enfeebled. It was as if I were saying: "Let me live!" and the next moment Jane was returning to me in my memory. I could see her running across the beach on our honeymoon towards the sea, I could hear her urging joyously: "Come on, Charles, *come on!*" and as the early morning sunlight pierced the window at Laud's the dead text was pulsating with life before my eyes. "Look, Charles—the tide has turned!" I heard her call, and as the book slipped from my hands I was aware of her love bearing me forward on the tide of my deliverance to the brilliant darkness which lay eternally beyond.

8

I REACHED Epsom punctually at noon on that Saturday morning and headed for the outskirts of the town where my parents lived near the race-course. Their house, built at the end of the last century, had six bedrooms, three reception rooms and an acre of garden, but my father had resolutely refused to move after his children had left home. This was his house, earned by his own hard work, and he was sticking to it until he was carried out feet first—or so he told my mother whenever she pined for a smart modern bungalow to cocoon them snugly in their old age. Attached to the house was an Edwardian conservatory, called "the greenhouse" by Ada, which had long been the centre of my father's aspirations as a horticulturalist and was now the ruling passion of his life. As I turned the car into the drive that morning and saw the sun shining on the glass roof, I wondered if he had yet succeeded in his ambition to grow oranges larger than plums.

I emerged from the car and pulled on my jacket. I had decided not to wear my clerical clothes, since my father so often made snide remarks about them, and was instead dressed in a pale grey suit and a plain shirt accompanied by my old school tie. I hoped I looked formal without being pretentious, smart without being flashy, well-bred without aspiring to be more than middle-class. In other words I was trying hard to convince my father than no matter what the truth was about my paternity, he had not laboured at fatherhood for over thirty-seven years in vain.

Ada opened the front door, and as she stood flat-footed and shining-eyed on the threshold my father's dog Nelson pranced barking across the floor.

"That dog!" said Ada crossly as Nelson waved his front paws at me in excitement, and in response to my inquiry about her health she produced the reply that her bunions were killing her. However, this was a traditional response; Ada's bunions had been killing her for at least twenty years, and after expressing the equally traditional words of commiseration I was finally able to ask: "How are my parents?"

"Ever so pleased you're visiting, Mr. Charles. Madam went out early this morning and bought a new dress. Make sure you notice it but don't say I—whoops! Here she is! God bless you, Mr. Charles, lovely to see you . . ." She thudded away towards the kitchen as my mother made a theatrical descent of the stairs.

"Charles—darling!"

My mother was a woman in her late fifties, still slender, with dark hair, dark eyes and a smart haggard look which was not unattractive. Her chief hobby was her appearance, which she maintained with an unflagging dedication. I was sure she dyed her hair and equally sure the idea that she might descend to such vulgarity had never occurred to my father, who adopted a naive attitude to the more esoteric mysteries of the female sex. Her taste in clothes was expensive yet restrained; she was wearing a navy-blue dress accompanied by an unobtrusive strand of pearls.

"I'm glad to see you still haven't lost the secret of eternal youth," I said smiling at her. "I like your dress."

"Darling, what wonderful flattery—I adore it!" As we kissed I noticed she was wearing a delicate scent, and suddenly I pictured her devoting her entire morning to burnishing her glittering image for my benefit. "And Charles, how divine you look without that clerical collar! Or will it make you cross if I say that? I mustn't make you cross . . . But come outside—I thought we'd have drinks on the terrace and I'm going to mix some champagne cocktails as a special treat. I know that silly old man told you not to bring champagne—how typical!—but why shouldn't we have some champagne, I'd like to know? I was so thrilled you'd decided to visit us—and so was *he* although he'd never admit it. Honestly, Charles, since he retired he's been exactly like a bear with a sore head—"

"I suppose he must miss the office a lot."

"Well, why should he, he's got his horrid conservatory! I keep asking him to grow orchids but he won't; it's sheer bloodymindedness. He could perfectly well grow orchids if he wanted to."

"How's Peter?"

"No help at all, I'm fed up with Peter at the moment. The least he could do is drop in every week to have a drink with your father and talk about the office, but he's always working late or going to the Test Match or playing golf or whizzing off to a smart dinner-party with Annabel. Of course I blame Annabel for being too possessive; I always did think she was a thoroughly selfish girl—oh, there's the telephone. Maybe it's Peter ringing up in remorse after neglecting us for so long. Darling, go and dig your father out of that ghastly conservatory and tell him we're about to have drinks."

Nelson accompanied me through the door onto the terrace and padded at my heels as I walked around the side of the house. However, outside the conservatory, which he knew from experience was too warm for his comfort, he sat down in the shade to wait. Meanwhile my heart had begun to thud at a brisk pace again. I felt as if every step I had ever taken in my life had led to this moment when I would open the conservatory door and face once more but with new eyes that fierce mysterious man who had brought me up.

I reached the door. I opened it. I crossed the threshold into the sultry heat. I was reminded of a jungle being colonised by a single ruthless British soldier intent on building his own private empire on which the sun would never set.

"Ah, there you are," said my father from the far end of the conservatory. "Glad to see you've arrived in one piece. That stupid woman says she's going to make champagne cocktails—why you're not utterly ruined by her petting and pampering I can't imagine, but there we are, she means well and it's not every day she has the excuse to waste my money on champagne. Where's your dog-collar? Nice to see you looking like a normal chap for a change. Suppose it's too much to hope that you've given up that damn fool superstitious pantomime that calls itself the Church of England."

I touched the cross hidden beneath my shirt and walked on down the conservatory to meet him.

XVIII

"Then as to success in life, I think that all turns on the meaning attached to success. From one point of view, I do not doubt that my professional career may fairly be described as successful, but that is not the point of view which at any time has secured my acceptance."

HERBERT HENSLEY HENSON,
RETROSPECT OF AN UNIMPORTANT LIFE

I

MY father was seventy years old but could have passed for a man in his early sixties. He had a trim neat upright figure, not tall, and he moved with none of the hesitation of old age. His hair, which had once been a mundane brown, was now an equally mundane pepperish-white; short, straight and ruthlessly parted, it receded sharply on either side of his high forehead. The eyes behind his glasses were blue. He had a long straight nose and a sharp pugnacious chin. His mouth drooped at the corners when he sulked and tightened into a thin-lipped line when he was angry, but he had a swift rare pleasant smile which revealed that he had kept his teeth; my father hated dentists almost as much as he hated doctors and was convinced they were charlatans intent on making money by the most dubious means.

As I approached him, I saw he was wearing his scruffiest gardening clothes. "Thought I'd change while your mother's pampering you over the first round of those damned cocktails," he said as we shook hands. "Did she send you to fetch me?"

I told him about the telephone call which might have come from Peter, and my father, giving an eloquent sniff, began to scoop a small pile of earth from the workbench into an empty flower-pot.

"Mother said you hadn't seen much of Peter lately," I added, removing my jacket in acknowledgement of the heat.

"He's been too damn busy. I'm just fit for the scrap-heap, of course, now I'm retired. And that stupid wife of his has been giving him extravagant ideas by bullying him into taking a holiday on the Riviera. 'What's wrong with England?' I asked him, but he just laughed as if I were senile. He never bothers to keep me up to date with what's happening at the office. Wish to God I hadn't retired but I always said no one should stay at the helm after the age of seventy so I had to stick to my guns and practise what I preached. And now what have I got? One son who doesn't answer my letters, another son who prances off abroad and a wife who nags me to grow orchids! It's enough to make one puke. I'm fed up with the whole bloody business of being alive. Roll on extinction, I say, and thank God there's no after-life. That really would be the last straw."

"I'm sorry I didn't answer that last letter of yours, Father," I said. "That was wrong of me. But can I now renew my invitation to Cambridge? I'd be very pleased if you and Mother—"

"Can't leave my plants. Various things at a critical stage. Need daily attention." My father scooped up the last fragments of earth and pressed them ferociously into the flower-pot before demanding: "Why all the sweetness and light? What's going on? Why are you here? Are you in debt?"

"My dear Father—"

"You don't have to soften me up before you ask for a loan. Come on, Charles—out with it! I knew as soon as you telephoned yesterday that you were in some sort of trouble—"

"I have indeed been in very great trouble," I said, "but it has nothing to do with money and I'm getting better now."

He pushed the spectacles high up on the bridge of his nose so that he could stare at me through the lenses. "You've been ill?"

"I've been through a time of severe strain but I'm now, with the help of my new spiritual director, beginning to—"

"Your new *what?*"

"Spiritual director. A specialist in spiritual health. Like a doctor of the soul."

"Very nasty. Sounds like quackery. You ought to be careful, Charles. Some of these quacks can do a lot of damage."

"I assure you he could hardly be more respectable—he's a clergyman as well as a monk, and—"

"A monk! I don't like the sound of this at all, Charles. No man in his right mind would be a monk. But what's the matter with you? Lost your faith?"

"No, I'd lost my spiritual way, but I'm finding it again, and Father Darrow—the monk—thinks you can be of enormous importance in helping me along the road to recovery. That's actually why I've come here today."

We stood facing each other, my father still holding his trowel, I still holding my jacket while my shirt stuck to my back. My heart was now thudding more briskly than ever.

"Well, of course I'll help you in any way I can, Charles. That's what fathers are for. But this all sounds damned odd to me and I'm not sure I understand what's going on. Stop talking about spiritual this and spiritual that and put it in plain no-nonsense English. Have you had a nervous breakdown?"

"Father Darrow refused to call it that. Perhaps one could say that my entire way of life broke down so that I found myself unable to go on without pausing to solve a number of severe problems."

"Severe—oh, rubbish, Charles! That nasty monk's been putting a lot of nonsense into your head! You don't have any problems—you're making the biggest possible success of that peculiar profession of yours!"

"That was the problem."

"My God, don't tell me you're going to chuck everything up and rush off to be a missionary in Africa!"

"No, before I can even begin to reassess my calling I have to get my soul in order, and that's why—"

"There you go again, talking in ghastly clerical whimsy-language! Why the devil you can't just say you're in a bloody muddle, I don't know. God, how you worry me, Charles! For years and years I've slaved to bring you up to be—"

"You did a wonderful job, Father. Before I say what I'm going to say next, I want to tell you how very much I admire you and how very grateful I am to you for all you've—"

"What the *hell's* all this? Nasty sentimental maundering—talking like a damned foreigner—pull yourself together, Charles, and for God's sake stop embarrassing me!"

There was a pause. I looked at him and knew the hour had come—and suddenly as he looked at me, I saw he knew it too; he knew that no fierce rebuke could stop me now from saying what had to be said. We stood there in the stifling conservatory, in that little jungle which he was doggedly colonising with his incorruptible British spirit, and it was as if we both saw the sun setting on the empire which he had been so valiantly sustaining for so long.

I said: "I've got to know. I can't live with the uncertainty any longer. Help me—you said you'd help me—that's what fathers are for, you said—"

"I'll help you best by telling you to wash your hands of that bloody monk and stop acting like a bloody actor in a bloody melodrama!"

"Are you my natural father?"

The sun finally set on the empire and the night began to fall.

2

MY father turned away to face the workbench again so that I could see his face only in profile, and then slowly, very slowly, he took off his spectacles. I felt as if I were seeing an actor remove his mask at the end of some long Greek tragedy. Then slowly, very slowly, like the old man he was, he sat down on a wooden stool and stared with unseeing eyes at the spectacles in his hands.

At last he said in a tired voice: "So it was all for nothing."

"How can you conceivably say that?" I was shattered. Automatically, hardly knowing what I did, I upturned a giant flower-pot so that I could sit down at his side.

"Didn't want you ever to know. Thought if you guessed it would mean I'd failed, and if I'd failed it would mean everything was a mockery—the marriage, all my ideals, everything. But you guessed. So I've failed. And it's all been for nothing."

"I don't think you've failed," I said. "I'll never think you've failed. And if I don't think you've failed, then it can't all have been for nothing."

He moved abruptly away. I knew why. He was terrified that he might prove unable to keep the depth of his distress to himself. The silence lengthened as he turned his back on me and pretended to examine one of the vines, but at last he said: "I suppose you want to know everything."

"I must. I'm sorry."

"Well, don't blame me if you don't like it!" said my father, making a frail attempt to recapture his characteristic truculence. "If you think he was a bloody hero, you're making a very big mistake." And then before I could reply he said in a rush: "His name was Alan Romaine . . ."

3

"ALAN ROMAINE," said my father. "Alan Romaine. Typical. Just the sort of name he *would* have. Maybe he picked it out of a French novel. Wouldn't surprise me. Nothing about him ever did surprise me. Alan Romaine . . .

"He was a doctor. But not your ordinary decent quack who runs gamely around the local houses with a stethoscope and is always a bit pressed for time. This quack was special. He had grand ideas. He was going to play the hero in a big London hospital and later he was going to have rooms in Harley Street where all the titled women could consult him about their aches and pains. He knew people. He name-dropped. He was about to begin a specialist's training in gynaecology at Bart's but that summer he had a little time to fill in so he came down to Epsom as a locum. Romaine liked Epsom. Near London . . . scene of the Derby . . . racing . . . smart people . . . glamour . . . just his sort of place. Once he'd arrived, he settled down in double-quick time and prepared to conquer everyone in sight.

"He was only twenty-seven. Obviously he'd done well. Plenty of brains. First-class at cricket and tennis. Modest, though—knew how to behave. All the women from nineteen to ninety treated him as a Greek god, but because he was such a sportsman he was popular with the men too—all the men except me. I just took one look at him and thought: Bounder. Cad. Too flashy by half. And I wondered about him. He never spoke of a family. Nobody really knew anything about him. He was a gentleman, of course, but . . . not to be trusted.

"He drank quite a bit. No one seemed to notice, but I did. Once at a dinner when the ladies had withdrawn he had a third glass of port after a heavy raid on the claret decanter and I said to him: 'You're drinking rather a lot for a doctor, aren't you?' That made him angry. 'Poor old Ashworth!' he said. 'So old, so staid, so dull!' But I said: 'You'd better watch your step. Hard-drinking bounders don't wind up in Harley Street. They wind up in the gutter.' For a moment I thought he was going to throw his glass at me, but instead he laughed and said: 'You're just jealous—and don't think we can't all guess why!'

"As you know, I'd wanted to marry your mother for some time," said my father, turning away at last from the vine and moving back to the workbench, "but I was much older than she was and I wasn't glamorous. I was just a plain man who wore glasses and worked hard. Of course I had my ambitions, but unlike Romaine I didn't go around advertising them, and meanwhile I wasn't happy in my job and I was tempted to make a complete change. I was also tempted to turn my back on Epsom for a while—I couldn't bear the thought of being an onlooker when Helen married a man whom I felt sure was no damned good—and when it seemed to me that the marriage was inevitable, I decided to volunteer for the Army.

"As you no doubt remember, I gave you a censored version of that decision when you were fifteen. However, what I didn't tell you was that the Army decided straight away that they didn't want me. There was no interval while they made up their minds; they just weren't interested in a thirty-two-year-old civilian with poor eyesight. Well, I was glad in the end that I didn't have to leave the law but sorry to be stuck in Epsom while Helen was still steering this disastrous course—and don't think I hadn't tried to alter that course, because I had. But she'd just told me to leave her alone. Finally I said: 'Always remember, whatever happens, that I love you and I want to marry you.' Perhaps I had a premonition that he'd jilt her. But on the other hand I'm not the sort of fellow who gets premonitions.

"And then . . . she came to me. I'd already heard from the Army but I hadn't actually told anyone that I wouldn't be leaving Epsom after all. She came to my house and broke down, broke down utterly, it was very terrible. I wanted to go after him and . . . But I knew I had to put first things first. He could wait. She couldn't. She'd come to ask me what to do. I don't believe she really thought I'd stick to my guns and marry her. She just wanted to know what on earth she was going to do. Romaine—" My father stopped.

I waited. By this time I was standing, leaning back against the work-bench and gripping the edge with both hands.

My father turned to face me. "He was already married," he said. "He called it a 'Jane Eyre' situation. Typical. He was equating his own sordid behaviour with a romantic novel—ugh! It revolted me. Anyway there he was with a wife hopelessly insane in an asylum, and there was Helen, completely ruined—oh, it was all so wrong, *so wrong,* I couldn't stand to think of it, and I knew at once I had to put things right. Well, what other choice did I have? I couldn't have let evil win. That would have been quite contrary to all my principles. I thought: I'm going to prove good always does win through in the end . . . Silly, really, I can see that now, but at the time I felt no other course of action was possible, and my decision was strengthened when she said—" My father stopped again. Then he replaced his spectacles, looked me straight in the eyes and said: "She told me Romaine had offered her an abortion.

"I said: '*You will not have an abortion under any circumstances whatsoever.*' Of course I'd realised that she wanted someone to tell her not to do it because she must have known in her heart that it would have been a disaster for her. I told her she'd never get over having murdered her own child—and that was true, I knew it was, I knew Helen, I knew how sensitive she was underneath all that brittle gaiety. I said: 'You'll marry me and no one's ever going to know.' Oh, how relieved she was, poor girl! She cried and cried and said she'd be the best possible wife to me . . .

"I had one interview with Romaine. I made sure I was absolutely sober and utterly in control of myself. Then I went to him and said: 'You're leaving Epsom and leaving England. Forget Harley Street. Forget all those glamorous dreams. You're going abroad within a month or by God I'll see you struck off the medical register—and if you ever dare come near Helen again,' I said, 'you can be bloody well sure you'll regret it.' I'll always remember that moment. He was dead white. He'd been drinking, of course. I could smell the brandy. But he was quiet. And suddenly I felt as if I were looking at someone whom no one in Epsom, least of all poor Helen, had ever really known.

"Well, the next day after he'd pulled himself together sufficiently to strike a glamorous pose, he announced that he felt called to work in Africa and so off he went, the noble young doctor, romantic to the last . . . and I was left to pick up the pieces.

"I pretended that I was on the brink of leaving for my military training so we had a good excuse for marrying straight away, but she insisted on having a white wedding and that meant a few days' delay while the gown was made. I tried to persuade her that we couldn't afford to wait but she said it would look too odd if she wasn't married in white and whatever happened we had to keep up appearances. However, finally we got to the altar, and that night after I'd consummated the marriage, I said: 'That's that. You're both mine now—which means that you're never, never under any circumstances going to mention that man's name again and you're never, never under any circumstances going to tell anyone that child's not just as much mine as any future children you may have. That child,' I said, 'is going to be my child from this moment onwards and I'm going to bring him up to be a good straight decent man even if it's the very last thing I ever do.' "

My father paused. Taking off his spectacles again he began to polish them with a grubby handkerchief. "So much for the preliminaries," he said tersely, "but then the trouble really began . . ."

4

"WELL, of course," said my father, "it was all rather different in the end from what I'd expected, but then I'm not sure now what I did expect. I don't think I'd looked much beyond the honeymoon, but Helen found pregnancy a great trial. Couldn't face marital intimacy most of the time. I told myself it was just her condition but . . . I suspected she was pining for Romaine.

"Then you arrived and she worried herself to death about what people would think—she'd convinced herself you'd be conveniently late but no, there you were on time. She wouldn't go out for a while, wouldn't see anyone, cried in her room—and it wasn't just because she was afraid people were talking about her. It was because she had finally woken up to the realisation that she'd jumped out of the frying pan into the fire—she'd avoided ruin but now here she was tied to a husband whom she . . . well, she wouldn't have married me if she'd had a choice. She never loved me as much as I loved her, and all the time . . . well, I felt increasingly sure she was pining for Romaine.

"She decided to have another child as soon as possible, and I knew why. It was because she couldn't stand the guilt, the guilt that she couldn't love me as she should, and she wanted to make amends, but although she became obsessed with the thought of another baby, she didn't conceive straight away. More tears, more unhappiness, more awful guilt—then finally, thank God, she had Peter and that put everything right for a while, but the marriage never really ran smoothly. She tried hard, but . . . I knew she didn't love me and I started to get resentful. And of course all the time there you were, growing up, the constant reminder, the cuckoo in the nest . . . poor little chap, not your fault. You were a nice little fellow, too. I said to myself: I'm not going to take it out on him . . . But I'd look at you and I'd remember Romaine.

"Then suddenly one day I realised that my own boy was getting overlooked because you were such an exceptional little chap. You really did have great charm. Everyone used to pat you on the head and dote on you, and no one doted more than your mother. But finally I woke up and saw you were getting very spoilt and pampered with ideas quite above your station so I knew there had to be no pampering from *me,* not if I wanted to be a good father, but of course your mother didn't understand, silly woman, thought I was taking it out on you. I wasn't. I just didn't want you growing up like him and I thought I saw all the ingredients there . . . So I got very strict and your mother called me a brute and we started having bloody awful rows, always over you, but I won, I shut her up, I even hit her sometimes, terrible, very wrong, shouldn't ever strike a woman, but I wasn't going to stand any nonsense from anyone in my household, not after all I'd been through, and anyway the net result of all this was that I wound up keeping you down with one hand while I paid special attention to Peter on the other. Not a good situation, but I didn't want my boy growing up thinking himself inferior because he had this exceptional older brother. Of course you hated me paying attention to Peter, you hated anyone paying attention to Peter, you liked the whole world revolving around you so that you could preen yourself in the limelight. Silly little fellow, but not your fault. You couldn't help everyone cooing over you, but I knew I had an absolute moral duty to keep the balance, and besides . . . I was so afraid you'd turn out like Romaine.

"However, as time went on I got both you and your mother under control and you really did begin to show exceptional promise. Very gratifying. But naturally I never believed it would last. I found myself becoming haunted by the worry not only that your heredity would triumph despite all my efforts to muzzle it but that you'd somehow succeed in discovering the truth about your paternity and go straight off the rails. You gave me a nasty moment when you realised you'd arrived so soon after the wedding, but I'd been prepared for that crisis so I was able to knock it on the head straight away. There's nothing more unstable than a moody adolescent, and I was sure you'd have gone to the dogs in no time if you'd found out then that I wasn't your natural father after all.

"You looked like Romaine by then. I used to see your mother gazing at you and I knew she was remembering, just as I was. I'd feel so angry then, so bitter, but I'd cheer myself up by thinking: if that boy turns out well, at least there'll be something redeemed from the mess. So I kept on at you, urging you to keep to the straight and narrow, until finally there you were, safely up at Cambridge reading law, and I thought: I've done it. That boy's turned out properly and he's all set to lead a thoroughly decent life, no glamour, no play-acting, no fantasy. But then—my God! You sidled home and told me *you wanted to go into the Church!* No wonder I nearly had a fit. I didn't think you were in touch with reality. You'd always been a bit of a romantic idealist—thank God the War ended before you could throw away your life dying gallantly in action! I thought this Church nonsense was just a pose, like Romaine telling everyone he'd felt called to be a doctor in Africa, and my God, that was the closest I ever came to letting the cat out of the bag about your paternity.

"But of course I didn't do it. Well, I couldn't have done it, could I? It would have been like hitting a man when he was down. There you were, wallowing in emotion, talking drivel about God—how could I have done anything but kept my mouth shut? You needed to be protected, not disowned, and besides . . . if I'd said to you then: 'You're not my son,' it would have been a lie because by that time you *were* my son. *I'd* brought you up, *I'd* knocked my values into you, *I'd* made you what you were . . . But now you were telling me that what I'd made you was a bloody clergyman! God, what an irony! I hardly knew whether to laugh or cry.

"Well, I battered away at you to try to save you from yourself, but you dug in your toes and wouldn't budge. I had to admire you for sticking to your ideals, and finally I thought: well, at least it's a good straight decent life. But then I thought: how's he ever going to stand it, living as a curate, unable to afford to marry, he'll go to the dogs, start drinking too much, get in a mess with some woman, and then all my hard work will have been for nothing and my marriage will be more of an unredeemed disaster than ever. But I'd underestimated you, hadn't I? You weren't the average ineffectual young padre who gets stuck in some remote rural hamlet preaching sentimental mumbo-jumbo. You were special. You had grand ideas. You name-dropped. And of course you wound up as the Archbishop's favourite poodle. Typical. Couldn't help admiring you. But oh my God, how you reminded me of Romaine . . .

"I couldn't believe it would work out. I kept waiting for you to get in a mess, but you didn't—you landed that amazing post at St. Aidan's and you married that thoroughly nice girl. Wonderful. But then I started worrying in case the marriage went wrong, thought she might perhaps have been a little *too* nice for you, thought you might later fancy someone tougher and more alluring . . . No peace, you see, not even then. When I married your mother and took you on I thought fatherhood would end promptly on your twenty-first birthday, but it didn't. Parenthood only ends with the grave. I went on worrying myself silly about you, but there you were, still doing well, and I could always cheer myself up by thinking: never mind, I did at least make a success of that boy. You were like a symbol in the end, a symbol that my ideals had triumphed over all the tragedy . . .

"But then last year . . . that awful row . . . I felt so depressed. I thought: maybe I've failed after all. I did cheer up a bit when you sent us that invitation to visit Cambridge for Easter, but the whole letter was much too smooth and I knew some old clergyman had been getting at you during Lent. I can always spot insincerity a mile off. So I wrote back that stiff reply in the hope that I'd needle you into writing something genuine, but no, you got up on your high horse and stayed there.

"Then I suddenly felt very old. I'd just retired. I had no work to go to any more, nothing to distract me from my unhappiness. You were estranged from me, Peter was too busy enjoying the life I'd once led to pay me much attention . . . I felt rather jealous of Peter, being young, leading the life I still wanted to lead . . . I was a bit sharp with him once or twice. Mistake. He took offence. Silly boy, henpecked by that awful Annabel of his . . . I suppose he's happy. Maybe he's miserable. Who knows? All I know is that *I'm* bloody miserable stuck in Epsom day after day with your mother, but poor Helen, I do feel sorry for her in so many ways. She's had a disappointing sort of life, not the life she had in mind. She would have liked a more glamorous husband, someone romantic, someone . . . well, someone like Alan Romaine.

"We never mentioned him, never, not even during all our rows over you, but he's always been with us. He's still with us. He's here now, invading my conservatory, smashing everything up . . . And after this, I suppose," said my father turning on me fiercely, "you'll want to trace him! I can just see you going all sloppy and sentimental, thanking God you've found your real father at last—so much for God! I slaved for years and years to be a decent father to you and now bloody Romaine will saunter along and reap the benefit! Disgusting! But that's typical of life, isn't it? The real bounders always bounce along into a happy ending while the decent fellows get trodden in the dust. Good doesn't triumph over evil, not in real life, good gets ground down and spat upon. Law of the jungle. No God. Nothing. Beats me how anyone can believe otherwise."

He sank abruptly onto the stool again and groped to remove his spectacles for another polishing. I waited to allow him time to steady himself; I bent my head so that he would think himself unobserved as he furtively wiped his eyes on the grubby handkerchief; but then I sat down at his side once more, and leaning forward I gently covered his trembling hands with my own.

5

HIGH heels clacked in the distance like gunfire to warn us of my mother's approach. We both started, both glanced at the door. I was quite beyond speech by this time, but fear galvanised my father into action, and shoving away my hands he struggled to his feet.

"Not a word, Charles. *Not a bloody word.*" He spoke in a fierce whisper, his face set in its hardest lines, every muscle of his frame rigid with determination. "Your mother's not to know you know. Absolutely not. *Never.* And if you so much as breathe one syllable of this conversation to her, I'll—"

My mother tip-tapped through the conservatory doorway before he could complete the sentence. "Well, really, you two!" she exclaimed in exasperation. "What are you up to? I'm waiting to drink champagne cocktails! Eric, go and change out of those filthy clothes and let Charles escape from this ghastly hell-hole of yours!"

I somehow achieved a smooth intervention. "Was that Peter on the phone?"

"Yes, he sent his regards to you and said he was so sorry he wouldn't be able to see you before you rushed back to Cambridge but he and Annabel were just off to a garden-party at Richmond."

"Typical!" said my father. "No time for his family!"

"When's he going to come and see Father?" I said, before my mother could put all the blame on Annabel.

"Tomorrow evening at six. You see, Eric? I knew it was nonsense when you said yesterday he'd forgotten you!"

"He's just coming to keep me quiet. 'Better keep the old buffer sweet,' he's saying to that awful Annabel, 'or he might do something nasty with his will.' Well, I don't care if he comes or not. It's all the same to me."

"Silly old man!" said my mother, grimacing at me to convey he was irritating her beyond endurance. "What nonsense you talk!"

But my father elbowed her rudely aside and stumbled off at a rapid pace into the garden.

6

"WELL, of course he's become absolutely impossible," said my mother. "I'm at my wits' end—have been for some time actually—and really, darling, when I heard you were coming today I almost started believing in divine providence because I feel that if I don't talk to someone soon about how awful life is at the moment, I'll start climbing the walls. Quick, come to the terrace and let's have a drink while he's changing."

"He seemed fairly pleased to see me—"

"So he damn well should! I said to him this morning: 'You'd better cheer up before Charles comes or he won't come down here again in a hurry,' but he only said: 'He won't come down here again in a hurry anyway, so why should I bother?' Ghastly old man, moping around like death personified, and it's so frightful for *me* being tied to someone who spends his whole time looking as if he's trying to find a coffin to lie in. Heavens, I'm not even sixty yet, and he makes life so dreadfully depressing . . . I wish to God he hadn't retired. He doesn't know what to do with himself, apart from pottering around in that frightful conservatory—and I'm sure the heat there's bad for him. He could have a heart attack. Maybe that's what he wants. I don't know, God knows what he wants, but I know what *I* want, and that's a decent holiday. Peter and Annabel are taking the children to the South of France, such a lovely idea, but Eric poured cold water on it and as good as told Peter he was an unpatriotic nitwit for wanting to take a holiday outside England—well, no wonder Peter took offence, I don't blame him, although I do think Annabel stirs him up. There's something very *common* about Annabel, but then we all know, don't we, that her father made his money out of trade."

We had by this time reached the wrought-iron table shaded by a white umbrella, and I was pouring the cocktails from the jug. "I'm sorry things are so difficult," I said as I sat down beside her and lit her cigarette.

"Never mind, darling, let's drink to a happy visit—mmm, what lovely champagne! Now don't let me rattle on about all my ghastly problems—tell me about yourself. I must say, you're looking a little thin and peaky. I do hope you haven't been working too hard."

"I've just concluded a long retreat with the Fordite monks at Grantchester."

"Poor darling, no wonder you're looking peaky! It's a miracle you're not worn to a frazzle—like me. Honestly, Charles, I can't get over how amazing it is that you should turn up. I kept hoping and hoping you would and I was going to write but I didn't want to pester you and I was so afraid of being one of those ghastly mothers who *cling*—and everyone knows nowadays that clinging mothers can do so much damage. Of course Eric's always accused me of spoiling you but I've tried so hard to be sensible, I really have, and the last thing I want is to be a nuisance or a burden or—oh hell, I'm embarrassing you, I can see I am, I'm saying all the wrong things but I'm so nervous, in such a state, please, please don't be cross . . ." And she began to cry.

"My dearest Mother . . ." I dragged my chair around the table so that I could put my arm around her shoulders. "I'm so very sorry—how dreadful to think you were afraid to write to me and how appalling to think I've left you alone for so long—"

"Oh, I'm all right," she said, drinking half her cocktail. "Heavens, I don't want to make you regret you've come! Everything's absolutely fine really—except that sometimes I think I can't go on any more—" She broke down again.

"How difficult is he? Is he just surly or—"

"No, he doesn't hit me, not nowadays. My God, he used to get so angry—but I did try so hard to be a good wife to him, I really did . . . It was just that whatever I did never seemed to be enough. Sometimes I used to despair so much that I'd tell myself I'd leave when you and Peter were grown up, but when it came to the point I was too frightened. He'd have been beastly about the divorce and I couldn't face being socially ostracised . . . Perhaps if I'd met some decent man . . . But I never did. All the decent ones were happily married."

"All of them? What about earlier in your life?"

"When you and Peter were little? Yes, there were one or two men who were very keen—although I was never unfaithful because I was so afraid Eric would find out and he'd already threatened me about that. 'If you're once unfaithful to me,' he said, 'that's it. Finish. And don't think you'd ever see either of your sons again.' Well, that settled it, didn't it? Actually I think Peter might have managed without me, but you . . . oh,

I couldn't have left you. No, no, that was quite impossible. I stayed with him because of you in the end—it was like some ghastly punishment but it didn't matter, I accepted it, I'd have done anything for you and you needed me, I knew you did, especially as Eric could be so . . . oh, how I hated him sometimes! But there was no question of leaving, and besides, I never in fact met anyone whom I could love as I wanted to love . . . as I knew I could love—" She stopped.

"You mean," I said after a pause, "there was a memory which acted as a yardstick?"

"Yes, I met a man once . . . before I was married . . . first love . . . and no one I met later ever measured up to him. It was as if I could see them only in black and white whereas this memory was in glowing colours." She drank deeply again from her glass.

"What happened to him?"

"I don't know. He had to go away, but it was so strange, Charles, because I always thought . . . I always thought—"

"—he'd come back."

She nodded, struggling with her tears again. Her mascara had smudged. The powder was streaked. I could see the deep lines on her face. "But he didn't," she said levelly. "Stupid of me to indulge in romantic dreams, wasn't it? But Eric always says I'm a stupid woman."

"Father makes a lot of wild statements that are unjust. Perhaps he feels that life's been unjust to him and he wants to hit back."

"Life unjust to him? But he's had a wonderful life, so successful! He's had everything he's ever wanted!"

"Yes, but . . . well, never mind Father for the moment, I'd much rather talk about you. Tell me more about this first love of yours."

"Oh darling, I can't. Eric would be so angry if he knew I'd even mentioned it to you, and besides . . . some things really are better not discussed."

"Are you sure? I've just spent days discussing my life with the clerical equivalent of a psychiatrist and I feel much better."

"Charles! Darling, what's wrong? Oh, if only you knew how much I worry about you—is the trouble to do with Jane? I know how terribly her death upset you, I've sensed you bottling up your grief all these years, never speaking of her—oh Charles, I did so long to help, but somehow I never knew what to say . . . I loved Jane. I cried and cried when she died—"

"My dearest Mother—"

"I did, Charles, I did! Such a good nice girl she was, always so kind to me, not like bloody Annabel who treats me like a drunken hag. Well, I know I do drink too much sometimes—and particularly when I have to face Annabel, but I'm all right, Charles, I'm all right—"

"I'm going to come back here next week and stay for a couple of days. I think it's very important that you should talk to me in detail about all your unhappiness—"

"Oh, if only you knew how much I long to confide in you!" she said. "But I mustn't. Eric would make life hell if he thought I'd been confiding in you behind his back."

"Eric's already making life hell. Let's see if we can change the gramophone record. Come on, Mother, we probably have at least another ten minutes together before he reappears—have a second cocktail and tell me all about this first love of yours who affected you so deeply for so long."

7

"*I MUSTN'T* say his name," said my mother, "because Eric said it was never to be mentioned again, but when I was a young girl still in my teens I thought it was the sort of name every romantic hero ought to have . . . Now I know what you're thinking, darling. You're thinking: what fools young girls are about men! But it wasn't as simple as that. I was going through a ghastly time and it was as if this man's wonderful glamour and his whole great spirit of high romance were in some magical way a negation of all the dreadful things that were happening to me.

"You'll remember me telling you that when I was eighteen, I went to Germany for six months to be 'finished.' Well, I always pretended it was great fun but the truth was I hated it. I hadn't wanted to go but Great-Aunt Sophie said it would be better if I went away from home for a while because my mother was so ill by that time with her TB and my father was keeping this mistress . . . My dear, nobody would think anything of it now, but this was 1898 and Aunt Sophie was deeply Victorian. Nobody explained about the mistress, of course, and I didn't understand why I was being sent away—oh, I was so unhappy! But in the spring of 1899 I was allowed to come home again because the mistress had left Epsom and now not only was my mother at death's door but my father was dying of cancer. I expect you remember hearing most of this before, darling, but I wonder if you've ever stopped to think how absolutely frightful it was for me.

"Well, Papa eventually died—I think old Dr. Barnes killed him with morphia in the end—and there I was, nineteen years old, in this house which was exactly like a morgue. My mother went on dying by inches and Aunt Sophie creaked around in her corsets and everything was prayer books and hushed whispers and I used to feel as if I were suffocating.

"And then . . . that summer . . . old Dr. Barnes broke a lot of bones in an accident and this young doctor came to Epsom for three months to take his place.

"I soon met him. He came to attend my mother in her illness. I remember I was embroidering yet another useless sampler when I heard the noise of wheels in the drive and on going to the window I saw this young man jump down from the pony-trap with his Gladstone bag. Then he caught sight of me—but he didn't just touch his hat and move on. He swept off his hat and he raised his hand and he smiled and . . . It was the breath of life, Charles. I ran all the way to the front door to let him in.

"He was a tremendous success in our set. Everyone liked him except Eric, but everyone knew Eric was jealous. I'd known Eric for years . . . and respected him . . . but he seemed so terribly old, over thirty—imagine!—and although I wanted to marry to escape from home I honestly couldn't see myself marrying an older man. I didn't truly know Eric then, of course. Later I discovered all his wonderful qualities and . . . well, I married him, didn't I? But earlier . . . after I'd met this other man . . . I couldn't think of Eric at all.

"Eric said I was just infatuated with the man's looks, but he was wrong. Of course this man was divinely attractive. But I fell in love with him mainly because he was the only person who seemed to understand what hell I was going through. He said he'd been going through hell himself because someone he loved very much had recently been certified insane. He said: 'Life's so frightful in so many ways, so many terrible things can happen even to the best people, and that's why it's so important to live to the hilt while one can and snatch all the happiness that's available.'

"I said: 'That's how I feel too.'

"It was rather a solemn moment, but then he kissed me—for the first time—and he laughed and he said: 'I have this *irresistible* urge for champagne—let's raid the cellars and filch a bottle!' Oh, he was such fun! It was only three in the afternoon—a preposterous time to drink champagne, but Aunt Sophie always took her afternoon rest till four so no one was breathing down my neck. We crept down to the cellar and found a bottle of champagne and sneaked off to drink it in the summer-house—oh, how we laughed and oh, what fun it was! But terribly naughty, of course—Aunt Sophie would have died. I said: 'I feel terribly naughty!' and he said: 'So do I! Isn't it amusing?' and he laughed again and began to recite some lines from Browning—that poem about how one mustn't miss one's opportunities—'The Statue and the Bust.' I can remember him lounging on the summer-house love-seat with the glass of champagne in his hand as he quoted: 'The sin we impute to each frustrate ghost is the unlit lamp and the ungirt loin . . .' Then suddenly he set down his glass and said: 'I feel a delicious urge to start lighting lamps and girding loins!' Oh God, how romantic it was, how exciting, I adored it, I was absolutely swooning . . .

"Well, as I've said, it was all terribly naughty and of course it couldn't last, and after a few meetings . . . well, to cut a long story short," said my mother, finishing her second cocktail rapidly, "it turned out that he was already married—the one in the asylum was his wife—so nothing came of my big romance and eventually he went off to Africa while I married Eric and settled down. But Eric always hated that episode in my past, and that's why you must never, never let him know that I've—oh God, here he is. Not a word, darling, promise me—*not a word*—"

"I suppose you're still drinking those disgusting cocktails," said my father, emerging onto the terrace with a glass of sherry in his hand. "Another bottle of good champagne murdered . . . Helen, why are you looking so odd?"

"She's wondering why she feels no remorse for committing the murder!" I said lightly, but neither of them smiled, and in the silence that followed this trivial but flawlessly smooth response I sensed they both looked at me and saw Dr. Romaine.

8

DESPITE the depth of my emotional turmoil I worked as hard as I could to make the lunch a success. I kept the peace whenever they began to bicker, I asked after their friends, I listened to interminable stories about Peter's omissions and the iniquities of Annabel. Finally we discussed the Coronation, and once the discussion had led inevitably to Dr. Lang, who had played such a leading role in the ceremony, we were soon talking about the Church of England's performance during the House of Lords debate on the A. P. Herbert Bill.

"I adore that Bishop of Starbridge!" said my mother. "He's the only one who seems to know what marriage is all about, and there was a madly attractive photograph of him in last week's *Illustrated London News.*"

"Bishops have got no business being attractive to women," said my father. "That man's paid to be a eunuch in gaiters, not Rudolph Valentino in a mitre. And anyway, what does he think he's doing, attacking his boss in public? Shady sort of behaviour, if you ask me, but then they say Starbridge isn't a gentleman. Never went to the right school."

"Do you know him, Charles?" said my mother.

I embarked on a heavily censored version of my recent activities in Starbridge, and the rest of the lunch passed in an atmosphere of hushed delight as my mother savoured the thought of me staying at an episcopal palace and my father mentally marked another lofty cross on the graph of my ascending career. However, after my mother had reluctantly observed the convention of the ladies' withdrawal at the end of the meal, my father said as he lit his pipe: "I shouldn't get too involved with Starbridge, if I were you. It might get you into hot water with Canterbury. Or as you clerics would say: stick to Cantuar and leave Staro well alone. You seem to be mixing with some very dubious people at the moment, Charles, and I'm especially worried about this peculiar monk."

"But I promise you he's a first-class chap, Father—there's no need whatsoever for you to worry!"

"Well, of course I'm bloody well going to worry! I spend my life worrying about you, Charles, and now I'm going to worry more than ever—my God, how I got through that meal just now I'll never know, but I've got to keep up appearances because whatever happens your mother must never, never know we've discussed Romaine."

"Why not?"

"Why not?"

"Yes, why not? Isn't it high time the three of us sat down and discussed him so that he can be exorcised once and for all?"

"I've never heard such a mad suggestion in all my life! Of all the idiotic, ridiculous—"

"Father, I do wish you could talk to this monk of mine—I really think he might help us both here. Why don't you come up to Cambridge and—"

"I can't leave my plants, and anyway I absolutely refuse to talk to some mad meddlesome old monk who should have been put in his coffin and buried years ago!"

"He's fifty-seven."

"That's worse. An old monk's bad enough but a middle-aged monk's a disgrace. Why isn't he living with a wife and several children in a nice house with a tennis court?"

"Well, now that his wife's dead and his children are grown up he's decided he can serve God best by—"

"The man's obviously unbalanced. I refuse to see him—and I refuse to go to Cambridge."

"Never mind, I've already told Mother that I'd like to come back here next week and stay for a couple of days. I think it's extremely important that we—"

"Don't make me laugh! You won't come back—we won't see you for dust now! You'll be too busy chasing bloody Romaine!"

I said: "If he's alive I'd like to meet him—just once, to satisfy my curiosity. But you don't seriously think, do you, that I'd ever want to be friends with someone who was willing to murder me when I was an inch long?"

"My God, you astonish me sometimes, Charles! How could a man with your brains make such a bloody naive remark? For God's sake stop and think before you open this frightful Pandora's Box! The rotter'll charm you and ruin you—I can see it coming—"

"My dear Father, I'm not a nineteen-year-old virgin female!"

"Wish you were. Then I could lock you up to keep you safe. My God, if you go down the drain now after I've spent nearly thirty-eight years slaving to keep you on the straight and narrow—"

"I can't go down the drain—Darrow's put in the plug, and if only you'd talk to Darrow you might start believing I'm not such a potential rake as you think!"

"Well, of course I don't think you're a—"

"Yes, you do, it's monstrously unfair! I know you don't mean to be unfair—I can see now that you don't mean it—but you just can't help yourself and it's all because Romaine's haunting this family like an unexorcised ghost—"

"Well, you won't exorcise him by digging him up and taking a look at him—you'll simply get in an even worse muddle than you're in already! For God's sake, Charles, go and talk to your mad monk before you do anything catastrophic. Perhaps you'll listen to him even if you won't listen to me!"

"I certainly intend to talk everything over with Darrow when I see him again tomorrow, but he's not mad, he's one of the sanest men I've ever met. Now please, Father—no more quarrels! Put out that awful pipe and let's join Mother in the drawing-room . . ."

9

AT three o'clock when I left, my mother hugged me and said with tears in her eyes: "You really will come back next week, won't you, Charles?"

"Yes, I promise." I kissed her and felt the tears spill onto her cheeks as she held me close.

"For God's sake!" exclaimed my father in a paroxysm of embarrassment. "Stop weeping over the boy! Disgusting!"

"Oh, shut up, you brute!" my mother shouted at him, and ran sobbing into the house.

"Stupid woman," said my father. "I can't stand that sort of nonsense. It's very bad for you and not at all how a mother should behave. Parents shouldn't let their children know when they're feeling upset and emotional. Irresponsible. Not the done thing at all."

We shook hands without speaking. Then I said: "Goodbye, Father. God bless you," and his mouth, already well turned down at the corners, began to tremble.

I got into my car and drove away.

10

I DROVE straight to the Epsom public library. The medical directory was waiting for me in the reference section and my hand was steady as I drew the book from the shelf.

Through my mind flickered the multitude of fates which might have overtaken Romaine. He had died of drink in Africa, died a hero's death in the War, died of old age in England after a long debilitating exile. Alternatively he was alive but no longer a doctor. He had been struck off the register years ago for hard drinking and seducing patients; he was keeping a tobacconist's shop in Eastbourne or a bookshop in the Charing Cross Road or a public house in Cornwall; he was in a lunatic asylum, an old peoples' home, a bed-sitting-room; he lived in a mansion with his fifth wife and ten children. Any fate was possible, but if he was alive and still practising in England as a doctor he would be listed in the book which was now in my hands.

The directory opened at the letter M. M for Mother, poor Mother, how she had suffered. N. N for Nativity, my birth on time too soon after that pathetic white wedding. O for the Orgasm which had created me, P for the Penis which had begotten me, Q for the Questions where is he, what became of him—

I reached the letter R. Of course he was probably dead. Or if he was alive he might well be abroad, settled happily in the Colonies.

ROM—ROMA—ROMAI—*ROMAINE*—

He was still alive.

ROMAINE, ALAN CHARLES—

Charles! My father could never have known the second name; he would have killed her if he had known.

—Oaktree Cottage, Starvale St. James—

I had heard of Starvale St. James. It was not far from my friend Philip Wetherall, the Vicar of Starrington Magna. It was a village less than twenty miles from Starbridge.

I had to sit down. I sat there for a long time while people padded to and fro among the bookshelves in the quiet room, but at last I replaced the directory, left the library and embarked on the long drive home to Cambridge.

XIX

"The difficulty of arriving at the truth when one has nothing but human testimony to depend on, is both apparent, and, from a religious point of view, terribly disconcerting."

HERBERT HENSLEY HENSON,
RETROSPECT OF AN UNIMPORTANT LIFE

I

THE telephone was ringing as I entered my rooms that evening, and when I picked up the receiver my brother Peter said: "Charley, it's me. How did you survive your visit to the Governor?"

"Just let me feel my pulse and make sure I'm still alive."

He laughed but said urgently: "Charley, what do you think's going on? Mother seems to be hitting the gin bottle for six every day, the Governor's deep in his beastly jungle of a conservatory and nothing I do is ever right. The Governor seems to hold it against me that I don't discuss the office with him in detail, but Charley, he *can't* expect to keep up with everything now he's retired! He's got to learn to let go, but somehow I haven't the heart to say that—poor old boy, I feel so sorry for him, even though he's being distinctly beastly to me at the moment. Annabel says I should take a firm line, but somehow I can't bear the thought of hurting the old boy. Annabel doesn't quite understand, and honestly, Charley, what with Annabel nagging me on the one hand and the Governor being beastly to me on the other, I feel in the mood to emigrate to Australia."

"I'll deal with the demented parents if you can deal with the militant wife. I'm returning next week for a couple of days to sort them out."

"Thank God. I knew you'd come to the rescue in the end, Charley. Don't think I didn't have faith in you, but the truth is I've been in such despair—"

"Hold fast, Peter, and cancel all your plans to emigrate. The Church of England's finally on its way."

2

I FELL into bed, slept till six, silenced my jangling alarm clock, spent the required hour on my exercises, dressed in my cassock, attended Communion in the Cathedral, breakfasted, returned to the Cathedral for Matins and the Sung Eucharist, saw my Bishop afterwards for ten minutes' conversation, accepted his invitation to mid-day Sunday dinner, escaped at three, discovered one of my undergraduates had turned up with his parents at Laud's, gave them tea in my rooms, returned to the Cathedral for Evensong at six, rushed back to College, threw a few essential items in a bag, staggered to my car, drove to Grantchester and arrived exhausted but still conscious at the Fordite mansion at half-past seven that evening. I had already arranged to stay the night, and the little white-haired monk, welcoming me like an old friend, said he had kept the same room for me. It seemed like the nearest earthly approximation to Heaven I had encountered for some time, and on attaining my sanctuary I kicked off my shoes, collapsed on my bed and lay inert as a beached whale for some minutes.

When Darrow arrived all he said was: "Obviously you've been working hard."

We smiled at each other. I had sprung to my feet as he entered the room, and now we shook hands. His first question was: "You've kept up with your exercises?"

I was aware of his priorities; his concern for my spiritual health preceded his curiosity about my parents.

"Yesterday I felt I might be getting somewhere," I said, "but this morning I was back in the desert after my view of the oasis."

"No doubt you were distracted by yesterday's events. And your paternity?"

"We were right. My father is Eric Ashworth but I was begotten by a disastrous doctor called Alan Romaine."

3

WE did not talk further then; he had merely come to the visitors' wing to welcome me, but later he returned and we had a long session together. His final verdict was: "You've done well with your parents and made more progress than I thought you would in such a short time. But where do you feel the battlefield now lies?"

"Starvale St. James."

Darrow was silent.

"Is that wrong?" I said, my confidence immediately dented.

"It's neither right nor wrong; it's merely inevitable. If I hesitate it's not because I disapprove but because I'm trying to decide the best way to approach this subject, which is a very dangerous one and potentially a breeding ground of painful illusions."

I was even more disturbed. I felt obliged to confess: "My father was thoroughly alarmed by the whole prospect and called it a Pandora's Box, but I thought he spoke out of prejudice and jealousy. Of course he thinks that Romaine's bound to send me straight to the dogs."

"Of course. I'm afraid we must expect your father to revert to his favourite nightmare when he's under strain, but what assurance did you give him that you would approach your Pandora's Box sensibly?"

"I told him what I told you the other day: I just want to see the man once. Then I can sit back and say: 'There! I've done it!' And that'll be that."

"You make Dr. Romaine sound like a sightseer's landmark, Charles, but is he really on a par with Buckingham Palace and the Tower of London?" And before I could answer, he added: "Why are you so determined not to see Romaine more than once?"

"It would be disloyal to my father, who I've now discovered didn't reject me at all but tried hard year after year in his own muddled well-meaning pigheaded way to be the best of fathers to me. I don't need another father in my life now, and I certainly don't need a broken-down old quack who tried to murder me when I was an embryo."

"Then why go to see him at all?"

I was taken aback. "But I must!" I exclaimed. "He's the source of my life—I must just see—"

"Yes, there's a psychological need. So you're in this awkward position, aren't you? You want to be involved yet you don't want to be involved."

"I don't in the least want to be involved!"

"If that were true, you wouldn't want to see him."

"All right," I said, becoming heated. "*All right.* I'm getting involved, but my involvement's going to be minimal. After all, he rejected me—tried to kill me—"

"That, I agree, is rejection. But do we actually know whether he would ever have performed the abortion? How much in earnest was he? It's a question your father can't answer because he wasn't there."

"I concede that I've only heard my father's side of the story—"

"No, you've heard your mother's side as well, and the two views of Romaine are very different, aren't they?"

"But that's why I want to see him! I want to hear his own version of what happened!"

"Exactly." Darrow sat back satisfied in his chair. "You're searching for the truth; that's why you want to interview Dr. Romaine and that's why, despite all your father says, the interview should take place. You need to establish a view of reality which will enable you to live comfortably with these difficult facts which you've uncovered this weekend."

"But all I need is one interview," I persisted. "Then I can turn my back on him and walk away."

"And may I ask," said Darrow, "exactly what you hope to achieve as a priest by rejecting him as you believe he once rejected you?"

There was a silence. The knot of tension expanded as my anger became infused with guilt. "Are you suggesting," I demanded at last, "that I turn him into a grotesque father-figure whom I keep locked up in a cupboard and inspect at regular intervals?"

"I'm suggesting you try to keep an open mind in a very difficult situation. Although Romaine's a stranger, he did nonetheless strike the spark which put you in the world, and this means that in a very real sense he's with you as long as you live. So obviously you've got to learn to live with him now that he's been identified, but how can one live successfully with a person if one remains in a state of anger at the thought of all his wrong-doing?"

After another painful pause I said: "What do I do?"

"What do you think?"

I had to drag the words out of my conscience. "I must forgive him."

"Yes," said Darrow, "you must forgive him in order to be at peace with him—and that may well be very hard indeed. So don't think of this visit to Starvale St. James as a little holiday to see a bizarre landmark, Charles. Think of it as a large rack in your continuing ordeal—and then, I suspect, you'll approach the meeting in something which resembles a realistic frame of mind."

Silence fell as I considered my quest in this new light. Finally I said: "Supposing I can't cope with him and wind up ruined, just as my father prophesies?"

"Ah, now we're getting somewhere. Here comes that demon, your fear that you're unfit and unworthy."

"Supposing I like him but he doesn't like me?"

"Here comes that demon, your fear of rejection."

"Supposing he doesn't even remember I exist?"

"Unless he's suffering from amnesia I doubt if he'll have forgotten the catastrophe at Epsom which destroyed his hopes of a Harley Street practice," said Darrow dryly, but I was barely listening. I was finally peering into my mind with a clear eye and being horrified by what I saw. I heard myself say: "I want him to like me so that I can hurt him by rejecting him, and I want to hurt him not just to pay him back for my mother's suffering but to prove to my father—and to myself—that I'm a loyal son . . . But just listen to me! What a muddle I'm in, I'm raving—"

"Better to be honest. Then you'll know exactly how hard you'll have to work to achieve a genuine forgiveness."

"What an appalling situation!" Feeling close to despair I asked him if I could stay at his house longer than we had planned so that I could spend the following day thinking and praying under his direction. "Then I'll leave very early on Tuesday morning," I added, "and drive down to Starvale St. James."

"So be it. Very well, Charles, get some sleep and tomorrow we'll start arming you against the demons."

4

WITHOUT making a huge detour I was unable to avoid Starbridge on my journey to Starvale St. James, but as I descended from the hills shortly before noon on that Tuesday morning I saw that the Cathedral was no longer glittering like an opulent decoration on a wedding cake but shrouded in a mist which was seeping through the water-meadows; here was no mystical sun-drenched city but merely a bedraggled county town in the rain. Winding my way into the marketplace I took the short cut through Butchers' Alley to avoid the shopping lanes around St. Martin's-in-Cripplegate. The main gates of the Cathedral Close flashed past me as I drove over the crossroads into Eternity Street, and then I was heading past the Staro Arms, across the West Bridge and into the open country beyond the river. In my driving mirror I watched the spire of the Cathedral recede and tried to imagine what everyone would be doing at the palace. I thought of Darrow saying: "You threw a big stone into that particular pond," and at once in my imagination I saw the ripples still travelling inexorably to the edge.

These thoughts diverted me for ten miles, but when I saw the name of my destination on a signpost I spent the remainder of the journey trying to steady my nerves. I reached the village at twenty-one minutes past noon. The rain had stopped, the mist had dispersed and the sun was trying to shine. Halting the car, I asked for directions and was told that Oaktree Cottage lay beyond the church at the far end of the street.

My destination proved to be a rambling house with a thatched roof; I guessed that the building had once been two cottages which some enterprising builder had knocked into one. A drive led from the lane through a well-kept garden where an ancient gnarled gardener was scratching peacefully at a border, and ignoring the sign which directed patients to the surgery at the side of the house I approached the front door. My fingers slipped on the bell. Automatically I wiped my hands on my jacket as I waited for a response, and after the inevitable eternity had appeared to pass the door was opened by an elderly parlourmaid. "Good morning," I said, handing her my card. "Is Dr. Romaine at home?" But before the parlourmaid could reply a woman's voice called from the shadowed hall beyond: "Who is it, Withers?"

"Dr.—Mr.—Dr. Ashworth, M'm," said the parlourmaid, who clearly believed any clergyman who wanted to be addressed as "Doctor" was behaving perversely, and handed my card to a plump golden-haired woman who now stepped forward into the light.

"Dr. Ashworth—I'm so sorry, have we met? Your face looks familiar, but I can't quite—"

"No," I said. "We haven't met. Mrs. Romaine?"

"Yes . . . Thank you, Withers," she said abruptly, dismissing the parlourmaid. She spoke in a no-nonsense contralto with a faint North Country accent. The golden hair was cunningly dyed. "Do come in, Dr. Ashworth."

"I was hoping for a brief word with your husband," I said as the door closed behind me. Naturally I had prepared a speech to meet all possible permutations of the situation which would confront me on Dr. Romaine's doorstep, but for a moment I feared I was going to forget my lines. By this time Mrs. Romaine was giving me a very hard look indeed. "He knew my parents in the old days before the War," I heard myself say after an awkward hesitation, "and when I discovered he lived here, I thought I'd look him up. The Vicar of Starrington Magna is a friend of mine and I'm not unfamiliar with this part of the country."

Mrs. Romaine decided to replace the hard look with a hospitable smile. "How nice of you to call! My husband's still out on his rounds, I'm afraid, but he should be back soon. If you have the time to wait—"

"Thank you."

"You'll have to excuse me," she said, leading the way into the drawing-room, "but I'm just about to go out to lunch. I'll leave your card in the hall for my husband and make sure Withers tells him you're here—would you like a glass of sherry while you wait?"

I declined the glass of sherry. She told me not unsociably to make myself at home, gave me one last hard look and departed.

I glanced around the room. It was expensively furnished to accord with the oak-beamed ceiling and the inglenook fireplace, but all the furniture appeared to be modern reproductions of traditional styles. Various knick-knacks in questionable taste were scattered along the mantelshelf but there were no photographs. On the wall hung several bad prints set in heavy gold frames, of the famous Constable paintings of Starbridge Cathedral, and on the floor the carpet felt plush to the point of sponginess as I walked to the window. I was unable to resist the conclusion that my mother would have judged the room vulgar in its moneyed attempt to ape a lady's drawing-room, and I knew she would have dismissed my hostess by that most damning of all middle-class epithets, "common."

Turning my back on the window with its view of the picturesque cottage garden I paced up and down until at last, like a drowning man, I saw my life flicker past as if that part of my self which Darrow had called my beleaguered psyche were engaged in some complex attempt to trace how I had arrived in Starvale St. James at this precise moment of my life. My memory was just recalling my installation service in Cambridge Cathedral with photographic clarity when far away across the hall the front door casually clicked open and equally casually banged shut.

I froze. There was a pause. I heard the parlourmaid's voice followed by a man's murmur, but after that there was a long, long silence. I knew at once—I needed neither to see nor to be told—that he was staring with incredulity at my card, but at last his footsteps crossed the hall, the drawing-room door slowly swung wide and in walked Dr. Alan Romaine.

5

I AT once experienced that sinister shock which follows a glimpse of oneself in a distorted mirror, and I knew then why Mrs. Romaine had given me such a hard look once she had had the chance to register the details of my appearance. The man before me was a long way from being my double, but nevertheless I felt I was being offered an uncanny glimpse of myself as I might appear in the unimaginable 1960s.

He was my height, six foot one, and far from being a "broken-down old quack," he was in a moderately good state of preservation. I recognized my curly hair, transformed from brown to grey but still displaying unruly tendencies; since baldness runs in families I was relieved to see that although his hair was sparser than mine it was still plentiful. I recognised the dark eyes with the creases at the corners, the mouth with the humour lurking subtly at the edges, the deep cleft in the chin which in childhood would have been described as dimpled. He was far heavier than I was; with his athlete's figure run to seed he must have weighed fifteen stone to my twelve and a half, but he carried himself well and in his unhurried graceful movements I glimpsed the charm which had enchanted Epsom in 1899.

I stood stock still in the middle of the room with my fists clenched at my sides and no doubt I looked the picture of extreme tension, deep distrust and appalled fascination. He paused by the door and looked the picture of relaxed amusement, his mouth curling humorously at the corners and his eyes bright with interest. I thought of my father saying as he fought his tears: "The real bounders always bounce along into a happy ending while the decent fellows get trodden in the dust." I thought of my mother saying: "It was like some ghastly punishment." I looked at this debonair stranger who was apparently unmarked by tragedy, and I loathed him.

He glanced down at my card, then looked up again with a quizzical smile and said: "Dr. Ashworth!"

"Yes. Good morning, Dr. Romaine."

Our voices were identical in timbre but different in inflection. Inflections are acquired by a child from those people who bring him up, and in my mind my voice was saying with Eric Ashworth's fierce stresses: still caddish, still flashy, still gliding along the glamorous road—*disgusting.*

Meanwhile his voice was saying with an admiration which repelled me: "A doctor of divinity at Cambridge! How proud your mother must be . . . And how is your mother, may I ask? I hope she's well."

"She's very well," I said. "So's my father. Both my parents are well."

I did remember Darrow talking of forgiveness. I did remember my hours of prayer and discussion at Grantchester. I did remember my resolve to open my Pandora's Box with a steady Christian hand, but at that moment I was beside myself with rage. I wanted only to brandish my loyalty to my father in every sentence.

"Still flourishing in Epsom? Splendid!" said Romaine warmly, but he had turned away from me and although the lines of humour still shaded his mouth, a stillness touched his face for a moment. Then he dropped my card onto a side-table and gestured gracefully to the cluster of decanters nearby. "Let's have a drink!" he said with a smile. "Or do you believe alcohol's the invention of the Devil? Our local vicar's very fierce on the subject—in fact he berates us so unmercifully so often on the subject from the pulpit that I always find myself longing to take a swig from the largest bottle I can find."

"You're a churchgoer?"

"Yes, I'm a churchwarden."

In the silence that followed I felt as if God had rapped me across the knuckles. Rage, remorse, guilt and misery began to shudder sickeningly through my beleaguered psyche in a series of emotional tidal waves.

"Whisky, sherry or gin?" Romaine was saying agreeably.

"Sherry. Thanks." It hardly seemed possible that I could speak but I not only spoke; I even sounded casual.

"Well, this is the most astonishing surprise!" said Romaine equally casually as he handed me my glass. "How did you find out where I was?"

"I looked you up in the medical directory."

"Of course! What an idiotic question—maybe I'm finally going senile. I see now that the question I should have asked was: when did your mother tell you about me?"

"Oh, it wasn't my mother who told me," I said. "It was my father."

"Dear me," said Romaine, shooting the barest fleck of soda water into his double-whisky, "how extremely difficult . . . My dear chap, do sit down—the chairs aren't nearly as frightful as they look. Have a cigarette—I hope you smoke as well as drink?"

"Not in my clerical collar."

"What magnificent self-control! I smoke like a chimney, terribly bad for me"—he was lighting a cigarette as he spoke—"what a bore one's bad habits are, but on the other hand how dull life would be without them . . . Now where were we? Ah yes, your father—such an extraordinary man! I underestimated him, of course, thought he was a dry-as-dust old fogey who enjoyed being a crosspatch, but the main problem in those days was not that I underestimated Ashworth but that I overestimated myself. I thought I could walk on water."

"Walk on—"

"Water, old chap. Terrible delusion. Only the very best fellows like your father can walk on water. The rest of us just sink like stones. Did he tell you about our final meeting?"

"Yes, he—"

"I thought he would, and I'm sure he didn't do himself justice. He was superb. I can see him now as if it were yesterday, very dapper in his wing-collar, not a hair out of place. What an executioner! And after he'd hung, drawn and quartered me he simply pulled on his gloves, donned his top hat and strolled away while I was left wondering whether to shoot myself. However, I didn't have a gun, I passed out with drink before I could borrow one, and when I recovered I found myself gripped by the most ungentlemanly desire to survive . . . But that's typical of life, isn't it? It's only in novels that the villain meets that scintillating bloodstained end which conveniently puts him out of his agony. In real life God much prefers him to toil away trying to live with what he's done—and talking of God, I must say I'm absolutely *delighted* that you should be a clergyman! Much more fun than being a doctor—all those interesting sermons to write and a beautiful church to work in and a nice wife whom everyone likes . . . You're married, of course?"

"My wife died in a car accident."

"How very terrible . . . Children?"

"No."

"Ah. I've been married three times," said Romaine after drinking deeply from his glass. "I—but no, I'm talking too much and I mustn't be a thundering bore. One of the worst things about getting old is that one's so often afflicted with the urge to talk garrulously about the past."

I said: "I've come here to indulge that urge, Dr. Romaine. I see no point in not being frank. I want to hear exactly what happened."

"Exactly? No comfortable euphemisms? Just the plain unvarnished truth?" He hesitated as if weighing the challenge but he remained unflustered. Then he said: "Very well, but hold on to your clerical collar, my dear chap, because this is where your Christian charity really gets exercised to its limits." And sinking into the nearest armchair he crossed one leg over the other and embarked with the most appallingly charming insouciance on the narrative I so urgently needed to hear.

6

"I WAS mad, of course," said Romaine. "Nowadays some kindly G.P. would have referred me to an alienist and I'd have spent numerous happy hours lying on a couch while I talked interminably about my childhood, but in those days one was judged sane unless one was raving so I got away with pretending to be normal. I was always pretending to be something or other. When I was a young man I pretended to be a romantic hero, and I suppose, looking back on my life, that was the most disastrous role I ever played.

"It all began when I was a child and started playing the poor little orphan. However, I'm not going to tell you some long story about how when I was seven my mother died in childbirth and my father expired in bankruptcy and even my toys were seized by the wicked bailiffs—it's all true but I wouldn't like you to think I had a Dickensian childhood because when I was orphaned I went to live in Starbridge with a doting maiden aunt who provided me with a delightful home, a nursery full of new toys and a nanny who thought I was the cat's whiskers. Did I go down on my knees every night and thank God for my astonishing good fortune? I did not. Like the horrid spoilt child I soon became, I took it all for granted and thought my aunt's sedate little house in the shadow of the Cathedral was the last word in dreariness. As far as I was concerned, wealth and success, not painstaking respectability, was the key to security; I never forgot the painstakingly respectable little room where my father had blown his brains out.

"However, I didn't want to think of my father blowing his brains out so I pretended it hadn't happened, and at school, when I invented some interesting clerical connections for myself based on my aunt's staid circle in Starbridge, I discovered I had a flair for telling stories which everyone believed. So then I realised that I didn't have to be stuck with my unromantic past because all I had to do to be accepted by the right people was to pick the right role to play.

"Up at Oxford I played the dashing young aristocrat, but I didn't have the money to sustain that for long and besides I did genuinely want to pursue that middle-class profession, medicine. But I didn't want to be just any old doctor. I wanted to go down in history as the doctor who had done the most to save women in childbirth. I was always so angry that my mother had died in her misguided attempt to give me a sibling, and perhaps the only way I could master the anger of bereavement when I was young was to put the blame on medical science and then vow to put right what had gone wrong.

"Eventually I wound up at Bart's to complete my training. How my aunt paid for it all I'll never know, but she paid until I qualified—at which point she died happy with no money in the bank. I was so disgracefully spoilt by that time that when I heard she was dead, my first reaction was: damn it, whom can I touch now for a loan? It took money to be a fashionable medical genius, and besides I liked to cut a dash up in town when I mixed with the right people.

"Detestable, wasn't I? But take heart—nemesis was waiting in the wings. I met this girl. She was a patient. I was still doing general work before embarking on specialisation and at that time I'd been assigned temporarily to what would nowadays be called the psychiatric ward. The girl was brought in suffering from delusions. She was very pretty—and very rich. The brain specialist thought the girl's prognosis was poor, but I didn't believe that. I just thought: silly old fool, I can do better than he can. I thought I could cure anyone, especially a pretty girl with a rich father. I saw the shining water in front of me and I said to myself: lovely! I'll walk on it! It never even occurred to me that such a thing couldn't be done.

"I told your mother I was the victim of the 'Jane Eyre' syndrome—a latter-day Mr. Rochester who married his wife for the best of motives in complete ignorance of her insanity. What a lie! And how deluded I was to think I could cure the incurable—although unfortunately I did manage to achieve a temporary cure. I made love to the girl in the old-fashioned sense of holding her hand and gazing soulfully into her eyes, and I got her out of hospital. She really did seem miraculously better. In fact she seemed just as sane as I did at the wedding, but of course the truth was we were both lunatics living in a fantasy. She attacked me with a knife on our honeymoon; a week after she was locked up she had a further relapse and never spoke rationally again. All the income from the marriage settlement was diverted to pay for the best asylum and the best doctors, so within a month of the wedding I was penniless again—and shackled, at the age of twenty-seven, to a woman who could live another fifty years.

"That was reality—and of course I couldn't begin to face it. I was a man who liked women, and the private life of a doctor is almost as restricted as the private life of a clergyman. How was I going to manage? I had no idea. I couldn't even begin to imagine. So I just thought: it didn't happen; it'll go away if I don't think about it. And like all people who need to keep reality at bay, I started to drink too much.

"I got out of London. I was due for a break anyway before I began my specialist's training and I'd already decided to do a locum because I needed the money, but what a huge relief it was to escape to Epsom to help out poor old Dr. Barnes! No one knew at Epsom, not even Barnes himself. He'd merely applied to Bart's for help, and when they referred me to him they didn't mention my marriage.

"So I went to Epsom and began a new life. I thought: it's just as if I'm a bachelor. I wasn't clinically mad but I was certainly deeply disturbed—although please don't think I'm making excuses for what happened next. Nothing could excuse what I did, but I just want to explain in accurate terms what was going on. Well, I met your mother and . . . Poor girl, what a rotten time she was having! I felt so sorry for her because no one seemed to understand what hell she was going through, her mother dying by inches and that old great-aunt clanking around like a walking coffin. I admired your mother so much for not developing some hysterical illness as so many young girls did in those days when everyone was too well-bred to scream with frustration. That's a brave girl, I thought, a girl of character, intelligent, sensitive—and very lovely . . . I started having fantasies that my wife would die—and after a while it was reality which seemed the illusion and only the fantasies which seemed real.

"Helen had a hard time facing reality too, and in my fantasies she saw an escape from the painful dreariness of her daily life. Later—much later—I realised what a good thing it was that I hadn't been free to marry her. I nearly destroyed her with my fantasies; I *would* have destroyed her if we'd ever married. She needed someone who could offer her the sort of reality she deserved, a decent home, a normal family life, stability—and all I could offer her was a string of day-dreams which hadn't a hope of coming true.

"Well . . . where do I go from here? You know what happened next—here you are to prove it. But perhaps you're wondering how on earth I let it happen. Had I never heard of that wicked word "anticonception"? Yes, of course I'd heard of it, but I believed that sheaths—which in those days were pretty damned awful—were for use only with loose women as a prophylactic against V.D. Sheaths weren't *romantic,* you see, and I was moving in this fantasy of high romance. I was also still trying to tell myself I could walk on water—which meant, in this context, that I thought I could achieve perfect control in a situation where control is famous for its absence . . . What a dangerous belief for a man who's fallen into the habit of drinking too much! Certainly that was the last time I ever fooled myself I could walk on water.

"After your father had hung, drawn and quartered me I went abroad, not to be a noble soul in darkest Africa—that was just the story I spun to make my Epsom friends tell me how wonderful I was—but to South Africa, to the Boer War. I stayed out there till the war's end but I didn't win any romantic medals because I was working in a safe dull military hospital. At the end of the war I decided to stay on, but as I couldn't afford to set myself up in private practice I volunteered to work in a Roman Catholic missionary hospital in Rhodesia. Well, all went smoothly at first but then I got in an awful mess with a nun—there's something about those white whimples which absolutely brings out the worst in me—so I ended up as a ship's doctor on a liner bound for India. I won't bother you with my Indian adventures but I got in a mess there too and eventually I wound up in Hong Kong—drinking far too much, I regret to say, and unable to hold down a job in one of the good hospitals. I ended up working for a Protestant mission in the slums where I had to deal with a lot of diseases which I prefer not to think about, and the result was I drank harder than ever because I hated my work yet couldn't scrape up the money to move on.

"But then the miracle happened.

"This nurse came to the clinic. She was Chinese and a Christian. She took one look at me and decided I needed rescuing, and I took one look at her and decided I wanted to be rescued. I spun my usual line—'Sleep with me and all my problems will be solved'—but that cut no ice whatsoever. I was very impressed. Then I said, trying to convince her that I wasn't such a bad chap after all: 'I only drink because I'm lonely,' and she said: 'Oh, no, you don't! You drink because you feel guilty and you can't forgive yourself for what you've done.'

"There's something very wonderful about the Chinese; they'd got the world sorted out when we were just dancing around Starbury Ring in blue woad. And there's something very wonderful about a Christian, a real Christian, the kind who practises what he preaches. I said: 'I *can't* forgive myself,' but she said: 'Christ can,' and quoted Confucius. My God, I was mad about her! Eventually I said: 'Can't we just pretend my wife's already dead?' But she told me we couldn't pretend to God, and if He wanted me to marry her, He'd arrange it. And damn it all—well, you can guess what happened, can't you? Two weeks later a cable arrived from England to say my wife was dead.

"So I married my Chinese lady. She was a lot older than I was so there couldn't be any children, but nevertheless for ten years we did live happily ever after. I stopped drinking altogether and finally got a job in a good hospital again. I used to work on maternity cases, and I was happy for the first time in years . . . But then my Chinese lady died and everything fell apart. I felt I couldn't bear to remain in Hong Kong without her, and I knew it was time to come home.

"I won't bore you with all the dubious adventures I had as I earned my passage back to England on a series of hair-raising old tubs, but eventually I did wangle my way within sight of the White Cliffs of Dover. I was forty-five and the War was on.

"As soon as I was settled, working in an East End hospital which was dealing mainly with casualties from the trenches, I hired a private detective and sent him down to Epsom to find out what was going on. Back came the report that Mr. and Mrs. Eric Ashworth were living with their two sons, Charles and Peter, in a very nice house on Epsom Downs. Then I had to make a decision. Did I wreck everyone's lives all over again or didn't I? Well, I knew what my Chinese lady would have said. She would have told me that if I really wanted to redeem the past, I'd put aside my selfish curiosity and leave the Ashworth family to continue their lives in peace. Of course if your mother had been a widow, I'd have raced to Epsom to look her up, but as it was . . . No, I felt I had no right to interfere.

"After the War I got a better job in a hospital in Manchester—I was always a little uneasy in London in case I bumped into Ashworth—and there I met my present wife, another nurse. I can honestly swear with my hand on the Bible that I didn't know, when I proposed to her, that her father was making a small fortune out of manufacturing corsets.

"Eventually the old man died and Bea found herself with 'a few thou of the ready,' as the swells say, so we hit on the idea of leaving Manchester and pursuing the ideal country life in a thatched cottage. I had this hankering to return to the Starbridge area; it's funny how at the end of one's life one yearns to return to the beginning . . . But it's a nice spot, isn't it? And whenever I get the urge to yawn, I remind myself I could still be working in a slum clinic and getting through a bottle of whisky a day. But don't think I'm complaining—far from it! I'm always telling myself how wonderfully lucky I am and what a lot I've got to be thankful for."

I knew that way of approaching reality. I had adopted it often enough myself when I had wanted to pretend that all was well in my life, and as I watched him pour himself a second double-whisky I said suddenly: "Do you and your wife have children?"

He added another fleck of soda water to his glass before he turned to face me. "No," he said. "I've never had children by any of my three wives. But I regard that," he added, raising his glass to his lips, "as all part of the judgement."

And then I looked past his glittering image to the sadness which lay opaquely beyond.

7

"HAVE another drink," said Romaine. "I'm afraid I'm rather hitting the bottle, aren't I, but I'm beginning to feel as if I've been walloped by a sandbag. Do have some more of that appalling sherry! I was in such a state earlier that I forgot to warn you that it was sweet and not dry."

"No, I won't have any more, thank you. I think I should leave so that we can each recover from our separate sandbags."

"Oh, but you can't possibly leave yet—I want to hear all about you! I say, I've just had the most delectable idea: let me pour away this ridiculous whisky and bring up from the cellar the most magnificent bottle of Veuve Clicquot which I've been saving for a rainy day!"

"Thank you," I said, "but I must refuse. I've got a long drive ahead of me."

"Well, you shouldn't drive on an empty stomach. Stay to lunch!"

I said with difficulty: "You must excuse me, Dr. Romaine. But I must go."

"Ah well," he said, drinking half his double-whisky, "just as you wish. But before you run off, do please tell me when I can hear you preach. I'd so much like to come to Cambridge and 'sit under' you, as they used to say when I was young."

"I'm not the Canon in Residence at the moment. I shan't be preaching until the first Sunday of next month."

"Splendid, I'll come up for the weekend. Where does one stay in Cambridge?"

"The Blue Boar is the most convenient hotel, but—"

"I'll telephone for a reservation. Now, you needn't think you have to entertain me—in fact you needn't even see me if you don't want to, that's all right, I understand. Just because I lost my head a moment ago and started talking about champagne you mustn't think I'm dead set on being a drunken old bore, making your life a misery. I'll just slip up to Cambridge, slip into the Cathedral to hear you preach and then slip away again—no fuss, no bother, no mess—"

I heard myself inviting him to dine with me in Hall after the morning services.

8

WHEN he escorted me to my car, he said: "How wonderful it must be for Ashworth that you've done so well! And your brother—has he done well too?"

"He's a partner in my father's firm."

"Lucky Ashworth! But then my Chinese lady would just say that the good get their reward. What an amazing man he was! When I was working in the slums of Hong Kong and getting through a bottle of whisky a day, I used to think of him surging triumphantly through life in his wing-collar. He haunted me, you know, and so did your mother—they've both haunted me all these years . . . I suppose your mother's still very lovely to look at?"

"She's kept her looks remarkably well, yes."

"I'm very glad, but I wouldn't want to see her again because I'd rather remember her exactly as she was. Sometimes," said Romaine casually, "it really is far wiser not to risk resurrecting the past."

I merely looked at him. I thought of my mother, longing year after year for him to come back, and no reply was possible.

At once Romaine realised he had made a mistake. "However of course I'm so very glad you came here today!" he said, obviously fearing I had interpreted his remark as a personal rebuff. He had taken his right hand out of his pocket but when he realised I had no intention of shaking hands with him, he pretended to flick a speck of dust from his cuff. "It was such a wonderful surprise!" he added desperately. "I feel so excited that I've met you!"

"In that case it was lucky that Ashworth stopped you aborting me, wasn't it?" I said, slamming the car door, and drove off with a roaring engine to blot out all possibility of a reply.

9

I WAS in such turmoil that two miles outside the village I halted the car on the verge and switched off the engine. Gripping my cross I tried to pray, but I was too upset. I wanted only to wipe Romaine from my mind, but there he was, imprinted for ever, a smooth, tough, wily old survivor who apparently knew exactly how to tug at my heart-strings. I thought of his valiant effort to gloss over his touching offer of champagne; I thought of his brave attempt to hide his distress when he realised I was determined not to shake his hand; I thought of his pathetic panic when he realised he had aroused my animosity, and I felt that my equilibrium, so painfully acquired at Grantchester, had been demolished. I could cope with his charming mask merely by disliking it, but the pathos beyond defeated me. I felt threatened by it. I was quite prepared to work out an intellectual formula for forgiveness which would put my beleaguered psyche at rest while enabling me to be a good Christian, but I did not want my emotions involved. My instinct was to lash out, push him away.

I decided that the sooner I returned to Darrow the better, but meanwhile I was a long way from Grantchester, I had had no lunch and I knew Darrow would have advised me to eat before wrestling further with my problems. Starting my car again, I drove back to Starbridge.

By the time I arrived all the restaurants serving lunch had closed, but I prevailed on the lounge-waiter at the Staro Arms to bring me sandwiches and coffee. After the meal I felt better. Reflecting that Darrow might well have recommended exercise at this point, I decided to take a walk along the river, but when I reached the West Bridge and saw the spire of the Cathedral I knew I had to make another attempt at prayer. I felt I urgently needed to pray not only for the strength to master my troubles but for forgiveness. I had hurt that pathetic old villain in Starvale St. James, and I wanted to lighten the burden of my guilt before I resumed my journey.

Remembering that my earlier attempt to pray in the car had been a failure, I wondered if I was being superstitious in assuming that a spiritual competence would miraculously return to me once I stepped onto consecrated ground, but superstitious or not I felt the pull of the Cathedral, and the next moment I was turning back along Eternity Street.

I had given Darrow my word that I would keep well away from the palace, but as it was now nearly half-past three I calculated that the possibility of meeting either Lyle or the Jardines was acceptably remote. Jardine usually spent his afternoons fulfilling official engagements, Mrs. Jardine, if she was at home, would be having a rest before tea, and Lyle would probably be relaxing in the garden after her usual busy morning. Thinking hard of Lyle I reached the crossroads at the end of Eternity Street, and I was still thinking of her as I passed beneath the arch into the Close.

Minutes later, as I entered the Cathedral, the cool dim light was immediately soothing, and savouring the pervasive air of peace I moved slowly down the nave towards the chancel.

At the far end of the south transept lay the chapel set aside for private prayer, its carved screen supplemented by curtains which covered the spaces in the wooden tracery and ensured the privacy of those praying within. Opening the door, I stepped softly inside. I had expected to find myself alone but a woman was kneeling in prayer and as I came in, she glanced up.

We both gasped. For one long moment we remained motionless, staring at each other, but when Lyle began to grope her way to her feet I said rapidly: "I'm sorry—I'm disturbing you," and retreated in shock to the transept.

XX

"Now one word in your ear. Perhaps I am mistaken: but I have sometimes thought that there was a suggestion in what you say and write, of some private and special worry of your own. If that be so, don't suspect me for one moment of the impertinence of pushing into your affairs: but I have a genuine affection for you, and should be glad to help you in any way that was in my power."

More Letters of
HERBERT HENSLEY HENSON,
ed. E. F. Braley

I

"CHARLES—" She stumbled after me but I had stopped before she called my name. Far away in the nave I could hear the faint drone of a guide as he showed a party of visitors around the Cathedral.

"Tell me I'm not hallucinating," said Lyle, still stupefied. "What are you doing in this part of the world?"

"I had to see someone in Starvale St. James." Pulling myself together, I added: "Look, we can't talk here—let's go into the cloisters."

The massive door opened reluctantly as I heaved the handle, and we passed from the transept into the sunlit quadrangle beyond. In one corner of the grassy square a garden-seat had been placed in memory of some Edwardian benefactor, and at my suggestion we sat down facing the cedar tree which shaded the lawn.

"This is the most extraordinary thing to happen," said Lyle, still dazed. "It's like a sign."

"It's certainly an opportunity to say how very much I've been thinking of you. Did Mrs. Jardine get my letter?"

"Yes, that was like a sign too—the letter made you seem real again. I was beginning to think I'd imagined you."

"My dearest Lyle . . ." I was quite unable to stop myself taking her hand in mine and she was apparently quite unable to stop herself tightening her clasp on my fingers. "Forgive my long silence," I said, "but I was in a colossal muddle when we last met and Father Darrow's been busy unravelling me."

"We were all so relieved when we heard you were safe with the Fordites . . . Is Father Darrow really as clever as everyone says he is?"

"It would be impossible for me to praise him too highly."

She said unexpectedly: "I wish I had someone like that to talk to," and at once I was concerned for her. The cry for help was muted but unmistakable. Realising that she would be reluctant to tell any of her numerous clerical acquaintances about a problem which concerned a bishop, I said tentatively: "Perhaps an Anglican Benedictine nun might help. I'm sure the Abbot of Starwater could recommend—"

"I hate nuns. I'm not wild about monks either, but if Father Darrow lives up to his reputation, perhaps . . . But he wouldn't want to see a woman, would he?"

"I'm sure he'd see anyone in an emergency."

"Oh, this isn't an emergency!" she said at once. "I'm fine."

"That's what I used to tell myself before I ended up drunk on Father Darrow's doorstep." I was now deeply concerned. "Lyle, if things get impossible, phone me at any time of the day or night and I'll do my best to help—and don't think this offer means I'm playing Casanova all over again because I'm not. I'm just trying to be something that resembles a clergyman, and if you ever do need my help, I promise I shan't demand any romantic payment in return."

She gave me a searching glance before saying cautiously: "You're different."

"You never really met me before. I was hiding behind a mask—the mask I call my glittering image—but Father Darrow's helping me to put that mask aside so that I can be the man I really am."

I saw the comprehension flare in her eyes. "Oh, if only you knew," she whispered, "how much I long to put aside *my* glittering image and be the woman *I* really am!" But before I could reply, she was saying abruptly: "What on earth does Father Darrow make of all this?"

"It's not his primary business to have opinions. His task is to see I form rational opinions of my own."

We were silent at last, and into our silence seeped the Starbridge mystery, billowing between us like a dark cloud to sever our communication. Glancing at her watch, she stood up. "I must get back. Carrie will be needing me."

"Lyle—"

Her eyes were suddenly dark with emotion. "Don't ask any questions."

"Let me at least give you some additional numbers in case I'm not at Laud's when you phone." I found the receipt from my lunch at the Staro Arms and wrote on the back my parents' number in Epsom and the Fordites' number in Grantchester. Then I added: "If I don't hear from you, I'll get in touch in mid-September in the hope of arranging a meeting at the end of the month. What's the best way of communicating with you? Shall I write?"

"No, don't do that," she said quickly. "Gerald gets to the post before I do and he tells the Bishop everything. A letter with a Cambridge postmark would be quite impossible to explain."

I somehow refrained from an appalled comment and said in the most neutral voice I could muster: "What's the best time to phone?"

"The afternoons. If you get Gerald, hang up, but if Shipton answers, ask for me and if I'm not in I'll ring you back. Say you're Donald Wilson—he's an old flame of mine who rings up occasionally, so I wouldn't have to explain any call from him."

I was unable to stop myself exclaiming: "You talk like a prisoner!"

"Of course I'm a prisoner! We're all prisoners of our circumstances, but for God's sake, Charles, *for God's sake,* don't storm the palace in a quixotic attempt to rescue me—"

"Don't worry, Father Darrow's taught me that the most effective help is always offered, never imposed."

We had left the bench and were moving down the north side of the cloisters, but when we reached the door into the transept she stopped. "It's best if we say goodbye here."

"Very well." I wanted to kiss her but knew she would recoil; she was already glancing nervously over her shoulder to see if we were being observed. Instead I took her hands in mine, and for a second an unmistakable reality blazed between us before dying amidst the miasma of despair which emanated from her.

I said: "Don't forget. You can phone any time of the day or night."

She nodded. I released her, and as we both stepped back into the transept I paused to watch her walk away towards the nave. I watched her until she had finally disappeared from sight through the door into the north porch, and then, feeling more deeply disturbed than ever, I returned to the chapel to pray.

2

I FELT too exhausted to complete the long journey to Cambridge that day so I spent the night in London at my club. Having anticipated a possible absence from home, I had brought with me in my overnight bag the books which I needed for my exercises, but even after a night's rest concentration proved elusive.

Darrow was not immediately available when I arrived without warning on his doorstep later that morning, but after half an hour I was escorted to the Abbot's Parlour where he was waiting for me. Aware that I might be diverting him from more urgent work, I apologised for my unexpected appearance and said I would return later to discuss Romaine. "But something very strange happened yesterday," I said, "and I did just want a quick word with you about Lyle."

"Sit down, take your time and please give me at least a brief summary of your meeting with Romaine before you vanish in a puff of smoke."

Realising I was creating a fevered impression, I made an effort to be calm. "I didn't acquit myself well in Starvale St. James," I said. "Romaine manages to be both a smooth wily old survivor and a vulnerable battered old man. He was pathetically thrilled to see me. I hated that. I hated him. But the worst part of all is that I've invited him to Cambridge next month and I can't wait to see him—and if you can make head or tail of all that, Father, you deserve some sort of cenobitic medal."

Darrow merely asked: "What did you do afterwards?"

"I stayed sober," I said, and recounted my movements up to the moment before my meeting with Lyle.

"At least you dealt with yourself competently when you were in distress," was Darrow's not unsympathetic comment. "Very well, we'll return to Romaine later. Now what's all this about Lyle?"

I told him every detail of my meeting with her, and when I had finished he looked so grave that I felt obliged to say: "Father, I swear I didn't break my promise and go looking for her."

"No, of course you didn't. Don't misunderstand. I'm not concerned about the meeting, which seems to have been unexpectedly beneficial; I'm concerned about her welfare. However, at least you've thrown her a lifeline, and that could well prove vital."

"Would you, in fact, agree to counsel her?"

"I'd counsel anyone in an emergency, as you so rightly told her, but beyond that . . . No, it wouldn't be advisable, Charles, for two reasons. One is that I'm counselling you and therefore I couldn't approach her in a truly detached frame of mind. And the other reason is that a difference in sex can often create difficulties in counselling, even if the two people concerned approach each other with the best will in the world and the purest of motives. She'd be better off with a nun than a monk."

"She says she hates nuns."

"When people make extravagant statements like that they may merely be struggling to voice a despair which can't be easily expressed. What Lyle may mean is that at present she feels her problems are beyond discussion either with a nun or indeed with anyone else."

"Surely the fact that she has such severe problems must mean—"

"We can't know for certain what it means. It certainly seems as if Lyle's involved with both the Jardines in a way that's emotionally and spiritually bad for her, but this still needn't mean she's Jardine's mistress."

"But even if she's not his mistress he must still be in error to allow such an unhealthy situation to persist," I said. "Obviously he's fooled himself into believing that the situation's not unhealthy, but then his error with Loretta proves, doesn't it, that he can be capable of gross self-deception?"

"I was wondering when you were going to notice that." Darrow sounded so relieved that he no longer had to keep his opinion to himself in order to maintain his neutrality that I was at once able to conclude: "I suppose I was so disturbed by my own error with Loretta that I didn't pay sufficient attention to Jardine's, but it's nonsense, in spiritual terms, to say that he didn't commit adultery with her."

"Dr. Jardine spoke as a good lawyer," said Darrow dryly, "but not, I'm afraid, as a good clergyman. Your own error with Loretta was severe but Jardine's was infinitely worse: a married clergyman, engaged in gaining a very carnal knowledge of one of his own parishioners—the whole episode's a clerical nightmare, and it makes one realise, I think, Charles, how shrewd His Grace the Archbishop has been over this business. Obviously he senses that Jardine's capable of colossal error and equally obviously, as we can now see, Dr. Lang is justified in fearing a scandal. But, Charles, none of this need mean Jardine and Lyle are lovers. So keep calm, don't rush to judgement and try hard to accept that for the moment, as far as Lyle's concerned, you've done all that you can do."

3

THAT evening I returned to Darrow to discuss my meeting with Romaine and we talked for some time.

"I do understand," said Darrow at last, "why you should feel hostile, but if you're not averse to seeing him again perhaps this indicates that you may feel more benign later."

"I doubt it. He's such an awful old villain."

"I'm quite prepared to believe you when you say that, Charles, but could you explain to me why you feel he's so awful and so villainous? You've actually made him sound delightful."

"Have I?"

"Well, haven't you? He tried hard, it would seem, to be truthful with you; certainly he didn't go out of his way to paint himself in a flattering light. He was nice about your parents. He bathed you in approval by saying how glad he was that you were a clergyman, and finally he could barely be restrained from diving into the cellar for the Veuve Clicquot. Is this really such iniquitous behaviour?"

"It was all an act to ingratiate himself with me! But I never forgot for one moment how he made my parents suffer."

"There's no doubt he did cause your parents considerable suffering," said Darrow, "but according to your account he suffered in the long run just as much as they did and possibly more."

"So he should. He wrecked their marriage."

"Who says their marriage is wrecked? It seems to me, from what you tell me, to have survived many outstanding difficulties. After all, here they are after nearly forty years, still living beneath the same roof, still on speaking terms and still, as far as we know, being faithful to each other. I'm not saying their marriage hasn't been difficult, but can one truly describe it as wrecked?"

"It seemed pretty wrecked to me on Saturday!"

"Obviously they're going through a bad time, but like most couples who survive thirty-eight years of matrimony they probably have their good times as well as their bad times. After all, has their marriage really been such unadulterated hell? Your mother's had the kind of affluent sociable life she likes and your father's had an attractive wife who's been a devoted mother to his children. Meanwhile the children themselves are a credit to their parents and are no doubt a source of much happiness as well as the occasional bout of misery. To me this all sounds reassuringly normal—although I'm not denying that there are abnormalities present. But I think you should consider very carefully how far these abnormalities have vitiated the marriage, Charles, before you start blaming Romaine for a marital disaster."

I was silent. I felt as if the truth had slithered through my hands and was weaving a new pattern which lay beyond my grasp.

"It's undeniable that Romaine's had an adverse effect on your parents," said Darrow at last, "but is this entirely his fault? How much of the responsibility should be assigned to your father, who by so ruthlessly suppressing the tragedy gave it this golden opportunity to fester at leisure? And your mother—how much is she to blame for clinging with such tenacity to this very romantic but possibly dangerously deceptive memory of her first love?"

After a moment I said: "She told me she always thought he'd come back. The thought of her waiting year after year seems so—" but I left the sentence unfinished.

"That's certainly tragic and you have every right to find it upsetting, but I think we should guard against assuming that everyone would have lived happily ever after if Dr. Romaine had tried to revive his disastrous love affair when he returned to England. We should remember that Dr. Romaine himself appears convinced that your mother was lucky not to marry him, and we should remember too, I think, that he's far better acquainted with the exact nature of their love affair than either you or I could hope to be. When he made his decision to stay away it seems he was trying to do what he thought was right, not only for himself but for you and your parents as well. It was a sad decision, certainly, but can you honestly say it was a wicked one?"

"No. But I still say he's an awful old villain and I hate him." I shuddered, crossed myself and whispered: "God forgive me."

"Tell me," said Darrow suddenly, "did he frighten you? We often hate the things we fear."

I was silent.

"Did he unnerve you in some way? After all, to confront one's unknown progenitor could well be a deeply unnerving experience. Was there a likeness?"

I winced.

"A strong likeness?" said Darrow, and added with a striking flash of his psychic intuition: "Was it like looking in a mirror?"

I shuddered from head to toe and covered my eyes with my hands.

4

"*I LOOKED* at him and he was just like me and I had to listen to him talking about all the drink and the women and how he'd made such a mess of his life—I saw him through my father's eyes, and—"

"That's all very well, Charles, but you have a perfectly good pair of eyes of your own—use them! Stop looking at Romaine through your father's eyes and make your own judgement!"

I finally let my hands fall from my face. "But my father must be right!"

"Why? He's wrong about you—we've agreed that you're a much better chap than he's ever been willing to allow. So why shouldn't he be at least partially wrong about Romaine?"

"But Romaine's drinking—the messes with women—"

"Yes, these are telling points against him, but now look beyond the image of the drunken wastrel and see if you can catch a glimpse of the man your father's far too prejudiced to acknowledge."

I made a great effort and after prolonged thought I was able to venture cautiously: "He had ideals when he was young. He wanted to redeem his mother's death by saving other women. I saw no evidence that he's not a successful country doctor."

"So his professional life hasn't all been a failure even though he failed to fulfill his early promise."

"His personal life hasn't been entirely a failure, either. He had his Chinese lady—and it was a Christian marriage—and apparently he's still a Christian—"

"How admirable! Despite all his difficulties, he hasn't sunk into cynicism or despair. Would it be fair to say, do you think, that he behaved in a Christian manner towards you?"

After another pause I said: "I doubt if he was driven by conscious religious considerations. Yet I can't deny he was kind." To my horror, Romaine's villainy began to dissolve. "He understood everything," I said in despair. "He understood how I felt about my father. He understood why I needed to know about the past. And finally I think he even understood that I couldn't cope with him and had to get out." There was a pause before I could add: "Despite all my resentment on my parents' behalf I was afraid that once we started drinking champagne I'd find myself liking him, and I can't afford to let that happen—it would be so disloyal to my father and I've got to be entirely loyal to my father or he'll be more convinced than ever that I'm unfit, unworthy, bound to go to the dogs, and as long as my father believes that, I'll feel driven to hide behind my glittering image in order to cope with him—and once I'm back behind my glittering image I really will go straight to the dogs—"

"I agree that at present you need all your emotional resources to deal with your father," said Darrow. "Until he can accept the real Charles Ashworth and trust him not to make a mess of his life, the glittering image won't wither away. But once you succeed in healing this exhausting relationship with your father, Charles, I have a feeling you won't need to see Romaine as an awful old villain any more."

5

WHEN I had recovered my equilibrium, I exclaimed: "How ironic that after years of chasing father-figures I should now have two fathers fighting for my attention!" and Darrow laughed before saying: "Very well, let's leave Romaine there for the moment and turn back to your father. Unfold your next battle plan."

"I'm going down to Epsom tomorrow for forty-eight hours. However, I fully expect it to be hell because once my father hears that I've met Romaine, he's bound to be at his jealous worst."

"I can quite see," said Darrow, "that your father will be tempted to behave badly if he's insecure about your affection for him, but you must be firm, Charles. You have a duty to be good to your father, but you're under no obligation whatsoever to allow him to dictate to you on the subject of your acquaintances."

A single word in this last speech had so riveted my attention that I could only repeat incredulously: "*Insecure?* But my father's the last man on earth to be insecure! He knows perfectly well that he's got this colossal hold on me!"

"He knows nothing of the kind. All he knows is that you've got a colossal hold over *him.* He sees you as justifying his difficult marriage. He sees you as providing the ultimate proof of whether or not he's been a successful father. Every move you make is of vital significance to him. You've just spent several months holding yourself aloof. Now you seem all set to walk off into the golden sunset with Romaine. Your father's terrified. You've correctly diagnosed that he's jealous, but the source of his jealousy doesn't lie in a mere petty resentment, Charles. It lies in an overpowering fear that you'll reject him in favour of this glamorous stranger, just as your mother once did."

"But at our last meeting my entire behaviour was directed towards reassuring him that I shall continue to think of myself as his son!"

"He can't believe you mean it. He's irrational with terror. In fact your father now appears to have two distinct difficulties: one is that you'll reject him utterly in favour of Romaine, and the other is the nightmare which keeps the glittering image alive—the nightmare that you'll go to the dogs. I think you can probably reassure him in the end about Romaine, but the second difficulty presents more of a problem because no matter how often you promise him you're not going to the dogs, he'll never believe you. He needs someone outside the family, I think, to put his mind at rest there."

"If only I could coax him to see you! But meanwhile what on earth am I going to do with the poor old devil when I arrive in Epsom tomorrow?"

"Let's include your mother in this battle plan, too—she always tends to get overlooked, but she's insecure too, isn't she, Charles? She's frightened of being a burden and a bore to you, frightened you don't love her half as much as she loves you. Here you have two people with an identical need: reassurance. You've got to let them know that you do love them, but on the other hand you mustn't pamper them, Charles. You must be yourself, not the ideal son spawned by your glittering image. Be genuine, be loving and be truthful—and then you'll be a far better son than any glittering image could be."

All I could say helplessly was: "Pray for me, Father—"

"Of course."

6

THE next morning a letter arrived from Starvale St. James.

"My dear Dr. Ashworth," Romaine had written in a slanting hand which bordered on illegibility.

> Of course I would never have gone through with it but your mother was talking of killing herself. I couldn't have stood by in silence. It was a desperate moment, so desperate that neither of us was responsible for what was said. I beg you to pity us both in our terror and shame, even if true forgiveness is at present impossible. Of course nothing I have just written detracts from your father's magnificent behaviour in dissuading your mother from tragedy—behaviour for which, during the course of time, he has been so justly rewarded by your very evident loyalty and devotion to him. Please believe me when I write that I do not in any way aspire to take his place in your affections; that would, as I clearly realise, be impossible. All I hope for is the occasional meeting and the chance perhaps to know you a little better than I do now.
>
> I suspect you thought I had consigned you and your mother rather too ruthlessly to the past, but sometimes one has to be ruthless in order to avert further suffering. Thirty-eight years ago I nearly ruined your mother's life. Certainly I ruined my own for many years afterwards. In those circumstances how could I have embarked later on a course of action where there was even the smallest risk of compounding the suffering I had already caused? Of course when I eventually returned to England I wanted to see you, but I felt I had forfeited all right to do so. I felt I had to content myself with the knowledge that you were safe with your mother, who no doubt loved you, and that you were being brought up in a good home by a man whom I knew to be decent and honourable. That in itself seemed to be a miracle, and the idea that I might lay a claim to either you or your mother in those circumstances appeared to me to be not only selfish to the point of wickedness but contemptuous of God's grace to the point of blasphemy. So I stayed away and I'm sure I was right to do so, but you mustn't think the decision was either lightly made or easily forgotten.
>
> I shall look forward so much to hearing you preach in September, and in sending you my best wishes may I assure you that I shall always be yours very sincerely,
>
> ALAN ROMAINE

I read the letter twice. Then I took off my collar, lit a cigarette and read it again. Eventually after several false starts I wrote:

My dear Dr. Romaine,
Thank you for your kind understanding letter which was far kinder and more understanding than my erratic behaviour on Tuesday deserved. Please forgive me for the pain I must have caused you, and please believe me when I write that I too am looking forward to our September meeting when I hope to show you that I'm neither so boorish nor so rude as you might justifiably imagine me to be.

Yours sincerely—

I paused to consider my signature. Then gritting my teeth I acknowledged our relationship by omitting my surname and merely signing myself: CHARLES.

7

". . . *SO* of course you thought he was wonderful," said my father, ferociously lashing a tomato plant to a stake.

"You couldn't be more wrong. I found him extremely upsetting and if you don't believe that, come to Cambridge and talk to Father Darrow."

"I can't leave my plants," said my father automatically, but added without pausing for breath: "I can't believe the mad monk approves of this stupid hobnobbing with Romaine!"

"He did remind me of my duty to you—"

"I should bloody well hope he did! For over thirty-seven years I've slaved—"

"But he also said—"

"I don't want to know what he said, I disapprove entirely of that monk, I think he's a bad influence on you. Now come along, Charles, stop slouching among the flower-pots and let's see if your mother's mixed a new batch of disgusting cocktails. I only hope to God she hasn't murdered another bottle of champagne . . ."

8

"*FUNNILY* enough," said my mother, after my father had retired to change from his gardening clothes, "your visit last weekend must have done him good because he's been much better—and if he's better, I'm better. I just couldn't stand living with someone who behaved as if he was perpetually looking for a coffin to lie in, but now he seems to be thinking that it could be worth his while not to die yet after all . . . Darling"—she hesitated before adding in a rush—"has something happened to you? I think it must have done. You seem different somehow, older . . . wiser . . . gentler—oh Charles, have you fallen in love again? Your father would be so angry if he knew I'd been pestering you with nosy questions, but I do so long for you to be happy with another nice girl—"

"I do have someone, yes, but please keep it a secret because it may come to nothing. There are great difficulties."

"Oh, I shan't tell a soul!" She was touchingly pleased that I had confided in her. "Darling, I do so hope it works out. I know the difficulty can't be that she's divorced or already married because of course, being a clergyman, you couldn't allow yourself to look twice at anyone who's in that situation, but is she perhaps shackled to a lost love as I always was?"

I smiled. "Perhaps."

"It was so strange the way you brought up that subject last Saturday and insisted on talking about it. It was almost as if . . . almost as if . . . But no," said my mother, "my imagination's getting the better of me. But when I looked back on our conversation, I really did feel it was as if—"

We looked at each other for a long moment.

"—as if you already knew," said my mother, and as she read the expression in my eyes, I stepped forward to take her in my arms.

9

"I CAN'T believe it! You mean you *saw* him—you actually *saw* him—but what did he say, what on earth happened, did he ask after me?"

"Yes, he said he was sure you'd kept your looks—"

"Oh, I must see him!" cried my mother. "I must! To think that he's alive—and in England! Has he only just come back?"

"Well, not exactly—"

"How did you find him? Was he listed in the medical directory? At first I used to search for his name in each new edition but eventually I told myself that was futile—I was so sure he'd contact me if ever he came back, and now that I know he's finally here—and asking after me—"

"Mother, darling, I do beg you for your own sake not to take too romantic a view of this! He's married to an efficient-looking blonde with a Lancashire accent, and I'm quite sure she wouldn't welcome—"

"Was he pleased to see you? You're so like him! Oh, he must have been so moved, so overcome—I'm going to cry," said my mother, and did.

I was still desperately trying to stem this tidal wave of feminine emotion when the drawing-room door opened and in walked my father.

"Good God!" he exclaimed as he saw my mother weeping. "You'll drown that boy yet! Disgusting! Pull yourself together, you silly woman, and behave yourself! What the devil's going on?"

My mother sobbed more loudly than ever and I felt obliged to kiss her before turning to face my father. "I'm extremely sorry," I said, "but she guessed that I knew about Romaine and I've just told her about my meeting with him."

"You bloody fool!" said my father, scarlet with rage. "How dare you disobey me like that!"

"Shut up!" screamed my mother. "I'm sick of you being cruel to him just because he reminds you of his father!"

"My father," I said, "is the one who's standing here behaving like an irrational jealous child. Now listen to me, both of you—"

"Never heard such colossal impudence in all my—"

"Be quiet, Father, and listen to me. Alan Romaine—"

"I will not have that man's name mentioned in your mother's presence!"

"—ALAN ROMAINE," I said, outshouting him, "has had a life which has often been profoundly unhappy—indeed, I think it's a pity you can't both meet him so that you can discover for yourselves how fortunate you've been in comparison. However, you won't meet him because the last people on earth he wants to see again are Mr. and Mrs. Eric Ashworth."

"Charles—*Charles*—"

"I'm sorry, Mother, but this is where the fantasy ends and the truth begins. Romaine doesn't want to see you. What happened between you nearly destroyed him, and I'm quite sure that the last thing he wants is the resurrection of all those painful memories at some excruciating reunion."

"I don't think your mother can stand you talking to her like this, Charles—you'll kill her—"

"Rubbish. I'm saving her a lot of pain by exploding this fantasy of hers that Romaine would be glad to see her again. Now the next fantasy I want to explode, Father, is that I'm a carbon-copy of Romaine. I'm not. I'm me. And the third fantasy I want to explode—"

"I feel dreadfully faint, Eric," said my mother.

"Here, have some of this filthy cocktail."

"Brandy—I must have brandy—"

My father obediently hurried to the brandy decanter. "Charles, get a glass from the cabinet and *don't argue.*"

I extracted a suitable glass. "The third myth I want to explode—"

"Shut up," said my father, grabbing the glass and slopping brandy into it, "or I'll explode *you.* Here you are, darling," he said to his wife, thrusting the glass into her hands. "Don't take any notice of that silly boy. He means well but he's crashing around like a bull in a china shop. It's the shock. He's not used to the idea of Romaine yet. Temporarily off his head."

"The next myth I want to explode while I'm temporarily off my head," I said, "is the myth that I'm going to turn my back on you and devote myself entirely to Romaine. I shan't. Regardless of what happens between Romaine and me, you and Mother are my parents and I shan't stop loving you just because—"

"For God's sake don't start talking like a damned foreigner, Charles. No wonder your mother looks as if she's about to puke!"

"What's wrong with talking about love?"

"Nasty un-English sentimental behaviour—"

"But wouldn't it save such a lot of misunderstanding in the future if I now make it clear that I do love you both very much indeed—"

"She's going to puke, Charles, and by God, I don't blame her. Quick, get the golf trophy—the silver bowl—"

"Not the bowl!" whispered my mother. "Ada's just spent all morning polishing it—"

"Please don't bother to puke, Mother," I said, handing her the bowl in the certain knowledge that she would never dare ruin Ada's hard work, "because if you think all this over carefully, you'll realise how much healthier it is to live in an atmosphere of honesty than in an atmosphere laden with lies, evasions and unexorcised ghosts. Besides, I think it's time you both stopped thinking about how much you've suffered from the Romaine disaster and think about me for a change. I've suffered too, and now I want both Romaines put away—and when I say both Romaines I mean not just the real Romaine, that battered old doctor with the unhappy past, but the mythical Romaine, that glamorous doctor with the brilliant future that never happened. The mythical Romaine must be given a decent burial in your memories at last and the real Romaine must stay tucked safely out of sight in Starvale St. James with his blonde wife and his double-whiskies, because I'm not prepared to stand by any longer while he spoils my relationship with you and spoils your relationship with each other. He's been hanging around this family quite long enough, and this is the moment when I insist that he departs. Out he goes this instant. Finish. The end. Now, I'm going down the garden with my dry martini and when I come back I shall expect to find you've both pulled yourselves together—for my sake, if not for your own. Come along, Nelson, you can come with me to inspect the tennis court."

And leaving my shattered parents speechless behind me, I walked out of the house with the Labrador at my heels and headed for the bottom of the garden.

10

IN the end I was the one who vomited. Beyond the lawn I stepped behind the yew hedge and neatly disgorged my breakfast into a flower-bed. Nelson regarded me with interest but seemed unsurprised. I myself was astonished. I had not vomited from nervous tension since I had departed for my first term at prep school at the age of eight. Scattering the remainder of my dry martini, I kicked some earth over the mess, slumped down on the seat overlooking the tennis court and lit a cigarette. I was wondering if the scene in the drawing-room had been a triumph or a disaster or merely a chaotic piece of bad taste verging on bathos, but I reflected that the only important question was whether I had communicated my message to my parents. I continued to smoke my cigarette and occasionally I shuddered. I wondered dimly how anyone ever survived their families.

I was just debating whether it was time to return to the house when I saw my father crossing the lawn, and as I drifted towards him I realised I now knew exactly how Romaine had felt when he had drifted into his drawing-room to meet me; I was outwardly casual but inwardly taut, exuding self-confidence but racked by the dread that the approaching scene might be a failure.

"Glad to see you're looking calmer after that shocking exhibition," said my father as we finally met by the net-post. "Encourages me to think you haven't gone completely off your head. Now listen to me, Charles. Your mother and I have been talking things over and we take your point so there's no need for you to be upset any more—and no need to keep shouting that you love us. Very embarrassing, that. Bad form."

"Yes, Father. I only wanted to make myself absolutely clear—"

"Quite. Now this is what your mother and I have decided: we'll all go on exactly as before. We won't talk about it, of course—"

"My dear Father—"

"—but that'll be because there won't be any need to talk about it—everything's been said. So although we'll go on as before, everything will be different."

"Well, I suppose that does sound more promising, but—"

"I'm sorry, Charles, but your mother and I are quite agreed that although we're very glad you went off your head and spoke your mind, we'd really much rather it didn't happen again."

"But how are you and Mother going to get on when I'm not here? Don't you think it would be better if—"

"Are you going to have the unpardonable impertinence to tell us how to conduct our marriage? May I remind you that we've been at it for thirty-eight years so we must be doing something right! I know your mother very much better than you do, Charles, and I can tell you that the last thing she wants is to hear me dredging up the past in the name of honesty. What your mother wants," said my father severely, "is that you should show her a little extra kindness occasionally to make her feel she's not fit for the scrap-heap now she's pushing sixty. However, you seem to have grasped that at last, thank God, so there's nothing else I can say on that point. You obviously didn't realise it earlier, but she felt lonely when you shut yourself up in your ivory tower, and of course when you refused to come home *I* got all the blame. Well, naturally I became depressed! Who wouldn't be depressed if they had a wife who was miserable and a son who treated his parents as if they were fit for the dustbin?"

"I really am very sorry about the estrangement, Father—"

"Of course you are. So am I. If we weren't both sorry, we wouldn't be here talking to each other. But, Charles, if you really want to make amends for worrying me half into my grave, you'll now wash your hands of that rotter Romaine before he ruins your life, wrecks your career and sends you straight to the dogs!"

"Oh, good heavens—"

"Well, what does the mad monk really say about Romaine, I'd like to know? I can't believe he approves of this reckless excavation at Starvale St. James, but on the other hand maybe he's mad enough to approve of anything. Did he put you up to that scene just now?"

"He told me to be firm, genuine, loving and truthful. Is that a crime?"

"Nearly killed your mother. Felt a bit queasy myself, to tell you the truth. I think I'd better come to Cambridge after all and get this monk under control. He's beginning to frighten the life out of me."

"What about your plants?"

My father stooped to pat Nelson. "Peter might look in on them for a day or two. Of course I'd have to leave him very careful instructions, but the plants can't all die, can they? Some of them would be bound to survive."

I recognised the unfamiliar note of optimism and knew another tide had turned. I too stooped to pat Nelson, but all I said was: "I'll make the reservation at the Blue Boar."

II

AFTER lunch when my father had retired to his conservatory, I said to my mother: "Forgive me for being so brutal earlier about Romaine, but I was in such a state trying to cope with Father."

"Yes, I realised that in the end."

I put my arm around her and we sat in silence for a while. "Is Alan's wife attractive?" she said at last. "A blonde with a Lancashire accent sounds perfectly horrid, and I can't imagine him being married to someone common!"

"That's because you can only picture him as he used to be. Mother, I do understand how much you must want to see him, but I honestly think—"

"Oh, I don't want to see him if he doesn't want to see me," said my mother quickly. "That would be frightful, so humiliating."

"I'm sure that in many ways he would like to see you, but perhaps he has a better grasp than you have of the pain involved. What would it really be like if you met him again? Would it be romantic? Or would it underline the tragedy and make even your cherished memories unbearable?"

She was silent, struggling to comprehend the situation in its entirety, and as I saw her set her fantasies aside at last, I tried to find the words to comfort her.

"At least if you remember him as he was," I said, "you still have your cherished memories."

She nodded. "I think you saw the truth earlier when you talked of the two Alans. It's as if the Alan I loved died and now today's Alan is someone else altogether."

"Well, that's a sad way of putting it, but—"

"Life often is sad, isn't it? But never mind, I had my great romance, nobody can take that away from me, and I still have you to remind me of it. Darling Charles," said my mother as I tightened my arm around her, "how very kind you were to Eric, treating him exactly as if he was your real father. No one realises better than I do what a difficult man he is, but he'll be quite all right, you know, so long as you show him a little kindness every now and then."

I kissed her and promised to be kind.

12

MY parents travelled to Cambridge by train on the last weekend in August and stayed at my expense at the Blue Boar. After lunch on Saturday my mother obediently retired to her room to rest while I drove my father to Grantchester; I had explained to her in private how important it was that my father should have a word with Darrow on his own.

"We won't stay long, will we," said my father restlessly as we left Cambridge. "I don't want to stay long—in fact I wish now we weren't going at all." And he added in his most fractious voice: "Can't think why I let you talk me into this visit, Charles."

"Father, you volunteered to come of your own free will—"

"Must have been off my head."

We met Darrow in the Abbot's Parlour, and when he took my father off to show him the garden I went to the chapel for ten minutes to pray. They rejoined me in the parlour later; my father had an uncharacteristically tranquil look but Darrow was characteristically serene.

"Interesting fellow," said my father afterwards as we drove back to Cambridge. "Served in the Navy. Nearly drowned at Jutland. Worked after the War in a prison where they hanged murderers. Doesn't approve of capital punishment. Very interesting. Didn't like being a monk at first. Said he hated being ordered around after all those years of being his own boss. He started out as a monk here in Grantchester but he got kicked out to their farm in Yorkshire because they thought he had too good an opinion of himself and needed to have his nose rubbed in the mud. He said he hated milking cows but liked being trained as a carpenter. I asked him why he stuck it and he said he knew it was the only way he could serve God once he didn't have to provide for his children—he said it was one of those situations where a man feels he has absolutely no choice but to act in a certain way. Reminded me of when I decided to marry your mother. Interesting. Very interesting . . . Of course he's off his head, but he's off it in the most intriguing way. Did you know that his son's an actor?"

"My dear Father, do you realise you've learnt more about Darrow in a thirty-minute visit than I've learnt after hours and hours of conversation?"

"We talked about our sons and about how bloody awful it is being a parent. He said he used to worry and worry about Martin—that's his son—in case the boy went to the dogs. Tricky business, being an actor. I asked him if he still worried about Martin and he said: 'No, I gave that up five years ago when he came to see me and said he had a small part in a West End play. I thought: here's this boy, doing well, happy, coming to see me regularly, why torture myself imagining a decadent life which may never happen?' Darrow says he still has the occasional twinge of anxiety, like passing toothache, but nothing compared with the agony he used to suffer. Very interesting. Most interesting chap. Made me think a bit, I can tell you."

My father paused. I waited, my hands gripping the steering wheel, my gaze riveted on the road ahead. Eventually my father said in a casual voice: "We mentioned you, of course, in passing, but we didn't say much. Naturally I said how worried I was about you as you were burrowing away digging up a man whom I knew to be an absolute rotter, but Darrow just said: 'Worrying takes an enormous amount of time and energy. Are you quite sure the time and energy couldn't be put to better use?' So I said: 'How?' and he said: 'Trust him and show that you trust him,' and I said again: 'How?' Then Darrow said: 'Let him dig up the rotter. Trust him to rebury the bones as he thinks fit.' But I said: 'Supposing he makes a mess of it?' And do you know what Darrow said next? He said: 'He's your boy. You've brought him up. You've made him what he is. Why should he make a mess of it?' And do you know, when he put it like that, I couldn't think of an answer. I did mutter something like: 'Well, if he's off his head anything could happen,' but Darrow said the main reason why you'd got in such a state recently was that you didn't trust yourself. 'But if *you* trust him,' said Darrow, 'then he'll believe he's trustworthy and everything will straighten itself out. Children are very much influenced by their parents,' said Darrow, 'and that's why we fathers have an absolute moral duty to make sure not only that our opinions are correct but that we make those correct opinions crystal clear.' Most interesting fellow. Wasted as a monk, of course. Tragic. He might have made a good lawyer. I can just see him having a clever way with the clients and making useful contributions to the partners' meetings."

It was the highest possible compliment. I was so lost in my admiration of Darrow's skill that I nearly missed the turning to Laud's.

"Well, thank God you're not an actor, Charles," said my father comfortably as we approached the College. "Then I really would have something to worry about, wouldn't I? But since you're a clergyman I suppose I can just sit back and let you get on with it. After all, despite everything you've managed to turn into a mature sensible sort of fellow, and with that interesting mad monk keeping you on course I see no reason why everything shouldn't come right in the end."

That concluded the life of the glittering image. It began to die, and as I remembered Darrow's metaphor I saw the whole noxious weed, complete with its excavated roots, start to wither away in the sun.

I somehow succeeded in parking my car in the College forecourt. "Thank you, Father," I said. I wanted to say more but no words came, and all the time the glittering image was withering away, no longer needed, dying on every level of my mind.

"Now don't start behaving like a nasty emotional foreigner again, Charles, because my nerves couldn't stand it. In fact just take me to your rooms as quickly as possible and give me a stiff whisky, there's a good chap, before my nerves give out altogether. God knows it's not every day I meet a mad monk."

The glittering image finally expired but I wasted no time saying a requiem over the corpse. I smiled at my father, said: "I think we could both do with a drink," and we headed in harmony for my rooms.

13

"MY only regret," I said later to Darrow, "is that I couldn't have hidden behind a bush in the garden and witnessed that miracle you wrought with my father."

"What miracle?" said Darrow amused. "He was an easy case—a simple decent man, not stupid, who was burning to know how he could put matters right. Of course I'm not claiming I solved all his problems, but at least I offered him a new way of looking at the problem which was foremost in his mind . . . And talking of Romaine, are you still feeling nervous about his visit to Cambridge next weekend?"

"Yes—although now that I don't have to spend all my energy trying to convince my father I'm not going to the dogs, maybe I've got a chance of survival."

Darrow said frankly: "Romaine could certainly make heavy demands on your new reserves of strength. I think a little nervousness is not unjustified."

"I wish he wasn't coming."

"Cheer yourself up with the knowledge that he's bound to try hard to make the occasion a success."

"That's what I'm afraid of. If it's a success, what do I do with him afterwards? I still can't see how to fit him into my life."

"Worry about that later. The situation may seem much clearer after you've talked to him on Sunday . . . "

XXI

"Friendship, however begun, is a voyage of discovery, full of perils and surprizes."

Letters of
HERBERT HENSLEY HENSON,
ed. E. F. Braley

I

ROMAINE sent me a note to say he hoped to reach the Blue Boar on Saturday evening but would not expect to see me until after the morning services the next day. I spent much time wondering whether I should call at the hotel to offer him a drink, but decided I was being sufficiently hospitable by inviting him to dine in Hall on Sunday. However, that conclusion made me feel mean, so to assuage my guilt I arranged that a bottle of whisky should be waiting in his room to greet him on arrival. As soon as this arrangement had been made I started worrying in case I was corrupting a heavy drinker.

In the midst of these tortuous psychological gymnastics I embarked on writing a sermon. I toiled away, constructing what I hoped would be a homiletic masterpiece, but was constantly racked by doubt. Were there too many obscure references? Did I sound hopelessly priggish? Was my thesis sufficiently stimulating to stave off the coughing of bored choirboys and the somnolence of elderly worshippers? Laymen have no idea what anxiety clergymen can suffer as they engage in their struggle to communicate the word of God, and even another clergyman might have had difficulty imagining the degree of anxiety I was now enduring as I struggled to communicate the word of God not only to my congregation but to the stranger whose ineffectual contraceptive skill during adultery had somehow resulted years later in the appearance of yet another clergyman in the Sunday pulpit.

The Bishop was absent, having been invited to preach in Durham, and the other two canons were on holiday, but the Dean was there to share the work of the Sunday services with me. Matins began; I noted Romaine in the congregation, and at last after the third hymn I mounted the steps into the pulpit and declared my text from Isaiah: " 'The grass withereth, the flower fadeth, but the Word of Our God shall stand for ever.' "

2

"*I ALWAYS* think that's the most moving text," said Romaine later as we walked back to Laud's. "I feel it puts all the triumphs and tragedies of life into a proper perspective, and of course that was your theme, wasn't it, or at least one of your themes—it was all so interesting and I liked the story of the monk who drew a cat carrying a mouse in its mouth in the margin of the manuscript. My Chinese lady liked cats; in fact I thought a lot of her as you spoke—and I thought of your mother too and of how I'd quoted Wordsworth to her—I was always quoting Wordsworth to your mother, Wordsworth and Browning—and when you said: 'The grass withereth,' I thought of that passage about the 'splendour in the grass' until past and present seemed to merge and I felt most uncommonly emotional. Well, as a matter of fact, I *am* rather an emotional sort of chap. I tell myself it's the French blood. My grandfather came over here to teach French to a London merchant's family and then he married an English girl and stayed on—oh God, there I go again, droning on about myself! It's time you got a word in edgeways. How did you set about constructing that splendid sermon? How hard you must have worked! I'm sure it took a long time to write."

We eventually reached my rooms at Laud's.

"What a marvellous place!" said Romaine, gazing around at the very ordinary main chamber which served as a drawing-room, dining-room and library. "How comfortable you've made it, how conducive to bookish labours! And look at your beautiful prints of Cambridge! If I had a fortune, I'd spend it all on pictures—so isn't it lucky that my present fortune, such as it is, belongs entirely to my wife, who has very proper ideas about how it should be spent! I'd have squandered the lot in no time."

I offered him a drink before we went down to Hall to dine.

"Well, I don't mind if I do," said Romaine, "although I feel a bit of a cad filching whisky from you after you've been so uncommonly handsome as to decorate my hotel room with a bottle of Johnnie Walker Black Label. What a treat! My wife doesn't approve of expensive whiskies and she watches the level in the decanter like a hawk—and quite right too, of course. I need someone to keep me in order."

"Did you tell her about me?"

"She guessed. When she first met me seventeen years ago, I was rather more like you than I am now. Her first question when she returned home after your visit was: 'When the hell did *that* happen?' but when I said soothingly: 'Oh, that was just a little awkwardness in Epsom in the Naughty Nineties, my dear,' she nearly hit the roof. 'Don't try to tell me it was a little awkwardness when it was obviously a bloody catastrophe!' she said, putting me in my place, so I found myself confessing everything. 'And how many more little awkwardnesses are going to crawl out of the woodwork, I'd like to know?' she demanded in a voice of thunder, so I said meekly that there weren't any more because this little awkwardness had taught me a lesson I'd never forgotten, and she then made that exasperated noise which in books is always written P-S-H-A-W. I have to tread very carefully there, I'm afraid, poor Bea, because it's a great sadness to her that she's been unable to give me children. I knew from the start that it would be much better if I came on my own to Cambridge this weekend because you'd simply remind her that some other woman had succeeded where she'd failed . . . But here I am, prattling on about myself again! Now, my dear Charles, this time you really must get a word in edgeways. Are you working on a new book?"

It was the question which my father had never asked. Halting in the midst of pouring myself a sherry, I demanded: "How did you know I'd already written a book?"

"I thought that as you were a doctor of divinity you might have published something stunning, so I telephoned Blackwells at Oxford and ordered your book as soon as they told me about it. I must say I was most entertained by your account of all those frenetic debates which raged about the Trinity! When one thinks of all the awful things that go on today—Hitler, Mussolini, the Spanish Civil War—one can't help but enjoy escaping into a faraway world where the one big topic of conversation was whether the Son was of the same substance as the Father!"

Here was someone who understood. The temptation was irresistible. Handing him his whisky I began to talk about the Council of Nicaea.

3

"*THAT* really was the most splendid meal, Charles, and the claret was out of this world—how you resisted the temptation to have more than one glass I just don't know. I say, I did enjoy myself! But should I slink off to the Blue Boar now? I don't want to get in your way if you've got more important things to do."

"I'm free till Evensong at six."

"Can I come to that too?"

"My dear Dr. Romaine—"

"Charles, I insist that you call me Alan. After all, since you were so generous as to sign yourself by your Christian name in that nice little note which brought tears to my eyes—"

"My dear Alan, if you want to come to Evensong, who am I to stop you? But first I suggest we have coffee—black coffee—"

"It's all right, I'm actually extremely sober—I could operate now and not even make a slip of the knife. Shall I tell you about the time I took out that very curious appendix in Bombay?"

"Well—"

"No, I don't think I will, I mustn't put you off doctors for life . . . Oh, here we are again, back in this nice room—did you have a house when you were married, or a flat? No, don't answer that, I don't want you to think I'm prying into your marriage—and talking of marriage, what do you think of the A. P. Herbert Bill—the Matrimonial Causes Act, as it now is? Divorce for insanity at last! Thirty-eight years too late for me, but at least I have the satisfaction of knowing some other young fool won't have his life wrecked just because he thinks he can walk on water. But what an exhibition the Church made of itself in the House of Lords! The only one who talked any sense was the Bishop of Durham—oh, and the Bishop of Starbridge, of course. Now *there's* a man after my own heart! Have you met him?"

I began to talk about Dr. Jardine.

4

"JOLLY nice brandy this is, Charles. Black coffee's never quite the same without brandy, I always think, and I'm glad to see you're having a little drop to pep you up for Evensong. Well, this is all absolutely fascinating. Probably it's just a schoolgirl's crush of Miss Lyle's, you know—unconsummated. Shall I tell you why I say that?"

"Tell me."

"If she'd been sleeping with him, it would have burnt itself out by this time. It's only the unconsummated passions of this world which go on and on like a never-ending gramophone record, and personally I always think it's better to leap into bed and have done with it—although of course I shouldn't say that to a clergyman. God, what a dreadful clergyman I'd have been! It was bad enough trying to behave like a doctor . . . Shall I tell you about the woman with the very curious breasts in Rangoon?"

"Tell me anything you like. Have some more brandy."

"Don't mind if I do, old chap. Marvellous host you are—but aren't you having any more yourself?"

"I don't want the Dean defrocking me after Evensong. Look, Alan, I shouldn't have told you about Lyle—I must be going round the bend—"

"My dear Charles, *don't worry*. I'm the soul of discretion—you talk to Bea. She has no idea who's sleeping with who in Starvale St. James, but I know it all right down to the last bedpost—"

"But I should at least have kept my mouth shut about Jardine—"

"Why? I'm thrilled to think he might have had a luscious young girl to cheer him up after a disastrous marriage—although in fact I suspect it's more likely he picked an older woman to soothe him, just as I picked my Chinese lady. I put my money on that mysterious Swedish stepmother, even if she did weigh sixteen stone. I rather like buxom women myself. Shall I tell you about—no, I most definitely shan't. Got to keep myself in control."

"I seem to have lost control altogether. I can't think why on earth I—"

"I shall take great pride in proving my magnificent discretion, and meanwhile I'm absolutely delighted that you've got an attractive girl lined up—but how are you going to lure her from that palace? Of course if you weren't a clergyman I'd tell you to seduce her as soon as possible; once you'd got her into bed she'd soon forget about Jardine, even if she was his mistress."

" 'Get thee behind me, Satan!' "

"I mean it, old chap! Any young sprig of thirty-seven can knock spots off an old warhorse of—how old's Jardine?"

"Fifty-eight."

"Well, there you are. Past his prime like me. I can still do it, of course, but I'm really only at my youngest now in the early mornings—and Bea can't stand looking at anything, let alone me with my pyjama flies open, before she's had her first cup of tea and read the headlines of *The Daily Express*. But that's marriage, isn't it? One long compromise . . . What did you say your wife's name was, Charles?"

"No, I'm sorry but I'm not going to tell you about Jane, not yet. I've already told you quite enough for one afternoon—"

"Let me slink off to the Blue Boar and give you a breather."

"Drink up that brandy and I'll take you for a walk along the Backs."

5

"THE Dean's sermon wasn't nearly as good as yours, Charles, but never mind, it was a very pleasant Evensong. Now I expect you've been thinking: how on earth am I going to get rid of the old bore? But don't worry because the old bore is now going to slink off to the Blue Boar and commune in reverent silence with that delectable bottle of Johnnie Walker—"

"Come back to College and we'll have some bread and cheese in my rooms. I don't like to think of you all alone with a delectable bottle of Johnnie Walker. My conscience tells me you need to be saved from that sort of fate very firmly indeed."

"Oh, I love being saved!" said Romaine. "Thank you so much—I say, can I have another sip of that nice brandy with my bread and cheese?"

6

". . . SO I go and see this monk two or three times a week and I talk about things and he sorts me out when I get in a muddle . . . Well, all right, just half a glass more—I don't usually drink twice a day—"

"A little extra claret will be very good for you after all your hard work. Now before I slink off to the Blue Boar—"

"I've heard that one before."

"—you must tell me all about this monk. I'm so glad you've got someone to talk to, Charles, because life's so bloody difficult sometimes, no one knows that better than I do, and I can see so clearly how difficult it must have been for you growing up with . . . well, with problems—"

"Oh, shut up and have some more claret. I wish I'd never told you about my damned problems. I can't think why I'm telling you all these private and personal things. I'll hate myself after you've gone—"

"No, don't do that. Go and see your monk instead and tell him how bloody awful I was, drinking you out of house and home and clinging to you hour after hour like some elderly incubus. Then once you've expended all your anger on me, you'll feel better."

We looked at each other over the claret decanter in the twilit room. After a long moment I said: "You're very shrewd, aren't you? I've spent all day giving myself away and now you've got me neatly summed up."

"Nonsense! Human beings are much too complicated to be summed up neatly after a few hours' acquaintance. Let's just say we've spent the day exchanging clues about ourselves—and meanwhile think of all the fun we've had, thanks to your kindness and generosity!"

"I just can't imagine how I'm going to cope with you. The whole problem's got quite out of control—"

"Impossible," said Romaine firmly, "because there's no problem in the first place. You don't have to cope with me. I'll just go on pottering around Starvale St. James and occasionally popping up to Cambridge to hear you preach and eventually I'll drop dead and that'll be that. Bea will have to cope if ever I become senile or bedridden, and all you'll have to do in those undeniably sordid circumstances will be to give Starvale St. James the widest possible berth."

"Not a chance. I'll be there at the deathbed feeling muddled up." I drank deeply from my glass.

"Oh, I shouldn't like that at all," said Romaine. "I'd be very cross. Promise me no deathbed visits! So Victorian, so dreary, so *dull*!"

"Not necessarily. I'd bring a bottle of champagne."

"My dear boy, what a lovely thought! It reminds me of Chekhov. Did you know that on his deathbed Chekhov tossed off a glass of champers and died with a beatific smile on his face?"

We started to laugh. At last I said: "Forgive me. I've been intolerably rude again."

"You put everything right by offering to bring me champagne on my deathbed! Don't worry, Charles, I understand. I know you don't need me in your life at the moment—I'm just distracting you from the things that are really important, but I'd like to think that one day I might be useful to you in some way. After all, God must have brought us together for a purpose, mustn't He, and if He'd wanted us to remain strangers He wouldn't have made it so easy for us to be friends. In fact in my opinion what's happening is crystal clear: He's redeeming my past by showing that something good came out of all that tragedy and failure, and He's giving you—for reasons we don't yet know—someone else in your life whom you can trust to be loyal to you no matter what the circumstances. Is that really such a sinister prospect? I don't think so, and if you talk it all over with that monk of yours I'll wager you a bottle of Johnnie Walker he agrees with me. And talking of Johnnie Walker I know you're thinking the time really has come when I should slink off to the Blue Boar—"

"Sit down," I said. "You need to be saved again. It's time for another round of black coffee."

7

AT three o'clock the following afternoon I once more turned up on the doorstep of the Fordite monks and sank into the nearest chair in the Visitors' Parlour. I had had a strenuous morning, celebrating Communion in the Cathedral's Lady Chapel, parting from Romaine at the Blue Boar and attending a chapter meeting presided over by an irritable Dean who was in the middle of a quarrel with the Head Verger. Lunch had been spent soothing the Master of Laud's (also embroiled in a quarrel with the Dean) and responding tactfully to the assertions of the Master's wife that all clergymen should be celibate. (The wife of the Dean was universally unpopular.) It was with profound relief that I escaped afterwards to Grantchester.

"I can't imagine why you thought the situation would become clearer once I'd seen Romaine again," I said irritably to Darrow after I had given him an account of Romaine's visit. "I feel in a worse muddle than ever. I don't deny I like the old villain, but he still frightens the life out of me."

"Some degree of distrust may well be healthy at this stage—in fact I'd be far more worried if you'd whole-heartedly embraced him as a father-figure and were displaying unmistakable signs of hero-worship."

This comment encouraged me. Once I was assured of my stability, I found I could try to analyse my feelings with more precision. "I do feel much better about my parents," I conceded. "No doubt they'll continue to drive me to distraction but at least I feel I've created an atmosphere of trust and truth which will enable me to deal with them without hiding behind my glittering image. But Romaine! I've got no confidence there at all."

"Are you still seeing him as evidence that you're doomed to go to the dogs?"

"No, that view just represents my father at his most irrational, I can see that now."

"But nevertheless Romaine still frightens you."

"Perhaps it would be more accurate to say he makes me feel acutely anxious. He really *is* an awful old villain, Father—I'm sure I'm not imagining it—"

"I think it's most unlikely that this judgement is entirely the product of your imagination, but you could be exaggerating out of sheer fright. Can you single out any detail which made you feel uneasy?"

"He didn't attend any of the Communion services."

"Ah. Yes, I'd wondered about that too."

Again I was sufficiently encouraged to analyse my feelings further. "After all," I said, "there he was, hanging on my every word at Matins and Evensong. Perhaps he felt the sung Eucharist was too High Church for him, but why didn't he turn up today or yesterday at Early Communion? Wouldn't you think he'd be eager to be first at the rail as I administered the sacrament?"

"Maybe he has a very Protestant inclination to attend Mass only occasionally. But yes, I do think it's odd he didn't decide that yesterday should be one of those occasions."

"Well, once I began to wonder if he was in a state of grace," I said, finally finding that I could approach the root of my distrust, "I began to wonder if he was entirely happy with his wife who not only holds the purse-strings but guards the whisky decanter. I know he's a churchwarden and ought to be respectability personified, but I've got a nasty suspicion that his Christian beliefs might not necessarily prevent him pursuing a life of adultery, heavy drinking and goodness knows what else. But perhaps I'm being completely unjust to him."

"Perhaps, but I don't think you're being ridiculous, Charles, or even excessively cynical. Your suspicions strike me as being real possibilities. Supposing in fact that you're right; how far would this shady private life of his impinge on your own life far away in Cambridge?"

"That," I said, greatly relieved that I could at last not only perceive but voice the truth, "is what makes me so anxious. If his marriage breaks up or if he finally gets struck off the register for sleeping with patients, I'd have to help him—but what a prospect! Tell me how I can stop myself having nightmares about him turning up ruined and penniless on my doorstep one day!"

"You could try telling yourself the nightmares may never happen."

"I wish I felt as sanguine about that as you apparently do."

"Well, consider, Charles. Romaine, as you yourself have told me, is a wily old survivor and wily old survivors, like wily old cats, usually have a very keen sense of when to make a mess and when to keep their paws clean. After many vicissitudes Romaine now has a comfortable home, a pleasant practise and a wealthy wife who provides him with a guaranteed source of whisky and sex. This, from Romaine's point of view, is as close to Heaven as he's likely to get on this earth and he's going to fight any temptation which will represent a one-way ticket to Hell. I think you can allow yourself some cautious optimism here, Charles, I really do."

For the first time since the start of the interview I was able to relax in my chair. "Awful old villain!" I said. "But what fun we had! And at the end . . . Well, I couldn't help feeling moved when he said God was redeeming the past by bringing me into his life. Of course I know it sounds appallingly sloppy and sentimental, but at the time—"

"—at the time Dr. Romaine was making a masterly attempt to capture your heart, and who can blame him? I must say, he sounds on very familiar terms with God, but then one never quite knows with laymen whether that indicates arrogance, reverence or ignorance."

"He seemed reverent enough but of course he fell into the layman's trap of assuming he knew exactly what God has in mind. However, since Romaine and I have only just met and we've no real perspective on what's going on, any discussion of God's purpose here can at present only be unprofitable—or at least," I added, fearing he might think me too dogmatic, "so it seems to me."

But Darrow said without hesitation: "I agree," before asking: "When are you seeing him again?"

"The shrewd old villain took care not to make me feel persecuted—he didn't pin me down to any date. But he'll be back. Of that I'm quite sure."

"Clever Dr. Romaine! And while we're on the subject of his shrewdness, I must confess I thought he made some interesting comments on the Starbridge mystery. Ought we to have a quick word about Lyle, do you think, before you leave?"

He had realised that since my parents were under control and Romaine had been safely dispatched to Starvale St. James, the Starbridge mystery was now grinding back into the forefront of my mind.

Leaning forward I put my three parents behind me at last and prepared to tackle the next stage of my ordeal.

8

"I KNOW I want to marry her," I said. "I knew for certain when we met in the Cathedral. There's genuine feeling on both sides, and I'm sure that when we next meet she'll tell me exactly what's going on."

"Will she? I wonder. The whole problem is riddled with the most serious difficulties, and before you make your final circuit of the Starbridge mulberry bush it's vital that you understand what those difficulties are. Can you come back and see me tomorrow?"

But I could not. My calendar was beginning to fill as the new term approached, and I was also burdened by my duties as Canon in Residence.

After we had agreed to meet on Wednesday evening, Darrow said: "Now be frank with me: are you tempted to rush off to Starbridge—or at the very least to telephone Lyle without delay?"

"I suppose the only honest answer to both those questions is yes. I know I threw her that lifeline and since she hasn't used it I can assume there's no crisis, but nevertheless I'm so very worried about her, and I was wondering"—I hesitated but was unable to stop myself concluding—"I was wondering if you could see anything. Can you look across at Starbridge with your mind and—"

Darrow said severely: "Charles, you'll treat me as a priest, if you please, and not as a charlatan in a fortune-teller's booth on some seaside pier."

"I'm sorry, but sometimes I feel so tormented—"

"Yes, don't think I don't understand how difficult this waiting is for you." He took pity on me. "If I knew what was going on I'd tell you," he said, "but my powers are in many respects very limited. I've a certain flair for picking up impressions from someone I can see, but I've never been much good at long-range intuition unless the other person in the psychic conversation is emotionally close to me."

"Do you ever see the future?"

"Yes, but there are many futures and not all of them come true." He leant forward on the table as if he wanted to reach out to ease my torment. "On Wednesday we'll picture the futures," he said, "and meanwhile try not to put yourself on the rack by picturing the present. Remember that you could be seeing the wrong picture, and even if it happened to be the right one you'd be unable to erase it. But the future is a different matter. You can draw a picture, erase it and draw another. What I'd like to do is to help you draw several pictures so that you can have a comprehensive insight into what may happen." He stood up to close the interview. "You've recently found the strength to endure the present by re-examining the past, Charles, but now that the past has been reviewed and reassembled, it's time to endure the present by viewing and assembling the future. And once that's been done, past, present and future will be set free to converge and the result will be the solution of the Starbridge mystery—although the solution may be a mystery in itself, leading to other mysteries, because as I said to you once the mysteries of life are rarely capable of clear-cut solutions . . . But I must stop talking like a mystic or—God forbid!—like a charlatan on a seaside pier, and urge you, as I must, to have faith in your gathering strength and above all to trust in God who alone can repel the demon of anxiety which is now tormenting you . . . Let me say a prayer now to help you in this ordeal, and afterwards I'll give you my blessing."

My torment was eased. Minutes later I was driving back to Cambridge, but long before I reached my rooms at Laud's I found I was strong enough to face the possible futures which lay waiting for me.

9

"FIRST of all," said Darrow, when we met two days later, "I want to remind you of the four major reasons why you shouldn't go cantering off immediately to Starbridge on the nearest white horse to rescue your damsel in distress."

"Four major . . . "

"Yes, I did wonder if you'd managed to count them all. Now, Charles, it's not enough to say grandly that you want to marry this woman. You must give me a competent analysis of the situation to prove you know exactly what you're doing."

I was immediately determined to demonstrate the rational equilibrium which he himself had helped me acquire. "I mustn't rush off to Starbridge," I said, "first of all because we haven't yet reached that date you set at the end of the month. In other words, I'm still too close to the disaster at the palace and I should wait a little longer to ensure that I can see Lyle without illusion."

"Good."

"This applies even though I'm now convinced, since the meeting in the Cathedral, that my feelings are based on reality and that I want to marry her."

"Even better. Go on. Reason number two?"

"She's a mature adult of thirty-five. I can't charge into her life uninvited—especially as she's asked me not to do so. I must stick to my plan to have a discreet meeting at the end of the month and trust her to phone me if she needs help before that."

"Well done. Go on to reason number three."

"I'm stumped. So much for my competent analysis."

"Let me put the question more specifically: why is it so important that you should allow Lyle every opportunity to end the ménage without your active intervention?"

"I might make a bad mess if I intervened."

"True, but I was thinking of a more distant future. Supposing you and Lyle marry but things go wrong between you. Then she could always turn around and say: 'You drove me into leaving when I didn't really want to go.' " Seeing my expression as this glimpse of an unpalatable future was revealed, he added swiftly: "We'll come to the possible marital difficulties later. Now what's the fourth major reason why you mustn't go cantering off to Starbridge on the nearest white horse?"

"I'm sorry, I'm completely failing this test—"

"No, you got the first two reasons right, but they relate only to the present. Think of the future. You may in spite of everything find you don't want to marry her—yes, I know that's unlikely but you must face the fact that it's still a possibility—and if you intervene actively now in the Starbridge ménage, you're going to find marriage virtually impossible to avoid. Let me just clarify my mind on one point: have you ever mentioned marriage to Lyle?"

"No, but of course she knows that's what I want."

"Yet you're not hopelessly compromised and if the worst came to the worst you could still back away."

"Yes, but—"

"I know you think I'm being perverse, Charles, but the truth is you don't know yet which way this mystery's going to break, and if the worst comes to the worst it may well break in a way which would make the idea of marriage to Lyle untenable."

"You think it would be untenable if I found out she was Jardine's mistress?"

"Let's hear your views, not mine."

I was silent for a moment before saying: "I could cope with that if I was convinced the affair was over. I wouldn't hold the immorality against her because I'm sure she wouldn't have slept with him unless she'd honestly believed she was his wife. She'd be like someone who married a bigamist in all good faith."

"That's a fair judgement. Very well, you're not going to recoil if you find out she's been fooled into adultery. But supposing your plausible theory of the informal marriage is in fact dead wrong. Supposing they're both apostates, both keeping up the pretence of being good Christians while knowingly committing adultery. What then?"

I said slowly: "I couldn't marry her. Marriage with an apostate would be impossible—there'd be no shared spiritual life—no clergyman could consider it . . . Of course if she repented and wanted to return to the Church, I'd forgive her and do my best to help, but no matter how far I forgave her it would be very debatable whether I should marry someone capable of living for years in adultery and continually abusing the sacrament. For the sake of the Church and my work a devout wife is essential."

"In other words the idea of marrying Lyle would have become untenable. Now I can see you're thinking that this possibility is too remote to worry about, but are all your problems really solved if she's a mere innocent victim who genuinely believes she's Jardine's wife? You may well picture yourself coasting across calm seas into a golden sunset in those circumstances, Charles, but in fact all manner of storms could be waiting for you. Think hard and see if you can identify these storms one by one."

I was aware that I was being put to the test again. "Jardine's memory could prove intrusive," I suggested cautiously.

"Yes, that's a hazard in all cases where the partner's been married before, of course, and it's not insuperable but nevertheless it should be considered. Go on."

"I think I might be haunted by the secret fear that she was switching horses—backing me because I could ultimately offer her more than Jardine. In other words, I'd be afraid she didn't love me for myself, and then my fear of rejection might crawl out of the woodwork again."

"Good. You're doing well on this test, Charles. Keep going."

"It's possible that I might always wonder if I knew the full story of that relationship with Jardine, and if I doubted that I'd scraped the whole truth from the bottom of the barrel, I might start to feel insecure."

"Excellent."

"I'm not sure I can go any further except to point out the obvious fact that somewhere along the line I'd have to deal with Jardine and that could prove a great stumbling block."

"Jardine, I agree, presents appalling problems. We'll get to him in a moment. Is that really the end of your list of difficulties? So far you haven't mentioned one of the most crucial problems of all."

"Haven't I?" I tried not to sound despairing.

"You've been considering the situation entirely from your own point of view, but what about Lyle? Let's again assume your theory's true and that she considers Jardine to be her husband. If she leaves him she's inevitably going to suffer some degree of guilt, no matter how justified she is in ending the liaison. Possibly she'll also suffer shock and grief—certainly there'll be a period of considerable emotional difficulty. Now, how is she going to cope with these feelings? How are *you* going to cope with them? How is your marriage going to survive their destructive effects? Charles, I'm not saying this problem's insuperable but it *is* formidable. You've got to be very, very sure you love her and very, very confident of your own emotional and spiritual stamina as you set out to conquer not just this problem but indeed all the problems we've so far enumerated."

He paused to enable me to digest this warning and eventually I said: "I'll have to persuade her that she needs expert counselling. Maybe she'd be better off with an alienist than a nun."

"I wonder. The trouble with psycho-analysts is that they can tiptoe around in a patient's childhood for years without getting anywhere near the spiritual dimension of the problem. I'm still convinced your best hope is to find a nun skilled in counselling who's been married or who's survived a long debilitating love affair—or both."

"How do I find her?"

Darrow said unexpectedly: "I'll have a look for you. I'm due to pay the Abbot's annual call soon on the Abbess at Dunton, and when I go I'll seek her help."

Conscious of Lyle's prejudice against nuns, I said: "It's a difficult problem."

"It is indeed and I'm sorry to burden you with it, but I'm sure you see how important it is that you should look beyond the golden sunset to glimpse what sort of marriage might be waiting for you in the dark below the horizon—if, that is, Lyle agrees to marry you. Another possible future is that she won't be able to bring herself to do it; she could choose to remain in the ménage."

"I'd make an intervention if that happened."

"If Lyle's psychologically unable to leave, an intervention would probably be useless. However, let's meet that difficulty when we come to it because it may never happen. What *will* happen is a confrontation between you and Jardine at some stage; I regard that as inevitable."

"If I eloped with her I wouldn't have to see him at all."

"He'd want to see you after the wedding."

"What for? Surely not to give me his blessing!"

"Why not? He might see Lyle's desertion as a punishment from God and visualise converting you into a son-in-law as a form of atonement."

"That's disgusting!"

"But not impossible, and we're surveying possible futures. Consider his psychology: I suspect Jardine collects son-figures just as you used to collect father-figures, and that one of the reasons why the two of you got on so well together was that you were each fulfilling the other's neurotic needs—you were both chasing a father-son relationship. If he now gives his blessing to your marriage, he not only atones for any past sin with Lyle and keeps Carrie happy by retaining Lyle in the family; he also permanently acquires a splendid son-figure whom he already likes immensely. And in addition, of course, he acquires the possibility of adopted grandchildren, a possibility which will be equally welcome to Carrie—"

"I'd emigrate to Australia before I let all this happen!"

"I sympathise entirely—if this unhealthy ménage is allowed to survive, even in a reconstructed form, it could be emotionally disastrous for Lyle and spiritually very dangerous for you both, but you do see, don't you,

Charles, that from the Jardines' point of view a ménage à quatre could be an attractive possibility?"

"Well, obviously there's got to be a clean break with them—"

"Yes, but how easy is that going to be to achieve if Jardine is bent on creating a ménage à quatre and Lyle is anxious to retain both Jardines in her life? The fact is this situation could quickly jeopardise your marriage, and if you do decide to go ahead it's vital that you and Lyle agree long before you reach the altar exactly what your relationship with the Jardines is going to be."

After a long pause I heard myself say: "Well, I've got the whip-hand, haven't I? I could ruin him in one sentence to the Archbishop."

"I was wondering when you were going to think of that." Darrow leant forward. "It wouldn't work, Charles—for two reasons. One is that Lyle would never forgive you and never forgive herself for Jardine's downfall. And the second reason is that if Jardine adopted a tough stance and denied everything, Lang couldn't force him to resign without a huge scandal—which is the one thing Lang wants to avoid."

"So Jardine gets away with adultery—again!"

"Not necessarily. Leave Jardine to God, Charles. God will deal with him far more efficiently than either you or the Archbishop of Canterbury."

"Well, God certainly seems to have turned a blind eye so far!" I said, but as soon as the words had left my mouth I was horrified. "I'm sorry, forgive me, but I was just so angry at the thought of Jardine getting away with all this and enjoying a supremely successful career—"

"Yes, the anger's clouding your mind; if you calm down I think you'll see that you're jumping to conclusions that are very much open to debate. After all, what do we really know about Jardine's past? We do know there was a gross error with Loretta, but are you so sure he got away with it? What does 'getting away with it' actually mean here? Jardine certainly met with worldly success after he parted from Loretta, but how far did that contribute to either his happiness or his spiritual welfare? The effect was to drive his marriage still deeper into trouble because his wife couldn't cope with her new responsibilities, and Jardine's misery must inevitably have increased. Indeed, if you equate worldly success with 'getting away with it,' Charles, I think you're on shaky ground."

I gestured to indicate I had no argument to offer.

"It's dangerous to make a judgement when one can't know all the facts," pursued Darrow, "and since only God can know all the facts, one can only conclude that it's best to leave the judgements to God. For instance, who knows but God when Jardine's present troubles really began? One might speculate that they began with his marriage, but why did he rush into that fatal marriage in the first place? Surely no mature man in his right mind proposes to a woman only four days after their first meeting! Such behaviour hints at instability, at some form of mental distress. Was there indeed an unhealthy situation with the stepmother? If one were speculating about a judgement one might advance the theory that the marriage itself was a retribution stemming from some previous error, but we don't know, do we? And we'll never know. It's impossible to know the whole truth about anyone, Charles, and all we can do is pray for as much enlightenment as God sees fit to grant us. So be cautious with Jardine. Beat back the demon anger. Even if he's entrapped in the grossest of errors you should still approach him with charity and refrain from judgement."

After a prolonged silence I said with reluctance: "I suppose I should also still guard against the temptation to assume that adultery's taking place."

"Yes, because it remains non-proven—and the last possibility here, of course, is that there's no adultery but Lyle's nevertheless locked up in an unhealthy psychological relationship with both Jardines which is preventing her from having a normal life of her own."

"But even if that were true, the situation would still be fraught with difficulty, wouldn't it? I'd still have to deal with the Jardines, still have to deal with Lyle's guilt—the guilt that she was leaving them—"

"—and you'd still have to deal with the dread that you never got to the bottom of the mystery and that maybe she did sleep with him after all. No, I agree this is hardly an improvement on the other possibilities. In fact, one could even argue that it would be easier to deal with Lyle's unwitting adultery than with some bizarre neurosis which keeps her in the Jardines' thrall."

"If the adultery exists, it must be bizarre enough in itself. Think of the complications!" I shuddered before adding abruptly: "Have we now exhausted the possibilities or are there any futures still to be considered?"

"There's always the future we can't predict. For example, Jardine might drop dead. But I think we've covered the futures which are foreseeable on the present evidence."

"It's certainly a daunting prospect." I looked up into his eyes. "But if I make the wrong decision after this conversation, it certainly won't be your fault."

"I'll pray there'll be no wrong decisions. And talking of prayer, we must discuss your spiritual life before you go. I want you in prime spiritual condition for this finale of your great ordeal, Charles, because I'm quite sure you're going to need all the spiritual strength you can get."

10

I REMEMBER very well when the end began. It was September 14, the day before I was due to telephone Lyle to arrange a meeting at the end of the month. I had spent the morning attending a conference of the University's theological faculty to discuss a new policy on tutorials; two of the professors had had a row about the Pelagian heresy, and that afternoon as I attended to some correspondence in my rooms I was just wondering idly if I could bring Pelagius into my next sermon when the telephone rang beside me on the desk.

I picked up the receiver. "Ashworth."

"Charles—"

It was Lyle. I rose to my feet as if I had been jerked by a rope. She said: "I need you."

"Where are you?"

"London. I want to come to Cambridge."

I glanced at the clock on the chimneypiece. "There's a train from Liverpool Street at three-twenty. I'll meet you at Cambridge station."

"Thank you," she said crying, and hung up.

The last ripples from my big stone had finally reached the edge of the pool and now apparently it was Lyle herself who was about to be washed up at my feet. At once I wondered if Darrow had foreseen this indefinably sinister end to my weeks of waiting, and the next moment I was telephoning the Fordites' mansion at Grantchester.

PART THREE

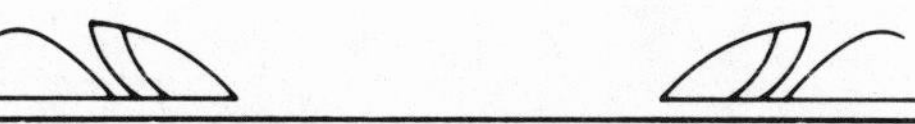

THE CALL

" . . . the possible final calls of individual souls are completely known to God alone, and to the soul itself, with some real knowledge, only and when it has advanced considerably on the spiritual way."

Spiritual Counsels and Letters of
BARON FRIEDRICH VON HÜGEL,
ed. Douglas V. Steere

XXII

"A perverted, confused or defective moral sense is yet reverently to be handled, after the manner of the Redeemer, Who would not quench the smoking flax or break the bruised reed."

More Letters of
HERBERT HENSLEY HENSON,
ed. E. F. Braley

1

DARROW was not available. "Father Abbot's gone visiting," said the monk who answered the telephone. He made visiting sound as if it were an act of great daring fraught with dangerous possibilities. His voice sank to a whisper. "He's calling on the Abbess at Dunton."

I saw us all moving into position like figures on a chessboard, I seeking Darrow, Darrow seeking a counsellor for Lyle, Lyle on her way to Cambridge to seek help. "When is he expected back?"

"Six o'clock, Doctor."

"Please tell him I rang." I replaced the receiver, thought for a moment, then telephoned the Blue Boar to reserve Lyle a room for the night. My next task was to cancel my social engagements, and once that had been accomplished I asked one of my fellow canons to substitute for me at the Cathedral for a couple of days on condition that I returned the favour when he himself was in residence.

Having concluded these essential telephone calls, I glanced at my watch. Then clasping my cross for comfort I calmed myself by reading the evening office. I still had over two hours to wait.

2

THE train drew into the station shortly before five o'clock and I was on the platform to meet Lyle as she left the last carriage and stumbled awkwardly into my arms. She was carrying only a shoulder-bag.

"Your luggage—" I was afraid she had left it on the train.

"I don't have any. I came up to London only for the day." She was very pale but appeared calmer than I had expected. There was no sign of tears. "Before I caught the train here I sent the Jardines a wire to say I was staying overnight. I didn't say where or why."

I kissed her briefly, led her outside and told her about the room waiting at the Blue Boar. "But we'll go to Laud's first," I said, "and I'll make you a cup of tea."

"I'd rather have a whisky," came the flat reply, and as I swung to face her she said: "Yes, ladies' companions don't drink whisky, do they? But I want to put aside my mask now, Charles—the glittering image, as you called it—and then when you see me as I am"—suddenly she was fighting her tears—"perhaps you won't want me any more but at least I'll have set you free to find someone else."

I said as I started the car: "Whatever happens in the future I promise I'll help you through the present crisis."

But she was apparently too overwhelmed to reply; she could only avert her face from mine as she struggled for composure, and in silence we drove to Laud's.

3

"MAYBE brandy would revive you more effectively than whisky," I said when we reached my rooms.

"I think it would, yes. Thanks. With soda." She began to search her bag for a cigarette. After I had given her a light, she added: "I haven't even said thank you for responding like this. I must be wrecking your social calendar and Cathedral duties."

"You're more important than calendars and cathedrals." I handed her the glass of brandy, and after siphoning some soda water into a glass for myself I sat down not on the sofa beside her but in the nearest armchair. I was wearing my collar so I was unable to smoke. Instead I sat well forward in the chair and gripped the glass with both hands. Outside in the quad the sun was shining. My rooms were very quiet, very peaceful.

"Sorry," said Lyle, "I seem to be in a sort of coma. I want to talk but I can't quite see where to begin."

" 'Begin at the beginning,' as the King said in *Alice in Wonderland,* 'and go on till you come to the end.' Have another swig of brandy."

"The trouble is I'm not sure where the beginning begins . . . Charles, could you sit beside me? Or have you planted yourself in that chair not just to reassure me you won't pounce but to help you to behave like a—whoops! I nearly said 'eunuch.' The glittering image is slipping. Ladies' companions in clerical households aren't supposed to know what such words mean."

"Surely if they read the Bible and have access to a dictionary they'd find their innocence rather hard to preserve?" I said mildly, and when she laughed I sat down beside her and gripped her trembling hand in mine.

"All that biblical sex!" she exclaimed, and suddenly I sensed she had seen the way forward into her narrative. "That awful use of the verb 'to know'! I remember saying to my great-uncle in Norfolk: 'Everyone in the Old Testament seems so well acquainted!' I didn't know anything about sex till fairly late—well, I didn't want to know. My mother said to one of her friends once when I was listening at the door: 'Of course no girl would ever face marriage if she *knew all,*' and my God, the way she said it! I crept away and vowed I'd never marry, never, never, never. I didn't want children anyway so marriage seemed not only repellent but pointless. I told you my mother was an invalid, didn't I? 'I was all right before I was married,' she used to say, 'but after the child was born, I was never the same again.' What a nightmare! Marriage, motherhood, and *knowing all*—ugh! I grew up wishing I'd been born a man.

"However, when I was twenty-four and still living at that ghastly rectory in Norfolk, I thought: there's got to be more to life than this, I'll go mad soon, I'll die of boredom unless I can make something happen. And I started thinking rationally about marriage. I was spurred on by the fact that my great-uncle was clearly on his last legs, and once he died I knew I'd be turned out into the street with no money. So I thought: maybe I should give marriage a try. Well, it just so happened that one of my admirers at that time was the son of one of the well-to-do farmers in the neighbourhood, not some blockheaded yokel but a well-spoken boy, reasonably educated, and I thought he could be a solution to my problem. I liked the idea of helping him run the farm one day, and there was a nice house attached to the farm too, Georgian, not some two-up, two-down hovel—it had *possibilities,* and I did so long for a real home of my own at last. I calculated that his parents wouldn't last more than ten years, his sisters would soon be married off and then I'd be free to rule the roost. So the only hurdle was: could I cope with *knowing all?*

"Well, I weighed everything up—I'm horribly calculating, Charles, you'll like me less and less as this narrative progresses, but I've had to be calculating, had to be tough, how else could I have survived after Daddy had gone off to die a hero's death in the War? Bloody wars! Bloody heroes! Why the *hell* couldn't he have come home instead of leaving me alone like that? He left me with nothing, *nothing* except a mother who wilted uselessly on a chaise-longue, and once she was gone I had to endure that ghastly hole in Norfolk with no money, no decent education, no real companionship, just cast-off clothes, boredom and despair—my God! I spent my youth feeling like a kitten flung into a rain-barrel to drown.

"However there I was, paddling away and somehow keeping my head above water, and I thought I could use Thomas to crawl out of the rain-barrel. But as I was so afraid of *knowing all,* I said to Thomas: 'Before I can possibly decide whether or not to marry you, I must know exactly what marriage entails.' Actually I thought it was a most sensible suggestion, but of course he was horrified. He was a respectable young man pursuing the respectable girl from the vicarage—only to find she'd turned into a trollop! He broke off the friendship in a fine flurry of self-righteousness, but he came crawling back later. Well, men usually do, don't they? They can seldom bear to resist a good offer when it comes to sex . . .

"Anyway I wound up in Thomas's hay-loft *knowing all,* and naturally it wasn't nearly as bad as the nightmare concocted by my imagination. I think what surprised me most about it was the sheer banality. I wasn't revolted, just amazed that anyone could be bothered to do it more than once. I certainly knew *I* didn't want to bother—no, thanks!—so I had to tell Thomas that marriage simply wasn't on. Poor Thomas! But I don't feel sorry for him, not now, because I know that if we'd married I'd have made him very miserable.

"Well, then the blow fell: my great-uncle died and the Church served me notice to quit the vicarage. But I didn't sink into despair. I was too angry. I thought: that damned Bishop in Norwich ought to do something about me! So I went to see him and demanded a job. The Bishop fluttered around in a purple panic, but by coincidence one of his guests at the time was the Bishop of Radbury, and the Bishop of Radbury thought at once of his new Dean.

"I went to Radbury for my interview. Do you know the Deanery there? A beautiful Georgian townhouse with ten bedrooms, much nicer than Thomas's faded rural home—oh, as soon as I arrived I knew the situation had *tremendous* possibilities! I was nervous of meeting Mrs. Jardine, but as soon as I saw her I recognised the type and was confident I could cope. Mrs. Jardine was a much sweeter, much more lovable version of Mummy—the sort of female designed by God to decorate chaise-longues and drive husbands to drink, or to die a hero's death in some hellish war. However, I could see Carrie liked me so I knew the first hurdle had been overcome. But then I had to have my interview with the Dean.

"Carrie took me to his study. I was expecting to meet a white-haired portly old buffer—have you ever noticed how many eminent clerics are white-haired portly old buffers?—so you can imagine how I felt when I first set eyes on Adam Alex Jardine.

"He was forty-eight. I was twenty-five. I took one look and finally realised what *knowing all* was all about. I think I actually went weak at the knees—can you imagine it! One never expects a clergyman to have an effect like a matinée idol, yet it's by no means a rare phenomenon—I remember reading once about a Victorian clergyman who inspired all the women in his congregation to faint in their pews, and I thought at once: that's like Alex Jardine. Clergymen have extra allure too because they're trying to lead a decent life, and every woman secretly dreams of a real stunner who can somehow stop himself rolling around in the mud like all the other swine—although of course she wants him to roll around in the mud with her. I'm sorry, Charles, are you absolutely appalled by my frankness? Maybe you'd better have some brandy too. But this is it, Charles, this is what I'm like behind my mask—cool, calculating and obsessed with sex. All that well-chilled propriety was just an act.

"Well, if this were a D. H. Lawrence novel, Jardine and I would have straight away leapt into bed together, but life isn't quite so simple as either the modern novelists or the Victorian novelists seem to think it is. In real life people are much more shadowy, and life is much more uncertain, more unpredictable, more mysterious; people can be a lot worse than they are in novels, but they can be a lot better too." She paused. Then she said: "Alex—" and paused again.

The two intimate syllables hung in the air between us. The curtain came down on the first act, the curtain went up on the second, but all I said as I added a dash of brandy to my soda water was: "Go on."

4

"*ALEX* was—and is—a good man," said Lyle, holding out her glass for a refill. "That's the point I want to make crystal clear because unless you understand that, you'll understand nothing. He's good—and he's devout. If it had been otherwise he couldn't have survived, Charles; he wouldn't be where he is today.

"But I didn't understand that when we first met. You see, although I'd spent so much time in a clerical household, I knew next to nothing about either devout clergymen or a truly religious life. My great-uncle was so old and only interested in butterflies; he just regarded being a clergyman as having a safe roof over his head and a duty to be polite to his neighbours. As for religion, I thought it was something people did on Sundays. I had rather a grudge against God, in fact, for allowing Daddy to be killed. Intellectually I knew about Christianity but spiritually I was illiterate, so when I realised Alex found me attractive I just sat back and waited for him to make a pass. After all, other men always had. But the next thing I knew was that Alex was trying to get rid of me.

"I couldn't believe it. I was stunned. It made me realise how ignorant I was and how the world was so much more complicated than I'd imagined. I felt very cheap. It was as if someone fine had shone a spotlight on me and revealed this revolting heap of flesh and bones. . . . Do you remember how St. Augustine felt about himself when he realized how he looked in the eyes of God before his conversion? Well, I felt like St. Augustine. And like him I hated myself and just wanted to be a good Christian. I can't honestly say I was immediately transformed by the call of God because I wasn't. I went on being much the same but I grew up a bit, became a little humbler, a little more aware of my own ignorance, a little more determined to find out what being a Christian was really all about.

"Meanwhile I wasn't sacked after all because Carrie had had hysterics at the thought of losing me, and suddenly I felt so sorry for Alex having not only this ghastly problem of his wife—of course I'd soon summed up the marital situation—but also this ghastly problem of me smouldering away under his nose that I thought: if I really love him, I'll help him out. So I told him I hadn't come into his household to wreck his career but to make it possible for him to go all the way to the House of Lords. I was so nervous that I sounded rude and defiant, and at first I thought Alex would explode with rage, but he didn't. In the end he laughed. He laughed and said: 'What a girl!'

"Then he became businesslike. 'You've been frank with me,' he said, 'and that took courage. Now I'll be frank with you. All I want is to serve God to the best of my ability, but my problems keep getting in the way. If we can form a partnership in which you take care of my problems and leave me free to serve God, then I swear you need never be homeless again. But the only way we can form a partnership, Miss Christie, is for us both to forget about turning our life at the Deanery into some wild cross between *Barchester Towers* and *Lady Chatterley's Lover.* Am I making myself absolutely clear?' I assured him that he was. 'Very well, I'll give you a new three-months' trial,' he said, 'and we'll see how we both get on.' I said: 'Splendid!' and we shook hands.

"That was how it all began. Innocent, wasn't it? And both of us only trying to be good and decent. The streets of Hell aren't paved with champagne, loose women and fast cars, as that old fool Bishop Winnington-Ingram said once. They really are paved with the very best intentions.

"Of course Alex should have stuck to his guns and dismissed me. But Carrie . . . poor darling sweetest Carrie . . . If I hadn't been there to run the Deanery and soothe her out of her nervous breakdown, she'd have ruined his career. I couldn't help being fond of Carrie—and it wasn't just because she was so hard to dislike; it was because she really did love me as a daughter. Never having wanted children myself, I had no idea until then what hell women go through when they want to have children and can't and Carrie had been through hell. Alex had suffered too, but he was in a better position to cope; he had his work to occupy him and he always had plenty of chances to work off his frustrated fatherhood among the choirboys and ordinands who trooped past him continually, but Carrie had no one to mother until I came.

"I asked her why they'd never adopted, but Alex had taken the line that one never quite knew what one was getting with a strange baby and he'd rather taken an unofficial interest in people who were older. Well, that was all right for him, but it was tough on her. However, she never argued with Alex, not by that time; she'd tried arguing with him in the early days of the marriage about his stepmother, but by the time I arrived at the Deanery Alex was God, in her eyes, and his word was law. Ironically that was part of the marital problem. Alex needs to be screamed at occasionally—he can't stand it when Carrie disintegrates into floods of tears because it makes him feel so guilty that he can't love her as he should. What a pathetic marriage! I felt so sorry for them both, locked together for life with nothing in common but their incompatibility and their double-bed . . .

"I expect you want to know where my obsession with sex had got to by this time, and the answer is: coming along nicely. As usual there was always some man writing me sonnets, but I couldn't look at anyone but Alex and I used to soak myself in fantasy; I'd lie in bed and have what the clerics call 'impure thoughts.' You're probably wondering how I stood the frustration, but in fact unrequited love can be great fun—ask any schoolgirl with a crush. One burns and one yearns in blissful comfort, and nasty brutal old reality never intrudes at all . . . The truth was I felt wonderful, doing a job I liked, seeing the man I loved every day, enjoying stunning sex every night in my imagination—and when all was said and done that was exactly where I wanted to enjoy it. Despite my feelings for Alex, I still couldn't rid myself of the nasty suspicion that real sex, even with him, was bound to be a disappointment, so the situation which had evolved at the Deanery actually suited me very well. I must be honest and admit I had my moments of jealousy, but they didn't happen very often, and that was Carrie's shining triumph. You see, she's the most Christian of us all—she loves Alex, she loves me, she's always so kind and good . . . In the end it wasn't Alex who brought me to a full Christian belief. It was Carrie, poor stupid helpless Carrie, but she showed me how to live a Christian life, and in the end I found myself loving her far more than I'd ever loved my vain whining self-centred mother.

"And so we came at last to Starbridge . . . But are you understanding what I'm trying to say? I think you have some idea that I'm the innocent heroine enslaved by the wicked Jardines, but you see, Charles, it isn't like that at all. Alex and Carrie are both good and devout. *I'm* the villain of the Starbridge mystery, and here's where my villainy really begins . . ."

5

I SAID as I lit her second cigarette: "Is it really a story of heroes and villains? Surely real life is never as simple as that!"

"Yes, I did say earlier, didn't I, that real life is so much less clear-cut than it is in novels . . ." She was calmer now. Her fingers were no longer trembling and the clasp of her hand was firm. "I feel better," she said. "I wonder if that's the brandy or the confessional? I suppose it must be the brandy because I haven't confessed anything yet except what a sex-obsessed adventuress I am."

I said mildly: "Do you realise that if you were a man your initiative in getting a good job, your ingenuity in keeping it, your desire to make a success of your work, your preoccupation with sex (a preoccupation which is hardly unusual among those not called to celibacy)—all these things would be considered either admirable or, at the very least, normal?"

Without warning her eyes filled with tears. "You mustn't make excuses for me. I'm so rotten, so undeserving, so unworthy—"

"Ah yes!" I said. "I used to play this scene before Father Darrow stepped in and revised my script. Cheer up! You may be unworthy but I doubt if you're more unworthy than I am, and anyway maybe we can have an interesting time being unworthy together. But let's get back to your story. You came at last to Starbridge—"

The interval was over and the curtain went up on the third act.

6

"WE came at last to Starbridge," said Lyle, drawing deeply on her cigarette, "and almost at once the crisis began. It had actually been brewing for some time. I was thirty, Alex was fifty-three and Carrie was forty-eight—and Carrie had begun the change of life. Physically this was nothing dramatic. She wasn't prostrated by dire symptoms, but mentally she went to pieces because the hope of a baby had kept her going in a difficult marriage. Alex is *not* the easiest of men to live with, and although she adored him, he'd often given her a rough time with his quick temper and sharp tongue. However, the desire for children had given her the strength to be what Alex calls 'dutiful'—what a sickening Victorian word that is!—and although sex had never meant much to her, she'd more or less managed to meet her obligations whenever she wasn't having a nervous breakdown. But how was she now going to face a childless future? That was the big question, and the problem was compounded by the fact that she was terrified of leaving Radbury where (thanks to me) she had her life in control, and moving to a whacking great palace with twelve servants at Starbridge. Of course she still had me to help her out, but I couldn't save her from being put on display as 'Mrs. Bishop' throughout the diocese.

"All this was desperate enough, but the turn of the screw came when Alex's sister died and his stepmother had to be imported to the palace. Carrie didn't hate old Mrs. J.—I honestly don't think Carrie could hate anyone—but Carrie was wholly convinced she couldn't cope with her. Mrs. J. gave her what I think is called an inferiority complex, and made Carrie feel stupid and miserable. Old Mrs. J. herself, of course, was a very tough lady indeed, and she didn't just hate Carrie; she despised her.

"However, when old Mrs. J. arrived she actually behaved very well—she was so pleased to be back with her Adam—and the real trouble arose not from her hostile behaviour but from the fact that Carrie couldn't believe old Mrs. J. was genuinely trying to be benign—you know how persecuted people feel when they're on the verge of collapse. I badgered the doctors for help, and after dishing out the pills one of them even suggested a psychiatrist, but Alex reacted as if the man had recommended witchcraft. Alex thinks psychiatry's rubbish, a sort of heresy on a par with spiritualism.

"Then finally the crisis reached its climax. Carrie, who was by now refusing to leave the palace and face the world, told Alex she had to have a separate bedroom. No more sex. What was the point, she said, when nothing could come of it. Well, Alex could live without the hope of children but he couldn't live without the hope of sex. I knew that. Carrie told me everything by that time—poor darling, she had no one else to confide in, but when Alex found out that she'd talked to me about their intimate life he nearly hit the roof. We had a row and he accused me of cultivating an unhealthily confidential relationship with Carrie. I said that was nonsense and he knew it. 'You're lucky she confides in me and not in someone else,' I said, 'because you know very well I'll keep my mouth shut till the day of judgement.' He said: 'I ought to get rid of you,' and I said: 'Oh, don't be such a damned fool!' He liked that. Alex likes a woman who can talk back to him. He said: 'What on earth am I going to do?' and I said: 'Stop being such a pigheaded Victorian and get her to a psychiatrist.'

"So he took her up to London—well, we all three went—and the psychiatrist was a nice man but of course he never got anywhere near a cure; he couldn't wave a wand to postpone the menopause. However, she liked him, so we all began to hope, and when he suggested that a little holiday might be beneficial the three of us trekked off to Bournemouth for a few days.

"Carrie in fact *was* a little better; the psychiatrist wasn't a complete failure, and when I coaxed her out of the palace to buy clothes for the holiday she was almost her old self again. Alex thought she was cured. Talk about wishful thinking . . . I said: 'You *are* booking three rooms at the hotel, aren't you, Dr. Jardine?' and he said: 'That's a very impertinent question, Miss Christie, and not one which I feel obliged to answer.' Well, we got to the hotel and of course he'd booked a double room for them. I knew it would be a disaster and it was. On the first night Carrie came to me in tears when he was having a bath and asked if she could spend the night with me in my room. She was in such a state, practically in hysterics, and when she sobbed that she didn't dare face Alex to tell him, I said at once: 'Don't worry, darling, *I'll* tell him.'

"They had a bathroom adjoining their bedroom—Alex always likes to be extravagant in hotels. I sat down in my dressing-gown on the edge of the bed and listened to him splashing away and eventually he wandered out with only a towel tucked around his waist. He didn't see me at first. He just assumed Carrie was there and he said: 'The Bishop of Durham has a good story about how he was once accidentally bathed in Sweden by a youthful masseuse—what a pity this hotel doesn't provide such an interesting facility!' Funny how clearly I remember him saying that. I suppose it's because I also so clearly remember thinking: this is it, I've taken her place, he's talking to his wife and I'm listening to him talk. And *that* was the moment when I knew I wanted real sex at last.

"A second later Alex turned and saw me. He went ashen. Then he very carefully put on his dressing-gown and tightly tied the cord.

"I told him what had happened. He said: 'I'd better talk to her,' and I said: 'I don't think that would be a good idea at all—better to leave her where she is tonight and tackle the whole problem afresh in the morning.' He said: 'And where are you going to sleep, may I ask?' and I said: 'Well,' I said, 'I'm very used to filling in whenever Carrie can't cope and this is all in a day's work for me. Why don't I fill in here too?' And Alex—darling Alex—said: 'My dear Miss Christie, we seem to have wound up in the pages of *Lady Chatterley's Lover*—may I suggest we return immediately to the pages of *Barchester Towers*?' And he added: 'Please go to your room and tell Carrie she must come back and sleep alone here in this bed while I sleep in the armchair by the fireplace. Tell her I shan't be cross, shan't lose my temper, shan't utter a single word of reproach because I'll be much too busy going down on my knees and asking God to extricate us all from this highly embarrassing, utterly catastrophic and apparently insoluble mess.'

"Wasn't he wonderful?

"I went back to my room and swore to Carrie she had nothing to fear. Then I told her exactly what I'd said to Alex. Her first reaction was: 'But of course! The perfect solution!' and she kissed me. Her second reaction was: 'But it wouldn't be right and Alex would never do it.' However, the next moment she was saying: 'It's so strange though, because I feel it *ought* to be right—do you feel that, Lyle?' and I told her I did. We all in the end felt it was right. But none of us could see how it could be morally done.

"We cut short the holiday and returned to Starbridge with the excuse that Carrie wasn't feeling well, but in fact Carrie was much better. She'd seen the light at the end of the tunnel and so had I, but I was so worried about Alex because I knew he was in despair. But after days of confiding in his journal and getting nowhere Alex finally scrapped his iron rule that he should never discuss his marital life with his stepmother, and of course old Mrs. J. sorted us out in no time. She *quite* understood that Alex couldn't live without the hope of sex, and she saw me as playing her own role in a re-enactment of her big romance with Alex's father. But the past never quite repeats itself, does it? Alex's father had been a widower, and Alex was still very much a married man.

"But old Mrs. J. had been brought up a Lutheran and she knew that Martin Luther had believed refusal of marital rights should constitute grounds for divorce. She'd also spent twenty-five years living with Alex's father who thought that clergymen were unnecessary, the legal bureaucracy was an impertinence and that any couple could marry themselves before God without conforming to all the man-made rules of Church and State. Old Mrs. J. had absolutely no doubts about what Alex should do, Carrie had no doubts, I had no doubts—

"But Alex was absolutely tormented.

"Finally Mrs. J. gave me her wedding ring—this ring, my signet-ring. Alex was there. She'd asked to see us both and we were in her room. She said to him: 'I want her to have my ring and I want you to put it on her finger.'

"She more or less married us. But in the end Alex had to do it more tidily; he's got a very legal streak and he likes ambiguous situations to be properly defined before being neatly filed away. He fetched Carrie. It was late at night by that time and Carrie was getting ready for bed but she came along in one of her stunning negligées—she looked better than she'd looked for months. I was wearing my evening clothes, a rather funereal black dress, but Alex took a rose from Mrs. J.'s vase of flowers and fixed it alluringly on my décolletage. He was wearing his episcopal clothes, apron, gaiters, pectoral cross, the lot. Mrs. J. was in her usual gunmetal-grey. What an odd crowd we must have looked! And what a strange scene it was! Alex made a short speech setting out the position—I think he needed to make a speech to convince himself that what he was doing was right, and of course by the time he'd finished it all seemed so right that one wondered why no one had ever thought of setting us a precedent. He told Carrie he wished to divorce her for refusal to consummate the marriage and said it was his honest belief that this refusal rendered their marriage a purely nominal affair; the spiritual core of the marriage had been destroyed, leaving only the legal formalities, and as far as these were concerned, God certainly didn't need a gaggle of lawyers to sanctify the dissolution of a spiritual nullity. Mutual consent alone was sufficient to dissolve any man-made ties.

"Alex promised Carrie that he would always maintain her and that for as long as she lived she would be his wife in the eyes of the world. He then asked her if she had any objection to what he'd said, and she answered no, she loved him very much and she was sure this was the best solution; she promised to do her utmost always to be a good wife to him in public. Alex said: 'Then before God I declare my marriage to Caroline dissolved,' and after a pause he gave her a kiss and asked her if she wanted to stay on while he married me. She said: 'Oh yes, dearest—I put on my best negligée!' and we all laughed, but it was a tense moment because we were all so close to tears. Old Mrs. J. said suddenly: 'Fetch some champagne, Adam, and some glasses for afterwards.' She knew he was temporarily too overcome to go on. So off he went to recover and Carrie went to the lavatory and I sat down by Mrs. J.'s wheelchair and Mrs. J. held my hand.

"When Alex came back with the champagne, we got married. Again he did it formally, spelling out all the details, saying it must be a secret marriage while Carrie lived. I agreed to the terms, we exchanged vows and he put the ring on my finger. Carrie cried, of course, in her role of 'mother of the bride.' It was all very peculiar and emotional. I hugged her and asked her to keep on loving me. She just said: 'How could I stop? I'll always love you both and want you to be happy.'

"After we'd all had a glass of champagne, ruthless old Mrs. J. ordered Carrie off to bed so that she could be alone with us. Then she kissed me and said: 'Now I can die knowing Adam will be happy at last'—and she did die, but not for another few months so she was actually able to see how happy he was with me.

"Meanwhile Alex and I had concluded the wedding night by going to bed together. It wasn't like my fantasies—he was in such a state he was impotent at first. He said: 'I'm afraid this isn't like *Lady Chatterley's Lover* after all,' but I said: 'Well, it certainly isn't like *Barchester Towers*!' Then we laughed and everything was all right."

Lyle stubbed out her cigarette. It had been a long time since she had looked me in the eyes and now she still kept her face averted from mine as she said rapidly: "I'm sorry to take my time over this but I want you to understand exactly how it was."

"That's what I want, too. Shall I make some tea now? If we go on tossing off the brandies like this we'll be insensible before the final curtain."

She finally dared to look at me. I gave her a reassuring smile. Then releasing her hand I rose to my feet and moved to the pantry to fill the kettle.

7

LYLE said when I returned: "Is the story turning out as you anticipated?"

"It is and it isn't. I guessed the bare facts, as you know, but I hadn't visualised the huge emotional strain involved—and I hadn't anticipated how everyone would play their parts. Of course I saw Jardine as the instigator—"

"No, it was me, in the beginning. Then old Mrs. J. pushed him over the edge at the end. I wish you could have met her, Charles. She had the most tremendous influence over Alex."

"What exactly—"

"I don't know," said Lyle. "I've played the model wife, waiting for him to confide, but Alex has always remained reticent."

"Maybe there's nothing to confide."

"I'm sure there's something. I suspect they had one of those intense relationships where sex is either unnecessary or unimportant—sibling relationships can occasionally fall into that category, can't they, although I'm sure Ingrid and Alex never saw themselves as brother and sister. I know he never saw her as his mother either—he told me he could remember his own mother too clearly, and anyway Ingrid wasn't maternal. While he was growing up he would have seen her as his father's wife, but when he found out about the informal marriage—that was when

Ingrid left home to keep house for him—I suspect he just saw her as the unattached woman who loved him. I still doubt if they ever slept together—Alex is so devout—but who knows? If the relationship was entirely innocent, why can't he talk freely about it to me? And why did he rush into that marriage as soon as he could afford to do so—as if he felt it was vital that he should put himself once and for all beyond the reach of temptation?"

"Perhaps something started in Starmouth, finished when she went back to the old man and then started up again later in North London after the old man died."

"I just don't know. You could equally well argue that he rushed into marriage because he feared the platonic relationship was finally becoming sexual. A man can't marry his father's wife, can he, and even though Ingrid's marriage was so peculiar Alex did in the end believe it to be valid in the sight of God. So he couldn't marry her—and as he was a devout clergyman no other relationship was possible. But I'll tell you this, Charles: although we can't know for certain whether she and Alex were ever lovers, I'm quite sure that old Mrs. J.'s loathing of Carrie was fundamentally rooted in jealousy."

"Was she never jealous of you?"

"She seemed to decide straight away that it was pointless. In 1932 when I married Alex she was over seventy, she knew she hadn't long to live and all she wanted was to see her Adam happy. Anyway she liked me. We got on. She adored the wedding—in fact, if I was going to advance a really bizarre theory, I'd say she got tremendous vicarious excitement out of pushing me at Alex and imagining us in bed together, but who knows what she really thought? Who even knows where reality lies? Think of all those philosophers—Berkeley and Hume and—"

"I'd much rather think of you. Do you take sugar in your tea?"

"Now *that's* reality! No, thanks. Just milk."

I poured out the tea. "So far," I said, "I still can't see any heroes or villains in this story, only victims."

"Victims of God?" she said. "Or victims of the Devil?" And she added unexpectedly: "That's a charism, isn't it—the ability to distinguish the manifestation of God from the manifestation of the Devil in ambiguous circumstances? Alex told me it's called the charism of the discernment of spirits."

We were silent for a moment, but then I said: "Ring up the curtain on the next act and let me test my powers of discernment."

XXIII

"Personally I incline to think that wherever a situation emerges in which the cohabitation of the husband and wife cannot reasonably or equitably be required, there a prima facie case for divorce must be held to exist."

"Before one could rightly order these folk to go apart, we must be well assured that they are not in spiritual fact married. *In the region of essential morals we cannot stake everything on the presence or absence of the legal certificate."*

More Letters of
HERBERT HENSLEY HENSON,
ed. E. F. Braley

I

"FOR a long time," said Lyle, sipping her tea, "everything was fine. Or perhaps I should say it was fine despite the peculiar circumstances which in fact made everything very difficult indeed. The first major problem was secrecy; I moved my bedroom to that remote nook in the south turret, but Alex thought it might look odd if he changed his bedroom arrangements at the same time, so he and Carrie continued with their shared room although now he always slept in the dressing-room. Then later they got twin beds so that they could occasionally sleep within the same four walls and present a facade of marital intimacy to the servants.

"The danger to our secrecy in fact came from another quarter altogether. Alex and I had had five years' experience of suppressing our feelings for each other, but it wasn't so easy to maintain a bland facade once we were also indulging in great intimacy—it was the switching backwards and forwards which was so tricky. We developed a strict rule that we should never under any circumstances embrace except in my room—and that was tough because we longed to snatch a kiss sometimes, but it just wasn't worth the risk. We also developed the golden rule that we were never to neglect Carrie—in fact Carrie was quite a problem to us at first because we felt guilty about her; we couldn't help feeling guilty even though we both knew she'd consented to the divorce of her own free will. Carrie was also a problem in another way, poor darling—both Alex and I were terrified she'd be indiscreet. I watched her like a hawk in the early months, but in fact Carrie never once let us down—she was so very conscious how vital it was that she should never make a mistake.

"The other major difficulty at first was the sex. This may surprise you—I expect you imagined us plunging away happily for hours, but we were both paralytic with fear in case I started a baby and for a long while after that first night we didn't go the whole hog at all. The advantage of that was that I was able to get used to intimacy without being overpowered by it, but eventually I went up to town, to the Marie Stopes Clinic, pretended to be a legally married woman and got myself a Dutch cap. After that everything was fine, but the sex always had its slightly sordid side—the hole-in-the-corner side of the clandestine love affair. For instance we both used to worry about the sheets so finally we always lay on a shawl which I could wash myself . . . Oh heavens, Charles, forgive me for dragging in these details but I want to be truthful, I want you to see the absolute grinding *reality* of it all—"

"It's much better that you should be entirely frank. Tell me, did Jardine never get caught going to your room? I'd have worried about that if I'd been him."

"Well, he seldom came at night. He reckoned that people always suspect the worst if a man goes creeping around the corridors at night in his dressing-gown but no one bats an eyelid if a man wanders casually around fully dressed in broad daylight. Usually Alex would visit me in the early morning, around six. The room next to mine had been converted into a bathroom so I never had to worry about a maid arriving with hot water in the mornings, and in the winter I lit the fire myself to 'spare the servants'—that went down well in the servants' hall—so in fact no housemaid ever came near my room until my bed was made between nine and ten. Early mornings were always the best time—or we'd meet sometimes in the early evening when everyone was changing for dinner . . . But when we met it was always as lovers, never as husband and wife. At the beginning it was all very exciting, but later I began to long for a whole night with him, like a real wife. However, he always said that was impossible; some wretched vicar might blow his brains out or the Cathedral might burn down—and then there'd be hell to pay if the Bishop wasn't found sleeping in the right bed.

"I expect you can guess where all this is leading, can't you? I became discontented. The discontent came on gradually, so gradually that for a long time I wasn't aware of it, but the more successful I became as Alex's unofficial wife the more ardently I longed to be 'Mrs. Bishop' in the eyes of the world. It was as if our situation had had the seeds of its own destruction built into it from the beginning.

"The discontent affected my spiritual life—I expect that as a clergyman you were wondering about that. Well, I was fine after the marriage; Alex had told me that there was absolutely no possibility that we were committing adultery and so of course I believed him. Why not? Damn it, he *was* the Bishop! So I had no pangs of conscience on that score and turned up at Communion every week, but when I became unhappy . . . and the good fortune began to go sour . . . it wasn't so easy. I began to wonder dimly if I was being punished . . . But I didn't like to talk about my uncertainty to Alex—not just because I was ashamed of doubting him but because Alex, if the truth be told, isn't a born counsellor. He's sympathetic and he's not incapable of intuitive understanding, but he finds it hard to resist the temptation to make a brilliant speech which solves the problem by temporarily converting one to his point of view. I knew that if I raised any doubts Alex would efficiently talk me out of them, but I didn't want someone to talk. I wanted someone to listen, and there was absolutely no one I could turn to.

"Then a very odd thing happened. As I've already said, I'd never been maternal, but one day when I was out in the town I saw this baby in a pram and suddenly I thought: if I was a real wife, I'd have one of those. And immediately I pictured this adorable little boy with golden eyes saying: 'Mummy! Mummy!' and holding out his arms to be loved. Can you believe it? I couldn't. I thought: how could I be so hopelessly sentimental? And the answer appeared to be: all too easily. I told Alex, but he only got upset. He said: 'Do you think I don't want your child more than anything else in the world?' but that sort of emotional statement was no help to me at all; it only made me feel worse than ever, and finally we had a row. That upset Carrie. She always knew if anything was wrong between us. One day I found her crying. She wouldn't tell me at first what the matter was but eventually she said: 'I expect you're wishing I was dead so that you could marry him properly.' I felt dreadful then, absolutely annihilated. I flung my arms around her and said no, no, never, never . . . But of course I often did wonder how long she was going to go on.

"Can you see how ghastly this situation was becoming? I felt as if someone—God or the Devil—had taken a giant spoon and was slowly stirring us up. I began to feel so muddled, muddled about Carrie, muddled about Alex, muddled about the marriage . . . Finally I went off sex. Alex hated that—and not just for purely selfish reasons but because he thought, poor Alex, that there was so little he could really give me that the least he could do was satisfy me in bed. It took me a while to realise that, but once I understood—oh, I felt so guilty, so unhappy that *he* was unhappy, and of course I let him talk me back into bed in the end. It was then—when he seduced me back—that he . . . No, I can't put it into words. Some things really are too bizarre to be talked about. But he made sure the sex was better than ever.

"Yet can you see how the triangle was coming apart at the seams? We all loved one another, but we were none of us happy any more. By this time—it was last May—what I couldn't bear was seeing Carrie play Mrs. Jardine in public, opening fêtes, presiding at charity committee meetings, getting all the attention from the important clerics and their wives at the big services . . . It was intolerable. I could feel myself becoming angrier and angrier, more and more bitter—*I* did all the hard work, *I* kept him happy in bed, *I* was the one he loved—and yet I was no one, just the aging spinster who was rumoured to cherish a pathetic secret passion for the Bishop. Oh, I often wanted to scream with rage and frustration, and all my feelings came to a head at the Coronation when Carrie got the wife's seat in the Abbey. Suddenly something snapped inside me and I poured out all my rage to them both . . . Then I hated myself because they were so dreadfully upset—and I knew at once not only how much I loved them but how absolutely *bound* I was to them both. It was loving the two of them at once—in such very different ways—which was so enslaving, and the weight of their joint love seemed to pin me in position so that there was no possibility of escape.

"Well, we patched up the quarrel, but I wouldn't go with them to London. I sat at home and thought and thought . . . I was in one of those awful states where one's thoughts go round and round in circles. Carrie could die tomorrow or she could live another twenty-five years. How much longer could I go on as I was? Was my marriage valid in God's sight or wasn't it? I could still tell myself it was but I was certainly beginning to wonder if I were entrapped in some frightful fraud. I was thirty-five years old, time was passing by and was I ever going to get my adorable little boy with the golden eyes or was he going to remain an unborn dream? I nearly went mad, torturing myself with those sort of thoughts, and all the time—all the time—I told myself: I can never leave them.

"And then . . . into this terrible situation when God—or the Devil—was really tightening the screws of my emotional rack . . . Well, you know what happened next, don't you?"

"Enter Dr. Ashworth," I said, "on his shining white horse. Can I pour you some more tea?"

2

"WELL, I thought I was on the rack before you arrived," said Lyle as I refilled our cups, "but that was nothing—that was just the introduction to the torture chamber. I took one look at you and thought—much as

I'd thought when I'd seen the baby in the pram: I'd like one of those. A handsome young canon with a golden future . . . I could see it all, right down to the new curtains I would order when I was Mrs. Bishop at last in an episcopal palace which was really my own.

"But then the guilt hit me like a hammer and I despised myself. I thought: If I were a real wife, I'd never succumb to such wicked dreams. And I felt so unfit, so . . . oh, so polluted by everything . . . But I made up my mind to fight the temptation very hard and be a good wife to Alex so that he and Carrie would never know how vile and disloyal my thoughts had been.

"But you weren't prepared to make fidelity easy for me, were you? My God, how you frightened me! You frightened us all. One of the worst moments was when I found you'd invaded my bedroom with the rose and the limericks. I kept all my contraceptive paraphernalia locked up in a jewel box so I knew that was safe, but the tell-tale shawl was just stuffed in a drawer, and if you'd searched my room . . . the stains . . . I was practically gibbering with terror.

"However, Alex calmed me down. We had a conference, he, Carrie and I, and he said: 'There's only one way to handle this and that's to act as if nothing's wrong. The more hostile we get, the more Ashworth is going to think we've something to hide.' Then he said to me: 'Be as cool to him as you always are with the infatuated chaplains and he'll soon see he's wasting his time."

"Of course Alex knew you posed a more serious threat than an infatuated chaplain but he did trust me not to be unfaithful, and at that stage you were just a colossal nuisance. However at the same time—and this was *very* bizarre—he seemed to find you fascinating. He talked about you a lot. He was convinced you had serious problems, all to do with women and your father—well, I just thought he was looking at you and seeing his own reflection. I didn't take him seriously, and meanwhile I was busy trying to convince myself that you were merely a dashing doctor of divinity who fancied himself with the ladies. But after that lovely evening at the Staro Arms I found it was impossible to remain cool and detached. That kiss outside the Cathedral . . . God knows how I didn't pass out. I wanted to leap into bed with you and make love till dawn.

"But as soon as I got back to my room I was crucified by my guilt again. I felt I'd betrayed Alex, betrayed myself—and the next morning I knew I couldn't face Communion. Of course Alex smelt a rat. We had no opportunity for private conversation before you left, but later he demanded a meeting and it was frightful. He'd guessed what had happened and he was beside himself with jealousy and rage . . . But we ended up making love and afterwards he said: 'You're my wife before God.

Never forget that.' And I didn't see how I ever could . . .

"Well, we were just recovering from your visit when the real ghastliness happened and you reappeared. I don't have to tell you how horrific that dinner was. It was bad enough that you'd guessed the truth, but what was worse was that you were obviously very drunk and very disturbed and might have bellowed your suspicions from the rooftops. I was also horrified to discover that Alex had been right in deducing you had problems, because it was now obvious that you were in a very bad way indeed.

"After you'd left, Alex said: 'We deny everything. The man's quite clearly unbalanced. It'll be his word against ours and we're the ones who'll be believed.' But then the bizarre element surfaced again—what a lot of bizarre elements there are in this story, or is life itself simply more bizarre than anyone's prepared to admit?—and he began to worry himself into a state about you. He was frantic in case you'd killed yourself driving while drunk. He couldn't stop worrying. He kept saying it was all his fault and that his charism had been taken over by the Devil—oh God, it was frightful! I packed Carrie off to bed and sat up with him while he crucified himself with guilt—and *all over you.* He even said you were just the sort of son he'd always wanted—and this was only a couple of days after he'd said he hated you for trying to steal me! Honestly, Charles, there was only one person who was more mixed up about you than I was at that moment, and that was Alex Jardine.

"Well, finally I got fed up with all this self-flagellation—I was worn out by that time—and I suppose I betrayed impatience. Immediately he changed course. He remembered again that you were a rival, and he said: 'Oh by the way, here's something that'll interest you, Ashworth admitted he slept with Loretta yesterday—are you sure he didn't sleep with you last weekend?' "

"Oh, my dearest Lyle—"

"We had a huge row. I thought he was lying. Then I realised it was true. And I felt so horribly upset and muddled and hurt—"

"Darling, I—"

"It's all right, I don't care now whether you slept with her or not—well, I do care, but I don't think it's important. Obviously you were in some very peculiar emotional state, and if you did sleep with her I'm sure it was a moral lapse you'd never normally have. But when Alex told me, I felt absolutely slaughtered—and of course I was livid with him too for accusing me of infidelity when I'd tried so hard to be faithful to him.

"The next thing that happened was that Alex discovered you were with the Fordites and he nearly expired with relief. But he was still terrified you might run to Lang with your suspicions when you'd recovered, and of course he *hated* the thought of Father Darrow knowing everything. Alex worried and worried . . . How he kept going with his work I've no idea. I turned up at the services as usual but that was just to keep up appearances. I was so confused, so unhappy . . . I didn't see how I could go on much longer, and one afternoon I went to the Cathedral to beg God to help me, but I couldn't pray, I was so cut off. I just knelt there in the chapel and said God, God, God, over and over in my mind . . . It was as if I'd dialled a number and was listening to the bell ringing—and I didn't really expect an answer, but then the miracle happened because someone picked up the receiver at the other end of the line.

"You came in. Do you remember me saying it was like a sign? I knew at once I had to leave Alex, but the only trouble was I couldn't see how I was ever going to do it.

"I told Alex I'd seen you. I didn't think we'd been seen by anyone I knew, but the last thing I wanted was for him to hear of the meeting from someone else. I also thought he'd appreciate my honesty, but he didn't, and there was an awful scene because he couldn't believe the meeting had been accidental. I tried to tell him the marriage was over, but I couldn't . . . He had such power over me, I can't describe it, maybe no words could ever describe it, all I can say is that I had to give in to him, *had to* . . . And so it went on.

"Well, as the days passed, Alex realised you hadn't told Lang and he began to feel better. So did Carrie. But I . . . oh Charles, this is where the going gets very difficult—"

I tried to put my arms around her but she pushed me away. "No," she said, "you don't understand. The going can't be made smooth by a well-meaning kiss." As she spoke, she rose to her feet and turned her back on me. I sensed she was nerving herself to confront some profound ordeal.

"Tell me what I can do," I said. "If you want my help in changing your situation at the palace—"

"It's already changed irrevocably." As she succeeded in summoning the nerve she needed, she turned to face me again. "My life at the palace has ended. There's no choice now. I have to leave."

I knew what she was going to say a second before she said it. "You're—"

"I'm pregnant," she said, and covered her face with her hands.

3

IN three seconds I saw it all, the inscrutability of God, the redemption of past tragedy, the backbreaking road into a barely conceivable future. Time completed some eerie circle; I was my father, Lyle was my mother and the embryo was me, waiting for the one man who had the will to give it the future God required. Yet all was subtly changed; I was not my father, Lyle was not my mother and the embryo was not and could never be me. The game was the same but the cards had been reshuffled and it was hard to perceive the dimensions of the hand I had been dealt. All I knew was that I was being called to play that hand. Of that I had no doubt whatsoever.

I touched the cross on my chest and took Lyle in my arms as she started to cry.

"I'll help you," I said.

She clung to me wordlessly. I stroked her hair, and then the shock began to bludgeon me, hammering my mind until I felt almost too battered to think. But I managed to form a prayer. I asked that I might be granted the grace to perceive the way forward, and the familiar words 'Let thy will, not mine, be done' were immediately comforting.

"Let's be practical for a moment," I said at last. "First of all, are you quite sure about this?"

"Yes, although it hasn't been medically confirmed." She drew away from me to extract a handkerchief from her bag. "I'm never more than twenty-four hours late. I knew at once what had happened. I felt different too, couldn't face coffee, it was just as if someone had thrown a spanner in the works and put everything slightly out of alignment." She blew her nose. "Today I went to the Marie Stopes Clinic and asked them if they could do a pregnancy examination, but they said it was too soon . . . Yet I know the baby's there."

I thought of false pregnancies and the power of the mind over the body. "When do you think it happened?"

"The day I met you in the Cathedral."

"But what happened to the contraception?"

"I didn't use it—that's why I know exactly when the disaster occurred. It was one of those rare occasions when he came to my room at night. Usually I always put the cap in before I go to bed so that when he arrives in the early morning I don't have to dash off unromantically to the bathroom, but that night although I was ready for bed I hadn't put the cap in and I was caught by surprise. Then before I could put matters right we were having our row over you, and afterwards . . . when he began to make love to me . . . oh Charles, I felt so helpless, so muddled, so absolutely *despairing,* that I didn't care about the contraception, I was beyond caring—"

"Have you told him about the baby?"

"No." She found the packet of cigarettes in her bag and clumsily shook one free. "I haven't told either of them—I felt I couldn't cope with their reactions when I could barely cope with my own. As you've probably realised by now, the great characteristic about my relationship with the Jardines is that I'm always the one who has to cope. Nobody copes with me—and of course that's why I'm here. I felt you could cope, tell me what to do—"

"How do you feel about the child?"

"I'm appalled. As far as I'm concerned, it's the most ghastly mistake. I've got over my sentimental dream of an adorable little boy with golden eyes, and now I'm visualising some plain little female crosspatch who'll be a millstone round my neck for the next twenty-one years—unless, of course, I have an abortion—"

"Absolutely not!" I said inevitably, and saw time encircling us both as the past repeated itself in a series of endless permutations. "It would be utterly wrong!"

"Oh, it's so damn easy for you to stand there and say that—you're a man!" cried Lyle, taking a very different line from my mother. "I don't think any man has the right to preach sanctimoniously about abortion!"

I had been unprepared for this feminist shaft. It made me realise how imperfectly I still knew her. "No man has the right to preach sanctimoniously about anything," I said, "but I'm not preaching and I'm not being sanctimonious. I'm trying to give you realistic advice. This is the child of a man you loved and it's a child you've often wanted. Wouldn't an abortion be a psychological as well as a moral disaster here?"

Her defiance crumbled; she broke down utterly. "Oh God, I'll never survive this, never—I thought I could but now I don't see how I ever can—I can't cope, Charles, I just can't cope—"

"But I can," I said. "I've been preparing for this for a long time, perhaps all my life. I can cope with you and I can cope with that child. You're going to marry me, Lyle."

4

I TOLD her briefly about my parentage. She was amazed, stunned and finally appalled as she saw the situation from my own perspective.

"But, Charles . . . Oh God, I don't know what to think! Obviously I've never understood the first thing about you—a man who could make such an offer without being coerced must be so utterly different from the sort of man I imagined you to be. Oh no, I can't let you do it, I can't—your offer's the most wonderful piece of idealism, but—"

"What's wrong with idealism?" I said, holding her close as she broke down again. "If there were no idealism we'd all be grovelling around in the mud with the animals. And anyway the best sort of idealism, the workable kind, is always firmly grounded in reality. I think I'm being exceedingly practical. I know you're the woman I want. You come to me with this huge handicap but as far as I can see I'm in a unique position to cope with it successfully. Of course the marriage will be plagued by the most unusual difficulties, particularly at first, but I think that with strength and will and by the grace of God the difficulties can be overcome. Why not? I'm supposed to be a Christian. Clearly I'm now being called to live out the Christian message of love and forgiveness in a very special way and besides . . . loving you as I do, how could I conceivably walk away?"

She could not answer. She merely clung to me again with a new intensity, and I knew how my father had felt long ago when he had witnessed my mother's overpowering gratitude and relief.

But I steered a different course from my father. I said: "We need help and we need it now. I want you to come with me to see Father Darrow."

5

DARROW was still out when I telephoned, so I took Lyle first to the Blue Boar where I confirmed her reservation and ordered some sandwiches.

"I couldn't eat," she said.

"Well, I can and you certainly should. Make an effort," I said firmly, remembering how ruthless Darrow had been with me on the subject of nourishment, so we sat in the lounge and ate chicken sandwiches. Lyle managed half a round and I consumed the rest; we divided the tea more equally between us.

"I've changed my mind about being keen to meet this man," said Lyle at last. "I quite understand why you need to talk to your spiritual director about the future, and obviously I have to be there too because I'm now part of that future, but to be frank I don't like the idea of him at all."

"I assure you there's no need to be nervous."

"I'm not nervous. I just feel that any woman can't help but regard a monk as a personal insult. What happened to his wife? Alex dug up the fact that he'd once been married."

"I've no idea what happened to her—Darrow's told me very little about himself, but that's in accordance with all the rules for good counselling. And talking of counselling . . ." I mentioned that Darrow had been looking for a sympathetic nun but Lyle again displayed antipathy.

"I couldn't talk about this to any woman," she said. "I don't even like women—apart from darling Carrie, and I don't like her particularly, I just love her."

This statement was so convoluted, so indicative of mental distress and psychological difficulty, that I thought it wiser to say nothing. I wondered how Darrow would approach the problem.

We drove to Grantchester, and as I turned the car into the Fordites' drive, Lyle shuddered.

"Darling . . ." Halting the car I leant over to give her a kiss. "Try not to regard this particular monk as a personal insult! I'm sure he's not a misogynist."

"Then what's he doing shut up in this place? How I hate the thought of people being incarcerated in closed orders! It's so damned eerie and unnatural."

I began to be seriously worried. All counsellors had their failures, and Darrow himself had made it clear that he preferred not to counsel women.

The happy young monk who had welcomed me to the house on the occasion of my first encounter with Darrow greeted us cheerfully and showed us into the Visitors' Parlour. "Father Abbot's just back," he said. "He won't keep you long."

"Poor old Darrow," said Lyle when we were alone. "I hope he won't wilt at the prospect of coping with your next huge problem."

"Darrow's tough enough to cope with anything."

"Well, he can cope with you but he'd better not try to cope with me! The last thing I want is to be coped with by someone who's given up sex."

The hostile note in her voice was now unmistakable, and I was just searching feverishly for the words which would soothe her when footsteps rang out in the hall.

Lyle at once looked as if she were about to face a firing squad. "It's him, isn't it?"

"Lyle, think of him as a friend—"

"But he's not a friend," she said, very pale. "He's the enemy, I know he is, I know it—"

And then in walked my exorcist to confront all the demons I had so persistently failed to recognise.

XXIV

"The power of self-deception is great in the case of all men, but I incline to think that it is greatest in the case of a popular official such as a Bishop, who never hears anything but his own voice, and the sycophantic acclamations which it evokes."

HERBERT HENSLEY HENSON,
RETROSPECT OF AN UNIMPORTANT LIFE

I

I HAD a surprise when I saw Darrow because he had not yet changed back into his habit after his outing in the world, and he was still wearing his clerical suit. The monk's habit had created an illusion that his personality merely formed part of a communal identity, but in clerical clothes the illusion of conformity was lost and his individuality became striking. He looked even more authoritative, even more confident—and he looked restless too, like an adventurer who was accustomed to sailing regularly in uncharted waters. It was as if his cool analytical serenity, which was such a feature of his monk's character, had been given a brasher, more volatile edge, and suddenly for the first time I could see him not only as a chaplain in the Navy but as a novice driving his superiors to such distraction that he had been exiled to Yorkshire to milk cows.

Beside me I heard Lyle's sharp intake of breath, and as I realised that shock had temporarily overcome her hostility, I knew she was astonished because Darrow was so different from the "white-haired portly old buffer" she had probably imagined. Darrow himself took one look at her and stopped dead. I stepped forward.

"Father, may I introduce Miss Lyle Christie? Lyle, this is Father Jon Darrow."

Darrow said swiftly: "How do you do, Miss Christie. Please sit down." He did not offer her his hand but instead pulled out a chair from the table for her.

"Thank you." Lyle sounded very cool, very suspicious. I knew the meeting had started badly but I was unable to locate the source of the awkwardness until Darrow said: "If I'd known Miss Christie was with you, Charles, I'd have paused to change into my habit. A monk should be a monk, not a somewhat eccentric clergyman with an ostentatious cross on his chest—it creates a disconcerting impression. Now, before I leave you in order to change, can I offer you some refreshment? Perhaps Miss Christie would like some tea."

Lyle firmly declined the offer of tea. I uneasily declined the broader offer of refreshment.

"Then if you'll excuse me for a brief interval—" He was gone.

As soon as the door had closed, Lyle swivelled to face me. "Why on earth didn't you warn me he was like that?"

"He's a striking sort of chap, isn't he? My father thought he should have been a lawyer."

"A *lawyer?* Good heavens, no! He should have been an actor—I can see him as a very sinister Prospero in *The Tempest,* or possibly as a very hypnotic Claudius in *Hamlet,* the sort of Claudius who makes it crystal clear why Gertrude could think of nothing but going to bed with him—"

"My dearest Lyle!" I was astonished. It had never occurred to me that a woman might see Darrow as sexually attractive. I had assumed he would seem too chilly, too austere, but I had forgotten that women are susceptible to an authoritative manner, particularly when that manner is wielded with an air of buccaneering self-confidence.

"I can think of nothing more bizarre," Lyle was saying fiercely, "than that a man like that should be a monk. It must be an act—that's *his* glittering image!—and underneath it I'm sure he's not monkish at all. Did you see how he absolutely recoiled when he saw me? Obviously I represent the biggest possible temptation to him—Jezebel reborn!"

I decided the time had come to take a firm line. "The reason why Darrow stopped dead when he saw you," I said, "(and I deny that he recoiled) was first because he was genuinely surprised to see you here, and second because he knew straight away you'd dream up all kinds of ridiculous fantasies about him unless he was wearing his sexless monk's habit!"

"But how can a man like that live without sex?"

"Darling, I hate to say it but I'm afraid you're prejudiced here by the fact that you've been on intimate terms with a cleric who couldn't cope with chastity—"

"That's right—throw Alex in my face!" cried Lyle, having worked herself up into a nervous rage. "I wish to hell I hadn't come to this beastly place!" And she burst into tears.

I was still trying to comfort her, still wondering how on earth Darrow was going to deal with us, still reminding myself that I could hardly expect to live happily ever after in a problem-free paradise, when Darrow himself walked back into the room.

2

LYLE leapt to her feet and marched up to him. "I think you'd better see Charles alone," she said. "I'm not running away—I just don't want a monk probing around in my past, that's all, and to prove I'm not a coward I'll tell you straight away that I'm pregnant and Charles has said he'll marry me and of course he's quite mad and mustn't be allowed to ruin himself like that. I don't care what happens to me, I'm too rotten to bother about, but Charles is good and decent and he doesn't deserve to be dragged down in this vile mess—and if you're as wonderful as everyone's always saying you are, you'll want to step in and save him from me."

"Lyle—" I began in despair but I was interrupted.

"Miss Christie," said Darrow, "what I want is of absolutely no importance here. The important thing is what God wants. Are you an apostate?"

"No!" shouted Lyle, tears streaming down her face.

"Then you'll accept that your first duty is to God, and that duty at this moment is to be calm so that you can hear Him if He wishes to communicate with you. Charles, give her your cross. Miss Christie, take the cross and hold it tightly . . . that's right . . . and keep holding it . . . Yes, you're being tortured by the demons of shame, guilt, despair, rage and terror, but no demon can withstand the power of Christ—yes, keep holding it . . . and now sit down here . . . Charles, you sit down too and put your arm around her . . . That's it . . . and now I'm going to sit down beside you both and we're all going to pray that in the name of Jesus Christ Our Lord these demons may be cast out and vanquished . . . and not just for your sake, Miss Christie, but for Charles's sake and for the sake of the child . . . Close your eyes and breathe very deeply . . . and evenly . . . and listen to my silent prayer, listen for any word from God, listen and listen very carefully . . . Lord, hear our prayer."

Lyle had squeezed her eyes shut and was shivering against me as I held her. I longed to tell Darrow to help the healing process with the power which he could channel through his hands, but although I never spoke he still heard me. He said severely: "Charles, concentrate on our prayer, please," and I said at once: "I'm sorry." At first I thought concentration would be impossible, but Darrow's training had not been wasted, and after praying hard I opened my eyes as he opened his. The words were "faith" and "trust." I had heard them clearly.

Beside me Lyle gave another shudder and opened her eyes.

Darrow leant forward. "Did you hear?"

"No, I heard nothing." She rubbed her eyes. "But I know I have to have faith in God and trust Him to look after me."

"That's it. What did you hear, Charles?"

"You were praying for faith and trust. I believe that I must trust you to help us and that I must have faith that I'll be able to serve God here to the best of my ability."

"Exactly. And it's God we all have to serve, isn't it, Miss Christie? I must serve God by helping you both to reach a correct response to this terrible ordeal, Charles must serve God by doing what he believes God's calling him to do and you must serve God by channelling all your energy into perceiving what He requires of you."

Lyle said shakily, still clutching my cross: "I want to marry Charles. But I'm afraid that's selfish and wicked and may not be God's will at all."

"It's not selfish and wicked to want to find the best possible solution to your dilemma. But what you must be certain of is that marriage with Charles is the best solution."

There was a silence. Then Lyle sobbed: "Oh Alex, Alex . . ." and once more broke down in tears.

3

"HOLD her close," said Darrow to me, and I was suddenly aware of his care that there should be no physical contact between himself and Lyle. I drew her to me again and kissed her cheek. She was still clutching the cross, and as I kept my right arm around her shoulders I covered her left hand with my own to confirm her grip.

When she was calmer she said to Darrow: "Alex is such a good man—you mustn't condemn him."

"It's certainly not for me to condemn him," said Darrow, "or for Charles either. Clearly we're dealing here with a tragedy where people have suffered greatly, but although I talk of suffering and tragedy, Miss Christie, you'll know as a Christian that out of every disaster can come a new beginning, a new hope, a new faith—and not just for you but for the Jardines too."

"But they can't manage without me!"

"Beware of falling into the trap of thinking that there's only one possible future, a future which is unfavourable to the Jardines. Such an assumption is actually a form of vanity; the truth is that no one's indispensable, so look to the future with humility and then I think you may be able to hope—and not only for yourself but for them as well. Think of our prayer just now. You must have faith in God and trust Him to look after all three of you in the difficult days ahead."

Lyle seemed soothed. After blowing her nose on her handkerchief, she said in a low voice: "My marriage isn't valid, is it?"

"Ah," said Darrow, "yes, let's sort out exactly where you stand. If you married Dr. Jardine in good faith you'd be adjudged an innocent party now that the marriage has turned out to be invalid. You would only fall into serious error if you went on with the marriage once you knew it to be no marriage at all."

"So it was all a lie."

"I suspect we'd come closest to the truth if we called it an enormous piece of self-deception by Dr. Jardine. Let me first explain why the marriage can't be valid. The defect is probably not in the marriage ceremony itself; it's arguable that in certain circumstances it might be possible to contract a marriage valid in the sight of God without the assistance of Church and State. For instance, if a man and woman were marooned on a desert island and wished to live in a Christian marriage, I don't think they could be called sinners if they exchanged vows reverently before God and set about being a good husband and wife. Dr. Jardine's father and stepmother apparently considered themselves on a desert island in Putney and certainly she would have been regarded as the old man's common-law wife, but their spiritual position is debatable and would depend very much on old Mr. Jardine's motives. However, possibly he acted sincerely and reverently. We'll never know. What we do know is that old Mr. Jardine was free to marry but his son, unfortunately, was not."

"But Alex thought—he was so certain—and Mrs. Jardine, his stepmother, she thought—and she was so certain—"

"I'm sure they were sincere in believing they were right. But old Mrs. Jardine was evidently capable of considerable spiritual elasticity—to put it kindly—and Dr. Jardine had apparently performed his famous trick of converting black into white with an elasticity which wasn't spiritual at all."

"But Carrie refused him his marital rights—Martin Luther thought—"

"Martin Luther wasn't God. Nor is that view of his on divorce consistent with the law of England."

"But if the spiritual core of the marriage has been destroyed—"

"I know there's a vocal party within the Church which believes that various circumstances can destroy the core of a marriage and constitute a spiritual dissolution, but refusal of marital rights isn't one of those circumstances, and despite Mr. A. P. Herbert's new law it isn't by itself a ground for divorce. Moreover I think it's impossible to argue here that the core of the marriage had been destroyed when Mrs. Jardine was still standing by her husband through thick and thin in order to save his career. An aspect of the marriage had certainly broken down, but in every other respect one could hardly find a more loving and loyal wife, and indeed I would judge it indisputable that Dr. Jardine had no remedy at law."

"But before God—the compassion and forgiveness of Christ—"

"I trust we'll all be praying that God looks upon Dr. Jardine with compassion and forgiveness, but it's quite unthinkable in spiritual terms, Miss Christie, that a bishop should be able to contract a valid marriage after an informal divorce by mutual consent. In fact many would say he couldn't justifiably remarry even after a formal divorce."

All Lyle said was: "He was so sure."

"Yes," said Darrow, "there was indeed great self-deception. He deceived himself into thinking that his marriage was spiritually null. He deceived himself into thinking that any marriage could be possible after an informal divorce. He deceived himself into thinking he was above the law of England and he deceived himself into thinking that a cohabitation bordering on bigamy was acceptable in the eyes of God. He also deceived both you and his wife by allowing you to think he was entitled as a bishop to make up his own spiritual rules as he went along and negotiate with God as he thought fit. This is the sin of pride and shows a degree of spiritual unhealthiness conducive to gross error."

Lyle was too overwhelmed to do more than whisper: "What's to become of him?" She started to weep again.

"That's a question which none of us can answer, but like you he has a choice of futures and we must all pray that he's guided to take the right one. However, at present you're more important than Dr. Jardine. Do you want to continue talking now or would you prefer to rest and return tomorrow?"

"What more is there to say?" Lyle put down the cross in order to wipe away her tears. "I know now I'm free to marry Charles—I know the truth in its entirety at last—"

"Yes, you do. But does Charles?"

She stared at him. So did I. I demanded at once: "What do you mean?"

Darrow stood up, moved around to the other side of the table and sat down opposite us in the counsellor's conventional position. All he said was: " 'Strait is the gate and narrow is the way.' "

The signal passed between us and suddenly I felt the dread sink to the pit of my stomach, but Lyle did not understand. She looked at him fearfully. "What do you mean?"

"Never forget," said Darrow to her, "that I want above all to help you and Charles to reach a correct solution here in accordance with God's will. And remember that this can't be done unless we know the whole truth."

"But I've told Charles the whole truth! I have, haven't I, Charles?"

"It certainly sounded like the whole truth to me," said my voice. I sounded emphatic but strained.

"Then in that case, Miss Christie," said Darrow, "you'll have no objection to enlightening me on one or two points which I still find obscure."

Lyle continued to look at him fearfully. Then she said to me: "I'm not sure what he means, Charles, but he seems to be implying I've deceived you in some way."

"I don't think he means that," I said with care. "After all, he doesn't know what you've told me. Think of him as holding up a torch to illuminate the dark corners—and always with your welfare in mind."

She considered that. "All right," she said finally to Darrow. "Ask away. What do you want to know?"

"Well, the first and most obvious question," said Darrow with great gentleness, "is: when did you decide to have this baby?"

4

I THOUGHT she was going to faint. I felt unsteady myself. Before she could reply I said rapidly to Darrow: "It was an accident."

But Darrow's first concern was for Lyle. "Charles, go into the hall and ask Barnabas to fetch a glass of water."

"No!" gasped Lyle. She clung to me. "Don't leave me alone with him!"

Darrow himself promptly called for the glass of water.

"Now, Miss Christie," he said as he returned, "have you considered your reply?"

She leant forward, her forearms on the table, her face hard and set. "I'm not telling you the details of my sex life. You must get your vicarious thrills in some other way."

"Lyle!" I exclaimed but Darrow said tersely: "Be quiet, Charles. Miss Christie—"

"You're prejudiced against women!" cried Lyle. "You're seeing me as a sex-obsessed bitch who's ruined one good man and is about to ruin another!"

"This is the demon of your guilt," said Darrow. "Pick up that cross again from the table."

"You're trying to prove to Charles that I'm just a calculating adulteress!"

"This is the demon of your shame and self-hatred. Pick up that cross."

Lyle leapt to her feet and shouted: "Shut up! You're nothing but a fraud, hiding here in this vile house because you're frightened that if you went out into the real world you'd seduce every woman in sight, so how dare you have the bloody impertinence to interfere in my private life, how dare you! Well, I won't let you vent your frustration on me like that, I won't let you destroy my last hope of happiness, *I won't let any man wreck my life*—"

"This is the demon of your rage," said Darrow, "but the rage isn't in fact directed against me. Tell me, how many other men apart from Dr. Jardine have so painfully disappointed you?"

Lyle gasped, grabbed the cross and hurled it at him, but as I leapt appalled to my feet Darrow caught the cross and sprang up so violently that his chair fell backwards with a crash.

"How many women did you put through hell before you castrated yourself with that bloody habit?" screamed Lyle, face contorted, her whole frame shuddering. "I hate you, *I hate you,* I HATE YOU!"

I tried to reach her but I was paralysed with shock. I felt as if some huge force had exploded, leaving a chasm between us, but the next moment Darrow was bridging the abyss. Moving swiftly around the table he said with great strength: "This torment must end. In the name of God—in the name of Jesus Christ—THIS TORMENT MUST END!" And he slipped the chain of the cross over her head as she flailed her arms to push him away.

"No, no, no—" She was screaming very loudly, but when he took her in his arms at last, the screams ceased, her whole body shuddered convulsively and she fainted.

5

THE young monk arrived a second later with the glass of water.

Darrow said sharply: "Get the brandy."

"Yes, Father." He thrust the glass into my outstretched hand and ran.

Darrow had lifted Lyle onto the long table. He moved swiftly and efficiently, laying her out full length and patting her waist with caution. "Thank heavens—no sadistic corset," was his only comment.

I roused myself from my stupefaction, set down the glass and demanded: "Father, what on earth's going on?"

"It's all right, she'll recover in a minute. Now before she comes round give me some quick answers to some quick questions. The contraception—is she claiming it failed?"

"There was one occasion when she left herself unprotected."

"Was Jardine aware of the omission?"

"She implied not."

"Do either of the Jardines know of her condition?"

"No. Incidentally the pregnancy isn't yet confirmed but she seems very certain. Father, I still don't understand what's happening—"

"Don't worry, Charles, I don't really believe this is a conspiracy between all three of them to produce a wanted child, but we've got to be sure . . . Ah, she's coming round. Now keep quiet and leave this to me—Yes, come in, Barnabas—Charles, pour out a little brandy, please."

"Will that be all, Father?" said Barnabas, intrigued by the woman prostrate on the table.

"Yes. Out," said Darrow, and Barnabas fled.

Lyle moaned.

"You're all right," said Darrow, stooping over her. "Have some water first. Then you can have brandy."

Lyle said: "Am I having a miscarriage?" She sounded dazed and childlike.

"No," said Darrow firmly. "Give her the water, Charles."

She drank obediently and after she had sipped the brandy, Darrow said: "See if you can sit up without feeling faint."

She tried. I was still supporting her. When there were no ill effects, she looked at Darrow. "I said terrible things to you," she whispered. "I remember."

Once more Darrow used the ancient symbolic language to express profound psychological truths. He said with complete authority: "The demons were very strong but they're gone now. You're not well yet but you're going to be well because now the healing can begin."

"Supposing the demons come back?"

"They can't so long as you're in touch with God. When you lost touch the demons were free to walk into your soul, but you won't lose touch now." He added to me: "Give her another sip of brandy."

Lyle sipped and said: "I feel better."

"Good. Charles, help her back into her chair." He made no move to return to his own chair but leant informally against the edge of the table.

Lyle said suddenly to him. "I want to talk to you."

"You want to tell me the truth about the baby?"

"But you already know, don't you?"

"Charles doesn't know and we both have to look after Charles here."

"I love Charles," said Lyle, still speaking directly to Darrow. I might have been a hundred miles away. "I want to be the best possible wife to him."

"And that's why you must be honest, isn't it? He's given you the gift of his love and you must give him the gift of your honesty to prove you're worthy of him. Very well, let's talk about this baby."

Looking steadily at Darrow, Lyle said: "I don't know exactly when he was conceived."

"You gave up the contraception?"

"Yes. I wanted to get pregnant."

"The only way out, was it?"

She nodded. Her eyes shone with tears.

"Can you tell me how you reached this decision that pregnancy was the only solution to your problems?"

Lyle said: "I'd gone to the chapel in the Cathedral but I couldn't pray because I was so cut off. Then Charles came. I knew then I had to leave the Jardines, but I couldn't see how I was ever going to be strong enough to end the marriage. Charles doesn't understand this part—the bizarre part—and I can't put into words the quality of the hold Alex had over me, but—"

"When did the love-making change?"

"Earlier this year. I went off sex. I felt in such a muddle about everything. But Alex talked me out of it. *Alex talked*—" She broke off.

"—and then the sex seemed exciting in a new way."

She nodded painfully again. "I can't explain to Charles, I don't want to explain—"

"Yet he must know. Otherwise he'll torture himself by trying to guess what you're concealing." He turned to me. "I'm afraid Dr. Jardine was again abusing his charism. He used hypnosis to enhance his power and then channelled the power into the sexual act with the result that the act became not so much an expression of love as an erotic subjugation of a prisoner by her captor . . . Do you recognise that description, Lyle?"

She managed to nod.

"Very well, we've explained to Charles that your mind was clouded and your will impaired by this hypnotic and profoundly unhealthy relationship. However, when you met Charles in the Cathedral, he temporarily acted as a barrier between you and Dr. Jardine with the result that you were able to catch a glimpse of your situation in its true perspective—and then you knew the relationship had to end. But once Charles was gone—once the barrier had been removed—you were again vulnerable to Dr. Jardine's will."

"Yes, that night when he came to my room I knew I wasn't going to be able to refuse him, but by chance the contraception wasn't in place, and . . . suddenly I saw that all I had to do was nothing. I was incapable of taking positive action by saying: 'I can't go on.' I was only capable of remaining silent, being passive, and while he was making love to me I thought: if I had a baby he couldn't keep me, not all the talk in the world would keep me, if I had a baby I'd have to go. And I made up my mind never to use the contraception again. Poor little baby, so wrong, I shouldn't have done it—"

"It's easy to be wise in retrospect, not so easy when one's enduring a desperate crisis . . . How did you see the future evolving once you were pregnant?"

"I thought I could get Charles to marry me. I knew I'd have to tell him I was pregnant—I never thought of deceiving him on a really colossal scale—but I decided to tell him the pregnancy was the result of a single ghastly lapse."

"Tell me how you set about coaxing Charles to propose."

"I kept saying how calculating and sex-obsessed I was, implying he wouldn't want to know me once he knew what I was really like—I thought that would make him even keener. Attractive men are always fascinated by a woman who can give them a challenge."

"But even so, surely you were worried that he'd baulk at the last fence when he heard about the baby?"

"Oh yes—I thought I'd have to force his hand at the end. But you see, I was luring him up the garden path until I could deliver the coup de grâce. And then . . . Oh God, oh God, he forestalled me—"

"How?"

"He told me about his parents," said Lyle crying. "He talked about his ideals, he stood by me, he lived his faith—oh, and then I felt so ashamed, so mean, so cheap, so absolutely vile—I could hardly speak I was so crucified with guilt, but I knew then I loved him. I hadn't loved him before. I'd found him physically attractive, but the truth was—"

"Yes—one last hurdle, Lyle—"

"I hated him, I was so angry with him, I wanted to make him pay—"

"And that was because—"

"He slept with Loretta," said Lyle, tears streaming down her cheeks. "I thought he'd just been amusing himself with me, I thought I'd been deceived, I thought he'd let me down—men have always let me down, even Daddy let me down, going away and never coming back, and I couldn't bear Charles betraying me when I liked him so much. I thought: I'll have my revenge on him, I'll make him pay, I'll tell him he's got to marry me or else I'll create a scandal by saying the baby's his. I was all set to do it, I'd drummed up the nerve, and there I was, mad with anger and loathing and wickedness, absolutely *infested* by those demons you recognised just now, and then . . . What was it you said at the beginning of our conversation?—"

"No demon can withstand the power of Christ."

"Yes, Charles was so good, so straight, so Christian—the demons all fell away and I was able to love him, but then the demons came back, they tried to reclaim me because they knew I was so undeserving of a man like that, they did reclaim me but by a miracle you cast them out—Oh Father, help me, please help me, I've been so sick—"

Darrow said at once: "If you can see that, you're already getting better."

"I just wish so much that all the terrible things I've done could be wiped out!"

"That may not be so difficult as you fear. Once a true repentance has been achieved the way's open for the start of a new life."

"But not with Charles. There'll be no new life with Charles now—I'm going to lose him, aren't I, Father? I'm going to lose what I want the most and it'll be a just punishment for all my lies and deception and wickedness."

Darrow said nothing. He merely turned to face me, and I shall always remember that at the end when the final decision had to be made, he was not only silent but inscrutable. The decision had to be mine and mine alone.

"If you can forgive me for Loretta," I said to Lyle, "I can forgive you for wanting revenge. And even if you can't forgive me, I'd still forgive you anyway now that I know just how deeply you've suffered."

"Oh Charles—Charles—"

"Let's go back to the hotel and make some wedding plans."

XXV

"The retrospect has much in it that is humiliating and that calls for repentance; but Christ, in His limitless mercy, has endured me all these long years, and I cannot doubt that He will be with me to the end."

Letters of
HERBERT HENSLEY HENSON,
ed. E. F. Braley

I

LYLE and I did talk about our wedding but not for long. She was exhausted, and at nine we parted in the foyer of the hotel. The following morning I rescued her from the dining-room where she had been trying to eat breakfast and we returned to Grantchester; she went for a walk around the village while I saw Darrow on my own.

"She's still tired," I said in response to his opening question, "but she's much calmer." I hesitated before adding: "How soon did you realise what was going on in her mind?"

"I could tell at once she was in difficulty, and when I realised she was using me to express all her anger towards the opposite sex I wondered if you yourself could be immune from that hostility . . . She needs much more help, Charles."

"Did you find a nun?"

"Yes. Fiftyish, widowed, very intuitive, very humane."

"I only wish I could believe that Lyle will ever agree to see her."

"I think that when the present appalling tensions have eased, she may well feel a new need to confide."

"How I wish you could continue to counsel her!"

"It would be too dangerous. You yourself witnessed the sexual edge the scene developed when she was disturbed, and if I attempted to counsel her on my own . . . No, Charles, such a session would only confuse her—and incidentally it would be extremely unwise for me. Monks are very ordinary men in many ways and were quite definitely not designed by God to counsel pretty women on their private lives." He smiled at me before adding: "Outline your next battle plan."

"We're going down to Starbridge. She needs to collect some essential possessions and I think it's best if she parts from the Jardines as soon as possible. I'll see him on my own first, of course."

"How do you think he'll behave?"

"That's exactly the question I was going to ask you. What do you think, Father? I'm not asking for a demonstration of clairvoyance now, just a prediction based on the evidence."

"Most of the time that's all clairvoyance is anyway." Darrow considered for a moment. "He'll be stunned—but not, I think, by the news that Lyle's leaving him; he must have been well aware for some time that they were in difficulties. But he'll be stunned by the news of the child, and the first question he's going to ask is how often he can see it. This is where you meet the problem of what part the Jardines are going to play in your marriage, Charles."

"Lyle accepts that there must be a complete break," I said, "and I confess that on this point I'm implacable. They've got to stay well away, and if they think they can come and coo regularly over my child in its pram they'll have to think again."

Darrow examined his Abbot's ring and was silent.

"Am I being un-Christian?" I said uneasily.

"Not necessarily. What do you think?"

"I think God's called me to make this marriage—which will certainly begin by being very difficult—and therefore my first duty is to make sure the marriage works. And I don't believe it'll work if the Jardines are allowed in."

"I must admit," said Darrow, "that I think this is the only conclusion you can reach while you and Lyle are both recovering from your ordeals and learning to love each other, but guard against inflexibility, Charles. Remember what difficulties your father's inflexibility caused when he was unable to jettison his conviction that you were an exact copy of Romaine."

Now it was my turn to be silent. Finally Darrow asked: "What are you going to do about the wedding?"

"That's another difficult problem. We're both agreed we want the quickest, quietest wedding possible—I shall get a special license, of course—but from the point of view of gossip it'll look odd if Lyle's not married from the palace."

"Will it? Don't lose sight of the fact that she's their employee, not their daughter, and employers and employees frequently fall out. Of course there's bound to be some degree of tittle-tattle if the Jardines aren't present at the wedding, but people have short memories and it'll soon be forgotten. The great thing is to behave confidently, as if you're taking the most natural course in the world—and that leads me to my next suggestion: why not get Dr. Lang to marry you in the chapel at Lambeth? What could be more thoroughly respectable than being married by the Archbishop of Canterbury? And that would also help to explain the Jardines' absence; everyone knows Lang and Jardine are estranged."

This struck me as a suggestion bordering on brilliance. "But how much would I be obliged to tell Lang?"

"Nothing."

"But what if he questions me about Lyle's relationship with Jardine?"

"My dear Charles, you're a clergyman—you're under no obligation whatsoever to repeat a word of Lyle's recent confessions to anyone, even to the Archbishop of Canterbury! All you need say is that both the Jardines were making such heavy demands on Lyle that she was quite unable to have any life of her own. This is so obviously unhealthy and undesirable that no further comment needs to be made."

My mind cleared. I realised then how exhausted I was by the strain of the past twenty-four hours, and Darrow's clarity of vision was even more comforting than usual.

He said suddenly: "Are you going to wait till the pregnancy's confirmed before you set the wedding date?"

"No," I said, knowing he asked the question to see if I were toying with the idea of escape. "I want to marry her anyway, pregnancy or no pregnancy, and the sooner the better."

He was satisfied. "And how do you feel now," he said, testing me again, "about being a father yourself?"

I smiled at him. "Now that I'm not wasting my time trying to be the perfect son to all my father-figures, I'm sure I'll have the energy to tackle parenthood!"

Darrow nodded, but when he made no comment I realised he expected me to go on. "I made myself so unhappy being the perfect son," I said soberly, "that I had a horror of creating anyone who might have to go through what I went through. And my father always made fatherhood seem such a colossal trial that I became subconsciously terrified of the burden it would entail."

Darrow nodded but continued to wait.

"I couldn't cope with my marriage," I said. "I couldn't cope with my family, I couldn't cope with myself. Of course I shied away from coping with anyone else, especially a child who would be dependent on me. But now I can cope, Father. It won't be easy. It'll often be very hard, but the truth is I don't feel unfit and unworthy here. I believe that this is the family life God has called me to undertake—perhaps to prepare me for a call to serve Him in some other field—and that through this great ordeal He's made me fit and worthy for this very special purpose."

Darrow leant back in his chair as if he had safely steered a ship into harbour after an exceptionally arduous voyage, but all he said in the end was: "May God be with you—and I'm sure He will. Well done, Charles."

2

WHEN we returned to Laud's I packed a bag for the visit to Starbridge and then while Lyle and I sat facing each other on either side of my desk I telephoned the palace. Gerald Harvey at once connected me to the extension in the library; as soon as Jardine responded, I embarked on my prepared speech.

"I'm telephoning to tell you that Lyle's agreed to marry me," I said flatly. "I'm speaking from my rooms at Laud's but we're about to leave for Starbridge so that I can call on you this evening to discuss the situation. I'll come to the palace at six-thirty."

A deep silence followed this declaration of war but at last Jardine said levelly: "I'd like to speak to Lyle, if you please."

"Until six-thirty—thank you, Bishop," I said, and terminated the call. I had no intention of giving him the opportunity to talk to Lyle unless I was able to monitor both sides of the conversation.

"What did he say?" said Lyle, frightened.

I told her.

"Did he sound shattered?"

"Not particularly." Ignoring her pallor, I added to divert her: "Did you write the letter?"

Opening her bag she produced an unsealed envelope which she handed to me.

"May I?" I said politely before I extracted the letter within. I thought it was important that my behaviour remained civilised as the pressure to become dictatorial increased.

"Of course," she said.

She had written to confirm that she wished to marry me and to inform him about the child. It was a cold, stark little letter; I suspected she had not dared admit any emotion for fear it might have permeated the entire message.

"Is it all right?" she asked nervously.

"Fine." Sealing the envelope I slipped it into the inside pocket of my jacket and in silence we embarked upon our journey.

3

SO we came at last to Starbridge, sunlit sinister Starbridge, the city which had concealed such a tormented reality behind its brilliant glittering image. The sun shone on the Cathedral again as we descended from the hills, and the waters of the river sparkled in the hot September light. Our separate rooms were waiting at the Staro Arms but I did not pause to unpack my bag. I drank some water to refresh myself and then left for the palace. Lyle saw me off. As we parted she was unable to stop herself saying desperately: "Be kind to him."

I at once wanted to lay waste the entire palace, but I gave a brief nod, beat back my jealousy with one last kiss and walked out of the hotel into Eternity Street.

4

BY the time I reached the palace I was more tense than ever but I had every emotion tightly in control. I had given Darrow back my borrowed cross at our last meeting, but I had bought a cross of my own which I was wearing beneath my shirt, and during the walk through the Close I touched the outline repeatedly to maintain my equilibrium.

On reaching the palace I was shown at once to the library.

Jardine was standing by the window and it was not until the door closed that he turned to face me. His face was pale and set. He looked tough. I stood my ground.

"Good evening, Dr. Ashworth." Evidently he had decided not to rake up memories of our previous meeting by calling me Charles.

"Good evening, Bishop."

He gestured that we should sit down and once more we faced each other across the desk. Eventually after an awkward pause he said with care: "I hope Lyle's well. I've been worried about her for some time."

"She's better now that she's made up her mind to marry me." I waited for him to defend himself; I was poised to deliver all the arguments against his informal marital arrangements; I was ready to grapple with the full force of his charism as we wrestled in debate. But he eluded me.

"The most important thing," he said, "is that Lyle should be restored to full spiritual health." And he touched the cross on his chest. At once

I knew he was tapping it for the strength to go on, and suddenly I feared he was going to undermine my enmity and plunge me once more into confusion.

"I'd very much like to see Lyle," he said, "because I think it's important that I set her free to be happy in her new life. I'd like to tell her that at best we contracted what the lawyers call a voidable marriage, a marriage which the parties can set aside if they choose, and I'd like to make it clear that I do release her from those vows she made five years ago. I'd also say that although of course I shall miss her very much she's on no account to feel guilty about leaving me, and I'd say that because as I survey the events of the last few months it seems very obvious, Dr. Ashworth, that you were sent into our lives for a purpose, and that I would indeed be the apostate you doubtless think I am if I failed to understand that it's entirely God's will that Lyle should now become your wife."

I was beyond speech. I was unable to decide whether he was being immensely clever, scheming to tame me into a pliable son-in-law, or immensely heroic, relinquishing the woman he loved in the best possible way, and I had the terrible suspicion he was being heroic.

"I'm not an apostate," he said, when he realised I was too confused to reply. "I reached my decision to marry Lyle because I thought I discerned God's approval. The rational arguments for the decision were weak but I'm a clergyman, not a lawyer, and I came to the conclusion that God had provided me with this strange solution to my troubles to enable me to continue to serve Him to the best of my ability. Obviously events have proved that I was in error. 'Truth is the daughter of time,' as the saying goes, but five years ago I did what I honestly believed to be right, right for me, for Carrie and for Lyle."

He paused, but when I still offered no comment he fingered his cross again and said: "It seems in retrospect that my error was very grave, but our errors are so often rooted in circumstances over which we have no control, and the foundation of my error here goes back a long way, as no doubt you realise. My father and stepmother had such a powerful influence on me, and although I've always congratulated myself on escaping from the world into which I was born, I see clearly now that my whole career has inevitably been coloured by my heredity and the very singular environment of my youth. However, please don't think I'm trying to make excuses for myself; I'm not. I'm merely trying to put my behaviour in a truthful perspective because I believe it's important that you shouldn't look at me and feel perpetually disillusioned with the Church. I'm not the first churchman to fall into error and I certainly shan't be the last, but you should understand that I'm not an emissary of

Satan but merely a devout man who's made an appalling mistake."

He stopped speaking again, and again I found I was impressed yet sceptical. The situation called for the charism of the discernment of spirits, but at that moment I was quite unable to tell whether his speech came from God or the Devil.

"Lyle will be concerned for Carrie and myself," said Jardine. "That's inevitable and that's another reason why I'd like to see her. I want to explain that we'll be all right. I shall, of course, resign my bishopric. I shall make some excuse about ill-health and retire to a distant village—somewhere near Oxford would suit—where Carrie and I can live quietly. I've always wanted to write a serious theological study instead of sermons and polemics, and retirement will give me the necessary time to do so. As for Carrie, no doubt she'll come into her own at last. She never enjoyed being the wife of a successful clergyman, but now I foresee her taking an active part in village life and becoming vastly popular while everyone secretly moans about her tiresome irascible old husband . . . And once Carrie's happier than she's been for years, our marriage may well take a turn for the better. At least I shall hope so, and perhaps in such changed circumstances I shan't hope entirely in vain."

I now had the confusion in my mind under control. With the strength developed by Darrow's training I had achieved sufficient concentration to wipe the blackboard of my consciousness clean so that God could write upon it if He wished. Then I prayed again for the gift of discernment.

At last Jardine said: "When are you getting married?"

"Very soon. I'm getting a special license."

Jardine looked puzzled. Cautiously he said: "Forgive me—I've no wish to interfere, but is it really advisable to rush into this? I speak as a man who himself married in haste, and I do most strongly urge you not to follow my example."

Without speaking I produced Lyle's letter and gave it to him.

He groped for his reading glasses. When he opened the envelope, the signet-ring fell out and I saw him flinch before he slipped it in his pocket. I went on watching him and eventually I heard the sharp intake of breath as he reached the crucial sentence. The next moment he was levering himself to his feet. On the side-table stood a decanter of brandy, the silent witness of the strain he had endured since receiving my telephone call that morning, and he now poured himself a stiff measure into the tumbler which I knew had already been used. All he said in the end was: "I've got to be alone."

I withdrew to the hall. I was still channelling my concentration into keeping the blackboard of my mind clear, but although I continued to pray for enlightenment, I remained confused. As Darrow had so truthfully pointed out, I was in many ways a very ordinary clergyman and I now felt quite out of my spiritual depth. Again I prayed for the grace of God which would transform my weakness into strength, and again the familiar prayer of Christ echoed in my mind: let thy will, not mine, be done.

The door of the library opened. I had probably been in the hall no longer than five minutes but it seemed that a far longer time had passed. From the threshold Jardine said: "Come back, please," but he was turning away as he spoke and it was not until I had rejoined him in the room that I saw his eyes were bloodshot. The gift of discernment at once overwhelmed me; looking past the mask of his heroic resignation which that faultless speech had so effortlessly projected, I saw not the Devil's emissary but only a good man struggling to master the most profound emotions.

"Thank you for letting me have those few moments alone," he said, and I was just thinking how self-possessed he sounded when I realised he was unable to continue. However, when we were both seated again he managed to say: "I'm sorry, I feel so overwhelmed, I still hardly dare believe it, it's as if the whole tragedy's been redeemed—it even makes Lyle's loss easier to bear, because of course this is the most miraculous compensation—"

I suddenly saw what was going to happen, and as I heard Darrow saying: "Leave Jardine to God, Charles," the chalk began to write at last on the blackboard of my mind. I could hardly bear to read the message but I knew I was powerless to erase it. I was bound by my call, and only one course of action lay open to me.

"I've always wanted a child," said Jardine. "I think it's the one thing, even now, that I want the most. It was so hard to accept when God withheld the blessing of living children from my marriage, and I've often felt acceptance would have been easier if there had been no children at all. That stillborn baby . . . That agonising glimpse of a future that never happened . . . It was almost unendurable to know one had created a child only to lose him before he'd even drawn breath in the world."

I could only watch him in silence, and in my mind the chalk was finally still.

"And how wonderful that you should want to marry her!" said Jardine, too absorbed by his emotions to notice my lack of response. "In the circumstances that too's miraculous—everything's miraculous—I felt so destroyed by this disaster but now I can start to hope again." Clumsily he poured himself some more brandy. "After your telephone call this morning," he said, "I didn't know how I was going to bear her loss, but gradually after much prayer I realised that my chief task was not to think of myself but to help Lyle by setting her free. So I resolved to put on a brave front—but it was so hard because I knew how much you must despise me—oh, how shaming it was when you walked into the room this evening, how terrible it was to look at you and *know that you knew* . . . Forgive me, I can see I'm embarrassing you by my frankness, but I've suffered so much, never think I haven't suffered, and that's why this news is so wonderful, because it transforms all that suffering and makes it bearable at last." He hesitated before adding diffidently: "I shall look forward so much to watching him grow up."

I said nothing.

His expression changed. He had recognised his executioner but could not quite believe the execution was at hand. "I trust," he said, "I'll be allowed to see the child from time to time."

I felt as if I were seeing a man facing a firing squad where all the bullets were being fired in slow motion, but when I spoke it was not because I wanted to but because I had no choice. The message had to be delivered.

"I'm afraid you must take it as settled," I said, "that the child will be mine and not yours. I'm sorry, but I've been called to make this difficult marriage, and because of the nature of the liaison you had with Lyle I don't see how I can possibly risk allowing you to play any part in my married life. It's out of the question"—I hesitated but made myself add—"for the present."

He grabbed at the lifeline. "But in the future—"

"We'll see. It depends very much how Lyle and I get on and that in turn depends on how conscientiously you keep out of our lives."

"I needn't see Lyle. But if I could occasionally see the child—with the help of an intermediary—"

"No. Don't get carried away by the sentimental notion that your biological connection gives you the right to treat my child as yours." I could hear my father's fierceness in my voice. Touching my hidden cross, I made a new effort to be calm. "Obviously he'll have to know the truth some day," I said, "and when he does know he'll want to see you, but until then you must keep your distance unless I feel it's safe to allow you to draw closer."

He struggled with his emotions and it was some time before he was able to say: "Could Lyle perhaps send me a photograph occasionally?"

"Lyle will send you absolutely nothing," I said, "and I forbid you to communicate with her." I had to steel myself to add: "*I'll* send the occasional photograph."

He tried to thank me but I cut him off. Having been compelled to take a tough stance I did not want him making me feel guilty by displaying humility.

Eventually he said: "Am I not to see Lyle—even to say goodbye?"

"I'll bring her here after dinner tonight, and you can make your set speech to her in my presence. Meanwhile perhaps Mrs. Jardine would be good enough to pack some clothes for Lyle to take away—and when we have our new address in Cambridge I'd be obliged if you'd forward the rest of Lyle's possessions at my expense."

He nodded. I assumed that there was no more which could possibly be said, but as I rose to my feet he added unexpectedly: "Would you like a drink before you go? This interview must have been almost as great an ordeal for you as it's been for me."

"Thank you, Bishop, but since I was so drunk when you last entertained me here I feel the least I can do now is abstain."

We both smiled, and suddenly against all the odds the spark of our compatibility flared between us. On an impulse he said: "I'm sorry I made such a mess of counselling you that night—I did want to help but I was so cut off from God by all my fear and dread that I had no help to give. I'm afraid it was a very great spiritual failure."

"We all have our spiritual failures."

"Well, make sure you learn from mine." He led the way to the door. "At least you've stopped asking impertinent questions," he said casually over his shoulder. "No doubt I should be thankful for small mercies."

"I could think of quite a few more impertinent questions to ask," I said, trying to match his lighter tone in order to soften my earlier severity, "but I see no reason on earth why you should answer them. You're never going to tell anyone the real truth about your stepmother, are you?"

"And what, dare I ask, do you consider 'the real truth' to be?"

"I think it was she who was the love of your life. No one else. I think Lyle was really only a substitute, someone your stepmother sanctioned when she knew she hadn't long to live. I think if you'd really loved Lyle, you couldn't have lived chastely under the same roof with her at Radbury."

"What singularly bizarre theories you conjure up out of your singularly fertile imagination, Dr. Ashworth!"

"Life sometimes *is* bizarre, Dr. Jardine—"

"—and sometimes it's merely innocent. Ingrid was my father's wife. The story begins and ends in that single sentence."

"But what a complex and ambivalent sentence it is!"

Jardine smiled at me again. It was painful to see the amusement return to those lambent amber eyes when they were still bloodshot. It merely underlined the pathos I had no desire to witness. "So you've resumed your customary impertinence," he said. "I'm glad to see that you at least have emerged from our battle unscathed!"

"No one ever emerges from a battle unscathed. I'll return later with Lyle," I said, and walked out feeling bruised beyond endurance and battered beyond belief.

5

I PRESIDED over the final dissolution of Jardine's ménage à trois later that evening. It was a sad, difficult meeting. Jardine spoke his piece but at a far more halting pace than he had achieved earlier. Lyle cried. I allowed her to embrace Carrie but afterwards terminated the meeting abruptly. By this time Jardine was ashen, beyond speech, and both women were in tears. Stowing in the car the numerous bags which had been packed for Lyle, I drove off at a great pace down the palace drive and pursued an erratic course out of the Close. Lyle wept soundlessly all the way to the Staro Arms.

After the porter had brought the bags to her room, I ordered brandies for us both and we sat on the window-seat in the gathering dusk. The golden light of the sunset had almost faded and I remembered Darrow talking of the darkness below the horizon which would represent the reality of marriage after the euphoria of the engagement.

As we sipped our brandy, Lyle said rapidly: "I expect you want to sleep with me. You can if you like. It doesn't really matter if we anticipate the wedding, does it?"

"Yes, it does," I said. "It would be like smoking a cigarette when I was wearing a clerical collar. There are some things clergymen just shouldn't do if they want to be respected, and if I'm ever to put right that disastrous error with Loretta—"

"Please don't say any more about that." She groped for my hand. "You've explained. I understand. We've forgiven each other for all the awfulness there. I only thought that perhaps—"

"Well, of course I want to sleep with you," I said, "but let's be realistic for a moment. You're offering out of guilt because you're ashamed you revealed at the palace how deeply you still care for him. If I accepted your offer I'd be accepting because I wanted to drown my insecurity by subjugating you physically, just as he did. But think, Lyle—just think! Do we really want to start our married life on those terms?"

She shook her head and gripped my hand harder than ever.

"You want to wait, don't you?" I said. "You've had quite enough of quasi-marriages. You've yearned all these years to be a real wife, just as I've yearned all these years to make a second marriage, and why should we now settle for anything less than the genuine article?"

"I thought you might want to try me out."

"What for? We hardly need premarital sex to tell us that at first the physical side of marriage is going to be difficult! What matters is not that we confirm this obvious fact before marriage but that after the wedding we're prepared to try hard to overcome the problem." I kissed her before adding: "Besides we both need time. You're exhausted. So am I. Let's finish our brandy, crawl into our separate beds and pass out. It may not be the most romantic ending to a gruelling day but I'm quite sure it's the most sensible one."

"I don't think it's so unromantic," said Lyle. "I think if you didn't love me so much the gruelling day would have an even more gruelling ending."

But in a flash of insight I saw my behaviour in a more complex and murky light. I recognised my desire to do what was right and my anxiety to protect her from further stress, but I recognised too my secret dread of being compared with Jardine and found wanting. However, that piece of self-knowledge was at present too difficult to master. Closing my mind against all troubled thoughts I embraced her in the gathering dusk, and later when I glanced out of the window I saw that although the night had fallen at last, the stars were beginning to shine.

6

DR. LANG married us in the chapel at Lambeth two weeks later in the presence of my parents, my brother, my sister-in-law, my two nieces, my nephew and a friend of Lyle's, an ancient charming clergyman who had been a canon of Radbury Cathedral during the Jardines' tenure of the Deanery. He gave the bride away while Peter acted as best man. Lang conducted the ceremony with his usual theatrical dignity and as he declaimed a short homily extolling the glories of nuptial bliss for those not called to the celibate life, it occurred to me that he might have guessed rather more about my life as a widower than I had cared to imagine. The Archbishop remained the canny Scot beneath his pompous English facade, and I reminded myself that time had proved Dr. Lang right in his estimate of the Bishop of Starbridge.

In the circumstances it seemed wiser not to have a prolonged honeymoon, so I decided we should go away for no more than a weekend to a small hotel I knew in the Cotswolds. We arrived there shortly before dinner, and later when Lyle said how much she had enjoyed the simple but carefully cooked meal, I knew she was trying as hard to make me believe she was happy as I was trying to be convinced. I told myself I should feel comforted that she so strongly shared my desire for the weekend to be a success, yet when we finally retired to our room I found I still needed reassurance. I heard myself saying rapidly: "Look, if you can't face it, for heaven's sake say so. We mustn't start play-acting and being dishonest with each other."

Lyle said: "I want sex. And I want sex with you. And I want sex with you now. Then maybe we can put a stop to this excruciating tension."

This was certainly unvarnished honesty and I did my best to achieve an equally candid response. "I feel exactly the same," I said, but I was hurt by her lack of warmth. I thought that if I had been Jardine, she would have called me darling and held out her arms.

A long unpalatable vista opened before me into my difficult marriage, but I pulled down the blinds in my mind to blot it out. I had hardly spent seven arduous years of flawed celibacy only to be squeamish on my wedding night, yet the demon of doubt was now crawling through my thoughts. I looked at Lyle, who appeared to be making such a brave attempt to sever herself from the past, and I wondered if she were even now secretly longing for Jardine. And as soon as this terrible thought had entered my head, I was tormented by the dread that she would always have secrets which would cut me off from her, secrets which she would never reveal.

I touched my cross and asked myself instead how far it was ever possible to know the whole truth about another human being. I thought of Jardine's final ambivalent silence about his stepmother, a silence which might well indicate not guilt but a desire to keep a cherished part of his life utterly private; no one would ever know now what had happened there, and perhaps it was right that no one ever should. I thought of Darrow saying: "All we can do is to pray for as much enlightenment as God sees fit to grant us," and suddenly I realised that Darrow was an even greater mystery than Jardine, a man who concealed all his secrets in order to disconnect himself from his past in the world. What lay behind his call to be a monk? Had he been happily married? Had he been a successful father to his children? Had Lyle been right in her intuitive conviction that the state of celibacy was unnatural to him, and if she was right, was his life a continuing struggle to maintain that serenity which always seemed so unforced? The likelihood was that I would never be able to answer any of these questions, and yet my relationship with Darrow was hardly vitiated because he was in so many respects an enigma.

I saw then that Lyle would always have her mysteries, and I saw too that the way to live with them was not to torture myself in pursuit of elucidation but to accept them as a limit set on my knowledge by God for His own purpose. The demon of doubt receded, and releasing the cross I began to prepare for bed.

7

I WAS face to face at last with my secret dread that I would be unable to match Jardine's illicit but alluring distortion of his charismatic power. Another searing vista opened into the future, and again the vista had to be blotted from my mind. I was being tormented now by that old demon my fear of inadequacy, and rolling away from Lyle I groped in the dark for the cross which I had left on the bedside table.

As I slipped the cross around my neck, I remembered Darrow again. I saw us in the herb-garden, remembered how the word "courage" had echoed in my mind, and suddenly without words I was able to ask for patience, for strength, for the will to endure all my difficulties and the wisdom to surmount them.

The demons departed as my mind stood open before God, and once more I passed through the strait gate to set out along the narrow way in response to my mysterious call. My new life in God's service stretched before me; I knew there could be no turning back. I could only go on in the absolute faith that one day His purpose would stand fully revealed, and in the light of that faith the darkness of my anxiety was extinguished. The glittering image of the apparent world dissolved into the great truths which lay beyond, and the truths were not a beautiful dream, as Loretta had thought, but the ultimate reality. Love and forgiveness, truth and beauty, courage and compassion blazed with a radiance which far outshone the cheap glitter of illusion, and I knew then with an even deeper conviction that in serving God man only fulfilled his need to strive to live in that eternally powerful light. St. Augustine's famous words echoed in my mind: "O God, thou hast made us for thyself, and our hearts are restless until they rest in thee."

At once I was at peace. My self-confidence returned, and as I claimed my wife and child at last I thought as my father had thought before me: they're both mine now.

Afterwards I said carefully to Lyle: "I think you really might come to love me one day," and at once she said: "Darling!" and held out her arms.

Without doubt some difficult hurdle had been overcome. I wondered what the next one would be.

I fell asleep and dreamed of a little boy tormenting me with his lambent amber eyes.

Author's Note

THE character of Charles Ashworth is fictitious.

The character of Alex Jardine is based in part on the life and career of Herbert Hensley Henson (1863–1947), one of the leaders of the Church of England in the early twentieth century. Henson was the son of a self-made businessman who retired early and proceeded to live beyond his means while he devoted himself to an eccentric and gloomy evangelical religion. Young Henson's mother died when he was six and three years later his father "remarried," although no record of the marriage has ever been found. When Henson was fourteen his German stepmother finally persuaded his father to send him to school, a step which set him on the road to Oxford where he was to become a Fellow of All Souls. He was ordained at the age of twenty-three; when he became Vicar of Barking in Essex, his stepmother moved to the vicarage to keep house for him.

After years of obscurity during which Henson was obliged to support his family and was consequently too poor to marry, he received his vital preferment: he was appointed Rector of St. Margaret's Westminster and became a canon of Westminster Abbey. Relieved at last from financial anxiety, he then married Isabella Dennistoun and a stillborn son was born to them two years later. There were no living children of the marriage. Henson became Dean of Durham in 1912, and in 1916 a young woman, Fearne Booker, arrived at the Deanery to assist Mrs. Henson; she remained with the Hensons for over thirty years. In 1918 Henson was appointed Bishop of Hereford but in 1920 he was translated to Durham, where he remained until his retirement in 1939. His stepmother spent her final days with him at his episcopal residence, Auckland Castle. It must be stressed that no impropriety existed between either Henson and his stepmother or Henson and Miss Booker.

The personality of Lyle Christie is my own invention and any resemblance to Miss Booker is coincidental.

William Cosmo Gordon Lang was Archbishop of Canterbury from 1928 until 1942. In 1938 during a debate in the House of Lords on Abyssinia, Henson opposed Lang with an unprecedented degree of fierceness, but their tendency to disagree had already been revealed to the public; a year earlier during the Lords debate on the Marriage Bill, Lang had merely adopted a position of neutrality, but Henson had spoken in favour of extending the divorce laws with an eloquence which was later recorded with grateful admiration by the Bill's author, A. P. Herbert.

GLITTERING IMAGES is the first in a series of novels about the Church of England in the twentieth century. The next novel, *Glamorous Powers,* opens in 1940 and focuses on Jon Darrow.

A NOTE ON THE TYPE

THE TEXT of this book was set in Bembo, a facsimile of a typeface cut by one of the most celebrated goldsmiths of his time, Francesco Griffo, for Aldus Manutius, the Venetian printer, in 1495. The face was named for Pietro Bembo, the author of the small treatise entitled De Aetna *in which it first appeared. Through the research of Stanley Morison, it is now acknowledged that all old-face type designs up to the time of William Caslon can be traced to the Bembo cut.*

THE present-day version of Bembo was introduced by The Monotype Corporation, London, in 1929. Sturdy, well balanced, and finely proportioned, Bembo is a face of rare beauty and great legibility in all of its sizes.

Composed by The Haddon Craftsmen, Inc.
Scranton, Pennsylvania
Printed and bound by Fairfield Graphics
Fairfield, Pennsylvania
Book and ornament designed by
Margaret Wagner